Critical Acclaim for Maureen H

"A *Lover's Almanac* inspires an infectious se
and exuberant winks at literary forebears . .
kind of risky book that comparisons to *Uly*
open all the windows and embrace its own
on the edge of the millennium, the views ar
—*The Washington Times*

"A funny, grouchy, madly nonlinear love story . . . a brilliant and convincing urban mindscape." —*Time*

"Infatuated with the world around it, and its own creative license, *A Lover's Almanac* is brazenly intelligent: daredevil clever and yet as innocent as a Wisconsin morning. Maureen Howard has adorned her seventh novel with narrative cheek and the passion for knowledge; she has also sneaked in a lot of tender romance posing as savvy, and that subterfuge gives away her heart."
—Gail Caldwell, *The Boston Sunday Globe*

"Splendid . . . an unforgettable delineation of how life goes terribly awry when a person fails to choose the one he loves. . . . Howard skillfully weaves literary and historical references in her rich, supple prose. . . . A writer of confidence and clarity . . . ambitious and uncompromising . . . approaches luminous heights."
—*The Dallas Morning News*

"A no-holds-barred, pyrotechnic display of fine writing within a romantic futuristic love story . . . wonderfully eclectic . . . complex, challenging, multilayered . . . dazzling . . . an exuberant look at where we have been and where we may be going when the present millennium is over."
—*San Francisco Chronicle and Sunday Examiner*

"Masterful artistry . . . With muscular prose shaping the wily skepticism of her postmodern project, Howard reaffirms the power of storytelling to translate the swirls and curlicues of intimate lives."
—*Houston Chronicle*

"A smart, sexy novel." —*Cosmopolitan*

"A literate love story, a bewitching winter's tale . . . Part almanac, part romance, part cautionary tribute to progress in its many guises, *A Lover's Almanac* delivers both sustenance and surprises." —*The Miami Herald*

"*A Lover's Almanac* is so rich and human a novel that it not only describes human nature, but recreates it. . . . [From the] whirl of images, ideas, quotations and references emerge real characters about whom we come to care intensely."
—*Chicago Tribune*

"Howard is a generous storyteller. . . . She tells tales in snippets, bits of esoterica, glimpses that feel preternatural. As with García Marquez's *One Hundred Years of Solitude* . . . it's not as if you're reading *A Lover's Almanac*; it's more like spying on a sprawling epic. . . . Powerful . . . A rollicking exploration of loneliness and destiny . . . Pack a slide rule, a compass, and a lot of heart."
—*St. Petersburg Times*

"Once again, Howard has written a book of great beauty and complexity. The result is a cacophonous burst of people, events, and quaint agrarian superstitions—a momentary convergence of recent centuries exploding like New Year's Eve fireworks."   —*Time Out New York*

"Rich propaganda for whatever's real, though it looks fanciful on the surface . . . Howard makes a modern version of the great panoramas of the past. . . . the product of obsessive craft."   —*The New York Times Book Review*

"Howard is a wonderful writer with a mind full of fabulous facts, and she lays them out for us to show the ways in which people slide by each other, bumping but never connecting."   —*The Washington Post Book World*

"Acute and haunting . . . Rich, crowded, metaphor-making prose . . . [that] catches us up and won't let us go. Eloquently and unmistakably a New York novel."
—*The New York Review of Books*

"Fascinating . . . Howard's prose brilliantly lights up passages. There is not a dull sentence in the book. One after another scintillates, taking the measure of generational clash, ambition and fulfillment, the harsh judgments of time, the ache of love won and love lost."   —*New York Newsday*

"Howard's voice is exceptionally true. . . . A *Lover's Almanac* contains one, and maybe two, of the most intelligent and affecting love stories in recent memory. . . . a careful, wry and winningly plotted novel."
—*The Hartford Courant*

"An intelligently written romance . . . Without her wisdom for organization, A *Lover's Almanac* would be just another love story. With her ingenuity and originality, though, her work becomes a testament, cosmic yet absurd, to the human condition."
—*Minneapolis Star Tribune*

"Evocative, intelligent, kaleidoscopic and witty . . . the literary detours are highly entertaining side journeys that enhance our understanding of the characters' lives."
—*Seattle Times*

"Truly beautiful writing."   —*Salt Lake City Tribune*

"Howard extends the boundaries of her love story into a broader meditation on Western thought."   —*Los Angeles Times*

"Vibrant and touching . . . Howard charts [the lovers'] course with her customary wit and eloquence. . . . a provocative novel of ideas."
—*Publishers Weekly* (starred)

"The richness and wonder of this work comes from the characters, relationships, and historical musings that Howard weaves into Louise and Artie's tale. . . . Complex and compelling . . . [it] deserves to be read more than once."
—*Library Journal*

PENGUIN BOOKS

A LOVER'S ALMANAC

Maureen Howard is the author of six other novels: *Not a Word About Nightingales*, *Before My Time*, *Grace Abounding*, *Expensive Habits*, *Natural History*, and *Bridgeport Bus*. *Grace Abounding*, *Expensive Habits*, and *Natural History* were all nominated for the PEN/Faulkner Award. Her widely praised memoir *Facts of Life* received the National Book Critics Circle Award for Nonfiction in 1978. She edited *The Penguin Book of Contemporary American Essays* (1984). In 1997 she received the Academy Award in Literature from the American Academy of Arts and Letters.

Ms. Howard has taught at a number of American universities, including Rutgers, Princeton, the University of Houston, Amherst, and Yale. She is currently teaching at Columbia University in New York City, where she lives with her husband, the novelist and lawyer Mark Probst.

MAUREEN HOWARD

A Lover's
ALMANAC

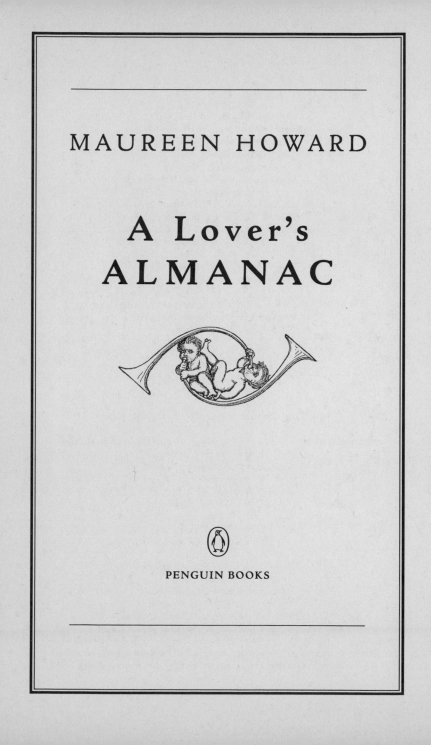

PENGUIN BOOKS

PENGUIN BOOKS
Published by the Penguin Group
Penguin Putnam Inc., 375 Hudson Street,
New York, New York 10014, U.S.A.
Penguin Books Ltd, 27 Wrights Lane,
London W8 5TZ, England
Penguin Books Australia Ltd, Ringwood,
Victoria, Australia
Penguin Books Canada Ltd, 10 Alcorn Avenue,
Toronto, Ontario, Canada M4V 3B2
Penguin Books (N.Z.) Ltd, 182–190 Wairau Road,
Auckland 10, New Zealand

Penguin Books Ltd, Registered Offices:
Harmondsworth, Middlesex, England

First published in the United States of America by Viking Penguin,
a member of Penguin Putnam Inc., 1998
Published in Penguin Books 1999

1   3   5   7   9   10   8   6   4   2

Copyright © Maureen Howard, 1998
All rights reserved

Page 271 constitutes an extension of this copyright page.

THE LIBRARY OF CONGRESS HAS CATALOGUED THE HARDCOVER AS FOLLOWS:
Howard, Maureen, date.
A lover's almanac / Maureen Howard.
p.   cm.
ISBN 0-670-87597-X (hc.)
ISBN 0 14 02.7512 6 (pbk.)
I. Title
PS3558.O8823A79   1998
813'.54—dc21   97–22191

Printed in the United States of America
Set in Electra and Cloister
Designed by Francesca Belanger

Except in the United States of America, this book is sold subject to the
condition that it shall not, by way of trade or otherwise, be lent, re-sold, hired out,
or otherwise circulated without the publisher's prior consent in any form of binding
or cover other than that in which it is published and without a similar condition
including this condition being imposed on the subsequent purchaser.

And you that shall cross from shore to shore years hence
are more to me, and more to my meditations, than you suppose:
Binnie, Carl, Jim, Joanna, Loretta, Rick.

Acknowledgments

Grateful acknowledgment to George Greenstein, the Learn'd Astronomer, and Gerald Weissmann, M.D.; to Rebecca Goldstein; to Brad Morrow of *Conjunctions*; to Janet Marks; once again to Lee Deigaard for her playful and practiced eye; to Ed Park, Peter Saidel, John Maddox and Anika Weiss. I am indebted to The Butler Reference Room of the Columbia Library. Barbara Grossman and Carolyn Carlson have been patient and inspired editors. Mark Probst and Gloria Loomis braved the fickle seasons of my Almanac with me, day by day.

JANUARY

More nice than wise.
Old Batchelor would have a Wife that's wise,
Fair, rich, and young, a Maiden for his Bed,
Not proud, nor churlish, but of faultless size
A Country Housewife in the City bred
He's a nice Fool, and long so vain hath staid
He should bespeak her, there's none ready made.

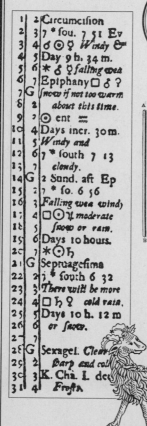

1	2	Circumcifion
2	3	7 * fou. 7 51 Ev
3	4	☌ ☉ ☿ Windy ☞
4	5	Day 9 h. 34 m.
5	6	* ☿ ☿ falling wea
6	7	Epiphany □ ☿ ?
7	G	Snow if not too warm
8	2	about this time.
9	3	☉ ent ♒
10	4	Days incr. 30 m.
11	5	Windy and
12	6	7 * fouth 7 13
13	7	clondy.
14	G	2 Sund. aft Ep
15	2	7 * fo. 6 56
16	3	Falling wea windy
17	4	□ ☉ ♃ moderate
18	5	fnow or rain.
19	6	Days 10 hours.
20	7	* ☉ ♄
21	G	Septuagefima
22	2	7 * fouth 6 32
23	3	There will be more
24	4	□ ♄ ☿ cold rain.
25	5	Days 10 h. 12 m
26	6	or fnow.
27	7	
28	G	Sexagef. Clear
29	2	harp and col
30	3	K. Cha. I. de
31	4	Frofn

*Instrument for
Taking Down Books
from High Shelves*

THE KOCH SNOWFLAKE

. . . your zodiac here is the life of man in one round chapter; and now I'll read it off, straight out of the book. Come, Almanack! To begin:

—Melville, *Moby Dick*

Being for the Bissextile or LEAP YEAR 2000 and of the 224th year of the American Independence.

Calculated for the Latitude 40 degrees, 42 minutes, 43 seconds North; Longitude 74 degrees, 3 seconds West. In the city and environs of New York, beginning January 1. Perihelion on the 3rd. Earth at 91,409,500 miles, closest in distance to the sun at 6 hours Universal Time. First quarter moon, 14th. Full moon 20th on which night TOTAL LUNAR ECLIPSE visible to all the Americas. The moon in our shadow appearing rose to red depending on volcanic dust and aerosols. Full sea at Coney Island 4:13 A.M.

> Lo! The year is new and cheery,
> Bright the snow, though dark the morn.
> And the black bird pecks till weary
> At the barren stalks of corn.

General Weather

Mild on the 1st. Fair and frosty on the 9th. Seasonable flurries. Winds from the Northeast—cold, erratic mid-month. Continuing inconstant to fickle before a January thaw.

Eclipse

A WINTER'S TALE

Louise Moffett cries in the ruins. Tears give way to bleating sobs, her sorrow run dry. She shivers out of her stiff silk dress, unhooks her froth of petticoat, throws both costumey garments on the pile of crumpled napkins and tablecloth stained with wine and ashes. At three o'clock in the morning she is quite alone, strutting in stiletto heels across the floor of her loft littered with confetti, streamers, noisemakers, shriveled balloons. Louise (Lou, Lou-Lou) is not to be seen by a soul in her lacy corset that pops her pearly breasts. As she stoops to retrieve a harmless cake knife from the debris of last night's party, garters stretch across her pink butt and swell of white thigh to the top of seamed stockings. No one will blink in disbelief at the scrap of suggestive white silk veiling her mons veneris.

Louise jabs at her wrist, but the blade of the long silver knife is serrated, dull. It would take force and determination to cut her flesh and why should she? The party's over, not her life, though she has been possessed by final thoughts from the moment when she found herself alone and shot the bolt of her door. Her tears for a man, of course, lying to herself that he has been an amusement, a convenience, nothing more. She teeters in those painful shoes to the bathroom, is shocked and saddened to see her scant underwear, her smooth blond page boy, cheery bright lipstick; the retro makeup and costume for a miserable party. Scandalous, so much snowy lace on white flesh, Miss January, a Calendar Girl, one of those saccharine cuties that hung in every feed store and gas station back in Wisconsin, girlie girls offering themselves to the inaccessible grease monkey or farm boy. Yes, she is such a smutty, unenlightened woman, though her little breasts would never cut it as fodder for male fantasy. Pert breasts admired by Artie Freeman whose toothbrush and razor confront her. And then don't the tears fall fast and furious, for he shaved so badly, always a bloody nick or a patch of stubble left by his ears, ridiculous floppy ears. And, having sworn off the man, she's into it again, choking back saltwater sorrow, for can it be that one night can unravel their years, one rotten night of Artie's misdemeanors. The answer is yes. Her Artie will never give up on his lightness. And the years that stretch ahead offer a diminishing view in which he will never change. Lightness is his affliction.

Louise Moffett is an artist, a painter now scrubbing at her lips as though scraping ill-conceived strokes from a canvas. Her hand quivering, she grabs a razor blade, begins to hack off her hair in dangerous swipes. When this disfiguration is accomplished she unhooks the corset, her body scored with red welts from its stays, and runs naked to the back of the loft, where the bed, lamp, rug made it home, sort of home, for her and her lost love, Artie Freeman. Home in the background as it were, hidden, relegated to a corner behind a screen. Lou hitches on overalls, sniffling as she buttons a paint-stained shirt, one of Artie's threadbare at the cuffs. He would be wearing it still had she not, but that thought as to her care and upkeep of the unworldly man turns her weepy. She will never again give in to his nonsense. Will not keep it light: it— the easy irony of their longstanding affair, their arrangement. As she hauls out a canvas, a sniff of wet paint revives her and Louise, kicking away paper horns and cheap wooden clackers, begins to work with a putty knife at a ruined painting, well, at one small corner that's all he has destroyed, of a large work. Now to undo the damage, so she paints through what's left of the night until the smudge is restored to a little apple tree in bloom resplendent. With her last stroke of sap green, the party is over.

Louise Moffett came to this city to make art. She is thirty-one years old and could not name the day when she got serious, oh, not about her painting, that's fixed as the stars, about Artie Freeman who has been her lover, nothing more.

Yet her work, her vision we might say, has depended on a correction of perspective. Large: her *Botanical Series* presents blowups—just one segment of leaf—oak, birch or maple—its veins, hairs, connective tissue in greens and yellow greens of chloroplast, amber palisade cells as seen through a microscope, a jungle growth unavailable to the naked eye. Small: on each canvas she paints an inset, the little "window" of computerese in which the tree is seen whole—bark, trunk, limbs leafed out, the tiny tree reflecting a landscape of memory. Louise has demoted the backyard maple in Wisconsin to mere detail, as though a postcard of the entire Sistine Chapel balanced on one finger of God, as though the habitat—rocky crag, fishy prey—of an Audubon eagle perched on one feather of the mighty bird. Moving from the huge segment of maple leaf, the living tissue, the viewer's eye quickly sought the comfort of the small static tree. This simple reversal of scale, amusing yet unsettling, has made Louise Moffett somewhat famous. The *Botanicals* had seemed to her a bold statement about desire for the object once valued and lost, lost beyond simple possession, some dumb Eden of the deluded heart and mind. She steps back to look at her reconstructed apple tree which Lou has not set in a cross-section of leaf. No, the mini tree blooms in a dark swirl of heartwood, the dead center of an old *malus*, and as she inscribes the Latin name where she usually signs her name, the whole enterprise appears sentimental, an impossible yearning for a time before knowledge, the world pieced back together, her little world of a farm in Wisconsin, and for the antics of a clown, Artie Freeman.

There is this: she wears an impressive emerald-cut diamond, third finger, left hand. Louise would have settled for dime-store, for zircon. Genderwise, her aims are no better than the empty promises of that booby, Miss January. With a shudder of self-loathing, she sees herself as a throwback to sweetheart left in the lurch, for she had so shamefully wanted this chip of blue ice; and when at last the ring was offered Artie played it as farce, for he was bound to be clever as though he had sworn in blood against the more revealing emotions. The cold sun rises, its brightness eerily opaque through snow on the skylight. Louise takes off the ring, smears its little blue velvet box with the white acrylic of her apple blossoms, and though her work is held in high regard and she is young, ambitious, talented and strangely more beautiful in spattered overalls and ragamuffin hair, she chokes back a sob, falls on the bed crying. That bastard has broken her heart.

In the Year of Our Lord 2000 — is that the year at last? — he wakes with a swollen head, two heads as it were, one twisting him back to the night of debauchery — to the songs, toots, cries and kisses which preceded his disgrace. He remembers the snapped stem of a glass, a busy white fizz of champagne splotching silk, running into a valley of breasts already damp with dancing. Whose breast? She is headless in memory, if memory is this befuddling pain.

There was snow. Of that he is certain, for the second head turns toward the assault of thick white snow plastered to windowsill. Plastered. Looking back, he remembers beating the trunk of a taxi with his fists, then slipping to his knees in supplication, studying the stamp of tire tread and the faint smear of exhaust on the new white world. Without scarf, gloves, overcoat, he had walked alone through Central Park, unpeopled by the storm, closed to traffic, a paper dunce cap dribbling crimson down his forehead. Concerts, fireworks, all outdoor revels had been called off in the city due to a freaky, calamitous storm. He did not consider that the lone cab, under no obligation to pick up a drunk, was driving the serpentine routes in the park illegally or had lost its way.

Yet here Artie Freeman finds himself, naked in his own bed, a bulging pressure behind the eyes, eyes no better closed than open to the excruciating light and to a view of sodden garments on the floor. Strange boots, coat, tie. The coat is an Eisenhower jacket with military emblems and campaign ribbons now stained. He had fallen a second time under a scaffolding, an armature surrounding his crumbling apartment house, a glamorous double tower erected in a year of disaster, 1929. In this shelter he collapsed in slush next to a barrel where street kids had lit a fire to welcome the incredible year. A girl, too young—twelve, thirteen—had propped him up. *Soldier,* she said, *soldier.* He remembers touching the wisps of her hair, limp hair of the undernourished, the ill. The spittle of her childish laughter sprayed his mouth in a mocking kiss, and he recalled the shallow wisdom of her eyes and his own wobbly stance, then his marching off with the hilarious rectitude of a drunk. He had thought the girl sickly pale and too young for any man.

Looking back that's not all Artie remembers: loose bolt of pain, a metallic shift in his head signals the coming day in the Year of Our Lord, Christ, it was Lou's dress he had ruined, the fizzle of his champagne sopping the blue silk from stiff pointed breasts down to a wasp waist.

"Forget it!" She had wrested the broken glass from his hand.

He no longer forgets her flouncing off like—like Mom in an old sit-com—tidy housewife, prim disciplinarian. The New Year's Eve party being costumed and set in the innocuous Fifties—she flounced in petticoats of that era, hooked into her stays—wasp waist she had named it—to flirt with another man, a pudge in tweeds, white bucks, spiffy argyles. The creep had wiped at Lou's breasts with a clean linen handkerchief. Artie swung at him, whamming his little foulard bow tie into his chinless chin. The women, all with bright lips and sleek hair, screeched at the crash of a lamp, drew off from their men, dark-suited men coming toward him in silence.

"See here, guy"—the voice of Artie Freeman's oldest, perhaps now his only friend—"you want to apologize to the lady?"

Yes, the familiar twang of the pal he beat at chess twenty years. They hitchhiked the continent, tripped together at the peak of Mount McKinley. And though they are of an age, that desperately youthful age, their early thirties, Bud Boyce is more or less

Freeman's boss. Once boys playing in cyberspace, now Boyce is a magisterial nerd, space salesman to galaxies, purveyor of time in the stratosphere, adman to corporate second-rate stars. Artie, sidekick to good buddy, was best man when Boyce wed the agreeable corporate wife.

"You want to apologize . . ."

Artie laughed, "To—our hostess? The little lady?"

All the while Big Band music and it seemed to him, the couples now turning from his tawdry heroics, shuffling into a samba, that they were all, indeed, from a forgotten day. In the high bright void of Lou's loft the century had ended, not quite the diverting re-enactment they had plotted. At midnight Lou ran the tape of Times Square that once was, pre–porn belt, pre–po-mo tourist trap, just the old dazzling crossroads of the world with thousands of clean-cut kids, clean-cut cops, assembled without fear, the countdown—minute hand jerking to the hour, the big ball descending, shimmering on the black and white screen. Flipping back in time, they drank to 1950, in accordance with Lou's plan—and Artie's; fed up with media blab—for years the city's promotional relations declaring New York PARTY CENTRAL; for months, for weeks the preview of satellite hookup—Alps to remote atoll, laser show from Mount Fuji, grizzled Beatles atop the Great Wall of China. The demoralizing history—info-techno, gender bender, Deco-Eco, Lenin to Lennon, Stravinsky to Sting, Moon Mullins to moon walk, Blimp to Bomb, cola to coke.

On a bright December day, Lou said, "Sure is the end of the world." She had been accosted by a bearded man in a toga who passed her a number—666, her number coming up in his cracked millenarian spiel.

Artie drew out his number, "Get in line." The soothsayer of lower Broadway had scratched yet another 666 on a scrap of spongy pink paper. Shuddering with cold in his soiled white drapery, he had appeared as yet another novelty in *People* magazine, as an item in the "Metro" section of the *Times*. There followed a

week in which everyone must have *their* number, always the predictable 666, from this wreck of a loon, once, it was rumored,
dean of arts and humanities at Cal Tech or MIT. When, before
Christmas, Artie Freeman figured the frequency distribution of
clichés over a sampling of three hundred newscasters nationwide
would result, median estimate, in "It was the best of times; it was
the worst of times," being mouthed, excluding Spanish, Korean
and Chinese, at least . . .

"Enough!" Lou cried, then went moony, quiet. As though she
faced a huge prepared canvas, she had sketched her notion in
lightly. "Why not celebrate the mid-century? Turn back," she said.
"Suppose we turn back. To my parents, their childhood. Chores,
Sunday School, 4 H, both of them safe on the family farm. They
might have been chicks in the incubator."

"A little hard to stage in the city." He said no more for it struck
him that her paintings were always of the farm, every silo and
barn and tree distorted or diminished to force observation, destroy
nostalgia, and that her view had prospered in Metropolis. Lou
was—at the moment, for the moment—wildly successful.

"Shirley and Harold, they would have been eight or ten," she
had no head for numbers, "my father at least . . ."

"No, in his early adolescence. So we can just play at being ourselves." She laughed at that one. "With zits and braces," he said.

"Be serious," a phrase she tossed at him from their first days together, lately without much amusement. "I only meant their
amazing innocence."

Which Lou and Artie agreed would not be much fun. So that
he had come up with the idea of his grandparents' sedate coming
of age, a scenario feeding off old movies, shadowy reruns, a cartoon of the Fifties, the postwar American dream. "At least they
knew who they were," he said.

"So, who were they?" she asked.

Artie dodged the question with a generic rundown of urban
upper-middle class, so that once again Louise knew little of them,

these prosperous grandparents, except that the dream had vanished. Their only daughter was dead. Their grandson, A. Freeman, was orphaned, named after no one, father unknown. Determined to claim no personal history, he might have been spawned by a mating of swanky schools and summer camps, or, as he reminded her charmingly—his life began when they met. So Louise, who was indeed serious, was much taken with these people who at least knew who they were in the funky Fifties, and with the sensible irony of a decorous party which might unlock a door.

Artie kicks aside the mound of soggy clothes, his costume of last night. At each step his right knee buckles, tibia grinding back into its socket. Unable to lift his head, he can't see himself in the mirrored medicine cabinet, just as well, for with his hair close-cropped for the party, he looks ravaged, skinned yet foolishly young and proper as he pees an inaccurate stream. At about eleven-thirty in the last century, the fun had gone out of the Fifties. For Artie at least, who had mixed and sampled the Manhattans, the martinis, the rye-and-ginger, the loft had started its slow swirl in which he could distinguish his friends and Lou's— their friends, he would say—and the inevitable extras, artists from her world half known to him, all passing before him in a solemn processional, though slow-dancing or eating the last of the historically accurate buffet—tuna noodle casserole, Waldorf salad, the damp ruins of a Boston cream pie—all twirling to "This Can't Be Love" on the portable hi-fi, vamping toward the millennium. Boozy, as in the old days he supposed, for he is of the recuperative generation, beer and wine, the mild toke, modest indulgences, take or leave your light pleasures, as he has taken Lou, she him, until lately when her unspoken proposition seemed to be that they should be getting on with their lives.

Such morning-after misery when he finally sees the pale stain which the party hat dribbled on his forehead, not the splatter of real blood, an unearthly dripping as from the bodiless heart of sweet Jesus, a bleeding heart crowned with thorns, framed in his grandparents' bedroom. Artie's torture, sharp almost visible. Puffed eyelids, swollen nose not a pretty sight. Lou had been exactly that, pretty in her blue taffeta dress held aloft with petticoats. Perched on high heels, she had displayed her mid-century finery to him. Her enormous canvases were stowed away, propped against their bed in the cozy area behind a screen—reference to privacy, domestic comforts. There was not a trace of turp or fixative in the workaday loft. Homey smells of supper, TV cart with the ten-inch set, a stack of scratched 78s. After that Biblical storm, the power had switched on in lower Manhattan for New Year's Eve and a chandelier only his Lou could unearth in a junk shop shone upon them, a fixture of such artlessness—frosted lights fitted to a futuristic galaxy welcoming the Space Age to the Levittown dining ell.

When he first arrived at the loft, as though her dress made all the difference, she rose on tiptoe to kiss him demurely, to touch the soft brush cut of his hair. Artie had looked down into the pretty dress. White lace poked her breasts forward, not necessarily for him in this getup. Lou's small pliant breasts he had soaped routinely in her, in their—he felt free to say in their Jacuzzi—though Artie Freeman did not live with Louise Moffett in the loft but kept, out of respect for his/their cherished independence, a bachelor apartment uptown. Waiting for their guests to arrive, she had looked to him shy, uncertain, fretting over arrangements of plates and cutlery. He was oddly elated that the great storm which canceled the fireworks at the Battery and at the North boundary of Central Park where the City virtually ended, had not interfered with their party. He had the ring in his pocket, and to Artie, who had left the dark streets uptown, it seemed that Consolidated Edison had conspired to illuminate the loft so that the diamond would dazzle his Lou at midnight.

A miracle of sorts, for at noon on this last day of the year the sky was luminescent grey, a negative. Howling wind swept up the broad avenues, clamored into side streets and blind alleys. Lights dimmed, flickered. Messages, in this city of messages, were half written, half transmitted, cut off in the troubled air. The mad prophet in his toga working the subways from Union Square to Chambers Street was exultant, his doomsday sign whipped into tatters, the last of his ominous numbers tossed like confetti in Astor Place. As the city shut down, so did the holiday air. Office parties dwindled. Not toasting that they had lived to this improbable day, workers—uptight, wary—wished each other safe home by whatever tunnel or train. By late afternoon the city was eerily calm, a short-winded bluster after all, but the last wild card of the century had done its damage.

Bothersome to Artie who worked at home designing plausible graphics for Bud Boyce—stylish bar charts and pies, seductive pictograms out of mightily inferential statistics. He punched at dead keys on the computer, on the phone. He could not call Lou to see if their time trip to the Unfabulous Fifties was still in place. The air in his apartment was suspiciously still, the dark street beyond a massive blank screen. The twilight zone that he (artfree @) dreamt up with Boyce (budboy @) had finally come about: the city had gone wireless. Cyberscouts playing WHAT IF on their screens: what if cables rotted in their decayed wood channels under the crumbling pavements of New York, what if the charged strands drew energy down signaling to resurgent mica in Manhattan's bed of granite, what if info ricocheted off the subway's charge or hyper optics were optioned by nibbling rats, jarred by shiftless tectonic plates. Twenty years since these meager fantasies entertained Artie and CEO Bertram Boyce who, bouncing messages of Product to the ever widening-narrowing world, had no time for such easy plots. Soon after Bud deleted the article before product, invested it with the capital P, Artie's faith went offline, a loss of youth in his microsoft heart, and he withdrew from Bud's enterprise, began simple piecework at home.

So, he was well out of the game, but thought seriously of Y2K unReadiness, the two blank 00s that erased a century, computers calculating the date as 1900, so belatedly searching and destroying each and every encoded day in the old mainframes at the cost of billions. And what if, somewhere around 1965, a neat-minded nerd had thought of the strategic imperative of a full four-digit date, but no one given the joy in the abbreviated language of tech talk, no one listened, for all such trivia would surely solve itself like a simple algebraic formula—$x =$ _____. Somewhere, a little guy, programmer retired—the U.S. Census Bureau, the actuarial troops at Allstate?—was laughing up his short sleeve in Scottsdale or hacker heaven. What if, but Artie is cut off, alone in his fantasy, and suppose it was only Mother Nature awarded her last chance to show them up, the communicants, corporate and casuals. To show Artie Freeman up as selfish, uncaring, for in the catastrophic silence he could not call the old man who did not want to welcome last year or the next, his grandfather who on the best of days, did not trouble himself to answer the phone, would not rise from his worn leather chair, or look up from his book, but read, read on, slowly drawing a magnifying glass across the page. The old man was Artie's family, all that was left, and his duty. His only duty to traipse across the Park with groceries, newspapers, clean socks and underclothes. Keep the old man going against the odds. Often, when Artie let himself into his grandparents' apartment—calling it that long after his grandmother's swift death—he feared to find the old man gone, last volume in his lap, head bent to decipher the last word. But his grandfather, turned out in a threadbare suit, stained tie, translucent finger marking the page in his endless pursuit of history, came toward him with a firm step. "Ah, dear boy!"

"Who else?" For Artie felt he was the only soul who knew that Cyril O'Connor was still alive and that he no longer honored the predictable seasons, forget the second millennium. As the power died in the city, Artie had looked at his dead telephone with some relief. His grandfather would reject his New Year cheer. Though courteous, Cyril O'Connor would dismiss the peculiar holiday, turn back in the fading daylight to recapture the lost line in his book, and once again the dear boy, boy now over thirty, wondered at the perfect tension the old man sustained between the will to die and the will to live.

January 1—Feast of the Circumcision:

At that time: After eight days were past, but already the text in the prayer book would seem to be an adjustment—the seventh day after the birth of Christ as Cyril counted it when he was a small boy, seven days since his electric trains were set up to run round the tree, to stop with the will of his finger at the crossing where the farmer herded his sheep through the village square. Monster sheep, sniffing at chimneys, at a tiny brass bell hung in the steeple. Stupid sheep, knocking the farmer's silo into the looking glass pond. At times he would let the locomotive run his flock down, let the clumsy ovine giants bleed plaster dust onto the green felt grass where the snowy cotton batting never melted, but switched tracks in the nick of time when his soldiers hid under the popsicle-stick bridge plotting to ambush the fort.

Seven days as Cyril figured it to the Circumcision, till his child's prayer book pictured a knife that was about to be plunged into the Babe, a knife large enough to scale a fish, to skin a rabbit, though he was a city boy who only dreamed of such outdoor adventures. Why did the knife hover over the Holy Child? At school the good sister murmured, "Is it not here His suffering begins?" A muffled question to his question. Nor was he told, as he counted down the days, why his father, come home from his beat smelling always of whiskey and still in his patrolman's uniform, began at once to disassemble trains, track, transformer, schoolmarm (rod in hand at the schoolhouse door), barnyard with farmer's wife throwing corn to the chicks out of her checkered apron. His mother had been given the whole expensive setup by a family she worked for, a couple whose boy had died of diphtheria. They could not bear the sight of these toys. Not to accept the charity of Protestants was a matter of his father's inebriate Irish pride, though the parents of the dead boy were Jews. In an apocalyptic siege of unplugging, wrapping, packing, shoving boxes to a topmost shelf, Cyril's kingdom was destroyed one day before custom declared the date on which the dead tree must come down.

A punishing feast for a kid in a West Side tenement with few pleasures.

Luke 2:21 *At that time: After eight days were past that the child should be circumcised* ... When he was fourteen, fine chap though a late starter, for some time prey to nocturnal emissions and perpetrator of shameful practices that might render him a drooling idiot or strike him blind, Cyril looked up a mysteriously forbidden word in the public library. *Smegma: an unguent or soap: a secretion of any of the secretious glands, specifically, the cheesy matter which collects between the glans penis and the foreskin, or around the clitoris or labia minora.* Well, that was a good deal of information for the head altar boy at St. Gregory's, a good deal yet not enough. What sort of soap might that be that soiled? And when had the cleansing act of circumcision been denied to the Christians? He dare not ask for answers, but Cyril O'Connor was learning his Latin. *Quod turget, urget*—what swells, impels—and did not lose faith, by which he did not mean his religion, until, ill-clothed, ill-armed, in cold outdistancing bitter, half the men in his unit were slaughtered in Korea to further inflate the imperial designs of Douglas MacArthur. Captain O'Connor, his zipper unyielding, finally zipped it down. Icy blue fingers adhered painfully for a moment to the soft fold of his foreskin; then Cyril pissed on the frozen chamber of his rifle as he had seen his men do if they were to defend themselves in this indefensible position. Their young leader under orders, he instructed them to go on with the killing in this Police Action, Yo-Yo war, for what else, in the frigid hollows leading to the Yalu River, could they possibly do. For fifty years, Cyril has not celebrated any holy day as holiday, though always a gentleman to those (most particularly his late wife) who delight in the hearts, masks, palms, eggs, crosses, doves, candles and trees that adorn their calendar of belief.

Isaiah 1:14–16. *Your new moons and your appointed feasts*
my soul hateth;
They are a trouble unto me; I am weary to bear them.

And when ye spread forth your hands,
  I will hide mine eyes from you:
Yea, when ye make many prayers,
  I will not hear;
Your hands are full of blood.

THE CELEBRATED SOUP

When Artie Freeman hobbles to Broadway foraging for food, the city is awake to the New Year. Shovels and plows undo disaster. Dogs squat in cold comfort. Children already at play—not the street kids of last night who have left, under the scaffolding of Artie's building, their Druids' circle of ashes, vials, limp balloons—his faint memory, the puckered mouth of a sallow girl. Real children stomp waist-deep in the magic element, a vast pudding of tainted water glazing in the sun. Warm, too warm—the snow will soon be gone, yet the stoplights are still dead uptown, Artie's neck of the woods in a city cut into jagged precincts of safety and squalor. The shops here closed, save for the Korean greengrocers and the Unhappy Butcher. He recalls his grandfather's response to a bloody steak—how often Cyril had turned their slabs of meat in a pan and proudly split open their baked potatoes, the years they hacked it alone. The old guy's scotch on the rocks, his child's tumbler of milk.

Often when serving withered peas, Cyril O'Connor said: "Your mother would not, nor your grandmother . . . would not believe . . ."

". . . would not believe"—the boy knew how the sentence, if spoken, would end—". . . would not believe we are so happy."

Here the Unhappy Butcher, ruddy, red-eyed. Powerless in the great uptown defrost, he fears for his livelihood. His counters have been cleared for the holiday and he will not open the ice chamber until Artie, spinning his data out of thin air, estimates the overwhelming probabilities of power returned within the hour and softens the butcher's heart with the tale of an old codger, half blind, neglected, unfed. When the cold vault swings open, there is the man's capital—stiff sides of beef, wee baby lambs, limp fowl with feathery necks, a piglet with frozen smile—happy, as the butcher is now, displaying rump steak and T-bone. He advises meaty aged rump for an old man and throws in a humongous soup bone, what Artie takes to be the cleaved thigh bone of a steer, ragged with meat. "Have a happy!"

> If it be too large for your vessel, strike a meaty beef bone with the kitchen cleaver. To two gallons of water add salt and the broken bone. Skim the scum as it comes to the surface. Add firm onion, carrot, parsnip—the predictable bay leaf and herbs. Simmer long and by this homey method you will make stock to make soup to take stock of your malingering Winter ills, not the world's.

Artie goes off with his bloody prize and some satisfaction. The metallic shift in his head has mostly abated, though his right knee locks with slippery uncertainty at each step. Yes, have a happy, he will cook for his grandfather. Purchasing a couple of plump potatoes, he recalls the dull grey skin of his computer screen. What has been lost? At most a parade of cows to please a dairy consortium, beasts of his design marching to colossal production, pails of their milk expanding to a promotable end. Lost—he had turned out the pockets of the soggy clothes, once Captain O'Connor's uniform, but could not find the jaunty overseas cap with its double bars. Lost—as well as those moo cows constructed out of a biased sampling (of Product? for Product?), constructed on the command of Bud Boyce to be aimed at the microtot market under his corporate rubric—Skylark.

Artie gets as far in his sluggish retrieval as sorrow, some inestimable sorrow, then draws a blank. A sense of serious loss overwhelms him. The petulant stamp of her foot in those ridiculous heels preceded a brawl. The loss can't be his Lou, yet some bloody brawl led to his eviction, to the heavy clunk of the dead bolt sealing him out of her loft. The tweedy man he had socked was Lou's art dealer a/k/a Dealer, whose lust was only for her work, no interest in her creamy breasts.

At the start of the evening Artie felt set up in his khaki shirt and tie, the wool of the Eisenhower jacket coarse and manly. His friends, their friends, the men looked docile in starched shirts and narrow ties, ready for mortgages, life insurance, the family sedan. While sober, he had seen a dreary domestication, unmistakably Fifties, in the women's pearls and pumps. Perhaps their girlish wondering over the food had kept him from eating. Then—a plate shoved into his hand, scrawny fingers pressing on his arm. Felicia, a harsh woman emaciated by choice. Was she perversely feeding him? An artist he barely knew, but knew she was notorious as Felicia with no further name, that she cut simulated documents—the Bill of Rights, the Nicene Creed, Magna Carta—into paper doll chains while lip synching extravagant arias, songs of love and death. For the millennial occasion she had tattooed the number 2000 in the blue-black ink of the death camps on her wrist.

"Wash it off," Freeman said.

"Permanent," Felicia spit her *p*, her *t*.

"Burn it off," Freeman said. At which point, he now remembers, he was smoking a stinky French cigarette, sophistication of an era. If only he could not remember the woman's transparent blouse of a prehistoric nylon. Her flimsy underclothes appeared jaundiced on her skeletal dark flesh. Felicia had been somewhere in the sun cutting papal bulls into doilies, but had made it to New York, by Jesus, to the scene, Lou's way cool party. Their tasteless party.

Sure enough—they had all come, Boyce and his buxom Heather, overflowing a strapless dress, a woman proud of her labels, "Ceil Chapman!"

He could not recall a movie, surely not of the Fifties, that featured Chaplin in drag. The media mavens, Bud's guys he had worked with at Skylark, made the trip into town from suburbia, each with a pretty wife, neither sleet nor snow, nor gloom of night—stayed these couriers of foreclosure. They had scooped Artie off the floor, lifted him high, music and laughter wheeling above his complaints, and when he looked down on the guests, his guests and Lou's, these men and their women were elated by his punishment. Something real had happened—raw, a touch psycho—and they were all in it at the end of a violent century. At the edge of this fury, Louise wept. Tough, angry tears.

Artie waits in the bus shelter at 86th Street, the big soup bone knocking his sore knee. The passengers on the crosstown, chatty pilgrims who have survived the spectacular Nor'Easter, observe the iced rocks shimmering black in the sun, toppled trees and torn branches, a shutter flapping at the barracks where patrol cars snort, ready to drive their routes where no dog or jogger or criminal element yet roams. A still, colorless world: ebony limbs, white hillocks severed sharp as canyons by the wind, lamp posts crowned with turbans of snow. Grand, the close-up as well as the panoramic view. As the bus skids toward the Museum, a woman in a leather hat, slick black hide pulled tight to her skull, follows the rivulet of blood which drips from the butcher's bag across the face of her New York Times, miraculously published this day, across the face of the Pope in his white robes blessing Artie's beef bone. He had no more wanted to stab Felicia than slaughter the beast in the bag, had mimed the act, taken a long elegant knife that cut a wedding cake back in the benevolent Fifties, the instrument of Cyril and Mae O'Connor, his contribution to the giddy, nonobservant gala.

"Burn it," Freeman had said to the artist with the Auschwitz tattoo, but when he came toward her, the glow of his cigarette melted, quite accidentally, a perfect little circle in her nylon blouse. Set on his charade, he had brandished the cake knife dramatically above Felicia's self-mutilated wrist, never for an instant intending . . .

A shrill cry. Some heroic postwar hero in a sharkskin suit wrestled him to the floor. Never intending . . . the serrated cake knife to damage the slick suiting, but one small prick of blood seeped to the surface of the man's finger. So, he had cut the man—Bud Boyce.

"A flesh wound," Bud laughing, not to spoil the party. "You want to apologize?"

"To—our hostess? The little lady?"

The crosstown bus spins its wheels, backslides, charges up to Fifth Avenue. The glass casing on the Egyptian wing of the Metropolitan Museum has been mostly swept away by one fierce current of yesterday's wind. As in a terrifying ice-palace dream, shards of jagged glass stick out of blue-white drifts. Some of the panes have skidded unbroken into the Park. Artie Freeman sees the Temple of Dendur, that artifact of a lost civilization, unscathed yet diminished. The ancient temple snowed in with its pool appears small as a bathhouse in a desolate off-season.

Quick as he can with his gimpy knee, Artie jumps off the bus, swinging rump steak and bone which lightly bloody the soft snow. At the blind eyes of each stoplight, the few taxis and cars play a civilized game as though entering a time of patience and respect and he's on to thinking that the showcase for the ruins of Dendur, which he so loved as a boy, can easily be reconstructed and on to believing it was natural in the military getup, his urge to erase an insidious number, not the number itself so much as the flesh that trashed it. He limps along sorry, though some mortal offense blacked out by the booze is unclear—all that surfaces is the stain dribbling to the hem of Lou's dress, the slap of her dead bolt. His eviction.

January 11—William James, American philosopher, born at New York City, 1842.

> Things tell a story. Their parts hang together so as to work out a climax. They play into each other's hands expressively. Retrospectively, we can see that altho no definite purpose presided over a chain of events, yet the events fell

into a dramatic form, with a start, a middle, and a finish. In point of fact all stories end; and here again the point of view of many is the more natural one to take. The world is full of partial stories that run parallel to one another, beginning and ending at odd times. They mutually interlace and inter- fere at points, but we can not unify them completely in our minds. In following your life-history, I must temporarily turn my attention from my own.

—Pragmatism

THE FLINTSTONES

Consider their affinities: both Freeman and his grandfather have withdrawn from the competition. (There is no father. That link is lost.) Their awkward bodies are strung together loosely. They stand above the crowd with high pokey shoulders, not the com- pact look of men who once fooled around on a basketball court, but they share an attractive energy—loners, not losers, not always. The dear boy is his grandfather exactly. Their loping long stride sets the hustling city at a distance as though they have arrived from an earlier time, both Artie and Cyril, as though they might easily saunter through swinging doors of the old Astor House on lower Broadway or into the feed store on Fulton Street, or rise re- spectfully at a meeting of the First Ward with a gentleman's re- quest. Shock-haired men, Artie's rumpled black, Cyril's stark white; they bear matching widower's peaks and startling blue eyes, the bright blue of untroubled summer skies. All in all, good looks somewhat botched by large, heavily lobed ears and by the narrow pinched nose of the craggy Irish. The old man cannot help his dignity, though it makes him seem a pretender seeking refuge in his old books, blindly pacing the dark rooms of his apart- ment, a pretender to better days when containment, reserve, inde- pendence and inquiry served a man well.

Consider that his grandson, dutifully trudging Fifth Avenue with an insupportable knee, would not have seemed such an ass at the New Year debacle if not cursed with a remnant of Cyril's outdated posture. And that Artie would not be so often ticked off if he did not sense that the words-upon-words barely visible to the old guy in his history books were kin to the glut of information on his screen, databases from which he fudged convincing facts; and that his grandfather's obsessive isolation was much like the lone hours at his workstation, where, most recently, he brindled, hoofed and uddered make-believe cows, one cow standing for thousands, her lactation engineered to the nth degree.

Not bad times, the many suppers with Cyril. Steak and potato on the menu, no vitamins as in the old days. In need of a remedy on this nauseous New Year's Day—hair of the dog, raw egg yolks in beer—Artie thinks of the primal cure, the pastel vitamins pressed in the shape of the Flintstones and their dinosaur pet. Each morning his mother had unscrewed the childproof cap and let him choose a chalky Fred or Wilma, Pebbles or Dino.

She had packed the kiddie vitamins in with his Yankee PJs and driven him into the city on a warm Spring day. In fact, his Spring vacation from school. All as usual—Cyril and Mae down at the curb to meet them so that his mother would not have to park on Fifth Avenue. That was a fiction: Fiona O'Connor seldom visited her parents in their apartment and his mother could not parallel-park, could not stop, if she stopped at a light, without a squealing of tires. In every particular a lousy driver. All as usual, the doorman taking his zip bag into the lobby. His grandmother leaning into the car. Two fair Irish faces—mother and daughter—facing off.

"Don't spoil my kid," his mother said.

"No more," a clip to Mae's voice, "than we spoiled you."

As usual his grandfather had turned him around by the shoulders to stand straight and wave his mother off. It could not have been as usual, for Cyril was still on Wall Street in those days. Unless that day was Good Friday and the market was closed, but Artie surely remembered Mae poking her head into the scarred suburban wagon, his grandmother's red hair fading to white. His

mother's hair brazen, that word picked up from Cyril, who said
with the faintest smile that his daughter was brazen. The boy believed it was therefore commendable that his mother's hair was
copper-bright.

He stood at attention that fine morning, held his hand high in
a salute, fearful that she might turn and wave back at him, killing
the dachshund at the curb. Fiona did turn with a wild hoot of joy,
both hands off the wheel, happy to be free of him. That is what
the boy thought. He was eleven years old. Freeman has not re-
vised that opinion. He remembers the station wagon screeching
off, turning east at the end of the block, right through a red light.
A parting view of the battered blue Connecticut plate.

It was the last he saw of his mother, who died that week in a
boating accident in calm West Indian waters. She was not at the
helm, knew nothing of sailing. The chances she would be totaled
on the Interstate, he had figured as one in five. That she should
capsize with her lover in collision with a tourist speedboat off the
tiny island of Nevis was a million to one. Each weekday of that
Spring vacation, his grandfather, dressed in a three-piece suit,
dealt out Wilma or Pebbles, unaware that the vitamins were for
toddling midgets. On the Saturday after Easter the news came
early. Cyril in a sporty jacket, Mae fussing over French toast. After
breakfast they had planned to go down the Avenue, to take their
grandson to the Temple of Dendur for the very first time.

But the news came early. His grandfather answered the
phone, then took the boy's hand which was nearly as big as his
own. "Vitamins," he said with great solemnity. "She would have
wanted you to grow. To grow up." A neutral statement, yet it was
how Mae knew that her daughter was dead. She had bounced the
Vermont Maid syrup in its plastic jug into the kitchen sink, re-
tracted their silverware and plates while the eggy bread burned in
the skillet. Clearing the deck, as it were, for sorrow, she tossed the
baby vitamins into the trash. For a while Freeman believed that,
denied the niacin, B_{12}, riboflavin of the Flintstones intended for
little people, he became a skinny freak, but at that moment his

extremities were palsied with fear, with rage, and in imitation of his grandfather, he found no tears.

Alone in the white clapboard house in Connecticut where he had lived with his mother, he had often imagined that he would answer the phone and the cops would say which barrier she had driven through, on which entrance ramp she had refused to yield. Even this role of dealing in manly fashion with sirens, doctors and tubular apparatus, taken from television drama, was taken from him. Fiona O'Connor was not rendered contrite in a hospital bed to be cared for by her boy, the child that a childish woman would have wanted to grow up.

Now he limps to his grandparents' apartment, never thought of as home though he lived there after the white house in Connecticut faded to no more than a set for old Hollywood flicks—the comedies of loving, quarrelsome couples that his grandmother found so reassuring. Movie homes that held forth the ideal of home in quaint shutters and shrubbery, pristine stove and sink, handwritten letters on a breakfast tray. Mae's big bland apartment was never home, for all the days he ran up Fifth Avenue from the Temple of Dendur to be back at the dining room table with his math or Latin textbooks before Cyril's key turned in the door. Faking it—homework and home.

Artie Freeman, the gimp, makes it to the lobby of that apartment house, finding there an untended dachshund simpering at the glass door which is also untended. "Poor beast," Artie says. Poor civilized beast, for when he lets it slither out, it is beached in snow well above its head and cannot figure how to lift its stumpy leg. He pulls the dog in, strokes it while she (puckered rows of tiny tits) relieves herself on the clawed foot of a gilt table Artie has hated for its fancy-pants glamour since he was a little boy. Elevators out, they climb the stairs together, the bitch's loose stomach whacking every step. At each landing she waits for Freeman who hobbles behind, and sniffs politely at rump steak and bone until she whines at the sixth floor to be let into the dark beyond. Paw scratch, click of a latch and she is home. Figuring life span of breed with modest turnover of old apartments on Upper East Side, he takes the low-slung hound to be a random variable, perhaps a descendant of the very dog he feared his mother would kill the week before she died.

Crawling the last flights in the dark stairwell, Artie fears that on this aftermath of a day, he will discover his grandfather asleep forever in the crocked leather chair or laid out in his Brooks Brothers pajamas under the genteel pall of Mae's crocheted spread, the gold pocket watch, which would now be his, ticking away on the night table, though . . . though, while Artie fumbles with his key, it would be like Cyril to read on, his wretched old eyes following word by magnified word—Jefferson, Monroe, Adams—plots of the past in which he loses the line literally. Often Freeman wants to shout at the unopened door—Here, I am here from the city of outlaws marauders unhoused tribes unknown to your floundering fathers their endless words writ out sealed posted to an old coot assembling big word by big word Double-Crostic for the insoluble grief forbearance here—I am here. But being so like the old man, he always enters without a word. Today, pain distracts him from anger. He sets down the meat and potatoes, leans his muddled head against the door.

"Here!" Artie cries. "I'm here!" Then the premeditated terror: he will find Cyril dead.

January 17—Benjamin Franklin born at Boston, 1706. Papa. Cher Papa. Though he has successfully concluded his diplomatic duties which bring to an end the War of Independence, he stands bemused, hat in one hand, spectacles in the other, while a most beautiful lady crowns him with laurel and myrtle in the grand salon of the Musée de Paris. It is 1783. She alone is awed, while ladies and gents of high degree, powdered and wigged, look to their American hero with bemused smiles of respect. He is the new Prometheus, the natural aristocrat among them, hero of the

New World from generous dome of bald head to plain buckles on his shoes. *One does not dress for private company as for a public ball.* —Benjamin Franklin

Or does one? Does one carry the Quakerish hat to make a point when it is replaced by the herbal tribute intended for emperors and gods? So that the laurels will not prick. Cher Papa, as Madame Helvétius called him, one of the many ladies to whom he was more fatherly than to his own children. Easier to play at family away from home and to be the public's darling, father of us all. Biographer's business: ferret out Franklin, the peevish husband, his drawing room dalliances, that love letter with a lascivious phrase; make philosopher and statesman real, human, flawed. Isn't that more comfortable in dealing with a man of genius? Franklin beat his biographers to the draw, shrewdly controlling the image of a simple man given to small theatrics, to harmless play.

Old Cyril, sipping from history that trick dribble cup of Time, admired Ben Franklin when, in his retirement some years before the millennium, he took to reading the Founding Fathers. He bought the anecdotal version of a near-penniless boy which appears in *The Autobiography*. Young Ben with three Puffy Rolls under his arm walking up from the docks in Philadelphia where, standing in her father's doorway, he saw the girl who was to become his wife. Bending to the book, Cyril puzzled out Franklin's story—an ambitious young man in his printer's apron setting type for *Poor Richard's Almanack*, which featured Advice and Amusement, Essential Information of the Sun, Moon, and Stars, printing his best-seller in downtime when the press was not running a job. At an early age, adept, as Cyril has been, at Making Money, and more than clever at his craft, though Cyril O'Connor was struck, reading between the lines, to discover that when Ben finally married the Puffy Roll girl he no longer loved her. Then hastily as he was able, Cyril read on to Franklin in gentleman's tricorn and weskit flying the famous silk kite, teasing Electricity out of a storm. Nothing daunted the old man until one unexceptional night (it is timeless in the dark apartment) Cyril understood that Franklin was seventy when Congress commissioned him as Minister to France, not many years younger than he is as he closes his book and feels his way to the bedroom, grumbling that the sun will rise next day.

Often he cannot name the day, but will wake with the first dull light, of that he is unfortunately certain. Still, he reads on — the great man's letters, bagatelles, political satires, his experiments and observations. Franklin awarded degrees from St. Andrew's, Oxford, Fellow of the Royal Academy, the first honorary degree from Harvard; tributes to a Natural Philosopher, long before the word scientist came into being. Finding that there really was no correspondence between the American Inventor–Self-inventor and himself other than the art of moneymaking, he reads on only to marvel. Then, as though time will be allotted so that he may turn back one day, Cyril takes up his pen to mark a passage —

> *If you would not be forgotten*
> *As soon as you are rotten,*
> *Either write things worth reading,*
> *Or do things worth the writing.*

but finds that disheartening, for he has never written or done, and is forgotten by all but the boy whose care packages come bound in guilt, and so marks another of Poor Richard's pithy maxims: *Let thy Discontents be Secret.* And further scrawls in the flyleaf of Franklin's delightful self-advertising *Autobiography*: Printer, Publisher, Statesman. Inventor of: Rocking chair, catheter, Franklin stove, lightning rod, bifocals, water wings — until the list of Practical Inventions runs off the page, leaving Cyril to contemplate Franklin's Long Arm, an Instrument for Taking Down Books from High Shelves, his Improvements on the Sea Anchor and the Glass Armonica. A thorough man, Cyril reads to the last page to discover it was not a bitter end for Franklin, who wrote to a friend that if allowed, he'd live his whole life over. And closing the book, Cyril

O'Connor considers his own Rags-to-Riches career, sorely limited to puts and calls and the shortsighted futures of Wall Street.

But on the first day of January, Janus allowing us to screw our heads back in this newest Year of Our Lord, Artie Freeman braved the snowbound city, crawled the black stairway to his grandparents' apartment, still unclear as to how he arrived in his own bed ten stories above Central Park on this powerless morning. Clever at guessing games—it's Artie's business to shape up unorganized data for Skylark, to chart and graph Product, as in overflowing milk pails, to coolly round off statistics into digestible, vendable pies, yet he stupidly leans on the bell, bangs crazily on the door wanting his grandfather, who is the fragile ghost of himself, wanting him alive while predicting with tears in his bloodshot eyes—a fitting end to that Christ-awful century—the old gentleman will be neatly laid out on the bier of his single bed.

"Here!" Artie cries. "I'm here!"

The woman who opens the door is tiny, will-o'-the-wisp. In the dim front hall, where the mirror and hat rack of old waver in candlelight, she calls out, "What kept you?"

Artie sees they have been waiting, they—for in the living room beyond, Cyril is buttoned into his antiquated chesterfield with the worn velvet collar.

"Ah, dear boy!" The routine greeting out of Edwardian novels or the Noel Coward revivals which his grandmother loved, pisses Artie off. Cyril is jolly, thumping his cold hands together as though in applause for the little woman all in white who pokes the decorative birch logs into a musty blaze suffusing the neglected room with flattering light. The leather chair is pushed to the window so that the history buff may read on, his endless pages.

Sylvie, that is the name of this blunt little enchantress, has arrived from Cyril's unimaginable past. Artie is outraged by her charms. The lovers (getting his aching head around that one) speak a bill-and-coo language—*old beau, sweetheart*—and laugh at the adventure of Sylvie driving through a blizzard, scrambling up the dark stairwell to find him, Captain O'Connor, to find him mercifully alone in the dark, yet so—so *available*. As the beau reaches for her hand, Sylvie is properly embarrassed and issues an emphatic change of subject. "Chances are an hour or so, the power will go on. You know about chances."

"I figure . . ." Artie Freeman figures to spite this minx who has transformed his grandfather with the kiss of life, "figure that the power in the corroded infrastructure of uptown Manhattan may not be restored in our time. We may not experience again the comfort of central heating, electricity, phone, the indispensable phone."

"Ah," she finds him amusing, "then it is better we go home to Connecticut." She is Sylvie, a sprite intent on running off with Cyril. Elope is the word of his grandfather's choice.

"Elope into the future, my—"

"My boy," Artie fills in.

"Hard to drop the old locutions," Cyril says.

"You are seventy-five."

"Seventy-six," says Sylvie.

"He never leaves these rooms. The basic functions. Sleep, walk, sit. Read. Barely reads," Artie hears himself shouting, "word by painful word."

"And yet he insistently stands on his head!" A rich rumble of mirth from Sylvie's small body. "You speak as though Cyril is not here. Isn't that what we do with the demented and little children?"

"His dotage! Elope into his dotage." Artie's rudeness cannot touch them. He doubts that his grandfather sees Sylvie's bridal white—boots, ski pants, parka, a powder puff of white hair—the snow princess who has waited for her lover how many frozen years? Thawed, the two of them, into giddy youngsters. Already secret smiles, words overlapping as they now speak their piece, a cornball, geriatric romance. One stolen night of luff in the Fifties. Artie detects a trace of Garbo guttural in Sylvie's recitation. While Cyril warms himself by the last embers of Mae's smoldering logs, this Sylvie reconstructs their passion at a little Hungarian restaurant—rhapsodic violin, potato pancakes.

Cyril sighs, "Red cabbage, veal paprika."

Artie slings the rump steak and bone onto Mae's noncommittal carpet. He is sorry for her beige wall-to-wall, for the bland fare of his grandmother's table, her weekly hair appointment, good works with the Grey Ladies of Charity and the yearly cruise to Bermuda. Harmless Mae, her touch of the ordinary on everything. An air of the exotic invades her living room—shadows of candlelight, a creamy silk scarf draping the button-back couch; the shimmer of Sylvie's glossy lidded eyes, crystal earrings of the seductress. Artie is undone by their story. He has projected gum loss in a colorful bar chart, pitching neglect against heredity for a dentifrice designed for oldies, great looking oldies like Cyril and his sweetie, who smile undentured upon him from the reclaimed height of their passion which has not been eroded by years of dutiful marriage to the wrong mates—to poor Mae O'Connor and to a blameless airline executive who expired, conveniently, on a golf cart in Boca Raton.

"Incredible, is it not?" Cyril fixes his grandson straight-on. He has lost peripheral vision.

"Fucking off the charts."

"Not so, not so." Sylvie revealing their pact. "We swore we would meet in the next century, so it is possible. I never forgot our foolish promise, how we cried when we parted"—Artie sees them on the steps of the Plaza, on a misty Waterloo Bridge—"the Captain, too, bawling for the world to see in Grand Central under the clock," Sylvie's coy hesitation, "the morning after. The morning after, fifty years seemed forever. You grow old. . . ."

Cyril gallantly dismisses his sweetie's age.

"So, you guys got a lot to talk about." Aiming this at his grandfather, who did not weep over the graves of his wife and daughter, but it now occurs to Artie Freeman that Fiona and Mae were counterfeits in Cyril's life of let's pretend. And their years together, aging man and orphan boy, a mere litter of homework, checkers, chess, frizzled minute steak and mealy potatoes, evenings his grandfather had not relished, nor had he delighted in Artie's stunning math scores or his array of diving trophies. All Cyril O'Connor's praise was fraudulent, meant for the son of a daughter born of desire.

The lights flicker, flick on. Sylvie looks to the dial of her dainty watch, prods her old darling, who lifts his traveling gear with effort. "We're off." In the dark hall Artie had missed the duffle, the very one Cyril brought back from his war, packed for the boy each summer when he was shipped off to camp. It bears both their names in black stencil.

When he rings for the elevator, Cyril turns back to Artie, who is curled in upon himself at the open door: "What of the young woman? The girl?"

"I gave her the ring." His croak of amazement that the old fella has remembered.

The victory sign from Cyril and then, "We're off," echoing Sylvie, the little imp in the driver's seat, who made it through one of the memorable storms of the century in an invincible old Jeep.

"Torque on the ice?"

She doesn't hear Arthur Freeman's feeble cut, words of a snotty kid, but he gets that she has shouted her romantic tale so that she might hear herself speak. The deaf old doll leading that blind, hoodwinked old man, the last living soul who knows who A. Freeman is—a bastard begot in the mud of Woodstock. He has never told Lou this likely story of his humiliating origin, though he had often computed the continuous density of the sperm bank which enabled one unidentified donor to succeed in becoming his father during Fiona's transcendent multiplicity of fucks. That he leapt into being at the legendary Love Fest was, of course, an unsound hypothesis. And by the time he met Louise, he had given up on it as a trite tale. She had seemed satisfied with *orphan* and with his remnant of family, an aged grandfather set in the wings, as though it freed her from her own—Harold Moffett, that heavy-duty father, and old Shirl, the dithering lightweight mom, set at their distance in Wisconsin. Until recently, he admits, when the idea of their New Year's party got under way and he called upon his grandparents as historical figures; then Louise had been curious.

At least they knew who they were. He had said that and been wrong, now sees that he produced Cyril and Mae as types, so damn sure he knew who they were that he rendered them lifeless to his shame. And feels the further disgrace of his grandfather getting it on—liver spot to liver spot with Sylvie, entwined varicosities. Off to Connecticut. Abandoned, left to nurse his throbbing knee in the empty apartment. He imagines Cyril in the Eisenhower jacket fumbling with Sylvie's zipper, trembling hand on wasp waist, not in a slick hotel scene. Their love nest is a home with green shutters much like the dreamhouse Cyril O'Connor bought for his unwed daughter, supporting Fiona in all her follies—the throwing of lumpy plates and pots, her untalented strumming of unmelodic folk songs. Though, on long Winter nights when the fire blazed in Connecticut, his mother sang prettily—

> *The snow may never slush upon the hillside,*
> *By nine p.m. the moonlight must appear.*
> *In short, there's simply not*
> *A more congenial spot*
> *For happ'ly-ever-aftering than here . . .*

—a song from the musical her own mother loved, her one concession to Mae's taste for Broadway maudlin, and he would join in— *Camelot, Camelot,* in his thin soprano . . . *The climate must be perfect all the year.*

The only time they sang together, until it dawned on him to ask: "Is my father's name Arthur?"

"It is not a saint's name," Fiona said.

"He was no saint?"

She turned on him, the red tangle of her hair flying. "It's not a saint's name and your grandmother would like you to be named for a saint."

An end to the weather *where once it never rained till after sun-*

down. No more duets. Though on his own he read Arthurian Legends of war, adultery, magic. Not his story, just grown-ups screwing around. Artie Freeman learned to live with the drawbridge drawn against his questions as efficiently as he learned to lay the kindling, leave a crack for air between seasoned logs. When the flames were high, his mother sat with her legs crossed to meditate, clearing her head of here and now, until, he knew this as a boy, until he was cast out, no longer present in the radiant warmth of her room.

Last night yet another dismissal. As his grandfather and Sylvie descend in the elevator, climb into the Jeep, head off through soiled city slush toward a house with green shutters, the painful moments blink on—oddly spliced like random camcorder footage. He had steered Louise to the back of the loft, his hand firm on her waist. The man leading, wasn't that how they'd done it? Stumbling in an awkward two-step, sure, he'd sampled a Rob Roy, thrown back a stinger and the sticky dregs of a Manhattan. He'd thought to take her behind the screen, where an easy chair, a scrap of rug, their bed gave a semblance of home. A giant canvas overwhelmed them, the one unfinished painting not stacked away for their perverse celebration. He knelt before Lou's dark vision of an apple tree's heartwood with a miniature inset of the tree in full flower. Astonishing, the thwunk-thwunk of his heart, years of cool blown away. A suitor on his knees, he had given some thought to this posture, this offering.

He had taken the ring from his grandmother's jewelry case, snapped open the velvet box to ask Cyril, "May I . . . ?"

Had Cyril seen the sparkler when he looked up from the page? A twitch of memory in the weak blue eyes: "Yes, by all means. She would want you to have it." Then skipped to the presumption, "You are going to marry!"

"Yes." Ordinary talk followed, absolute flow of conversation breaking the reticence of all their years, the old man curious about the girl.

"The woman."

"Of course, woman."

And Artie was quick to praise her, in fact a girl from the heart-land, eager to bring Louise home—calling the apartment home where Cyril sat reading, tidy but unclean. He felt somewhat un-comfortable, his easy words promoting the attributes of Louise— her beauty, humor, competence—not the woman herself but single white female: caring, loves art and a good laugh. Over-selling himself on the proposal, for lately the M word was written in invisible ink all over Lou's calendar, a drop of lemon juice and it would surface. "Be serious" had narrowed in meaning.

"Marriage," Cyril said, "is an honorable state. I felt the need of it and your grandmother did surely. Not my Fiona. She was en-tirely free of such institutions. I often think she might have come round, though I would not have encouraged her."

"Come round?"

"In those days—"

"Come round? Who'd she come round to? My father?" Which cut the pleasant talk, always had.

"If I knew. If I knew—"

Artie ending that one. "—I would have told you long ago who the bastard was." Then, feeling ungrateful, he set his grandfather's magnifying glass to the top line of a page from which it had wan-dered. "Thanks," he said, snapping the box closed on the ring, "I'm sorry."

"No need for that," Cyril said. "It's a sorry world."

"Better dealt with in sayings? Things others have said?"

The magnifying glass slipped to the carpet. Artie put it in the old man's cold fingers. "Sorry," he said again. "Thanks for the ring." And Cyril began an anecdotal account of the diamond's purchase.

"In those days—"

Walking home through the Park, Artie ran off what he should have said, a habit of long standing, the should-have-said-to-Cyril: *Contortionist's stiff upper lip hiding my withered limbs, the*

crippled kid, you know crippled, having once trained me to walk
like a little soldier, stand up like a man, words from your boy stories,
pluck against adversity, value of the ring in my pocket no more to
you than my weekly allowance, more than a year's take in my cot-
tage industry, always money to heal the wound of what might be
called, I suppose, my inner life, my blind rage at being fatherless
turned to a gentle myth, one of your wife's dotty ones, transubstanti-
ation. Numb the injury with ice, pay up. So, do you see me, Pops,
kneeling, a suitable suitor? Part of me hoping the ring might be
worthless, a gag.

But the ring, like his grandfather's hard currency, had its
value, was there for the taking, though Artie believed the arcane
token no part of his life. Yet last night he knelt on one knee in the
shadow of a tiny apple tree. Its snowy petals showered promise as
though pages of the calendar fluttered forward to Spring and he
was suddenly worshipful, as he dug the velvet box out of his
grandfather's pocket, though unable to judge the distance to his
loved one's hand.

"Hey! Love you, my Lou."

At a distance, on the other side of the screen, the New Year's
revelry continued. He had wanted the magic moment to be midnight. That moment had passed. He had wanted the accompani-
ment of his grandmother's music, maybe — "Begin the Beguine,"
"What Is This Thing Called Love?" Someone had put on the
pounding Electro Funk of a more immediate past. The gummy
smell of turpentine rags mixed with the heavy sweetness of hash-
ish, the night smoking its way into a timeless future. Balanced
uncertainly, Artie saw with selective clarity the dribble of champagne he had dealt to Lou's taffeta dress.

"Love my Lou-Lou!"

She plucked the diamond from its velvet safety in a snit, put it
on her finger, taking it as one more prop for their millenarian
masquerade. "Oh, Artie! You're polluted."

He stayed a supplicant, kissing the stained hem of her gown.
"Serioushly, Lou!"

"Not now, when you're sauced."

The painful moment surfaces, Louise jabbing him with her stiletto heel, a swift kick to the knee. He topples, streaks of verdigris and raw umber on Captain O'Connor's uniform, Lou's apple tree felled. She weeps uncontrollably. He hears her call above the throbbing music, call out for Bud Boyce and his henchmen. Then he is lifted ceremoniously, held up to ridicule as in a tar-and-feather ritual. Heaved out of Lou's loft.

THE ALICE BLUE GOWN

Louise Moffett sits on a straight chair. In her empty white space not a crumb of New Year's remains. Early afternoon. She listens to her calls, abbreviated, one-sided commentary, the guests of last night checking in: "far out," "thrilling" (Heather Boyce), "assault on the official culture of temporality" (Felicia), "quite a *rumble*" (Dealer attempting the language of hip), "wild," "shocking," "in-your-face blowout," "a blast." Lou sees that Artie's bad behavior is a party favor they have taken home. They have witnessed. Their version of violence, almost the real thing, is souvenir, has value on the street. So she's the victim and that has value, too, more than the mild rebellion of her work which seems a confusion of art and commerce. No more, this lucrative preaching to the converted. See. See what you cannot see, life and death converted to . . . but she will not think *deadwood of apple tree*, leave it to others, the sappy pun of her *malus*. Occasionally, she walks to the front window to look down at the trash she has set in the melting snow at the curb—the moderno lighting fixture, old linens, TV cart, LPs. The ancient stereo is first to go. The merry-widow corset stands stiff against a fender. The skirt of the pretty blue dress dances in the wind, rhythmic flutters.

"Happy New Year!" (Lou's mother calling from Wisconsin.) "We want to wish you . . ." (The *we* is untrue. Harold Moffett is at odds with his daughter.) "We miss you!" (As though her husband hears this cheery note, Shirley signs off quickly, a kiss in the air.)

Louise waits patiently for Artie's call. It comes when the street-light first shines like a spot on the pile of anachronistic junk in the gutter.

"Sweetheart?" Artie murmurs. "You were never more beautiful. Think a dress can change your nature?" Not what he meant to say. "You think there was that danger, losing ourselves in dress-up?" He speaks from the bourgeois ruins of his grandparents' apartment, nursing the blue egg that has risen on his knee. "I'm sorry. It's a sorry world, Louise. Louise, I know you're there. Have mercy." In the long silence which follows, his desire for her becomes urgent, unpredictable the rise of his pecker. "Lou, I have this bone," even on closed circuit unable to play it straight, "this bloody useless bone."

She unplugs the phone, stands at the window. Someone had punched him to keep him in line, a light blow. She wonders if his nose hurts, a high-bridged Irish nose like—like Samuel Beckett's. He would not know to ice it. Yes, there was a danger in dress-up, but it was not that they were different. She had played the heavy, reverted to such a conventional woman, to the nature she had rightly denied, while Artie was airier than ever in zip cut and tight little jacket, a toy soldier. If anything they were more themselves in masquerade.

Louise watches a woman tug at a miniature dog sniffing the stiletto heels, then pick up the smoky-blue dress bought at Second Hand Rose, hold the stiff silk to her large body. Silk of such quality Louise had placed the dress above the slush, set its swinging skirt with care on a hydrant, now her last sight of it swept away with a yelping dog down Broadway, taffeta snapping like a flag in the wind, her false colors receding. And believes she is well rid of it, the loveliest dress she'll ever own.

A dress such as I wore, ankle length, puffed with net petticoats. Underneath a merry widow strapping me in with metal stays, confining me in an excess of blue silk stuff. A fashion of the Fifties looping back to the Viennese waltz. The cocktail dress, cocktails aplenty.

Confined in the Midwest, where my husband taught bright boys. I had no children, but picked up a little boy, eight or nine, a slow child who walked home from school trailing others through our yard. A lone boy with a droopy hangdog head, vacant eyes that came to attention when I spoke kindly.

This is what I knew: The father was a rigid mathematician carrying on an improbable affair with a dicey young faculty wife who was not like me. A wild Spanish girl, not laced in, not constricted. The mother of the boy was French, a plain woman of the people, thin and tough. Her mother had been landlady to the mathematician when he was a student in Montpellier—brilliant, inexperienced and poor. It seemed out of a novel, all this information at my disposal, this foreign plot, yet it was only village gossip. The town I was billeted in was small and it was noted that I gave the boy cookies on a fall day, that he came into my kitchen without knocking when the weather turned cold.

I did not know what to say to him, what to do with this needy kid, but in some way loved his exclusion from the gang who also took the shortcut through my yard on their way to the football field or to the hour allotted them in the college gym.

The boy drank his milk in fast gulps as though he had just learned to hold the glass and was glad to set the burden down. Together we looked at picture books and at maps which he took to at once, even pretended to understand. I saw that he had an eye for the little red numbers by the side of each route and could with effort and pleasure add the miles from town to town until he arrived at the distance between Columbus, Ohio, and Cleveland, between Cleveland and Detroit, between (his greatest challenge) this little college town and New York, where I came from, where I wore that cocktail dress with perfect ease, not as a fashionable dress to set me apart as the stamps set me apart, stamps on the letters I received from friends in London and Rome and Istanbul, in a continuing foreign correspondence as though I was more than a wife—perhaps a professor of government, as it was then called, or, like my hus-

band, a proper critic—the postmaster when I picked up my mail cracking a sour joke about my un-American activities.

And my boy quite liked the colorful stamps of the young Queen, the old Ottoman Sultan, the classic profile of La Republica— clipping them carefully off the tissue-thin envelopes with my nail scissors, so intense his concentration, so devoted to painfully completing the task any kid could do snip-snap. That was how the stamps began and I bought a leatherette album in which he placed the stamps on what (we both learned) are called hinges. This continued through the Winter and I found myself waiting for school to be out, waiting for my caller, who was getting bold with my refrigerator and cookie tin, drinking Cokes out of the bottle.

I sent away for stamps to the Philatelic Fulfillment Service requesting familiar issues, not the exotic, which he removed with care from their fragile packets, completing the pages of centimes, half-pennies, 50 lire, which gave us a private language. He was quick, nearly clever figuring the distance from Rome to Paris to London to Ohio, distances which had no meaning to him beyond our afternoon study of the stamps. His features were large, somewhat rubbery, and he learned to tilt his head, throw me a bright smile before looking with a magnifying glass to see watermarks, perforations, to see the many delicate lines forming the tiara of the Queen, the laurels crowning La Republica, the torch of La Belle France, seeing what no one saw when casually opening a letter—the exquisite small etchings. And the boy, his plain name Johnny, squinted in wonder, amazed at what he could discover in the magnified picture—the black pit of nostril, the arabesque of lash, the crosshatch of a foreign number seen close, yes that close, like the segment of bark with nodule and striation or the dead tracheid cells of heartwood, which Louise Moffett renders in her big pictures. But I had not kept the big picture in mind. I did not see, as the artist sees, the Moffett inset of a tree in its field or out by the barn—small as a stamp in relation to the huge canvas.

Johnny came no more. He walked home the long way.

At one of the end-to-end cocktail parties, I was wearing the inappropriate low-cut dress which my husband, a Victorian scholar, called Alice Blue, the exact blue of the dress which Alice wore under her pinafore at the Mad Hatter's tea party in the Tenniel drawing which hung in his study, a British Museum reproduction. I was wearing the blue silk dress with the excellent New York label when the woman stood in my way, the stern mother of Johnny. "Eh bien," she said, "he is not such a fool."

"Not at all."

"He knows the stamps are of no value. I send him now to a tutor. You will see."

She was claiming the boy, I saw that. I saw that she could withstand losing her husband for a season, but to also lose the boy I was certain she did not love, certain as the monthly blood from my vacant womb. I knew perfectly well that the stamps were a come-on advertised in the back of a silly magazine, a cheap distraction. I knew they were undesirable, never mailed or canceled to order.

You will see.

Indulgent Reader, I never saw him, though the town was small, never saw the leaps and bounds he would take into the mainstream of schoolboys, given a proper tutor. When we returned for good, for better or worse to live in the city, returned the 532 miles to New York, I found I had lost track, that the cocktail dress, an iridescent taffeta, the Alice Blue of a vaudeville song, and the merry-widow corset were of another time and place. I thought to give it to a thrift shop along with Bermuda shorts and a kilt skirt, and, in a lonesome entertainment, took care to choose a charity that supported research in heart disease.

THE FOOL'S CAP

After a bleak Winter dawn, the morning settles into gloom. Sissy sees the soldier scrape a lump of dirty snow off the park bench. She watches the spaced-out, automatic swivel of his head tracking taxis, cars and two rich kids riding out from Claremont Stables.

Their horses dump loads, shit steaming in the muck. She knows Freeman as the soldier who fell at her feet, Sissy pulling him up, her arms hitched round him as in an embrace. That made Tony and Little Man laugh, so she pressed her mouth to the soldier's, stuck her tongue past his cold lips and cold teeth to the liquor taste. New Year's hanging with Tony and Little Man under the scaffold, warmth where a grate melted the snow and Little Man set a stinky fire in a tar can, tar being what they patch the old building with or else, Little Man says, rotten stones crumble, crap down on your head. For Sissy, beer and a couple a blunts was no party. Then the soldier fell at her feet wearing his clown hat.

Sissy watches from under the bridge, where the drain trickles black sludge, careful not to spoil her sneakers, to look neat like she is, uh-huh, going to school. A cop car slows to a pace observing Freeman, who is not a bum, not even a guy out early for the doggie run, just space case icing his ass on a bench like it was some fine day. Sissy thinking *soldier* though he's not in his soldier suit, runs down the slope to the bench now the cop car has passed. She sits on his bench, far side. Freeman sees the vapor out of her mouth, but not Sissy, not as he saw the girl for an instant on the night of his fall from Lou's grace, her indulgence. Lack of indulgence. He was wasted, fell, a child picked him up.

Romance to Sissy—how she was hatless, her knit cap hung on the tar can to dry, so the soldier combed his cold fingers through her hair, soft, like daytime sex on TV, no gropes, grabbing her skull like a bowling ball. "Lou," he'd said, "Lou-Lou."

Little Man laughing, "Fuckha, man. Fuck the bitch."

And she went with the game, forcing herself at the soldier so Tony and Little Man would see how she laughed in his face, but let the warmth of his tongue linger on hers.

Soldier walking wounded into the crumbling apartment stuck together with tar like Little Man said. The grate on the sidewalk blew hot air smelling of oil, smelling bad when Tony took a piss.

"Dumb fuck," Little Man said, "now you gonna sleep in that shit?"

"Where's the party?" Tony said. Little Man took out a pack, the last crumbs of cheap shit. From upstate Sissy remembered a cake, favors, party hats and that particular foster home where she lived for a season with one of her brothers, one shift among many. The favors had little charms and dopey fortunes. In the paper hats they had looked silly and different, even the strict woman they must call Mother barked out a laugh like they were having some fun. Beer and weed were no party.

The soldier is hatless. She knows his red elephant ears, his black hair. Her knit cap is pulled over her own lank hair he combed with his fingers. In her gear she has his hat, not the conical hat with torn paper rushing and soggy pom-pom which fell in the fire when Tony snapped the elastic under the soldier's chin. Sissy has the overseas cap Little Man swiped from his pocket. Only a twenty and loose change. The soldier hat, thrown, lay in wet grime. In her gear she has that overseas cap from a war, and sitting on the bench with Freeman thinks she will not give it back but keep it since he does not see her, see Sissy, keep it to remember Cpt. O'Connor, his name stamped on the hard wool.

She sleeps with her gear, knapsack as pillow though Sissy could have a pillow for these past weeks she sleeps with Little Man and Tony in Day Care, stealing in after cleanup. Little Man takes care of Tony, a dumb fuck, calling him that maybe a hundred times as he covers his friend with a scrappy little blanket the kids use for naps. They sleep behind stacked milk crates of blocks and toys and in the early morning make it perfect like they were never there. Six o'clock before the first kid is dropped off by the first mother, before the fat lady aide comes shoving in the door they are out the toilet window, over the jungle gym into the alley. Sissy breaks for a tunnel in the park.

The rich kids on horseback come round again, clopping in the mud, two blonde girls in velvet hard hats and Sissy thinks bitches have school days, no truant officers watching their cute asses bumping up and down. Now Freeman looks at the waif, a boy or girl. Mopey, she thinks he is mopey for himself, like he was that night, and smiles at him knowing how her warm tongue felt the ridges of his palate, how the liquor taste licked off the smooth enamel of his teeth. He gets up, O'Connor, name stamped on his hat. The cop car orbiting slows its pace to take a look at the kid and Sissy skips, her feet numb with cold, skipping beside the soldier as though he is something to her, or she to him, grabbing the sleeve of his down jacket, presuming a connection. There is no connection and she runs ahead through the grit-covered snow, disappears into the black maw under the footbridge. Artie Freeman, who has suspended time, days mounting to weeks, worrying his losses like Mae O'Connor's beads—his mother, Cyril and that absence that kicks off all misery, his father—is shocked, draws away, scared for a second, by the simple touch of the kid.

Mopey, yet he will not count Lou as a loss, though when he went downtown to the loft a new lock had been installed above the old one. It looked insubstantial in the heavy metal door, a factory door. Artie put his useless key back in his pocket. He did not call her name, listened for a time to the sound of her silence. Fair's fair, he would say if she'd hear him out, then romance her with the absurdity of Cyril and Sylvie, "Twilight zone, one night of *luff*, Louise. A tale from outer space." She'd laugh at him, "Be serious." He would be, and even a touch angry. "The new lock is a cheap move, Louise. It has about it a flimsy finality, like your unreasonable judgment against me." Strong words well arranged in his head.

January 20—Eve of St. Agnes, Virgin Martyr, d. 304, a Christian girl, who at the age of thirteen was ordered to marry the son of a rich Roman. Agnes said: "I have chosen a Spouse who cannot be seen with mortal eyes, whose mouth drips with milk and honey."

They marched the child naked through the streets, confined her to a brothel where her honor was miraculously preserved. Agnes was feared as a witch for she walked to the place of her death with as much joy as most women going to be wed. She was then tied to a stake, but the faggots would not burn. An officer of Diocletian's guard struck off Agnes' head. You'd think there might have been some willing maid for the rich man's son, but the saint's legend is not about reasonable choices. It's about Agnes' unreasonable claim to her body, saving herself for the passionate marriage, about the anger of men not served. The story of St. Agnes, like that of Ursula and her eleven thousand virgins, is about the strict ordinance that a woman must come unsullied, unwrapped, though to sweeten the prescription, on St. Agnes' Eve a girl, if she lies still as a statue and looks to the ceiling, will discover the face of the man she will wed.

Mae O'Connor, née Boyle, prayed nightly to the smooth plaster above her head that Cyril would be her lover. There was no guesswork, no heavenly revelation. By lover she meant the man who would be her provider, the father of her children. They met at a dance, Cyril, not a society Catholic, by some chance on a list of young men to partner pretty girls, drink good whiskey, cop a feel, get lucky and make out—not likely. Penniless Cyril, on scholarship at Georgetown, gave his brown shoes an unconvincing swipe of black polish, snapped on a black leather bow tie his father, a patrolman in Hell's Kitchen, wore to department funerals. Yet he was handsome enough in his rented tux, standing on the sidelines. Maesie Boyle saw him as serious and soulful but some dancer, that gangly stranger, when he asked her at last, waltzing her round. It was only the fathers who waltzed with their daughters, and the stuck-up dancing-school boys who knew Mae from the cradle as Miss Goody Two-Shoes, freckled and shy. She flushed with pleasure, sweating out "The Blue Danube" with this O'Connor who bowed when the music stopped, who drank ginger ale. She had known him at once for her man. He need not appear on the ceiling of the Boyles' Park Avenue apartment.

Often, crocheting one of her loopy afghans, Mae O'Connor watched her husband open his briefcase after dinner, settle to his financial reports, and thought of the awkward young man in the brown shoes who danced divinely, who told her over lemon ice that he was studying history, American history. She had thought it grand, his formal, bookish speech, and grand not hearing the gossip of her crowd. When he told her he was reading each day in the public library, each day of his Christmas vacation, about the Draft Riots during the Civil War, she had nodded her bright red head until the pins fell out of her upsweep, which had been set that day at Elizabeth Arden.

"History?" she asked with flirtatious interest.

"So we know the sort we come from."

Maesie knew she was the daughter of Frank Boyle. The Draft Riots had to do with the poor Irish in this very city in which she was chauffeured to the cotillion with her parents in a limousine. She understood that Cyril was shanty Irish and that speaking his history at her he was comfortable, though somewhat put off by the debutante scene. So they had written, her notes on pale blue stationery soon assuming a future. As Cyril assumed, visiting the Boyles at Park Avenue and out on Long Island, assumed that he loved this convent-educated girl who passed her days in good works, who occasionally read a book he recommended—assumed that after his graduation, after his tour of duty as an officer in Korea, after being promoted in the field for bravery, after the inevitable whorehouses in the Philippines, that he would return to New York, perhaps go on with his studies. And marry.

The many afghans were given to the Sisters of the Sacred Heart; Mae's fingers a busy machine, yanking the next length of wool from her basket as the television played her nightly shows. Something went wrong during that dreadful war or just after. For a while Mae's cheery blue letters had gone unanswered. Then she heard he was in New York again. That his mother had died. She wrote to say how sorry, though she had never met Bridget O'Connor who cleaned and sewed for people who lived across the Park, the West Side, which seemed so far away Cyril might as well have been at war. When he finally came round still in uniform, he was stunned by her tears and her expectations which were reasonable. Cyril said he did not know what he was going to do. Mae took it to mean what he would work at. He had meant what he was going to do with the rest of his life. It was that small misunderstanding that brought him to reach down, touch her damp freckled cheek to comfort—"That's it. I'll be out of a job." Which was arranged by her father, who set him up on Wall Street and at the Athletic Club with the prosperous Irish, though when he gave her the lovely emerald-cut diamond he wore a cheap suit from his undergraduate days which no longer fit him. They waltzed for the world to see at their wedding. Mae came to their bed a virgin and lay beside her gentle husband. It was Cyril who looked to the ceiling before touching her white gown.

Louise Moffett, alias Lou-Lou, grew up on a dairy farm. It was like really astonishing not to lose it in junior high. No big deal, which now seems to her the ultimate devaluation, hustling, at the ready, trying to be one of the boys.

Like her mother's maidenhead and that of the woman who spurns her son, the price set on Fiona O'Connor's chastity was appropriate to her day, to an exuberant exploration of sex, a sloughing off of the bourgie traces, and to her own timely sexual rebellion in the Summer of Love, which might set her free. Love with its capital letter as in—*There are no ugly Loves, no handsome Prisons.*—*Poor Richard,* 1737

In her innocence Fiona was a virgin many times over. Her deflowered power, which her son once believed as a legend of the Sixties, U.S. of A., seems more reliable than that of the strong-willed Agnes (Agnus) who was awarded her very own symbol, the sacrificial lamb.

Sylvie, Sylvia Neisswonger Waite, now a widow with a handsome house in Connecticut, was not given a choice. When the Germans came in 1938, her uncle was mayor of Innsbruck. Her father, a vague Catholic Socialist, was naturally taken off to be questioned, along with his son. Professor von Neisswonger's wife and daughter were placed under house arrest. Inge Neisswonger packed a suitcase, making sure it was light enough for a child to carry, and directed the serving girl to set it by her daughter's bed. From the clothes thrown out of that suitcase, strewn on her carpet, the thick-set guard who raped Sylvia stole only her green velvet dress. Her new dress, as yet unworn, with lace collar and cuffs, cut in the princess style which flattered her narrow breastless body, for she was twelve years old. So like her mother, who loved the gaiety of evening parties, to pack that useless dress.

Sissy is the age of little Agnes. As of this date, her unredemptive story is not fit for the Proper of the Saints. The records relating to a neglect petition, the placement of the child in foster care, her disappearances, apprehensions and the misuses of her body are on file in Sullivan County.

DEAD LETTERS

> In the early dawn while the sluggard yet turns upon his bed and yawns for another nap, the industrious author should be up with pen in hand and courting his thoughts for his own future use, if not for the press, for the good of mankind. Our spirits rise with the sun as with the eagle who wings his flight toward that brilliant orb.
> —*Stoddard's Diary of New, Useful & Entertaining Matter*, 1828.

January the 22nd. I am seventy-six years old and do not see well. I make out the colorless dawn as it turns gold, a blur of sun to the east of Sylvie's hill. Dabs of light changing like paint freshly worked on the palette. I am thinking perhaps of the Sunday painters with floppy hats who set up their easels in Central Park and mixed their colors to get the Sheep Meadow or the Great Pond, to get nature which cannot be had by the untalented. I am such an amateur of the morning sun and of flora and fauna. As a sickly boy I was limited to indoors in winter, imprisoned with books. How I wanted to run free down the dark stairs of the tenement into the cold light of day.

The distant fields I see more clearly than objects close to hand. I make out a film of snow covering all but the fenceposts swept clean by the wind so that birds may perch there. I am ashamed I cannot name the black birds, but presume they are common. I hear their piercing caws.

Sylvie hears only the amplified word, the clatter nearby. We are the perfect pair, are we not, Arthur? For if I were to pick up the *Audubon Guide*, I would not be able to distinguish one black bird from another, to read of its habits without the magnifying glass, and in our haste to get on with the new life, I left my glass behind. If you find it slipped down in the leather chair, do not send it. We will procure another, though I have little time to read. Forgive my use of old forms which keep me from saying it's one hell of a trick to write of my happiness, to write at all—feel my way across the pages, knowing that my words float free of lines. It is my pretense that this illegible scribble will be sent to you, for I write in a ruled blank book which I think of as my business ledger for I was, as you know, a man of business all my life.

Sylvie will name the black birds on the post and name the tree, a tangle of branches scratching at the windowpane. With effort I find my way to the bedroom of this house, one that I should have lived in for some years, known the creak of these floorboards, the draft noiselessly sweeping the stairs. I am more than content being with her all day, yet, tiring easily of wholeness, I welcome the dawn when I am alone. From where I sit, through the scrim of my infirmity, I see Sylvie restored to a girl, a spray of blond curls on the pillow, a milky arm thrown across her eyes to hold back the light. Who would have thought a late sleeper when she exhausts my old bones every day? I mete out desire, naturally. All natural here. The sun on the snow becomes more blinding than the page addressed to myself. If I could see to go back over the words, I would cross out *should* and *ashamed*. *Mea minima culpa*. All evidence of this undeserved happiness is admissible as I sit at the little desk where my dear one pays her bills, as I paid mine, paid up every month of my life. Cyril, do not make a spoil of the present with the past.

Last night, to speak of the recent, comforting past—we observed the full eclipse of the moon. They came to Sylvie's field, the highest, clearest spot for miles around. "My trespassers," she said, smiling upon schoolchildren who rushed out of a bus to join the amateur astronomers, newspaper folk, the curious and plain crazy—a woman in a wizard's hat, a clergyman flipping holy water on the frozen ground. All assembled before the night began to dim. As darkness descended, we drove upfield and there, above the crowd, she sat up on the hood of the Jeep, Queen of the Mountain, seeing for me—the inevitable astrologers with charts and arcane paraphernalia—metal wands, magic stones; seeing for me—and I hearing for her the disapproving words of the reverential crowd at a mother with a sickly child holding it to the heavens. Opera glasses, telescopes—a fine one on a brass tripod set to view the eerie disappearance. I saw little of the moon as it came from the West into the earth's shadow. A silence fell. Each minute was prolonged, extruded, then the rustle of human breath, the shift and click of equipment.

I saw the darkness. What a scene of science and theatrics, a professor calculating the duration of penumbra while the sick child whimpered and the priest with his crew mumbled their prayers and the loonies fell upon the ground moaning, embracing the white snow against the black of night. Though spectacular, this event plotted in the sky seemed less extraordinary than our being together at the top of Painter Hill, my old girl and I. Then the moon moved East, assuring us of our precious little time, our favored place.

When the last moon gazer drove off her land, Sylvie said, "I hope they get what they came for." The answer to prayers, perhaps, not the astounding predictions come true. Being one with the universe during the eclipse, I suppose we were less than a pebble in the drive, more than a vaporous breath in the cold air. Better take that baby to a doctor than expose it naked on a frozen hill. On Painter Hill, as they still call it, cleared for a cornfield, where no American panther has roamed for two hundred years.

Blind as I am, I saw the darkness.

Monday 26 January

The day after my birthday; in fact I'm 38. Well, I've no doubt I'm a great deal happier than I was at 28; & happier today than I was yesterday having this afternoon arrived at some idea of a new form for a new novel. Suppose one thing should open out of another . . . only not for 10 pages but 200 or so — doesn't that give the looseness and lightness I want: doesn't that get closer & yet keep form & speed, & enclose everything, everything. My doubt is how far it will <include> enclose the human heart. . . . For I figure that the approach will be entirely different this time: no scaffolding; scarcely a brick to be seen; all crepuscular, but the heart, the passion, humor, everything as bright as fire in the mist. Then I'll find room for so much — gaiety — and inconsequence — a light spirited stepping at my sweet will.

— *The Diaries of Virginia Woolf*, 1920

This mania for writing. Oh, fine for Franklin and his imitators with their profitable volumes, and for Mrs. Woolf, who had her happy-birthday breakthrough, but now there's Cyril up with the sun, his words running off the page onto the pink blotter which tops Sylvie's desk. A skid of his hand off the blank book sends his record of delightful discoveries of the natural world into oblivion; and Artie Freeman writes love letters to Louise, begging her forgiveness. Louise remains incommunicado. In any case e-mail, voice mail cannot express what is in Artie's heart. Finding the last of Mae's old blue stationery, he takes up a pen: "Dearest Loop de Lou." Artie confesses his astonishing love, for so long he has been blind, etc.

And whether it was because he wrote to Lou from his grandparents' apartment still smarting from the sight of Cyril revived, deluded old fool so easily dusting him off—or simply that this home was never quite home, Freeman was suffused with a sense of continuing loss, time itself lost over the years. He knew exactly how many years (10) he has doodled his working life away manipulating the stats for Skylark, how many of those months (55) he has preferred not to, that is, has preferred to animate pretty images at home, chosen not to see close-up the targeted approach to the specific user of Product and ancillary services which differentiate Bertram Boyce from his failing competitors, as if forty city blocks unhooked him from Bud's exponential growth and efficient morality. It's been 1,820 days since he first set eyes on Louise Moffett, fresh as a prairie rose, the wasted days of his life with her, wasted on waiting for the heart's release . . . but there he stops, none of this written . . . settling instead for a dull play of words: *Let's address, as they say, our 2000 problem. Was it the dress, Little Lady?* The best he can do—*How's about you forgive, I forget?*—his tongue thickening with the tender emotions. And Arthur Freeman did not sign his name, but drew himself as a little owl.

The very signature which once got him in trouble when writing in hieroglyphs, his teachers complaining that Artie was in another world. His book reports and math exercises bore the indecipherable mark of this very owl, a wise-eyed bird, and it was further discovered that the boy wrote notes to himself in ancient symbols. He haunted the dim halls of the Egyptian collection which were, according to the headmaster, lugubrious, the funereal bric-a-brac fostering a preoccupation with death, understandable given that his mother . . . given the alarming coincidence that soon after the tragic accident his grandmother, it was said, succumbed in her sleep to sorrow.

When Cyril brought up the unfortunate matter of the owl, they were alone with their minute steaks. "And what is it about the Egyptians you like best?"

"Their tools—chisel, adz. The broken head of a queen."

"All of it?"

"The boats," Artie said. That was his mistake, telling of the miniature barques, peopled and brightly colored, so alive. He had loved the fowling skiff best, with square sails, gangplanks, sixteen paddles. Midship a canopy was raised over a king of the Middle Kingdom and his small son. Before them the foreleg of an ox roasted on a spit. "They're going hunting and fishing," he said with such feverish excitement he was shipped off that summer to a lakeless camp where his gaudy Indian beadwork bore no resemblance to the splendid dead things of a museum, where the chlorinated pool suggested neither the unearthly inventions of Luxor on the Nile nor memories of his mother's pleasure trip to a watery death, where senior counselors were said to be healthy substitutes for the king of the Lost Kingdom, the father he would never have.

Camp was O.K., but did not break Artie's bad habit. Back at school, he continued his secret messages to his mother in glyphs, discarding slithery ballpoint pens. For this practice he took to sucking the ends of reeds which grew wild by the Belvedere Lake in Central Park, chewed and sucked till a brush was formed which he figured to be nifty as that of Ramose, the honest scribe. A leather pouch which once held his jacks became his pigment bag, a chipped saucer his palette. Thus outfitted, he wrote when Cyril sent him to bed, stashing his implements and computer-paper scrolls behind Scrabble and Ouija boards during the day. And what did he write that was so very wrong? The date on each page, an account of the money he spent on candy and comics, the number of laps—free-style and butterfly—he swam in the Horace Mann pool, his first trophy for the running dive, his grades in all subjects, the names of favorite teachers and of his enemies and friends—the daily facts of his boy's life as though they were an accounting for stores of grain and gold to sustain the dead in the Great Place of Thebes.

It was for Fiona that her son wetted his brush and drew on his scrolls, though she was not buried in a glorious tomb with helpful amulets of carnelian and lapis lazuli, but in a narrow grave in Queens marked by a sunken headstone which bore the name

O'Connor. Buried without her guitar or favorite sandals, without her little jam pots and bud vases, useless for storing corn. He drew her as a vulture, which was the proper hieroglyph for "mother," one who sees far, one who provides. She had fed him on millet and brown rice in their meatless house in Connecticut, on fruits and nuts, the gentle vulture who would not feed off the dead; and he remembered their suppers as good, and her singing, the false notes of her folked-up singing, but how true her flecked brown eyes, her brazen hair. And believed (still) that his mother enjoyed all that he inscribed, small and large events of his every day, that she listened to the son she had saddled with an allegorical name.

"Who was Mr. Freeman?"

Her fierce clearing away of supper dishes.

"Why did he leave us?"

"No one left me. Or you. Sometimes it happens that way." A heavy strum on the guitar; Fiona's misfortune (and his) not up for discussion.

Evenings when she was not preparing to go out with one of her men, as they ate their wholesome fare Artie told her what sport he played, what math problem he solved—it was that sort of daily chat that was drawn in his pictograms that she might continue to read in the afterlife, suppertime talk which made up his library of paper scrolls hidden behind the game boards, and all vanished as the papyrus rolls had—just disappeared from their cubbies in the Library of Thebes. One day the marauder, the infidel upon this occasion an industrious cleaning woman, tidied up Artie's closet, the closet in the spare room of his grandparents' apartment, and all his messages to Fiona in the otherworld were gone.

A heavy loss. In the face of the Egyptian prohibition, he could tell no one that his precious records had disappeared, perhaps consumed in the great incinerator in the belly of the apartment house, as swiftly turned to ash as the 70,000 scrolls set aflame on the banks of the Nile, the sacred texts which Cleopatra gave to Caesar out of love or fear. Artie had known for a long time that the owl's writing for the vulture was a kid's stupid game and gave up the glyphs as quickly as he would at a future date abandon his talent for higher math, but for the time being he consoled himself, for he was having schoolboy fun with such simple problems as—

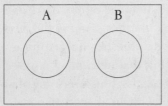

Exclusive Events:
A   Fiona dies on the Interstate, 2.3 miles from home.
B   Fiona capsizes in the Bahamas, 100 feet from the guest house in Nevis, the house where Alexander Hamilton was born.

And Freeman drew a Venn diagram of disjoint sets, A and B, so obvious it is stupid, and besides, as he grew older he developed a distinct bias toward B, the romantic choice which happened to be perfect, for he discovered that Hamilton, most mysterious of all the Founding Fathers, was born under the bar sinister. A bastard like himself, good at numbers. That was encouraging, though apparently Hamilton was far better at words than Artie Freeman.

Louise does not answer his letters, does not pick up on his amusing calls.

THE BEST MOLASSES CANDY

Stir two cups of molasses and two teaspoons of vinegar in a granite or Scotch saucepan until the syrup forms a ball when dropped in cold water. Remove from the fire and quickly add two tablespoons of butter. Sylvia Neisswonger remembered the rich decorated chocolates of a particular sweetshop in Innsbruck. She was often treated to one of her favorite truffles by the confectioner who attended her flirtatious mother, hoping that Frau Neisswonger might throw him a departing kiss. The black chocolate was so dense and rich, the daughter's little mouth puckered with expectant joy. When, after the scrambling life of a refugee, she married in America, Sylvie had long been used to accommodations. Her husband, a widower with small children, brought her to his house in Connecticut, his family home which, for this country, was old. He had been a squadron commander in the Second World War, a chicken colonel who flew with his men. Bob Waite was now an airline executive. One cold night at the end of January, after he put the kids to bed, he discovered Sylvie at the kitchen sink, singing to herself in German, her tears mingling with the soapy water. He found the bottle of Br'er Rabbit Molasses and the vinegar, stirred it in a pot over the flame till the ball was formed, all as his people had done it, with no cream or chocolate in the cupboard. "Come," he said to his young Austrian wife, and he took his pot out the back door and poured the syrup on the snow. It formed a sheet of brittle amber. He broke a piece and gave it to Sylvie. The pale sugar frosted with snow was watery as it cracked against her teeth. She smiled down at her husband kneeling before her with his pot and spoon, and said: "This is the best molasses candy."

January 30—Franklin Delano Roosevelt born at Hyde Park, New York, 1882.

> At a quarter to nine my Sallie had a splendid large baby boy. He weighs ten pounds without clothes.
>
> —James Roosevelt, Sr.

And on the next-to-last day of January 1933, after an uncertain night though fully prepared to press ahead with his evil cause, Adolf Hitler was declared chancellor of Germany by President von Hindenburg.

THE ENDLESS PAGE

We have suffered reversals, Courteous Reader. Tomorrow is To-day. We are in the rubberized suits of sci-fi gliding through our streets, full of hope and aspiration for our bodies. The city is and is not divided. We may wander where we will in Cosmopolis. Sissy

(Little Man, Tony) surface in citylife which Louise Moffett and Arthur Freeman do and do not own, own up to; the child's scrawn and pale pinched face is there, not there, lost in crowd scenes, the multitudes. For a moment the lens of a cold Winter moon isolates Sissy shivering in an asphalt playground waiting for Little Man to slip from the alley with dumb Tony, waiting for the Pine-Sol to wash away the daily soil in Day Care, where they take shelter at night, each night in their timeless day-by-day pact with peripheral life. The cruel moon captures them under the jungle gym, reveals three kids to a security guard pacing the project. They scatter, Sissy making it to a demolition bin where she lies in the plaster dust and splintered lathes of a gutted building, crouching in this foul cauldron as though she, too, is fungal dust to be carted off, dumped out of the city. Much has been written about her, each fragment of her story reveals a systemic problem. As a runaway, she is the subject of the state's protective oversight, no longer particular; her anger/indifference and sexless boy body areas of investigation. We repeat, repeat her case like and unlike others. When a cloud blanks the moon she meets up with Little Man and Tony, forgetting to crouch in the bushes for the lights shine all night on the playground, yet they are unafraid jimmying the window, as they have done these cold Winter nights. As always the city is illuminated, *one brief shining moment that was known*, once famously beckoning as in the Stieglitz photo *Evening, New York from the Shelton, 1931*, or still beguiling us in a garish tourist postcard, skyline concealing the almshouses and prisons and charity wards which mark our progress as sure as health clubs and the flags rippling at our museums. We are up for it all, only select, wired beyond our dreams which never outdistance reality. New news every day, every instant if that's our desire.

> Time is so eager to talk of novelties, that he never fails to give circulation to the most incredible rumors of the day, though at the hazard of being compelled to eat his words — tomorrow.
>
> —Hawthorne, *Time's Portraiture*

In which the writer debunks the picture on the front of the *Farmer's Almanac* wherein Father Time with his scythe is half clad, for in fact he is a man of fashion keeping up with the times. To write of the future at this blessed moment (9 1/2 minutes before 2 P.M. of this 23rd day of August, A.D. 1996) is to flirt with Time, tease the old man. The ultimate control may be to conjure the future, its doom or salvation, pass out the predictions, *give breath to the image of the beast and cause those who would not worship the image of the beast to be slain, also to call both small and great, rich and poor, free and slave to be marked on the right hand or the forehead so that no one can buy or sell unless he has the mark, that is the name of the beast or the number of his name, let him who has understanding reckon the number for it is a human number, its number is six hundred and sixty-six,* Revelation 13:15–18, 666 with its variant apocalyptic readings, only select, though clearly the beast named is commerce and those marked for the buy and the sell call upon themselves the wrath of God, the cup of His anger, yet all millenarian words must be withdrawn. Desperate for celebration we have come to a false end, while the movie got it right, *2001* beginning the odyssey. The calendar, as A. Freeman knew, having been fucked by religious and civil adjustments and the millennium, the real one slipped by unnoticed four years ago—but who's Artie to spoil the party. The ongoing party: *My theory is that the author might be the maker even of the body of his book—set the type, print the book on a press, put a cover on it, all with his own hands; learning his trade from A to Z—all there is of it.*—Walt Whitman. *We are competing with paper.*—Bill Gates, November 23, 1995. Only select: the professors at the Media Lab, the money magicians at Dreamworks admit they do not know what the products of their metastasizing technology will be called, term superseding term—a breathless lexicon. Withdraw to plain words, inedible, outdated, words silted with detritus of the past.

Only Cyril and Sylvie in their country idyll live with no news. She cannot hear the television without troublesome aural apparatus.

He sees only the faint outline of the newscasters, politicians, stars. No matter, they are busy with the affairs of the day. Often they time-travel to the memorialized Hungarian Restaurant, where a gelatinous breast of duck, crisp potato pancakes and sweet red cabbage lie uneaten on their plates. Their meetings that Winter and Spring remained companionable, discrete, until the first hot day of Summer. She is overdressed for the humble workaday translation pool at the U.N. She has come into the city to meet Cyril. She lives in Connecticut with her husband and his children. Her skin is freshly tinted, a light country-club tan. He is engaged to marry a sweet thing, Mae Boyle, and wears the jacket of a new serge suit, for he is now on Wall Street learning the business.

Her kitchen in Connecticut, Sylvie buttering Cyril's muffin: "A dark blue suit. You went from uniform to uniform."

"Yes, and I'd had a streak of beginner's luck on the market. I might have chosen a better restaurant."

Sylvie's line: "There was no better place." Though the hearty meal that had sustained them through the cold season of their delayed lust was too heavy and the restaurant hung with hunting horns and dusty antlers was stifling.

"Saturday." Yes, he had worn the navy blue suit jacket with a soft shirt and suntans from his war in the Pacific. Saturday—her rendering from English to German of "The Legal Status of the Continental Shelf as Determined by the United Nations Conference on the Law of the Sea" was an unlikely excuse for Saturday in town. Her leather portfolio sat on an empty chair. Looking at her dainty watch set round with diamonds, a gift from her husband, Sylvie spills a drop of wine on her dress of white piqué. He reaches across the table, across the paper rose and sprig of fern, not to the small stain growing on her breast but to her burning cheek, and strokes, strokes down to the pale golden throat thrust forward for him to stroke like the neck of an agreeable animal . . . complicit, yet she must leave to catch the late train to her husband and his children. Sylvie must leave . . . but went to the public phone with a handful of change from her lover, from the pocket of the man who will become her lover within the hour. A Saturday, red cabbage darker than the paper rose, than the blot of wine fading to pink on white piqué.

"Bull's blood," Cyril shouts to her deaf ear and they laugh as though the bottle of Bikaver faced them at the breakfast table in Connecticut, the rough Hungarian wine called bull's blood of Eger that finally gave them courage, Sylvie feeding her lover's coins to the pay phone, calling long-distance, no laughing matter, to Bob Waite, speaking boldly of immediate revisions called for in the German translation lest the continental shelf be forever entrapped by the laws of the sea, though speaking without shame for one night of love, never. Cyril had already paid the bill when she came back from the phone. Enough to go on, the bull's blood and their urgency, enough to sustain them in the restaurant scene so that they do not turn further back to memories of childhood, to the von Neisswongers' handsome villa in Innsbruck with its lofty view of the Tyrolean Alps, or to the O'Connors' firetrap on Columbus Avenue with swayback stairs. The squadron commander, Bob Waite, and Mae Boyle, the Park Avenue debutante, are bit players, easily written out of their script. It remains to be seen if this selective calendar has a faulty device, for in devotion to their past, Sylvie and Cyril, eating their morning muffins, have only one feast day to honor and now. Now, the insatiable present.

Louise shuffles the blue letters, sets them, unopened, next to the velvet box with the ring. Reading them, she would hear Artie's mild self-deprecation, a tug of laughter under serious words, then laugh herself and be lost forever, caught up in his intolerable lightness. So much was already lost, even her ability to draw. Infuriating to think her talent has anything to do with Artie, his post on the sidelines, nursing the happy injury that kept him from the game. Nothing comes right. Botched sketches for yet another botanical, the oblate leaves of a weeping willow too big, the pond it sits by too small. *Salix babylonica*, her horticultural guide tells her: *shallow rooted*. She has forgotten the old tree her father called a nuisance, how it crippled the septic system, toppled at a great cost on the old barn. Perhaps her imagination can no longer be fed by Wisconsin. Perhaps she is finished with New York, yet if she left the city where would she go, to what place, what people? She has come to the coast from landlocked fields and now finds herself stranded on the glitzy shores of Bohemia.

Screening her calls: "Daddy's bought into a condo. Florida, Louise, come on down."

"To Florida?" Louise gasps as though Shirley Moffett proposes the gaseous rings of Jupiter.

She speaks to Dealer, who has scheduled a show.

"I've had inquiries." Curators, *Art in America* "await the new Moffetts."

Louise hangs up on Bud Boyce, who is tracking down Artie.

"Say, you doing all right? You want—nothing complicated, darlin'—a little company?"

At his machines, Arthur Freeman reconfigures the Blameless Cows, making them friendly brown and white.

"Lou, are they Swiss? Are they Jerseys?"

No answer.

Artie knows cowcake about cows, but gets into it coloring a grassy green isle for them to graze. They chomp and cluster freely, though he suspects they are confined to antiseptic stalls. For the video presentation he massages the figures in favor of the animals, lets his flock yield plentiful gallons, but keeps their output humane. At that rate per gallon of Product, per head, per day, per year, he comes out with half a cow, the butt end weighed down by a full udder.

"You're cutting it close." Bud Boyce stands next to Artie in the executive pissoir. They shake, zip, wash with no words. When the bisected bovine and the silvery little pails sloshing fluorescent milk are screened, they do not entertain the client of Skylark. O.K., with a few strokes the cow will be made whole, milked to the max, lactation turned milk-white and fat-free, if not pure.

Next day Bud throws Artie a bone: work out the preference in the Pacific Rim for scented or unscented Product. The preordained preference—hibiscus with a touch of patchouli. As Bud turns him out of the pillared postmodern boardroom, he says, "And lay off Louise."

Artie swings, misses—no end to his shadow-box violence. The big boss feints, dodges in full view of his crew at Skylark, so . . . So, as the month nears its end, Artie is unemployed. He longs to tell Lou that he's free of Bud Boyce, off the consumer index; longs to see her in a paint-stained shirt on the videophone, catch a glimpse of her broad Midwestern smile which has not hardened these years in the city.

"Were they Alderneys, Lou? Holsteins?"

Louise is unplugged, though each night she unlatches the new lock on the door assuring herself she's not that mean-spirited or that literal. A dozen times a day, she shifts the box with the ring so that it stands to the right or the left of the unopened letters. Neutral moves, or cheating, like a girl telling the petals of a daisy.

At his workstation, Artie shuts down the machines. He takes to walking across the Park to his grandparents' apartment. Picking up Cyril's mail is his final chore; sending it on to a strange address in Connecticut engages what's left of his pride. The mail is not all Cyril's bills, research reports and monthly statements. There are pleas from a number of Catholic charities still addressed to Mae; and the private schools that expelled Fiona, presuming she has matured, invite her to fund-raisers—homecoming games and cocktail parties. The stale rooms of the Fifth Avenue apartment are clueless. What was the mystery? He cuts to the lasting injury: who was the coward, the stiff absent without leave? The father nameless as his son? He runs to this problem for comfort, a solution to emptiness. But today, today the demands of the absent seem needless mystification, an evasion of real questions: Will it ever come right with Louise? Who was the fool who failed to love her? Loneliness lies in Mae's afghans nibbled by moths, in the magnifying glass left on the open page, in a floppy dinosaur disc from his first computer, in the miniature swimmers poised for the diving start on his school trophies and in the drawer with his life-saving badge. His mother's bright hair drenched, dark, calmed at last, he had thought to drag Fiona to the impossible shore, pummel the sea out of her until in death's rattle she spewed out a name that remains unheard. In the faded paper and paint of these walls the family curse, silence. Yet as Artie opens the jewelry case in which he found the engagement ring tucked in its velvet box, he recalls the surprising chat with his grandfather.

Holding the diamond up to the light, "May I . . . ?" he had asked.

And Cyril roused himself to tell a story: "In those days Frank Boyle set me up on Wall Street, making me a likely prospect for his daughter. It was the Fifties. I bought the ring with my first big score—Polaroid. We all wanted to see ourselves instantly. The stock took off in a parabolic rise and I hopped a cab uptown to Tiffany's."

Half-truths, Gramps, the-should-have-said-to-Cyril, *no better than lies.*

On a mild morning Arthur Freeman heads off to collect the next accumulation of O'Connor mail. He walks into the Park, climbs up from the bridle path to come upon the glittering circle of the Reservoir which lies before him. Overwhelmed by the drenching silver light, he is healed by hope. At least his Lou has not returned the ring. He walks on a few muddy steps, then turns, runs back, back to his expectant screen. *My Dearest Louise, If you can find it in your heart . . .* And again, *Dear One, I do not know who I am. . . .* And yet again, *I'm a bastard, Lou, no kidding.* Words, rusty as Cyril's *Dear Boy*, fail him. Then Freeman begins to draw, one line meets another and another, forming the Golden Rectangle, so pleasing in its proportions. Inside he places two interlocking circles, A and B.

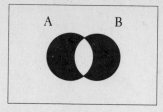

A   Louise Moffett has Arthur Freeman's
     diamond ring.
B   Surely they will marry.

These are known as exhaustive events, Lou. One must occur, has occurred. Both may occur. Exhaustive events cover all possibilities. So that's where we must be, Sweetheart, on the island of overlap in the beauty of intersection. He prints out, signs his love letter with a pen, tucks it into the last of Mae's pretty envelopes, posts it by snail mail. As he turns from the reliable blue mailbox, he looks up to the bright Winter sky. This last day of the month, exactly as predicted, a January thaw.

FEBRUARY

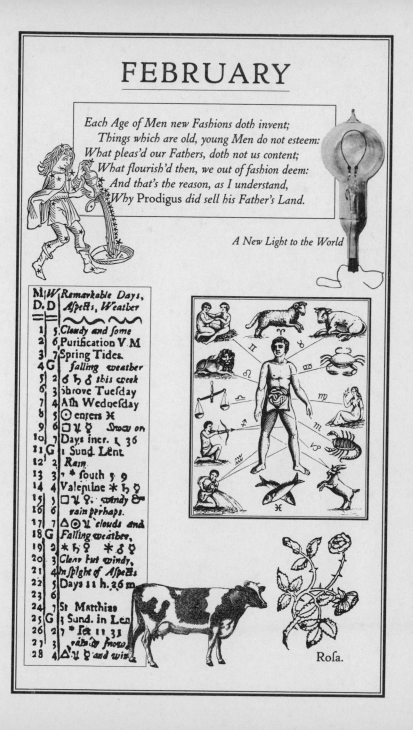

Each Age of Men new Fashions doth invent;
Things which are old, young Men do not esteem:
What pleas'd our Fathers, doth not us content;
What flourish'd then, we out of fashion deem:
And that's the reason, as I understand,
Why Prodigus *did sell his Father's Land.*

A New Light to the World

M	W	Remarkable Days,
D.D		Aspects, Weather
1	5	Cloudy and some
2	6	Purification V.M
3	7	Spring Tides.
4	G	falling weather
5	2	☌ ♄ this week
6	3	Shrove Tuesday
7	4	Ash Wednesday
8	5	☉ enters ♓
9	6	□ ♃ ☿ Snow on
10	7	Days incr. ♄ 36
11	G	1 Sund Lent
12	2	Rain
13	3	♃ south ♄ 9
14	4	Valentine ✳ ♄ ☿
15	5	□ ♃ ♀ windy &
16	6	rain perhaps.
17	7	△ ☉ ♃ clouds and
18	G	Falling weather.
19	2	✳ ♄ ♀ ✳ ☍ ☿
20	3	Clear but windy
21	4	In spight of Aspects
22	5	Days 11 h. 26 m.
23	6	
24	7	St Matthias
25	G	3 Sund. in Len
26	2	✳ set 11 33
27	3	rain or snow.
28	4	△ ♃ ☿ and wise

Rosa.

Who knows if in three or four thousand years, the current history of the Americas won't be as muddled, as inexplicable for its inhabitants, as the history of Europe prior to the Roman Republic is for us now?

—Diderot, *Histoire des Deux Indes*

In Dead of Winter

Ashes sift through the grate, potatoes growing their eyes—
winter tramps round the millstone
grinding discontent—the pond not frozen, snowless hills—
sport denied and the puzzle done,
a last piece of blue pressed into the seamless sky.

The imagined season unruly—
hybrid of breast stroke and lobs,
catalogue of bugbane, rosehips, angelica, squash;
In bumper crops seedless fruit resists flavor,
plump for shelf-life, not our life, our affection.

Groundhog, coaxed from his hole,
scared of the sun and its shade,
reveals nothing that is not foretold—
In February there is always one fine week.
Unbuttoned, hatless with joy,
we sink to our hubcaps, wallow in thaw.
Then the cold sets in—
more than we bargained for, the dip
to zero and below, the root of the matter.
Oh, how can they live further north
in the shadowless land
where tedious stars shine all day?

To check off the date is simply to have done with.
Useless to flip the page,
yet how we look forward to each branch of each tree
balancing the white stuff, a drift against the door
                              poised for the ravishing noon.
Years past—the silence of calendar art
                              prettied the field and shed.

We have to ask is it worth it—
turnips sprouting their beards—the pinochle deck is found—
worth the long longing? The strain on perfection.

Now is the month—
bring in a branch of the plum, of the quince,
force the fiery bloom.
Now—save woodash for the rose.

Clouds

February 1, 1770—Thomas Jefferson's library burnt on this day at Shadwell, County of Goochland, Virginia.

There were forty volumes in his late father's bookcase: Bible and prayer book, the essays of Addison and Steele, works of English history, astronomy, geography and eight maps of the most inhabited part of Virginia and of the larger world, all gone. "Would to God," young Jefferson wrote, "it had been the money, then had it never caused me a sigh." Ten years later he was to lose all his books and letter books in the British raid on Richmond. He borrowed back and recopied his letters to General Washington with a goose quill, sharpening it with his pen knife, though he owned one of the new "fountain" pens with its reservoir of ink and knew that the future lay with his (or the venerable Dr. Franklin's) perfection of James Watt's portable copying machine, or more likely with that "most precious invention," the delicate polygraph of Charles Wilson Peale, which so delighted Jefferson he caused one to be made for the Secretary of State and the Bey of Tunis.

The lost cannot be recovered; but let us save what remains; not by vaults and locks which fence them from the public eye and use, in consigning them to the waste of time, but by such a multiplication of copies, as shall place them beyond the reach of accident.

Our first archival president would delight in libraries available to historians and hacks which have sprung up from Independence to Austin to Yorba Linda, with catalogue letters, transcripts, medical reports, audiotapes, film, visual aids and backup discs. Though as a man of the Enlightenment Jefferson might be put off by the sentimental displays of personal paraphernalia—boots, spats, crutches, capes, eyeglasses, Stetson, top hat, fedora, pens that signed treaties of peace, declarations of war—fetishism as history.

On the first of February, Artie Freeman crosses the line of permissible behavior by settling into his grandfather's reading chair, which is not too big as always imagined, but a wee bit too small. In the evenings when he was a boy, Cyril was enthroned in the leather chair by the unlit fire, reading annual reports and the weekly newsmagazines. The chair is now by the window, where the meddlesome Sylvie has placed it. Order is further disturbed by Artie's belongings heaped on Mae's carpet—unwashed bedding, burnedout kettle, gooseneck lamp—the ruins of a dormitory life. He has not been a student for all of ten years. To be kind about his academic career, A. Freeman was a dropout. Looking upon his pathetic goods from the vantage point of Cyril's chair, he recalls painful episodes of dispossession: the dark day he was shipped home from prep school having tapped into, posted on the electronic bulletin board the headmaster's lusty correspondence with a buxom mom; and his dishonorable discharge from Yale, the result of a graphic lark, his picture puzzle of Bulldog Dan, the True Blue mascot, hiding within slobber and fangs of digital dogface, the answers, for whoever might make use of them, to a senior math exam.

Artie's dismissal a month before graduation wounded Cyril, who understood that the unrepentant boy had not cheated, merely mocked authority. "Nothing was asked of you, only that you stay on course."

"Whose course?" Artie asked.

"Is it really that insufferable, the little tyranny of testing and scoring?"

"Not insufferable. Beside the point," repeating his smart-mouth argument presented to the undergraduate dean. "What's important, see, the problems not the answers. The answers are," he'd said with an indifferent shrug, "only as true as you can get."

What he had wanted to say was a current mathematical truth. "What does the proof prove? Seeing that arithmetic is incomplete, not provable or disprovable." The accusing parties cut him off in the muddle of mid-theory, which was no theory at all, just an urge to flunk their test.

What he had really wanted to say had little to do with Gödel's theorem or unprovable verities. It was his tremendous secret that numbers—formal, informal, hifalutin—were no longer a comfort. When he was a kid, he could redress his losses with cool arithmetical games, raising his mother from the tomb, conjuring a father without tears or anger. The speculations of higher math had suggested an alternate world that was less fantastic than a dead end of dreaming Fiona's return with Mr. X as though his parents had been out to an evening party and he lay awake waiting to hear hushed voices as they came in the door. So, he had networked the answers to a final that would pass him degreed, authenticated into the real world, a bravura display. He had taken that chance.

"What's the proof prove?" Artie said to the doctor called in on his case.

"To be caught? Was that the thrill?"

"To fail on my own."

A folder lay on the psychiatrist's desk. She was exotic, he knew he should not think that, a darkly beautiful Indian, black hair loosely knotted, spilling love curls, heavy-lidded eyes, a sultry slur to her spoken questions. He knew that he should not think she was miscast for her profession, and that if he had committed his crime earlier in the semester he would have fallen in love with her. They might have worked together on his insoluble problem.

"To fail or not to be entitled?" she asked. "All on your own?"

He knew that the folder on her desk laid forth his history, ripe with the answers. Unfathered orphan. At college, no social or athletic achievement, only the spectacular grades.

"Look," he said, "I'm outta here. Why are we talking?"

"Because you were good enough to come at the request of your college master." She was almost lazy, tilting back in her chair, opening his file, the lovely shrink-in-training who had at most ten years on him. "And perhaps you thought there was a reprieve."

"You mean like I could get off death row?"

"No. Like you could continue doing what you're good at, adding and subtracting—whatever. And we're talking to cover the legal bases."

He remembered the legality of their interview, that it was in no way treatment, the note she would write to let the university off the hook—A. *Freeman: self-destructive, avoidance disorder, reenacting loss of the mother:* That note would replicate earlier notes in earlier files. She came round the desk, now that they would have no more to do with each other, and slowly extended her hand in a purely social gesture. It was Spring, of course, and he had walked back to his belongings already packed, cutting through the old campus where, out of the trodden mud, the university was growing grass that all might be presentable for parents and trustees. Quick impermanent grass that his grandfather would not see at his graduation and he thought to say to Cyril: *You didn't get your money's worth.* Over the smooth shallow run of the past ten years, Artie had not, until his recent dismissal, remembered the sultry psychiatrist who knew everything or nothing about him, but set him free to establish his career as the amusing fuck-up who survived amusing disasters.

So that frayed towels and single socks, a fractured biking helmet, his mother's unstrung guitar, his holey sweats and ravaged sneakers might have been dumped in this pyre years ago. Somewhat wiser, Artie has set his techy equipment carefully aside in the hall. A wintry melancholy descends: he might have paid his rent on this first day of the month, but having split finally with Bud Boyce, no money coming in . . . money is not the answer. Had he wanted to move back, back home? Guilt and grief, the emotional combo withheld from the lovely doctor in New Haven; or the avoidance noted; naturally, he'd blow it, the love scene, sport a dunce cap at the one moment in his life that was meant to matter, act the re-enactment. Get rid of her before she gets rid of you. That woman knew he would cart his junk back to this bleak stopping place of his childhood. Sent back to the bland living room of forgiveness. Penalty in the game with no answers: Why, since he no longer plays the fool, does Louise take him for a fool? How can Sylvie hear the outmoded endearments of the blind? The blind see the sly maneuvers of the deaf?

And could his mother, who outfoxed them all, really have played a harmless board game on this carpet—Clue or Stratego—outwitting nice girls uniformed by a private school? Did Mae allow their slight contempt? Their Cokes and cookies on the broadloom? His mother, a mystery child whispering secrets, giggling in the back bedroom papered with Bo Peep lambs lost in yellow haystacks. He has moved back to this place for the unattainable Fiona—for her charm and cruelty, her imprint and erasure. As though lulled again by her *happ'ly-ever-aftering*. She is his distraction from Louise, from serious numbers.

The punishing leather chair grips her boy. Cyril's magnifying glass pokes his behind. How can the old guy live without its necessary enlargement? To read had been life until the seductions of Sylvie further clouded his grandfather's vision. Artie studies his palm under the glass—life line and heart line, furrows of past and future illegible as the whorls on his finger—then reaches for the book his grandfather has abandoned:

> *The white bear of America is as large as that of Europe. The bones of the mammoth which has been found in America, are as large as those found in the old world. It may be asked, why I insert the mammoth, as if it still existed? I ask in return, why I should omit it, as if it did not exist? Such is the economy of nature, that no instance can be produced, of her having permitted any one race of her animals to become extinct. . . .*

He flips through Jefferson's account of the natural world in *Notes on the State of Virginia*, which his grandfather read and reread: atmosphere as measured by the barometer at Monticello, superior weight of our hogs and horses, habitat of the crane, house swallow, turkey buzzard, each bird given its Latin moniker. Cyril's weak eyes have tracked down the common ledge of schist in the Alleghenies and that sublime work of nature, the Natural Bridge. So much gathering, listing, recording; Jefferson's boasting of each river and mountain, broad leaf of tobacco, each fatted calf. A documentation of paradise—is that what his grandfather was after?

In the heap of Arthur Freeman's possessions carted across Central Park, there are no books. The sci-fi novels, which always fall short of reality, he's thrown in the trash with idiot computer manuals. He discards the open book, *Notes on Virginia*, leaving off as Jefferson is about to inquire into the Militia—before the sticky bits about women, aborigines and slaves. Early winter-dark, he's without a clue as to what kept his grandfather in this uncomfortable chair, in the death grip of history.

But that is history of the family sort, muddied by love, pride, by false stories. Or no story at all: Cyril never let on that he once intended to continue his study of American history, to understand the country in which Mae's God had set him down, or to confirm that he had actually served that country by killing (and salvaging) men in Korea, a skirmish buried in the public archives. When Fiona was a kid, or Artie for that matter, it was their history homework Cyril would not help with. "Look it up," he'd say, tapping the authority of the *Britannica*. Look it up for whatever summaries of time's passage—Abbasids to Zwingli—might be collected in that useful book. It is merely history of the personal sort that in a moment of grave indecision he gave up both his passions, Sylvia Waite and American history, as not worth the risk or the pain that accompanied knowledge. It was the Fifties, in hindsight that shameful and careful moment in which Cyril's failure of nerve happened as we might say history happens. By the time he found the time to get back to his books, he had lost the thread in his readings of our national history, a story of curious and alarming discoveries but, he still believed, of progress over time, which often slowed to a halt given his myopia or to a loss of perspective in which he perceived Franklin's silk kite flying light-years above the vanished mammoth, not to mention the American bear.

Artie makes nothing of Jefferson's musk melons and quinces. *Our grasses are lucerne, st. foin, burnet.... 2,500 peas to fill a pint measure; a horse eats 1,170 bundles of fodder during a winter; 50 hills yield 200 cucumbers a season.* Boyce would call it Dada data, Bud Boyce, who graduated with an inflated B average from Yale and soon after was able to employ his unambitious pal, had kept him on the payroll these many years. Tossing Jefferson's *Notes* on the windowsill, Artie once again launches the search — automatic, dead-end — for Fiona. Bo Peep repeatedly loses her sheep on the back-bedroom walls, a room kept for a good little girl who never really lived here. The closet is a shrine — ethnic dresses and shawls, jeans patched with American flags — tidied once and for all by Mae O'Connor. After his mother died, Artie was spooked by the expectant hangers, the hopeful shoe rack. He preferred Fiona as a vulture eating nuts and berries in her Egyptian tomb. Touching air in an empty vinyl go-go boot, he discovers that this chamber of antiquities holds no fear and that he wants Louise, not a raveled end of yippie scarf, love beads, signs of his mother's mainstream rebellion that so perfectly fit a puzzle. He wants Louise Moffett in the flesh, not the haunted-house story of a ghostly child. A month and 2 days since he last touched the hem of Lou's gown; 32 nights of a cold season; the pulse beats of the new year he figures to an astronomical magnitude: Artie's calculations are as precise as Jefferson's, but to no purpose tracking his time in a landscape of personal loss, a territory so small, notes for no one.

February 3, 1874—Gertrude Stein born at Allegheny, Penn-sylvania.

> What is the relation of a calendar to the human mind even
> if one means to say an almanac.
>   An almanac has a relation to the human mind because
> every day tells us what it is.
>   An almanac has no relation to human nature because
> every day human nature tells it what it was and therefore
> human nature can not write but the human mind can.
>   It not only can but it does.
>   —*The Geographical History of America*

If one means to say an Almanac, every day tells Louise Moffett this is the Winter of her discontent, and though it was once in her nature to leave, it is now in her mind to stop in her tracks. Days meld into nights, nights into days in their order with no relation to her disordered state of mind as she attempts to draw, crumpling page after page of cheap newsprint, each stroke a misstroke, the pencil cramped stiff in her hand, yet fingers nimble with the un-opened letters. She knows the heft of each thick blue envelope by heart, the postmarks dating back to January, which might be years ago, or yesterday, her name and address in a barely decipherable scrawl as though the act of writing was logged out of his system—Artie's.

She will say: "You see, I always presumed there was more. Your letters, I haven't read them," she will say, "not opening your damn letters is a refusal, sort of like leaving," she will say, "if I am making myself clear, a bitch, maybe, a cunt, but I've been mostly a coward, the glue on the flap perhaps all that gums up my work, my words . . ." But she will not say, for his phone is out of service and when she goes to the crumbling double tower uptown, Mr. Freeman has left no forwarding address. "If that's your game," she will say but not say, shuffling the blue envelopes, setting them neatly to the side of the Tiffany box with the ring, "that you do the leaving. You are better at games, always were."

February 8, 1957—John von Neumann died at the Walter Reed Hospital, Washington, D.C.

Von Neumann computed in his head faster than the machine, the digital computer he developed after the Second World War. His *Theory of Parlor Games* (1928) established game theory as a reputable field of mathematical inquiry. Which came first, computer or the game? The theory. Ask a silly question—but how serious the games when taken out of the parlor, out of the think tank in the early Fifties and into the political arena where two superpowers set against each other like gladiators of old in old Biblical movies, the Pagans and early Christians having a bloody go at each other in glorious Vistavision. The analogy doesn't hold: in the Hollywood version always the special effect of divine intervention—Light from Above, the Holy Ghost as well as the musical vamp to the afterlife which trivializes earthly triumph or defeat.

1950, as celebrated by Arthur Freeman and his Louise with close attention to decor and food, to the "look" of an era, was not burdened with language—brinkmanship, chicken, fail safe, Preventive War, surprise attack, open skies. Their New Year was a celebration, the only disasters personal. Cyril's campaign ribbon and his medal awarded during the Korean incursion for a sniper's bullet which caught him in the butt, were worn by his grandson as decorative items. The police action or Yo-Yo war toyed with the nuclear race in which game theory fit to a T, though that image is incorrect, for the carpenter's tool is true whereas strategic deception lies at the heart of war games, much like games Artie played with Bud, video shenanigans, two Yalies virtual slumming in a West Haven mall—collegial escape to joy stick, blasting each other off a garish screen. Artie has reached a stalemate in real time. Slouching into the dawn of the century, it occurs to him that he's playing an age-old game against Lou and Lou's playing against Artie, a tic-tac-toe of messages sent, unanswered, intercepted. A zero-sum game that he does not want to win. To win may be to lose.

Von Neumann's conception of the H-bomb (1955) could not have been developed without the behemoth of a computer at Princeton, his brain still working faster than the machine. Faster than MANIAC1, the machine that he believed could be programmed to imitate randomness as it functions in memory. As his prolonged and painful death by bone cancer approached, he is said to have cried out, "What will happen to this brain?" The brain that could quote all of *Faust* from memory on its deathbed. In his last days, von Neumann converted to Catholicism, hedging his bets, a loss of faith in the numbers game.

MILKY WAY: I

The Egyptians took comfort from the vault of the sky, tracing in the heavens a cow, her belly full up with stars like so many bright eggs, barnyard produce imagined by farmers. *Bos taurus*, a gentle herbivorous beast domesticated to man's purpose, grazed the valley of the Nile, and at night when the sun god dipped into the netherworld, the cow's matronly figure floated above, yielding stories of the gods' commerce with kings and with the seasons. (Bossy—a bulky, earthbound creature—why the little dog laughed to see such sport when she jumped over the milky, the buttery moon.) Magic stones, sacred trees, the fabled rise and fall of the Nile could not compare with moving pictures in the sky, spectacle after spectacle, a shifting narrative of 365 days. Pharaoh's Almanacs declared auspicious days for planting, for mining of copper and turquoise, others to be of ill omen for inscribing birds and fishes in the dun-colored mud of the royal tombs, or days favorable for painting in bright tones the sheaves of wheat for bread, sacks of barley for beer—foodstuffs for the lively world of the dead.

Astrological symbols were demoted by early Christians as inferior to the iconography of saints, yet there persisted in many translations the Arabic treatise *Secret of Secrets*—"Of Winter. Winter begins when the sun enters the sign of Capricorn and contains eighty-eight days, fifteen hours, fourteen minutes. . . ."—secrets connecting rationally enough to the regulation of days.

> *"Those impostors then, whom they style Mathematicians, I consulted without scruple; because they seemed to use no sacrifice, nor to pray to any spirit for their divination."*
>
> —St. Augustine, *Confessions*

But the heavens with their messages for man could not be suppressed and mysteriously there was inserted in that most exquisite of calendars—the *Très Riches Heures* of Jean, Duc de Berry (d.1416)—a picture of the astrological man, which in this case was a naked woman decorated with the signs of the zodiac as they correspond to the parts of the body, thus the Crab upon her breast, center of the emotions; Scorpio lies over her sex; and Aries, the Ram, sits upon her head, wherein the intelligence.

Madison, Wisconsin, 1989: A promising student, Louise Moffett, takes notes in the dark as her instructor in Late Medieval Art lists the four humors which influence man—phlegmatic, melancholic, etc. She puts down her pen, for what strikes her about this slide of the Duke's calendar was the secondary figure, the man who faces away from the Zodiac woman. They stand ass to ass and, no matter what the rap on the female figure depicted as softer, weaker, perhaps one of the three arty graces, she looks to Louise strong. Her calves, where Aquarius spills his jug of water, are thick as the man's and the astrological woman's form is oddly contemporary—articulated deltoids, biceps, small breasts— as though she works out with weights or runs miles each day on the shore of Lake Michigan. Her pubic hair might have been waxed for a string bikini. Attractively androgynous, as is the backside of the man with his small waist and full hips. The instructor projects the months as rendered in the Duke's rich hours, flipping quickly past the royal banquet of January to dwell on the peasants of February in their barnyard scene—sheep huddled for warmth, light snow capping the beehives and haystack. How this young instructor, a latter-day Marxist, favors the peasants warming their legs by the fire, pleasantly sitting the season out. The picture an elaborate lie, of course, for the lice-ridden serfs are down to their last buggy sack of meal, the death rate rising in this cold season under the influence (influenza) of ducal neglect and their misguided belief in the confounding stars.

February. Winter on the farm. The projection of the *riche heure* shines bright; the gauzy dusting of snow, clear grey of a silo and the strong blue dress of a woman toasting her legs by the fire might have been painted yesterday. Louise thinks of the moist warmth of heated barns, of riding out to the school bus on the plow with her father through heavy drifts, the clutter of cross-country skis and hockey sticks in the mudroom. In Winter, she had liked more than anything to stay inside and draw. Once, in the time of her copying, when she lost touch with the free strokes and honest fantasy of a small child, she had drawn the Zodiac Man out of the Almanac. She had wanted to be correct, to reproduce her subjects exactly. Then she had traced pictures out of her mother's household magazines and her father's farm journals, but mostly Louise had loved the *Farmer's Almanac* that hung in the kitchen, for it had flowers and fruits, illustrations of fat ladies and clowns, of Uncle Sam, Cupid, old bicycles and sailing ships, lobsters, snails and her favorite—a rustic cottage reproduced each season, appropriately leaf-laden, rose-covered, snowed in. She had copied the Winter scene, quaint as the Duke's, chickadees pecking at suet hung from bare branches, comforting woodpile, smoke curls from the chimney defying a cold white sky. She had copied Winter to perfection.

Each year the Almanac showed Zodiac Man, his stomach flapped open, displaying a tangle of intestines, liver and bile. He was a sullen-looking guy stretched out by lines which led from his squat body to all those weird astrological signs. Her brother, on Winter break from the university, said with a creepy voice that didn't scare Lou, "Zodiac Man was a nut job, a serial killer."

Perhaps not the mild figure she drew and pinned to the wall of her room?

"Bumps off his victims for the crime of their signs."

Well, wasn't that Glen with the put-down of Little Sister. So she had blown up the naked man, a mild man after all, spilling his guts. In her meticulous drawing he was larger, much larger than the small figure on the Almanac page. Her sister, a farm girl, was amused by Louise's substitution of heavy ambiguous cross-hatching for penis.

It was not many years before the free hand guided by imagination returned, but Louise still flipped through the little yellow Almanac, for she had started to figure the horoscopes of her family, by which she set a control on their world, their adult world always out of her reach. She suspected such predictions were only stories, yet there was always a satisfying element of truth—that gorgeous Glen (Scorpio) would get what he wanted, leading with his dick; that wishy-wash Heidi (Libra) was fated to be boring. Mom, under the sign of Cancer, a perfect household drudge. At supper Louise was often deliberate (Sagittarian) in her pronouncements, until her father, a man of science, who in that year had split quality embryos small as grains of salt to implant multiple births in dairy cows, dismissed her from the table.

"When you can speak to us sensibly," Harold Moffett said, "that is rationally, about this family, we will welcome your thoughts. Until that time you may go to your room." Lou went in a huff. Her mother, soft heart decreed by Venus moving in on Virgo, smuggling her daughter's dinner up the back stairs.

"He doesn't mean it, Lou."

"Oh, yes he does."

"Doesn't get it, then."

"Get what?"

"That you're kidding." Louise wasn't sure she was kidding, but her mother laughed, a squeak cut off in mid-titter. Shirley Moffett looked caught out, as though they were in a small conspiracy. Her mother whispered, "Hal's not long on humor."

Why whisper when no one was about? Fear, a slight blink of fear crossed Shirley's face as she turned to hustle downstairs. On the third night her mother looked so worn with the argument as she set the supper tray down on the quilt she had sewn for her daughter's bed, Louise popped the thumbtacks out of Zodiac Man, marched down to the kitchen and with adolescent drama tossed him in the cast-iron stove, making sure that her father bore witness.

"That's more like it," Harold Moffett said. "We have no need in this house for your ungodly stories."

"Ungodly?" He never attended First Methodist with her mother.

Her father came to where Louise sat, reinstated at the dinner table, smoothed her yellow hair, then tipped her face up to see that her beauty had set in, this late child of his with a passion for pictures and stories. Her good looks were stronger than his wife's, Shirl once a pert sorority girl. Louise, thank the good Lord, was his fatherly thought, as yet had no bust. He saw the resistance in her eyes to being reasonable and the curl of her pouty lip at his words. "I mean your farfetched stories," he said. "The influence of the planets and the stars is hogwash. When to plant corn. Geld the bull in the waxing moon. Astrology does not give you leave to criticize your mother."

"I know," Louise said. "It's a dumb way of saying what's on my mind."

"Of being unkind."

"Yes." She no longer wanted to argue. Her father was bound to win, perhaps this time with a Leo's violence. Her mother, true Crab, was nervously serving meat loaf and three-bean salad while she, who was destined to be bold, remained silent. Zodiac Man was ashes, all his aspects consumed in flames. The windows wept in the steam of the Winter kitchen. Virgo had come into . . . it was February, the waning second phase . . . she could not stop the celestial creatures from telling their stupid stories in her head, predictions which set her at odds with this family who loyally drank whole milk with their supper. Her brother had gone back to Madison after the Winter break; Heidi was doing it with the basketball coach, so for the sibs there was no further interest in making fun of her. Fun was in neither of their signs. She tore at the bread her mother had buttered, imagining herself under the sign of Jupiter, a traveler far from this dull Winter place, an unregistered blip in her parents' successful breeding.

This astrological disturbance passed with the season. There followed cloud cover of a moody Spring, and when the Summer stars emerged for Louise Moffett they were above the head of her junior-high lover, winking at her beer breath, blessing the safe sex of her era. Mechanized farm kids still making it to Billy Joel or Steely Dan, even Joni Mitchell, the outdated harmony of their sphere.

Louise, it then seemed, was to become the best of ordinary, the milkman's lovely daughter. Her father could level no complaint against her other than the growing oddness of her pictures, until, upon graduation from the university, she dismissed the young man she was to marry with bullshit concerning the inharmonious aspects of their celestial signs. That was unkind, for she did not give a sweet fuck about the stars, but could not tell him that all she loved was his athlete's body and to some extent admired the generosity of his good mind that made room for her career, no doubt a back room. He was not in an advantageous house, she explained. Louise spoke to the glorious running back of astrological opposition, a dithering rundown of quadrants and cusps, of Venus in an unfortunate conjunction with the Sun. He lay naked on her bed. Though she had looked at the all-star's perfect body many times, he seemed now a god who might have miraculous stories told about him, not to him.

In the uncertain light before dawn, he lay with his eyes closed, having seen her as his own for the last time. They made love crazily the night before. Or had sex, for now he understood that her riding him high, her cries for more and mercy were a sexual finale. She was dressed for a journey, swinging her backpack expectantly. In Madison they had fallen in love, naturally; and it was natural that they never spoke deeply to each other, or falsely. He fumbled for the quilt to cover his shame, thrown out of their collegiate paradise, though only Louise was leaving. Huddled, he listened to her with attention as though she was calling the last desperate plays in a losing game. Then he rose with the quilt wrapped around him. "Bitch," he said.

"Yes. Cunt. Slit." Beating him to the words so they would spring like toads from her pretty mouth. She was resolute: "Sagittarius is impulsive, often cruel."

For a split second it seemed she would laugh, they would both laugh. "Give it up," he said.

"You see, that's it. I can't give it up." It being as amorphous as the morning fog that clung to her father's fields; it—her painting or worlds never seen? Or her nature under the sign of the Archer, pigheaded, wounding, on target? And Louise was out the door, thinking what crap, yet amazed at her recall—houses, cusps, aspects—for years had gone by since she had angered her father with Zodiac Man, a hideous drawing copied out of the *Farmer's Almanac*, kitchen kitsch that let her speak the spite of a childish mind. Eight years, she reckoned, since she was sent to her room, the room in which her abandoned lover now lay. As she walked toward the State Road by fields of rye and early clover, she understood she would be banished, a word that suggested bitter estrangement in a tragic play, though she banished herself, was even unkind to herself, for she was not a cunt. A coward, a liar.

Each year Shirley Moffett readdressed the Christmas card from the handsome running back to her daughter. Winterscapes of Wisconsin followed Louise from one roach-infested hovel to another in New York City. In recent years, photos of his identical twin boys in twin snowsuits found her in the loft. This past Christmas, preceding the year in which she declared she would never see Artie Freeman again, though he has her key and she his ring, the sturdy blond boys were set on a couch in matching blazers propping a frothy bundle, an adorable baby girl. She did not think he was mean sending her these greetings. When she had her first one person show, she put his name down for an announcement to be sent to the best damn law firm in Milwaukee, where he was already junior partner.

She wondered, when that catalogue was mailed, what he made of *the foreshortened ground plan* of her paintings. At that time she painted picture postcards, small jewels in which *the primacy of distance*—the way the critics went on about her work—*the notational figment of a lost sublime*, how that inflated language registered among the practical legal documents he dealt with. *The variable syntax of Moffett's Cow Palace Series*—what gas it must seem to a litigator making a clear, effective case. He was not a dumb man, and if he looked for only a moment at the color reproductions of her work finely printed in Japan, he would see that she painted one subject, the farm, shrinking the landscape to what the heart could handle—a reduction, an ephemeral reproduction with postmark of place and date.

"Hey! You're the tourist?"

From their earliest days she had loved that Artie asked the right questions, questions that would never occur to the lawyer in Milwaukee, she was sure of that.

"Yep. A tourist of what I know best."

Her stamp of authenticity was the flip side of each card on which Louise wrote her address and message. They were messages to herself from the home she had left, messages of her making about the haying, the calving, the school board election, birthday, toothache, the new combine, blessing of rain, fear of Summer blight. Never about loss, her words were short and not, in their slight mockery, so sweet. Private hurt gone public.

When dreaming ahead to her *Botanicals*, huge paintings as yet unpainted, Louise thought of the good prospect she did not marry. She would send the catalogue to his firm in Milwaukee, her big canvases unfolding on thick, slick stock would reveal the enormity of her ambition. He would understand her scale, be pleased that she made the right choice for the both of them. Her father, on the other hand, might never see that her work was addressed to him, her every distortion of the farm. *The familial made foreign, probing the interiority of generic*—what unnatural gas—he had sent her to her room so that she would not be unkind. For Harold Moffett, she had consigned Zodiac Man to the flames— the ancient humors and polarities she never did believe in. Her father sent her to her room so that she would not speak her mind. A small flame burned in her always, steady as the pilot light in her mother's kitchen stove. She could not leave the man-made ponds, the rich improved earth, the fresh dung-smelling air of the farm. Like how many painters and poets finding their way to the city, a few with talent among the pretenders, Louise Moffett, at once yearning and rejecting, has worked with the landscape of home. No, the professor of animal husbandry would not approve of his daughter's obsessive vision—kind and unkind—her hard correction of memory, reduced or inflated, forever speaking her mind. Her pictures seemed to him unsound, as foolish as favorable days on which to seek pleasure, ungodly as the celestial order to plant root vegetables by the dark of the moon.

These were the only men of note in her life until Freeman. She loved Artie's first approach, which was not the onset of love she knew, just that she was struck by the direct unshuttered look of his eyes, cerulean straight out of the tube, blue irises that might need a wash of transparent white to seem real. He was real enough in the phony reception area of Skylark, taking her in as she swiveled toward him in her zinc-grey chair. Louise, a cute throwback to secretarial, twirled in Scandinavian wool upholstery behind the polished granite and steel desk with flowers fresh-every-other-day, stark blooms *à la japonaise*, flowers from no field she had ever seen—but then, her first grubby years in the city she had not seen the likes of Skylark. Ms. Moffett was a purely decorative item in the amusing installation that admitted petitioners to the world of Bertram Boyce. She did not have to dissemble, pronouncing Chairman Boyce to be "in conference" or "unexpectedly called away." Regulars passed to the inner chamber, their palms were read by the magic door while a humanly inflected voice screened the uninvited from the privileged. So, when Artie Freemen first saw Louise swiveling, adrift from the heavy hand of Skylark style, her welcome smile gone slack, Ms. Moffett's boredom was refreshing. Not playing her bit part, she had doodled on a dog-eared pad the button face with sharp acquisitive eyes, the buoyant emptiness of Bud Boyce. Artie noted ghoulish green paint caked in her cuticles. "You're new? Brand-new?"

"Temp," she announced with pride, not to be taken for permanent or every other day, but for one of the thousands of office temporaries shuffling around the city awaiting their real lives, a pilgrimage which had led Louise from legal brief to insurance claim to invoice of outer and underwear, from terminal to terminal. Skylark was to be Ms. Moffett's final stop. Her destination was that vast bright space in which she would paint big pictures she only imagined, for what could be accomplished in her studio apartment beyond her miniatures painted by lamplight when she was free of the temp life or on weekends in the shaft of soiled sunlight at her window, unable to step back between dresser and bed into the tangled wires of telephone and coffeepot? She could not distance herself from small landscapes no bigger than postcards from home, *Postcards*—what she named them when hung in her first show. A dirt road bisected fields of wheat, corn, rye. Clover nuzzled out the sky. At times a telephone line sliced across the silo, cropped the barn, disturbing the view and the viewer. The *Postcards* sold like postcards, but not before her attachment to Artie Freeman blossomed into more than temporary, less than permanent.

Many big canvases later, Louise paces the high white space once longed for. She stops to play the shell game with the blue love letters and the ring. If it's over, her enchantment with that lumbering feckless fool . . . valued for what? His ironic detachment from the galloping greed of the city? If it's over, then why does she finally, why sniffle as she finally tears at an envelope to give herself to his nonsense, so sweet his illegible attempt at the handwritten letter—*forgive, forget, then you, then I*—his overlapping circles in which they are explicitly one. Soliciting her as he had with honest blue eyes at Skylark. Artie still laughing at the surreal city where he finds no place, no home—she makes no mistake—is a floater, teen-time. She should have stayed on the farm, bred with some local, one of those bionic aggies who worked for her father, shown pleasant watercolors at the county fair. She could be fucking delighted with herself outside of this provincial black hole, this hopeless hub that sucked her in with hype. She is Ms. Moffett who can close the whole damn shop, laugh all the way to the airport. Except that she loves him. A love not fatal, more an urban disease, or the passing misery of a heavy Winter cold, yet, sleeping long hours, dosing herself with order-in Chinese (packets of soy and lethal mustard mounting in the empty fridge), she makes no move to go where the air is clean and clear. Artie is her lingering sickness. She fancies she hears the metallic turn of his key in the steel fire door of the loft, which remains unbolted. At odd hours, she throws the door open, leaves it ajar. She plucks his ring from the velvet box and wears it each day. His old messages play like the top twenty on her machine.

"Are they Jerseys, Lou?"

"Only asking, dear one—they keep on chompin' when they squat?"

Please!

> Now if there was one thing that could save the situation
> it was the cow on its little swatch of land
> I give my milk so that others will not dry up
> it said and gladly offer my services to the forces
> of peace and niceness
> but what really does grow under that tree
> —John Ashbery, "About to Move"

"Holsteins, Louise?"

She listens to the city boy, the begging note, not unlike the sodden bleat in his voice when he knelt before her—Love you, my Lou-Lou—with the fool's cap on his head. At least he's not toasted, slurring his dumb questions. Yes, she says to empty air, probably Holsteins, black and white picture-book cows, but what's she letting herself in for, loving him for years though she never backed up to see it; their independence once prized long devalued in her books. What's with the frigging cows? Cows are her father's business. Some funny business, these men in her life conspiring. Louise, in her will to paranoia, missing the obvious: no male plot, just the macrosystem. Home on the farm was megafarm, the neighbors' farms gobbled, thousands of acres now run by Harold Moffett's expensive equipment for some Commodifide Creamery which naturally accessed the services of a Skylark thereby employing the dual talents of Arthur Freeman, not knowing their data were farmed out to one man in one solitary room morphing their moo cows. For if a lone technician can extract 20,000 gallons of Product in one hour—if a pedometer implanted in the milk line—

"Louise, this is strictly business. The brown one, Bossy? Is she Alderney or Swiss?"

"Manure, sweetheart? Random or plotted?"

Shit. He knew nothing of cowcakes which multiplied in one year to tons of manure, or of the soft ammonia smell of the Winter barn cut with the sweet scent of hay, or farts popping stall to stall, the methane layer hovering heavy above Wisconsin. He is no longer at the other end to receive her cow intelligence: damn you, Freeman, not Bossy, cows by the thousands not even registered by number. Only the prize stock affectionately named—Beulah, Auntie Mame. Or Bonnie Belle, the cow shown at State Fair, curried until silky smooth, Lou shining her hooves till they gleamed for a blue ribbon. Ever the farmer's daughter, in the first cramped rooms of New York, when roaches crawled her brushes and tubes of acrylics, when water bugs big as toads shared her moldy shower stall, the livestock of this infested city, she thought not one Lower East Side kitchen was clean as Harold Moffett's barns.

Field mice, which were not adorable nibblers, had not troubled her mother's pantry for twenty years. High-frequency sound sent them back to their burrows and her father's crops were harvested in air-conditioned John Deeres by men and women out of the ag school where he taught—Dr. Cheese, Professor of Ice Cream, Advocate of Additives, at times State Representative (R). The dairy farmer's daughter was a passing curiosity in the city, where no temp came with much history. She let the ignorant city folk assume a milking stool, cow bells, a churn, let them imagine rusty chickens pecking in the dooryard, not her mother's prize perennial bed, her sister's Mercedes, the heated swimming pool. These people she had come to live among did not know her. They presumed her pictures, big and small, were cultural commerce executed out of bloodless theory, technical acrobatics, heartless. And the man she lived with, sort of lived with, knew her least of all.

The Moffett children married well and in good time, all but Louise, who left them, their handsome daughter with skin her father called top o' the milk. Sweetheart of Sigma Chi, all but engaged to the all-star, honors in art, fine art, and there Harold Moffett had no complaint, for Louise had sketched the family dogs and cats, her mother's posies set in the Waterford vase, drawn since she could grasp a crayon in her hand. He had given the walls of his house over to her fleshy nudes and her excoriating self-portraits and to her last undergraduate phase, minimal white-on-whites which set him at ease—milky canvases with slight variations of butter fat. He had not counted on his daughter's "acceptable drive turning the corner to raw ambition." With these words, delivered to a tearful Shirley, he dismissed her.

The day Louise left the farm, her mother had been at the bedroom window as the shining silver tank of a milk carrier pulled up by the long barn. Dawn, not early on the farm. A flock of oven birds swooped into the unmowed field where they built their tidy oven nests the cats would discover. Sunday, but there was never rest from the milking. Hal was out with his crew, students hired for the Summer, and he could not allow them a go at the new separator. It was the last week in June, the heifers grazing in the

East pasture. Soon they would be inseminated in the seasonless round of production. Shirley Moffett believed her daughter slept safe and sound with her lover under the flowered canopy in her girlhood room. They would marry when he was through law school. A farmer's wife, she could not help but think of him as a superior stud. Louise would teach children color values, the rudiments of art in some clever up-to-date way. Shirley Moffett was fond of such projections, which came true for her older children, but was not secure in her plot for this last child, born when she was near forty; and could never have predicted her shock as the first light glanced off the Big Pond, the sight of Louise hitched into a backpack walking down the long drive to the State Road. The clock read 6:25. Hal would have pumped half the day's gallons into the processor's gleaming tanker at this hour. Louise was heading for the six-thirty bus that would take her to Milwaukee. Shirley threw on a robe, was running in floppy terry cloth mules the quarter-mile drive only to see her child, her dearest child, flag down the Badger bus, turn round to take in the spread of the farm, to see her mother flapping her arms wildly, an unnatural creature in the calm domestic landscape.

Then it seemed to Shirley Moffett no surprise at all, only heartbreak, and what to do, to cook ham, eggs, potatoes—the hearty farm breakfast no longer allowed, the comfort food of her early marriage, when Hal fed the stock before dawn and drove off to the lab to analyze the emulsifiers written into his dissertation, leaving her to her first baby in diapers and to shoveling manure in the barn.

"What's this?" Harold Moffett noted the butter, the cream for his coffee. "Shirl?"

The young man came into the kitchen, set down his nylon sports bag as though it was a great burden. The massive all-star—good-natured, lacking the killer instinct. His defeat filled the room. He had never been turned away from any prospect.

"She's gone." Shirley Moffett fussed with the place mats and silver, stalling, yet when she spoke she sounded forthright, bold.

"She's gone. On the morning bus. Louise has left us." Leaving her graduation present, a red Camaro.

"She said"—the young man looked down at the breakfast he refused to eat—"she said she must travel. She . . . she's a Sagittarius." He did not use her name, for it was as if Louise could not have said she was in transit from Venus or the ninth house, if it was houses or aspects in Saturn. He attempted to speak the language she laid on him to make it easy, her inexplicable walking off.

"That's bullshit," the professor said. "I'm the expert on bullshit."

Cradling his sports bag, the young man moved to the back door, where an Almanac hung next to a feedstore calendar which informed him that on this day Mrs. Moffett would attend the League of Women Voters. Tomorrow her reading group: *Innocents Abroad*. Thursday, First Methodist choir. Suddenly a grunt, the stomping of scrimmage as Dr. Cheese, the distinguished dairyman, rushed to tear the Almanac off its nail, where it had lived every year in this farmhouse where he was born. His hands, once firm for milking, were limp from years of academic conferences, writing up grants, directing his staff in the lab. With a scholar's soft hands he ripped ineffectually at pictures of the Archer, the Crab, of Aries dribbling water on the cheap newsprint of the Almanac, of the Bull that was bullshit. He turned to the iron stove to burn this nasty scrap of nostalgia, to burn the book's simple jokes and puzzles, its herbal cures for hair loss, impotence, acne, ancient balms against the toothache, pox, bunion, its quaint quatrains that denatured the very seasons with singsong rhyme, its age-old ads for trusses, wine presses, fungal and love lotions, its adages and moral fables, its digest of history, predigested as feed in the second stomach of a cow. Harold Moffett wanted the book which his daughter used against him consumed in flames, the poor *Old Farmer's Almanac*, its astral divination, factual and foolish, reduced to ash. But it was the end of June. The potbelly stove, a cheerless artifact, was cold to the touch of his furious hand.

THE SNOWFLAKE IN HELL

The chances of finding two snowflakes that are identical are one in a billion, maybe more, but that's what happened to Dr. Will Bottoms. Bottoms, a crystallographer at UCLA, was looking one lunchtime at the wrapper of a frozen Milky Way with his trained eye when the miracle happened and so forth, Almanac repeating form, monthly quip comforting, melting quickly away.

Februare: to purify. From the Roman festival of expiation. Had it been February, the month of our story, bleak days for young lovers set up- and downtown on overheated islands of yearning and remorse, separated by anger, humiliation and pride, had it been the foreshortened month in dead of Winter when the Sun with mild promise surfaces from the lower latitudes, the charred Almanac might have warmed the unreasonable heart of Harold Moffett. His daughter is alone in her high white space, at times dreaming of reconciliation, no way as lofty as purification, for the turn of the century remains an era of adjustments, accommodation. She must work, work on, and so Louise abandons the newsprint, the dull No. 2 pencil, and in one of her few trips to the world buys charcoal and a drawing block, supplies valued in her student days. On the way back to her desolate loft, she is stopped by a book in a window, the self-help trash they laughed at in the old days, they. The author looks a fraudulent Santa Claus who will stuff your stocking with cheap toys that break in an hour, still . . . still, she buys the book to spite herself or Artie Freeman. It promises salvation: seven roads to self-assertion; seven deadly sins of self-denial; seven selves as seven elves, Grumpy and Dopey not included. The book works on Louise like a poultice burning to the place that is sore: a remedy of salvage for the credulous, not salvation. In shame she finds herself on every page, so rampant is the disease of . . . what to call it? Emptiness, the human predicament so general anyone might discover their nature, their need — as in a daily horoscope — *you are intuitive, risk all, exude magnetic charm.* She assigns the book to the garbage so that it will never be recycled, calls Dealer to insure that her show is scheduled for Spring, shaves her charcoal to the point. Louise begins to draw.

By the first week in February, millennial fluff is thrown into the discount bin—apocalyptic angels, rectilinear crosses, misappropriated Zen and Zodiac. Astrological Man is temporarily discarded with Nostradamus. Their prophecies of doom, milked dry by the media, did not come to pass. But the *Seven Roads* to wherever so pleases the multitudes it continues the blockbuster sell.

POSTCARDS

A cop presses Tony's big head stuffing him into the squad car.

"Dumb fuck!"

Like they have just spilled out of school Little Man and Sissy walk along with kids from Joan of Arc High. The sky threatens rain. Sissy thinking the dumb fuck will be dry. Little Man splits, down the ramp into a garage. A cousin there, plenty of boys on the block. His man Tony, shithead came with him down from a squat. Stuff got wonky up there, maybe two, three months ago. Time in Little Man's book connects to duration, where he is for how long—how long till it cools in Fort Tryon, how long he trusts his cousin who jockeys cars in the parking garage, how long he is on probation, how long the cops hold a dumb fuck. Tony, all his life he has watched out for Tony, who follows him like a dog, big boy, his fat head wobbling yes, yes, yes above Little Man. Yes, Tony would kneel to suck his cock if Little Man did not slap his fat head.

"It's words is all! *Dumb fuck. Suck my cock.*"

Tony gone with the cops, lost baggage. They gonna send a retard, dumb fuck, to Riker's stealing a slice off Kosher Pizza? Fat boy stuffing his mouth, only Tony keeps his dumb mouth shut in detention, stupid dumb fuck. And the girl who hooked on to them gone, extra baggage. So what? Little Man shit talks his cousin, who hoses down a Volvo grey with the salt and grit of Winter roads.

While Sissy runs into the Park, squad car following. Tony locked behind the grate in the car, animal, dumb fuck fingers her. Running up by the Reservoir for her life, not her health, she's not worth it, not worth getting a tight ass out of the squad car, chase a skinny kid through the mud. What are we talking about here? A slice, Parev Pizza Pie. The day unseasonably warm. Under a veil of persistent rain footpaths have thawed to slippery mush. Moving out of range, almost to the East side of the Park, Sissy finds a rock to set down her gear, for this moment not afraid, then sees him on a bench, *soldier*, his face gleaming wet, far from his crumbling apartment, out of her precinct. Little Man taught her the 24th—West 86 to 124, Park to River. She got here with an address, connection to Debby she knew upstate, this older girl instructing Sissy what story you tell in counseling. Tell them, girl, like its oh, yeah, first time, last time, they're writing it down, a baby, you could tell them nice this, nice that—whatever. My friend Debby, she called her. Debby sent a postcard to a way station, the only mail ever directed to Sissy, ever, postcard of a kitty nose to nose with a mouse and this address in big block letters, but when Sissy got off the bus in Port Authority, walked the blocks uptown, Debby was gone with her kid and there was this project, this playground with Little Man, Tony, this precinct. So Sissy is far from home watching the soldier, who looks like he sits all day—one bench or another. The drizzle never melting his bubble of gloom; he is hatless, black hair matted, grown longer over the top of Dumbo ears, not funny. Even the first night, she never thought the ears funny. His mopey blue eyes do not see her.

The rain is spit, spit in her face. She unzips her gear, feels down into ragged jeans and lumpy sweaters for his cap, the army hat she has vowed never to give back. Relenting, she will say she has kept it for him since the night he fell at her feet and she, Sissy, helped him. She will say *lost*, which is true, not stolen, though she's done worse than steal an old hat. Sissy on the lookout, as Little Man—dwarfish, hunched—slashed menu boy for the cash, Chop Suey bleeding in the gutter. Her own fast fingers after old-lady coin purses tucked in flappy cloth bags, old ladies shuffling the supermarket aisles. Blonde girl dressed as a boy, Little Man pimped for her on the beeper. No way *now*, is only when she came looking for Debby, earning her keep the first time, last time, tell them, girl, words is all, sweat their shit.

Feeling the captain's bars, she pulls the rough wool hat out of her gear to confront the soldier and he looks at the kid a split second, then with practiced urban gaze disconnects.

You don't know Sissy helped you out?

He is up from the bench, not heading back across the Park, trotting in the wrong direction and Sissy running after.

Dumb fuck, I kissed your mouth.

When he crosses Fifth Avenue, she loses Artie Freeman in the confusion of buses, runs between cars to see him enter a white building, awning and doorman, glass doors through which potted palm, gold table. Doorman smiling at the soldier, he does not smile at Sissy beached with her gear under his silver awning on polished brass poles. Almost dark enough to move on, back through the Park to her precinct, now safe. Tony has stuff to tell, they slap Tony's fat stupid head, hold him for more than a slice. Three minus one in the Day Care, their squat, better than a condemned ratscrap apartment. They are always in the dark. She hears Little Man and Tony, hears them other side of kiddie blocks, laughing, fooling around, though quiet as mice, for such is the discipline that must be maintained, the strict order of toys and juice cartons, coloring books, bright numbers and letters which must be lifeless till morning, though Little Man pays the security guard. Payoff, like rent for the squat, so why does he keep her around? Baby doll, her body no longer useful? Tonight she will be with this clever little man. Two, the two of them behind the tot toys in Day Care.

Sissy moving on, pulls off her wet knit hat and puts on Cpt. O'Connor's to scramble up over the black rocks to the transverse. The overseas cap slips on her narrow head, at times clownishly covering her eyes, but she knows where she is going and saunters past the police barracks in Central Park, not her precinct so she is, for the moment, unafraid. Pleased that she met up with her soldier, a sharp kid on the run given a crumb to peck at in the city where she is unknown. She has seen *soldier* again, then again. Their story line incidental.

7,200 runaways enter the city (1996), populace of a small town, the rate rising each year, downtown rockers and rich kids unabused, artsy types in SoHo and the theater district. Many hang out in dedication to purposeless hanging. Some for the blast, trash, freaks, drink, fuck, fight and dance, dance to vast music du jour of the clubs. Sissy has come off the bus with a postcard, still in her gear the cute kitty sniffing the mouse, a photo not a drawing, so it is real, the peaceable kingdom, nice this, nice that, you tell them, girl, the wisdom of Debby. She has come for survival, not numbness or excitement, yet so much incident in her city life, so much in the moment to moment she expects something to happen with the soldier, nothing big (dark stranger, helium high, big kiss), just next time he will know her. Next time, not tonight with Little Man. Next time, the romantic presumption of her plot.

This sodden twilight of early February is the end of the goddamn world to Louise, as hard a judgment on her adventures in the city as a dark Winter day some years ago when Shirley and Harold Moffett stood staunch as pitchforks, appearing to all the art scene like husband and wife in *American Gothic*, which they were not, yet Louise could not correct the impression that her father's stiff tweed jacket, the broach at her mother's throat were of a distant, unaffected place, a lost country of straight talk and worthy tasks.

The occasion her first show, the opening. Louise thought her success would afford a moment of reconciliation. The Moffetts flew
in from Wisconsin on their way to a Cow Conference, her father
made that clear, on his way (Shirl in attendance) to advise the
squalid outposts of the world where dairy farmers bumbled along
without automatic feeding fences, without a single pneumatic
machine to plug an udder. So it was, as always, Harold's show.

At the airport the porter ripped her parents off. The hot water
boiler in their hotel was on the fritz. When at last the travel-soiled
Moffetts pushed through the gallery glitterati to approach their
daughter's small pictures, her *Postcards*, they saw their landscape
diminished. Harold stooped to look at his first steel silo, which
rose slick and engorged from the flat land, x-ed out in the artist's
view with black telephone wires. In the dusky foreground a small
windmill lay discarded like a broken toy, while the background
flared in a bloody sunset.

"That silo is to the east!" cried Harold Moffett. "To the east of
the Big Pond!"

"Yes," murmured Shirley, "and now there are twenty-five.
Perhaps—"

Harold turned from his wife to scout out Louise, to discover
that his daughter's hair was dry as corn tassels left in the sun, her
beauty withered in dank indoor air with these brittle women and
lithe men who looked him over in ignorant amusement.

Shirley thought, *Perhaps, the fault is not Lou's memory. Her
farm is that of a child.* How could she say it when Hal spoke, as he
did so often to the children, of his pride in that first steel silo,
praised its shinning blue shaft as though ... Shirl thinking *he
can't see the farm of an angry child*, when the bulk of her husband
pushed her aside, Harold squinting.

Squinting now to read the *Postcards*, which were flippable,
these city people turning them round, desperate for any entertaining message, for a sophisticate's laugh at his life on the farm.
"Aunt Bea here for Glorious Fourth. Crackers as always." What
could his daughter mean? His sister, whatever might be said of

her, was a prominent oncologist in Chicago. Beatrice Moffett had been awarded her first honorary degree. Her niece should redden with shame, though he imagined Louise beyond blushes living among these bloodless people who could not comprehend a word of Dr. Beatrice Moffett's papers on the structure of miscreant cells. No, they would prefer to read an exhausted myth—neurotic spinster in poke bonnet or Kmart polyester—into this frivolous note on Aunt Bea. As though avoiding a cow pie, he hopped back from the little painting, a desecration of his first lonely steel silo.

"Beatrice!" Shirl laughing with her daughter. "Crackers, absolutely."

"We have an early plane," Harold Moffett said.

"But I *love* Aunt Bea—" Louise did not defend the aunt who left the farm for her share of scientific glory, left her envious brother to his mechanized cows. She led her parents to the door of the gallery flung open to the storm of a Winter night and then she did blush, for there was Artie Freeman on West Broadway in Huck Finn straw hat and laceless tennis shoes, fumbling to pay a cabby. His arms were full of funky sunflowers and farmy wheat stuck in a glamorous milk pail. Artie hallooing, "Lou-Lou, my Lou." The intimate peck of her lover's kiss stiffened both Moffetts before Freeman thrust his barnyard tribute at their lost child, "Hi-ho the dairy-O!"

Yes, she loved this unambitious clown, a marginal man entertained by probabilities. His aim, if any in life, to dog-paddle behind the champs in the morally muddy waters of cyperspace. She had been at the reception desk the day Freeman shot through the programmed door of Skylark, Bud Boyce in pursuit. When did Big Boyce trail in distress? When look hot under the collar of his dove silk shirt? Freeman careening across the carpet with its larky Skylark logo said to Boyce: "And how dare you chain this prairie princess to a desk?"

To Louise: "Remember! Temporary, not of this artificial light."

She never knew what fancy corporate footwork finally detached Freeman from Bud's imperial plots. Skylark tentacles extended to plastics, waste disposal, energy systems, baseball—minor-league. So, upon the exploitation of workers in Southeast Asia or the pitch of a spitball, Artie set himself free, though not entirely, hedging his bets with piecework, targeting markets for Bud Boyce, fairly harmless calculations and groovy graphics for the old ad agency, a sweet remnant of Skylark, once an electronic mom-and-pop store.

"Why continue with Boyce?"

"We go back, way back."

By this time they were sleeping on her skimpy futon in the roach room. When the *Postcards* and the first *Botanicals* paid off, they moved to the loft—not entirely, for Artie nestled into ironic detachment in the uptown layer with the endearing machines and she had her space, workspace, dedication to work. He seldom spoke of his mother, Fiona the dabbler, and often Lou thought he loved her own love of work more than he loved her. He understood the little paintings of the farm that brought her first fame. "I see. Home. The crippled viewer, the crippling view."

He claimed no home. They had been somewhat together for five years, and though she had seen his barren pad with rumpled bed and techno-tools, he had never taken her to the old man's apartment. The grandfather remains fleshless, a fleeting name hidden from her. In the aftermath of the sorry proposal, wearing Mae's diamond each day, Louise is deeply wounded that Freeman never took her home as though she was—a chick, low-life, slut—sentiments unreasonable as the fact that she set her heart on this man one fated day in the five years—five, a magic number— the day, perhaps, when she cropped her hair for the fashion and he cried for the loss, for the boyish figure he held in place of her. She had grown her hair in to please, now chopped it to spite him, to reclaim her body. It is growing, growing in untidy clumps as she begins to draw an arm with Artie's mere bump of a bicep, then his widow's peak and sharp Irish nose . . . remembering the night the violinist played schmaltz while they cracked lobsters, just the two of them on her thirtieth birthday, and his amazement when confronting the first of her *Botanicals*—an enormous microscopic view of a maple leaf with the small inset in which she painted whole the domestic shade tree fluttering its limbs over still water.

"Big picture, little picture. A story. Tell me the story," he said three years before a bingo-brained critic got her number on *Acer saccharinum—the dialectic narrative of Moffett's misprision*. Yes, there was a story, she told Artie, that tree, that very tree, a silver maple, grew on the far side of the Big Pond, where the dry cows follow their leader, lie down before a storm. . . .

Half a decade, five years, five—the odd number of love, Venus, *Veneris* retrieved from some dusty astrological corner in her head, rejected as nonsense though it prompts Louise to call her improbable lover, a digital voice again reporting the phone no longer in service. All receptors dead, she calls (poor judgment) Boyce, who suggests she drop by the office. The reception area where once she was installed in chill luxury, is a plaster and concrete bunker with steel beams and wires exposed; inkwells, their little pots cemented over, pencils and pens cast in useless glass decorate a white elephant of rolltop desk; typewriters affixed to the walls, their keys splotched with paint, alphabet obliterated. In the warm glow of genial monitors, she feels a bumpkin, not up to the Skylark game.

"Like it?"

"Love it."

"Amusing."

Bud consoles her and suggests they get it on. At least that's what she thinks a bottle of Dom Perignon later, fending him off in the limo.

"Freeman is a loser. The guy lost track, dangled off the end of the system."

"Your friend?"

"My former associate," Boyce says. "A throwback to monkey morality. See no evil, speak no evil, doodle no evil. I hold with Etcha Sketch, Miss Moffett. Tip the magic slate and the nasty picture disappears."

"He wants to play it straight. Virtual integrity." Now her

moment for an Artie routine, Operation Skylark—*beam aboard client, suckass to client, read you*—but the black windows of the car confine her in the slick setup of a tidy controlled man, skin and hair a uniform taupe ordered to go with the kidskin of his Italian shoes. Bertram Boyce, photographed as youngest of the Schoolboy Millionaires for the cover of *Money* magazine, came off older than Artie. Polished and untrustworthy as a diplomat, he had not wanted her, a sexual proposition tossed at the woman he knew to be his friend's.

The Buddy smile begging yet confident, "Forgive?"

"Forgiven."

"In any case, your hero has disappeared."

"Yes," then sweetly probing, "he's not at O'Connell's."

"O'Connor's," Boyce's sharp laugh, "not at the grandfather's apartment?" He switches on a reading lamp which shines a circle of light between them, but of course she's in the dark, wondering how often Artie had been outsmarted in his long history with Boyce, longer than five years.

They are driven through the city—off the ramp at Grand Central down Park Avenue South, coming to clean and prosperous Union Square. Union, she had thought crossroads, perhaps a railroad station, until Artie, scanning Citylore, came up with the Civil War, that Union, and Search, skipping a half-century, displayed a graphic of shabby old Commies raising the Red Flag—MAY DAY IN UNION SQUARE. He printed out, stuck the picture to her refrigerator with a Minnie Mouse magnet to prove them no longer innocent of that history—not their common history of Union Square with favorite bistro and flower stall. The agitators in the old clipping were stern men in bowler hats, furious women in dainty white shirtwaists menaced by mounted police in brass buttons, paddy wagons at the ready . . . which should have instructed Louise that history was not a costume party. When reinventing the dull Fifties in dress-up, she forgot that Union Square thereby lost . . . nothing, nothing at all, for hadn't Artie honored history in a dumb show, slashing at that cadaverous woman, Felicia, who dared to decorate herself with the tattoo of a death camp.

Boyce dialing the restaurant where he is to dine with his wife and a client: "Running late." His voice hushed, secretive to wife or client. They draw up to a cast-iron building with Late Roman pillars and cornices, the building that houses Moffett's loft. The driver opens her door, wind whipping back his coat, exposing the livery of a serving man. Louise recognizes him from Skylark, a man always uniformed, always waiting, waiting now in a slanting cold rain. She cannot let Boyce win. "Monkey morality. Isn't that monkey see, monkey do?"

O'Connor. There are a glut of O'Connors in the telephone book, Upper East Side (she guesses East Side) ten, twenty. One day Artie sat on a park bench, a laundry bag with clean underwear for his grandfather—fragment of story—an old man who did not like servants in his house, the underwear stolen the instant Artie closed his eyes. Which park? Riverside, Carl Schurz, Central? There is a slim chance she will hear his voice if she calls all O'Connors.

MILKY WAY: II

John Dee, astrologer to Elizabeth I, forecast the auspicious date for his sovereign's coronation, sold the horoscope for profit. Dr. Dee built a flying machine fitted out with a picnic basket to deposit him on Jupiter, taught the Euclidian mathematics while claiming discovery of the philosopher's stone. Our time and our position, plotted with an accuracy by Kepler, Galileo, Newton (astrologers all) which discredits . . . that which all our enlightened centuries fail to discredit—the wisdom writ in stars.

Louise Moffett had not thought of her flirtation with astrology since she was a pesky kid and here was Zodiac Gal, still glittering on the lid of a coffin: Nut, Egyptian, 2nd Century B.C. Nut, the sky goddess, arced over the earth, touching down her fingers and toes. The Milky Way formed the stars on her long royal gown. She is circled by the signs of the Zodiac. Louise ran across Nut flipping through slides for an art history exam. That sets her in Madison, Wisconsin, ca. 1987, the year, if we are keeping track of time, that the market crashed, that van Gogh's *Sunflowers* was sold to the Yasudu Fire & Marine Insurance Co. of Japan for £24,750,000; the year and month (February) of the supernova, the first exploding star visible to the naked eye since one seen by Johannes Kepler in 1604. So, 1987, in which the slide of Nut illuminated with bare breasts, sandals, bracelets and a contraption like a halo set over her head was discovered by Louise mixed in with Florentine Virgins receiving the angel of the Lord. Louise halted in the dark before turning the carousel to the next Mary, smiling at the Egyptian goddess with indulgence.

DON'T YOU BELIEVE IT! She could hear her Aunt Bea, see her in the Harley Davidson jacket, black leather boots, the studded belt and tight jeans, see her squaring off with Zodiac Man, that lousy defiant drawing tacked up on Lou's wall. Aunt Bea seldom left her patients or her lab, but came out from Chicago for the holiday, any holiday of her choosing. She owned the back acres and while she was at the farm would walk her property at Christmas or Easter or the Fourth of July. She came on her motorcycle out from Chicago and slept on a cot set up in Lou's room, that custom started when the house was full of Moffetts.

Louise assured her aunt that she did not believe in Zodiac Man, but she would say or do most anything to please Bea, ride over the rutted frozen ground or through the muck-soft cow paths, hugging her aunt till they arrived at the electric fence that set off her land. As they walked, Louise listened about Bea's work at the hospital, the little children with weak blood, or bad blood, about children who inherited such problems.

Beatrice's bright jingly words: "And this is my problem. These acres. My inheritance." Everything about her was compact, delightful to her tall, farm-fed niece. When Bea straddled the

Harley, her feet barely reached the pegs. "We should all be so lucky, to have my problem."

They looked back across the land to the farmhouse and barns and silos, to the grazing cows like squarish blots floating in the pastures, to the toy trucks and tractors. "Distance fools the eye," Aunt Bea said. When she looked through her microscope at injured cells back in Chicago, the farm was even smaller. The girl understood that Aunt Bea had left the farm which Harold Moffett mostly owned and that her parents were unprepared for these visits, that her father did not like his daughter walking the fields with Beatrice. One night, when the silver hoarfrost cracked under their feet, Lou looked up to the bright stars of Winter sweeping her hand across the path of the Milky Way. Aunt Bea called through the dark, "WE ARE IN IT," wanting the child to know our address in the cosmos, our home the little solar system lying thirty thousand light-years from the center of our galaxy, the Milky Way. She ran far out through the crackling litter soil of her fields, far out, her niece following. Bea spun in the moonlight, "ADAM AND EVE BLEW IT." The child stopped at a distance. "It's nothing," her aunt said, "I'm just crackers as always." Once, when Lou wondered over the age of a wagon spoke picked out of the Spring thaw, Bea threw the recent hand-hewn wood aside, wanting her to know the age. "This is the Holocene, WE ARE IN IT."

As Louise grew older, Beatrice talked to her at night, girls together. They were both late children, she said. How they wanted to make a pet of you, little sisters. Harold had almost cried when finally he understood she was smarter by a long shot, smarter in school. It was then he hunkered in with the cows so he would never leave this place, make it bigger, better, cutting edge of cow culture, so Bea's big brother would be Mighty Milkman.

Bea liked men and women as well, but married the Polish Intellectual. They met in Berlin at a conference on Science and Theology. Science had nothing to do with theology, no way, but oh boy she was up for a free ride to Europe. She brought the

Polish Intellectual home. That is what she called him in a FedEx
sent to Harold on her wedding day. She brought him home
to Chicago, only once to the farm. Not a success. The slight
young man hitched behind little Bea, they were like two black
birds alighting from their perch. Lou thought him adorable,
out of his biker's costume wispy and pale as the first florets on
the sugar-maple tree. It was not even a holiday, just Spring in
Wisconsin. She was fourteen and she taught him . . . NOT IN THE
HOUSE . . . she taught him old American dances, the hully gully,
the frug, out in the barn, the original barn, unhygienic, out of use.
Louise had come into a girlish beauty and the P.I. touched the
buds under her sweatshirt, ran a swift hand over the fringe of her
cut-off jeans.

NOT IN THE HOUSE . . . Harold, beside himself, treated the Polish Intellectual as if he was a dork from the regional high, for he
was a good deal younger than Aunt Bea. "He doesn't *work!*" This
repeated to Shirley many times in an hour. Lou laughing with the
P.I., hoping he did not hear or understand Dr. Cheese. And it was
true, the agile little man thought his thoughts all day while Bea
studied sick blood late and long hours in the lab or tended to
those poor hopeless, hairless kids. At the farm, that one uncomfortable night, they slept, the married couple, in Heidi's room.
Lou heard them drop boots, one then another, heard Aunt Bea's
laugh, not melodious, and something like a thump of pillow
against the wall, a shrill cry, but in the morning her aunt beamed
satisfaction over Shirley's farm fresh eggs. She had shown them all
the Polish Intellectual and did not bring her man again.

Louise knew as she listened to the night sounds of Summer, the
frogs burping methodically in the pond, a barn bat flapping at the
screen, that he was gone. It was the Fourth of July. Aunt Bea lay in
her cot curled round a pillow. Now and again what seemed to be
the last rocket shot into the sky. That would be the ag school kids
working the summer farm. Their music was folksy, distant, but
suddenly all was silent as though her father had ordered—not in

the house. Earlier this night Aunt Bea rode out to her inheritance, walked the land alone in her hot leather jacket. Louise had been out with a boyfriend, come home to find her parents glum by the side of the pool. Now she waited, girls together, for the story.

"What did he think?" Lou asked.

Aunt Bea did not answer.

"What did he think about?"

Aunt Bea came into her bed. She hooked around Louise as though they were careening down the highway, her birdy head nestled in the girl's thick golden hair. "It was true he did not work," Beatrice said. "He came from another kind of city. He thought about nations and wars, global economy, population curves, indigenous people. I do science. He thought about science. I analyze chromosome aberrations, basophils in the bone marrow, block the sticking of good cells to bad. If we can clone the genes, their sequence, track the DNA bands . . ." Then Bea remembered she was pouring her heart out to her niece, a high-school girl. "I do abnormalities," she whispered to Louise, "antisense—crackers as always. He went to a conference. He thought about genetics and ethics. I do science, Lou, science in the lab. The woman he met does religion. Religion and Polish intellectuals."

Louise lay in Aunt Bea's arms like a big child. This woman who did religion had a child, a boy by an absent father. She did religion and science, how Galileo, having found our little earth in the Milky Way, blind and sick, gave his truth up for the Pope of Rome. How Einstein fumbled toward the end: "God does not play dice."

"She undoes science," Bea said. "What a lousy mealy-mouth game." How Michael Faraday, with each magnetic discovery, professed the written testimony of the will of God. How Darwin, awed by the Great Design . . .

DON'T YOU BELIEVE IT!

"I won't." Louise said. "I won't believe it." Then she led Aunt

Bea back to her bed, pulled the sheet over her shame, for the flamboyant little woman was now stripped naked before her niece and the world. The girl stooped to hear her aunt's laugh, a laugh or dry murmur: "Yes. Oh, yes. We are in it."

And so Louise (slide room, year of the supernova) lingers over Nut triumphant, in full control of the Egyptian stars painted on her belly, before turning to the assigned Florentine Virgins, who kneel in humility, presented by the angel of the Lord with their symbols. Louise will be examined on the lily, lamb, rose, on the dove and flame of the Holy Ghost, on the newly discovered use of perspective. In the dark study hall as the slides of great art click around her, Louise looks hard at the Italian hills and valleys seen through gothic arches of Fra Lippi and thinks his idyllic countryside is at a great distance from his beholden Mary, as far away as she is, taking notes in Madison, from the neglected fields of Aunt Bea.

ZODIAC II

Louise draws seven-pointed stars, fiddling with the planets so that they connect to each day of the week. The seven points of each star reach to the circle in which she encloses her hope. She has called Dealer to look at new work, as though talent will return with his studio visit. He warms his plump white fingers with a mug of herbal tea but does not bother to take off his sheepskin cloak, wondering how best to cancel, that is *reschedule*, Moffett's show, for there is no new work to see, only this washed-out blonde with red-rimmed eyes and a bruised heart. Dealer has presumed her alliance with Freeman to be a useful arrangement, never liked the man's aggressive dishevelment, his superior smile, and since the thug attacked him on that downer of all New Year's Eves . . . but there is no dealing with this woman's sorrow. He pats the artist's hand without a comforting word. Her wiry knuckled hand that so cleverly wields a paintbrush is soiled by the ooze of a ballpoint pen, her worktable littered with stars, clones of stars, proliferating

copies, copies of copies with Sun-Sunday, Moon-Monday, Mars-
Tuesday and so forth, written at seven sharp angles. What to say?

"Is the moon a planet?"

"It is not," Louise says and opens a block of fine rag paper. She
holds the drawing to her chest like a proud child. Zodiac Man.
That fellow who can be seen in the windows of dusty curiosity
shops, the old-age New Age, still an arresting figure weeks into the
new century that was to launch the great leveling, healing; charts
reproduced in the popular press, astrologers interviewed prime
time, taken to be wise as senators and macro-economists, as quantum physicists who are delighted to address a larger public on
whatever cable expounding the Theory of Any and Every Last
Thing. Miss Moffett has drawn the splayed man of all centuries, of
all our natures and that of the universe, drawn him badly. Dealer
has dealt the art of the moment, often transitory goods of the untalented, but he sees nothing in Louise Moffett's exacting pencil
strokes other than an uninteresting copy of the creature that can be
found in any cheap Almanac.

"A scherzo? You *are* good at the performative gesture."

"It's Artie," Louise says with the assertive voice of an earnest
child.

"I mean your generation, so adept at appropriation. Perhaps I
mean counterfeit—your *Postcards* and *Botanicals*—so deliciously
retrograde. And new work, is it to be the pulpy illustration?"

"It's Artie."

Dealer's schlock of recognition, seeing that the astrological
man's head is that of her departed lover. Does she presume he
controls our universe, our lives? Indeed, it is Artie, thatch hair,
mocking eyes, blue watercolor of his irises washing into the
graphite, those unfortunate ears and the simple smile of a man
the dealer understands to be anything but simple. The likeness
is startling as portraits done by children often are, yet in this
head there is such loving attention to line of the nose, shadow
of the bright eye. *Portrait of a Youth*, Giorgione. Dealer is
reminded of that young man looking out at the world with a

self-incriminating smirk—we are all of us in it, are we not? Which reminds the dealer, too, of someone he had once cared for without reservation, judgment thrown to the wind, reminded not by this ragged sketch of Artie Freeman, but by the youth in the exquisite painting in which the shadow of a flared nostril so beautifully echoed the mood cast by a dark Italian eye. Yes, the loss of a Giorgione boy who ditched him in Venice, that loss of the loved one's arched neck, a pale neck suddenly more particular in memory than any old master. He had waited for that boy in the bar of the Daniele, waited at the perfect corner banquette reserved for two.

"New departures," he's anxious to leave on that false note. Sweltering under sheep pelts, Dealer sniffs the acrid floral tea and studies Zodiac Man as though it is a seminal work. He sees that this poor child has idealized her lover's genitalia and once again throws judgment to the wind, for there is something mighty in Moffett's attaching that prick's head to a mythic body. Yes, we are all of us in it.

Louise meets his falseness with hers: "New departures!" In a defiant moment she had summoned Dealer to look at new work, and when—on this strange lost day among days—when he actually came with his silly rap on retrograde, she hadn't a clue what she was up to, nothing to show but Artie stretched on the rack of the year, poorly drawn as though cribbed out of an old Almanac.

"Why, Lou!" as her mother might say. "You've got Heidi (or Dad or Bowser) exactly."

Yes, she had captured A. Freeman, a small crafty talent. And she'd made use of the planets once again, this time to stay in the city, but oddly it was like getting on the bus again, leaving Wisconsin. As bad as that, scary. Poor Dealer, he had come to cancel and bent—to her will, she supposed, or to the pathetic pluck which covered her heeling in for the long run. She tears Artie as Moon Man to bits, smooths a blank page but makes no mark upon it. Now passionless, blind as a beast in one of her father's *in vitro* gestations, yet she must count the days till her show.

February 11—Thomas Alva Edison born at Milan, Ohio, 1847.

The (second) American Prometheus. The Edison script a recycling of the self-made man: genius simmers in the inquisitive poor boy who tinkers in his father's barn, a mere telegraph boy working city to city during the Civil War, tapping urgent messages in the Morse code which travel no more than two hundred miles. A large, lumpish young man, his broad forehead swollen with brains, his hearing impaired from an early age but sharp: like Franklin, never missed a dollar or a trick.

Who was the greatest person, living or dead, in world history?
—Gallup Poll (1945)

The answer in order of preference: Jesus, Franklin Roosevelt, Lincoln, Washington, General MacArthur, Edison.

You have to wonder why they posed the foolish question in the year of the great Allied victory, demoting heroic enterprise to a random sampling of opinions from man on the street or woman on the phone. I knew the name of every great man living and dead on that list, even as I unwrapped the improving book, a Christmas gift in no way enviable like the chemistry set and half-scale pool table which appeared under the tree for my brother. Pleased, mildly, by my first pumps with flat grosgrain bows, by yet another Parchesi board with its colorful paths to the winning circle, but actively bored by the dull blue cover of my book, its stars and stripes forming a garland interrupted by gold lozenges which framed young fresh American faces of great good kids, their stories designed to inspire me to industry and learning.

1946. The sluggish winter of my thirteenth year: As February tramped through gloom, my brother who'd shot up like an unseasonable weed made the basketball team which played the junior high circuit. Saturdays—and he was off with his fan club, our parents suddenly speaking rebounds, layups, personal fouls. Saturdays—the matinees at the Rialto featured a series of brooding films, dark plots with calculating women (so I was told), tawdry romances recently of much interest to my friends, not to me, never. There was nothing for it, for my distaste of junior hoopla and steamy celluloid kisses, but to inflict further punishment on myself, so . . . a Saturday, 2 P.M, the Bridgeport Bullets facing the Fairfield Falcons— upright piano pushed aside converting the school auditorium to gym; the velvet curtain, bloodred muted with dust and decay of the unfrivolous war years, was about to part at the Rialto, my chums hunkering down with popcorn as the house lights dimmed . . . so, so it was then I cracked the cover of YOUNG HEROES FOR YOUNG AMERI- CANS, *knowing I should read about Clara Barton or Amelia Earhart, yet I was drawn to the baby face of a boy—Thomas Edison in cap, rumpled jacket with a white scarf like a drool bib, though in the murky photo he is sixteen years old. His bright black eyes engage with the camera.* YOUNG HEROES *confessed that of all American heroes he is the most unlikely, but instructed me to look about my living room at lamps, the radio and phonograph, to consider what fun I have at the movies, to recall the mimeographed tests (some fun) distributed at school and to be grateful for the gum tape and waxed paper which keep sandwiches fresh in my lunch box, for the alkaline battery which lights my way in the dark. Every day I have reason to thank this poor, ill-educated boy.*

Young Tom's gumption and grit were hardly a comfort on a dim winter day. The Saturday was lost as I turned on the lamp by my bed, the likes of which this tinkering genius could not imagine until he came upon the carbon filaments to set in his bulbs, which "burned with a bright, beautiful light that is a little globe of sunshine, a veritable Aladdin's lamp."—Dec. 21, 1879, The New York Herald. *The tedious chronicle skipped from one early Edisonian achievement to the next, for its trials and triumphs tell of the boy, not the man, therefore sparing its young readers Edison the cold potato, distant father and husband, the Wizard of Menlo Park playing his role of hayseed to perfection, the anti-Semite, the litigious sweatshop boss who co-opted the clever minds of his workers, the anti-intellectual. Disdaining scientific theory—Edison believed alternating current would kill us all—believed too much knowledge a hunk of baloney, though at least, at last, under pressure, he discredited the electric chair.*

YOUNG HEROES, *which brought each prelude to each heroic life to a neat dead end, quoted the great man, "Genius is ten percent inspiration, ninety percent perspiration." If it is Edison who said that and not Ben Franklin, but the writer of my uplifting Christmas book, uninterested in dismantling myths, presented only glib reflections upon the past age of whichever young hero, which now leads me to note that Franklin took out no patents, believing that scientific discovery was to be shared among gentlemen, while Edison took out 1,093 including the electric pen (unfortunately marketed at the same time as the first typewriter), the musical telephone, cement works and an electronic turntable on which to present displays of food, though he existed for years on a diet of apple pie and, when in ill health, on curdled milk from one particular cow in Parsippany, New Jersey.*

But the bio in YOUNG HEROES *ends with the most notable achievement of the man, the biographer being neither for nor against technology, just in dreary pursuit of his story, which is the same old story of adversity overcome, the early call to greatness. The dutiful yarn spins to the grand finale—Edison, accused of fraud, thousands assembling in disbelief to witness and wonder at his magic. It was New Year's Eve. The arrogance of the man saying, "Let there be light," but ah, when the lights went on! The admiring headline:* THE MOON GOES INTO MOURNING. *Saturday almost entirely wasted by the time I drop the book, kick it under the bed, where it will lie for many months with dust mice and forbidden soda bottles, and go downstairs in the empty house at early dusk, turn on the radio in the living room and listen to a story, a terrific last act of story quickly told by a man with a slippery smooth voice, a tale of Rhinemaidens and a dwarf and a hero, of a magic ring and potions, of a true wife and a false, of love that ends in suicide, love beyond the fiery grave of immolation. Better, infinitely better than young Tom burning the barn in some cockamamie experiment, being smacked* on the ear by his Dad, forever deaf but not as a doorpost; and when, after the grand summary of story, those Rhinemaidens sing, I listen, for it was really something.

Crouching, knees high, by the speaker so that when they come home, my brother full of team loss, my mother chirping with desperate cheer, they found me listening solemnly to the opera, shush them, shush and they dared not laugh for my eyes brimmed with tears as the true wife sings on and on, the one who was to die, my tears for the lonely, unproductive day, for my loathing of those girls who had moved ahead to groping flesh, to lying femme fatale kisses, my contempt somehow spilling over to that fat-jawed boy in the cap, Edison. I would not singe my pinkie on the gas stove for that young hero. The full glory of Brünhilde's flaming rock is best accomplished by theatrical lighting (smooth announcer explains in swooping glissando), what's more I would never have heard the Wagnerian dusk fade into the night without Young Tom's restless pursuit of daring devices, without old Edison's two thousand five hundred notebooks of ongoing notions, ideas, plots, plans for a comfortable material world, though I soon heard my brother harharring in the kitchen, forcing a crude guttural imitation of Heldentenor (a term I did not know). I turned off the lamp and the radio, the audience in New York still cheering, their applause drowning the plug for Texaco, to savor the hush, the dark . . . but the streetlight on the corner invaded the room and there was light just beyond in the hall and in the bright kitchen, where my mother was dishing out macaroni and cheese, my favorite, calling my name to come, come eat your supper, and still high as a silk kite on grand opera, I didn't mind them looking at me as if I was sick or plain nuts and sure, I'd have macaroni and cheese.

A second helping.

The following weeks in February I took my place by the radio on Saturday afternoon to prove a self-pitying point. They came home early and victorious during Carmen's last defiant aria—"At least," my father said, "it's not that Kraut." They came home late, grumbly, defeated in overtime as Mimi coughed her last sweet spu-

tum at the end of La Bohème. *And then there was a shift, like a heavy weather system moving in, a rise in barometric pressure having to do with a boy in a cap, his big brother's flight cap, a notorious bad boy with a Bogart lisp, having to do with his arrogant black eyes upon me and the flash of my response quick as Edison's Perforator, Tasimeter, Electromotograph or Quadraplex, for our messages received and sent were various, multiples. And I found that the matinees with those girls so recently reviled is what I yearned for, a projection of my lust seen exactly in dark mirrors, brooding shadows, the angled shots of moist lips and large chins, the tear's glistening descent. My heart leapt with the movie music underscoring doomed love and betrayal. Sharing my first cigarette with the surly bad boy in a bomber jacket was as far as passion took me: the scenes of noir classic played in the back booth of Spanner's Soda Fountain.* The Big Sleep, Blue Dahlia, The Killers—*these flicks were my stories in plain English. Veronica Lake, Jane Greer, Lana Turner—such wanton women my heroes, not the distant divas, multo agitato, or a boy wizard grown to the famous white-haired old man with the sound of his ratchety camera heard through the talking-picture device which failed in 1914, the actors' lips too slow or too fast, the plaintive words of a woman squealing from the mouth of a man.*

And there remains always the question. It is a polling of the heart—Who has failed, living or dead, at the larger emotions?

"WE MIGHT HAVE MET IN THE PARK"

When they first came to America, Sylvia Neisswonger and her mother lived in a room on the Upper West Side of Manhattan. Herr Neisswonger, a mathematician of some distinction, and his son were presumed dead. Even as Sylvie led her mother down into the servants' quarters of the villa in Innsbruck, through the tiled kitchen into the pantry where many gleaming pots and pans sat in order on their shelves along with the labeled canisters of sugar, flour, cocoa, rice and the little white beans that floated in the Italian soup her father loved, she knew those unimaginable deaths would soon come to pass.

Through this splendid pantry seldom visited, Frau Neiss-wonger was led by her child into the first light. Sylvie, carrying her small suitcase, knew the way through a break in the garden wall. Her mother, swaddled in grey fox, looked like a big stuffed toy, one of the expensive Steiff animals Sylvie had left in her nightmare room with her china dolls, all silent at their low table, about to sip tea from tiny Dresden cups. Toys she had outgrown, it's true, and she would not play with toys again until she played clumsily with the plastic G.I. Joes, the Barbies, Tiny Tears and Hula Hoops that entertained her stepchildren. Inge Neiss-wonger's route through Vienna to Paris to Dover was bold. Often, Sylvie thought it was the cut of the elegant fur coat, more than the expensive Austrian exit permit, more than her mother's perfect French or her charmingly accented English, which got them to London, where immigrants were not allowed to work, and there-fore across the Atlantic to the square room that looked at a tarred roof and wooden water tower on the Upper West Side of the over-whelming city. The city was New York. To the empty room—nothing but one bed, two cups, two plates and the fur coat. A communal telephone in the hall connected Inge to a distant von, a Habsburgian relative who installed her in the millinery depart-ment of Saks.

Inge's glamour was quick money in the bank. "Is it not per-fect?" settling a jaunty tam-o'-shanter on her crisp blond curls. At once the silly hat was Parisian, desirable. "It is the mode," the authoritative tilt of her smile as she displayed a stiff pillbox or snap-brim or snood—wartime headgear designed for these safe Ameri-can women. And when the saleswoman with the trace of Brit in her Austrian accent modeled a hat, her swift gesture with a feather or veil conveyed the assurance of her class and something that might be bought after all, a sexual presence. Home from work . . . what an idea, Inge Neisswonger home from work! Her husband never worked, had lectured when invited, when a particular abstract game pleased him. It was that sort of family—silver mines, copper mines in the limestone Alps. When it pleased him, the professor sat home with his equations. Home was the nineteenth-century villa, bourgeois ostentation in stucco. He had been a student at Göttingen with Oppenheimer and von Neumann, of course not of their cut, and, unlike the great bombardiers, decidedly unpolitical, unworldly. Inge married up, with pleasure. She was schooled to give pleasure and gave it at Saks, but was sour and silent at home, home being the single room where Sylvie watched her mother's transformation. Home from work, Inge's swollen feet soaking in epsom salts and warm water.

Sylvie prepared their meals in the kitchenette behind a brocade curtain, a touch of faded elegance that made the rickety chairs, the scarred table with dime-store vase and a castoff cathedral radio look shabbier. She was not allowed to play the radio while Inge lay with a damp washcloth on her head, but played it when she came home from school each day for the words, the English words she did not understand in the classroom, played it to possess those words, for the tutors who came to the villa were for her brother to learn more than the *Gymnasium* dished out of mathematics and Latin. The nuns gave Sylvia a bit of French and much decorum. At the public school in New York she wore the clothes packed in the little suitcase she had carried through the garden wall, dirndls and an embroidered Tyrolean jacket with silver buttons. Sylvie did not covet American skirts and sweaters, begged only for a phonograph. And bought one record.

How is the weather today? Is it cold? No, it is hot. Is it sunny? No, it is raining. Repeat. Cold? Hot?

How are you? Very well.

Repeat. You will please repeat. Very well. Good morning. Is it hot?

While Inge sold hats and discovered the émigré doctors, professors, artists, or they discovered Inge, her handsome head thrown back, abandoning herself to laughter though it was known she had sorrows, Sylvie observing the further work, her mother's further work with these men, Inge listening as she never had to the political arguments that finally invaded the villa, Inge forever distracted at the long dining table supported by carved angels. A delicate inlay of edelweiss and stunted alpine roses wound round their plates of soup, their white bread with sweet butter, while Inge toyed with her rings as her husband, the dreamer, said it would never come about in Catholic Austria.

February 12, 1938—*Hitler to the resistant chancellor of Austria at the Berghof: "Perhaps you will wake up to find us there—just like a spring storm."*

Inge directing the broad-backed girl from the Obersdorf, her thick braids pinned up to wait on table, to pass round the strudel, the *Schlag*, while the men talked, but in New York she argued in cheap smoky restaurants or studied under the fox fur coat far into the night, schooling herself on Buber, Schlegel, Nietzsche, Herzl, Freud, a quickie course for the next transformation while her daughter drilled herself in dreams: *Do you know this word? I do not know it. Do you know this man? I know him. He does not know me. Repeat.* Vergawa. *I do not know the word. It is cold.* Nutte. *I do not know that word, that filth.* The sallow daughter, her pinched frame seemed not to grow the curves of a woman. In New York at an émigré bistro, she might have been placed at the end of the table to set the mother's beauty off.

"Sylvie, that is the child?"

As though not seen with her schoolbooks, a sleepy, distrustful girl, listening to their useless talk, listening in wonder to Inge's fierce defense of aesthetic exile as the sole means of spiritual survival, her mother vamping Wilhelm Marks, the expressionist producer who was on his way to the West Coast to make lighthearted movies, first marrying, then transporting Inge. The glamorous mother moving on, going, gone—boarding her daughter out. A scrawny peripheral creature.

We might have met in the Park. The entrance at 86th Street?

Yes, that is where I walked into the Park to study. I sat on the bench by the drinking fountain. You see, I could not bear them, the Sisters Kapp. . . .

Sylvie, being kind to her old lover, suggests the might-have-been which for a split second erases the years, as though Cyril, a devout high school student at Loyola, might have saved her the humiliation of the family Kapp, Jewish refugees with three long-beaked, hirsute daughters who leafed through fashion magazines until the pages were ragged, as though they had fled to this country to learn depilatories and the uplift brassiere, to swoon over Franchot Tone and Paul Henreid at the Trans Lux. The worst of it was Saturday at sunset—the old people with candles, old Kapp with prayer shawl, the Three Furies squawking, curlers in their henna hair, white mustache bleach pasted above wide pink mouths, their broad beams and mighty breasts in soiled kimonos, jostling in the hall as they prepared for their dates, a changing cast of older men got from a pool of widowers and mamma's boys sent by the rabbi.

Sylvie as Cinderella in what was once the maid's room in this moldering middle-class haven from the free city of Danzig, and from Innsbruck, where the abstracted mathematician predicted that the malign painter of pretty landscapes, his unhinged screaming would never . . . , the dreamer's daughter cast as stepchild came out of her dark corner to watch grotesque preparations for marriage, the Kapp girls' polishing of toenails, sweetening of breath, oppressive gardenia scent applied to oily crevasses behind ears, in canyons of cleavage, as the jaunty wartime songs played on the bedroom radio. Hairpins, bracelets, stockings without runs were fought over in backstage hysteria before the grand entrance of each girdled, gloss-lipped sister into the mud-brown living room where the man waited of a Sabbath eve in the un-Orthodox electric light, Jewish custom abandoned for the prospect of movies or even, God forbid, the *trayf* of a cafeteria, jitterbug, dance-hall booze.

The wan Catholic boarder watching with sharp eyes, trained to be passive, noncommittal, observing the Three Furies' efforts—

final hitch of a garter, brilliantine on an unruly curl, rouge where the natural flush . . . once rose to her mother's cheeks in the chocolate shop on Sankt Jakob Strasse, as well as more recently in the coffeehouses of Greenwich Village. The Kapp sisters might have been schooled by Inge in work, in the arduous maneuvers of woman's work. In L.A. Inge exuded an aura of health and well-being. Not only the suntan and the new brass glint to her hair, the daughter felt all of Inge Marks was now attractively hard as though dipped in gold, no competition for Garbo in the flesh, yet a centerpiece for the distinguished émigrés—Brecht, Wilder, Lang, Vicki Baum, Werfel. Inge managing their correspondence, revising scripts from German, from French with such intensity she might have been rival to the tense little daughter she had all but abandoned, the student of languages, for that is what Sylvie was up to, the possession of words, words that might pass her from one scene to another, one life to another, a matter of speaking your part, surviving a role, let's say of little princess of the Villa, of bookish Cinderella, of Shabbas Goy switching on the electric lights, turning raw into cooked on the gas stove for the old dears she loved at a distance, Mamma and Papa Kapp, who, suffering the afflictions of a foreign land, still lived by the Sabbath Laws, their silent backroom boarder dreaming fluently in many tongues the scene in which the Nazi guard entered her childhood room, dolls and animals sipping their cocoa or tea, fat pink roses on the wallpaper balancing blue birds on thornless stems, butterflies sailing free, this dream in French or Italian, in American English (never in her native tongue), never with the base German words whispered to the child's ear, words the little girl could not know, could never repeat, the soldier's huge beefy hand clamped over her mouth . . . dreaming in a babel of survival—*chemise, valligia, estupro, letto, bed*: bed, the little white bed, a confusion of words, the dream stopping short of the hard rod of the man pushed at the child's body and of the *serviette* of soft linen with which she wiped the man's spill mixed with the blood of her torn flesh. The dream stops wordless, untranslatable. She wakes, still wakes sixty-two years later with a muffled cry, fearing she will wake the house, whichever house—Villa, room on Columbus Avenue, the Kapps' back bedrooms weighted with the heavy breathing of those tremendous girls, or the tidy one-room in the anonymous high-rise, one of those ugly brick apartments thrown up in the first building boom after the war, the bed-sit where she lived, bachelor girl, simultaneous translator at the United Nations. Sylvia Neisswonger Waite, it is the work of her life to suppress the scream, in part woman's work as she understands it, not to repeat the humiliating words, never to tell the end of the story.

So that even now, lying in a cherry four-poster in Connecticut, in a handsome frame house built a hundred years before the pretentious Villa in Innsbruck, waking under an electric blanket next to her half-blind, brittle-boned lover with swollen feet, only a gurgling of terror rises in her throat, a sound inhuman, almost comic when Cyril hears it, like the whimper of a dreaming dog reliving the thrill of the chase.

Might have. We might have, not six weeks into the present and already the old man tinkers with the past, sweet revisions Sylvie will not allow, so the past is now with them daily in her corrections. "We might have met in church," he says, "with your mother, with Inge."

"No. She was on her feet all Saturday at Saks, then out late, discussing with her men. At the Kapps', yes, I got out early on Sunday not to hear the Three Furies rising, flopping to the toilet, not to hear gossip of their unfortunate men. When it was cold, as it is now, I sat through more than one Mass in more than one church, a pilgrimage from Blessed Sacrament to Holy Name to Gregory the Great."

"Then I might have seen you," Cyril tells her clear and loud. "Like one of the blond angels above the altar at St. Greg's."

Pretending she does not hear, for he would not have noticed a drab student in drab grey coat, hood pulled over her head like a mendicant. Sitting in the last varnished pew, she would not have been seen by the tall boy serving on the altar, not one chance in a thousand, not even in that world of probabilities his grandson lives by, an unreal world like that of Herr Professor von Neisswonger, who said (even as Cardinal Innitzer fell in line, rang the bells of St. Stephen's welcoming the first Nazi troops into Vienna) that once the rational strategy was chosen, the result of the game was certain, any surprise move by the squealer with the music-hall mustache could not approach Innsbruck in Catholic Austria. She might not have seen Cyril in his youth, for the immigrant girl would not look favorably upon any boy or man for years and the altar boy would not have caught her nodding off in church, kerchief on her head in the summer. She'd had her fill of hats with Inge—the bobbing feather, the smart bow, not adornments for the anemic student who lived with the Kapps those years, the three ballabustas actually marrying, moving out to the Island, to their expectations of competitive living-room suites, to babies and labor-saving devices and shvartzehs, leaving Sylvie in the maid's room with her grammars and dictionaries under the unflattering light of a student lamp.

I would not have spoken to a stranger.

You were never shy.

The big talk came later.

Later, when she finished Hunter, when she was at the U.N., when she prettied up for the parties, so many parties celebrating hope over history, the innocent sense of being on the spot as history is being made, the privilege of being at those parties, one of the many girls out of good women's colleges hired as adjuncts, translators, though none as quick with a word as Sylvia Neisswonger restored to her heritage among the Austrian observers. At the parties she employed Inge's laughter and Inge's solemnity, attending to men, her mother's work, finding that she had after all inherited that womanly attribute—attention as a charm, seductive attention. Seeing herself as a clever survivor, blooming with words, not a stunner like the mother but with the mother's grace distilled to a wry acceptance of the game between men and women, a catering to the dignitaries at these receptions, though only the elderly diplomat from the Republic of Austria remembered the enchanting Inge and the vague theoretician . . . a lunch at the Villa, Frau von Neisswonger dispensing gold rimmed snifters of Benedictine before the gentlemen went off in leather breeches with their skis. This old man, with silky white hair and the exemplary posture of a palace guard at the Hofburg, recalled the loss of Inge's company as they drove off in the mayor's limousine to the best run on the Zweitausender, the lunch and the skiing a cover for his visit, which was purely political—a warning he delivered, what horrors might be perpetrated under the thin guise of Austrian cooperation, what dangers in outspoken resistance, and that Neisswonger might come to understand political realities rather than fiddling with the clamps on his skis. The mathematician, his host, fared no better than the polite son who had helped him with his gear as Madame Neisswonger waved them off, a diminutive girl at her side who was now this translator, this skittish bright Sylvie.

Sylvie, who had no use for the men who would have her, therein the great difference from her mother, who divorced Marks (his lighthearted movies betraying a bitter undertow didn't play well in this country, which prefers its dark dark and bloody), a great difference from Inge, who set her next cap for an oil impresario with a taste for the arts. Inge receiving nothing, really a pittance by way of reparation, was building an enlarged replica of the Villa in Houston and aging as successfully as a heroine in a best-selling romance in which love and money are interchangeable currency in the panoramic plot, while her daughter, still dreaming in tongues of beefy fingers clapped on her mouth, sour breath at her ear, stink of hairy parts strong as the bison cage at the Alpenzoo . . . could tolerate only casual sex after one or another reception with one or another member of a European delegation. Fluent, there was a clarity in these encounters which admitted no shaded meaning, no future tense, though inevitably she fell for a like-minded Italian, knowing she was one of his adventures, the hard core of her linguistic precision blurring for a few weeks into reckless romantic talk, a devastating man with a name she no longer remembered as she lay next to her only love, Cyril O'Connor. Inge of the Art Collection, of the mock-Austrian-baroque mansion in River Oaks, Houston's extravagant shelter from real life, Inge Boots of an international horsy, doggy set who sloughed off husbands, daughter, the chronicle of her flirtations in the cafés and chocolate shops of Innsbruck, London, New York, L.A., who dropped her earnest émigré studies as though she had excused herself from the philosophical dilemmas proposed after dinner by the wool-gathering mathematician, who deleted her historic flight through the gap in the garden wall, wrapped in grey fur, following the sensible footsteps of a child, scrap of a girl who never told that she had been torn, soiled, her blood left behind on a *toalla, asciugamano,* on the fresh linen towel which hung always by her washstand embroidered with a cross strangled in the elaborate *von N.*

And Sylvie, viewing her own history so far, that is as far as those hopeful days at the U.N., saw that Inge Boots—ridiculous names, Inge and Billy Ray Boots, wintering in Cap d'Antibes—that her mother's gift of tongues was to slip from language to language without memory of meaning—children, kitchen, church containing nothing of *Kinder, Küche, Kirche.* It was Inge herself that was translated. While her daughter was perfectly suited to her profession of simultaneous translator, words spilling from her mouth as they were heard. In whatever learned, possessed language, public words, which were her business, and private words—pain, lone, fear—fused with Sylvie's native Austrian tongue in an unnatural coexistence, in a double-speak running too fast. *Repeat. Please repeat.* Too fast for love or contemplation.

"No," she says to Cyril. "We would not have met in the Park."

When the airline executive, heroic pilot in the European Theater, appeared at one of the many receptions, the bristly bright woman attended to him in colloquial English, a man with small children and, sadly, a dead wife, she attended to his every word, trained as she was to listen, woman's work, and understood he spoke of measles and whooping cough, of his grinding half-aspirins with sugar and orange juice to quell a fever in the night.

"How old are the kids?"

Four and six, the ages of the children that were to be hers, the boy and girl of this decent man who should have been working the room, contracting for his commercial flights to land at the scruffy airports of whatever delegation, but there was a problem in these countries with untrained land crews, with safety regulations, the problem somehow skidding to the safety of his children while he was away from home.

"They're in danger?"

She had not considered steep stairs, hot stove, lethal household powders, the many domestic dangers, and thought how odd this American hero who had bombed the late enemy, actually escorted his squadron to the fire bombing of Dresden, how odd Colonel Waite's proposals for a safe world: a chair must be placed by the side of a sleeping child's bed, the fire screen set against the stray embers of a burning log. The hired woman had let a temperature rise to 104°. What extraordinary value he set on these lives, on their safety, such safety, and his care seemed an attractive proposal to Sylvia Neisswonger worn by years of survival. Soon after, it was a proposal and a fairy tale marriage, this of convenience, an accommodation learned at her mother's shapely knee.

"What beats all," Sylvie says to Cyril, "is that I ever ran into you. Forget the park bench, the church pew. There's your miracle, that I ever came into the city that lousy winter day. It was about to snow."

In their romantic present, the presumed millennium, snow mounts in Westerly drifts as it always has on the Waites' land in Connecticut, at least since some undated continental shift, or the subsiding of tides poked Painter Hill up from the grasslands that run into Long Island Sound. Winter is always a touch operatic on what is now Sylvie's hill, sleet and snow making a great fuss, wind swooping up from the mild shore. She leads Cyril out to the Jeep. The thick lenses of his glasses fog up in the cold. They are going to fetch Artie Freeman off the train, that bewildered young man who comes to them with a pack of mail, a humble courier in the days of his beloved electronic devices. He carries a canvas bag with an accumulation of third-class notices, quarterly reports and bills. The Pony Express, she calls him, no longer mailing the mail he comes to be fed, to be cared for. They simulate family, what family has come to after all her safe years in the Waite house, two old people living in sin and an orphan, an unlucky, lovelorn boy.

Miracle . . . meeting in that storm.

Shifting to second, she does not hear Cyril's words above the rumble of the Jeep. *That* storm, the one they have made famous, was fifty years ago and no more than a flurry, a soft powder silvering the Plaza of the U.N., silencing traffic on First Avenue. A gull called gently from the East River as she stood in the portico with her briefcase of documents to translate. She had come into the city from Connecticut, maintaining that degree of independence from family life. There was nothing urgent in the documents, which might have been sent to her, but it was a day in town, a day without the children who were not hers though she had taken to them, cared for them—expressions avoiding the word love.

The General Assembly was in recess, and for those first moments only the translator and a young American army officer looked at the city transformed. Then a cab drove up with African clerks in overly tailored French suits tucked to their bodies, no overcoats, so there was one cab for two people.

"Get in," the officer said, "I'll drop you." Though, in fact, he had no place particular to go. It was his last week in service. Before they were halfway to Grand Central, he told her that, declared it. She perched on the edge of the seat, very proper, the briefcase clasped to her chest with those documents—preliminary compromises of Anglo-Norwegian fisheries—soon to be lost in three official languages in the vast overflow of reports. He saw at once the determined set of her mouth, the prim thrust of her delicate chin above a fur collar that looked like a soft toy around her neck. It was fox, she said, wild fox.

"My mother had a coat of them. An entire coat. I only have this collar." Wondering why she said this to the Captain, young to wear the double bars. "Captain," she had said, "if you are not going . . ."

"Where you're going," he'd said, seeing the wedding ring under a tight kid glove. She was small as a girl, not a girl's face, no trace of innocence in this taut woman who guarded herself against him in the cab.

Sylvie looking younger to him now that she is old, at ease in her snow-white parka. The events that made her wary long settled into history, the generosity of years easing the injury that lay under the confident smile once turned on the young Captain. Still confident, she drives downhill through the second storm of the century, less surprising than the first with its legends of Biblical doom. They wait at the station in the steaming heat of the car. She does not hear the wipers beating furiously. "The train will be late," she says.

Fifty years ago, her train back to Connecticut was on time. She had simply missed it to have a drink with the Captain, to celebrate his return to civilian life, the peacetime world. He had thought to stay in, had been transferred to staff, United Nations Korean Reconstruction Agency, which sounded fine, as though we could put back what had been taken from those people. He was not sure what that meant but, while stuck in crosstown traffic, said that it was giving them a slice of American pie. The whole ball game was *status quo ante*. Did she get that?

"Back where we started," she said. "A loose translation."

"But where was that? Before Hector Ramirez died?"

"Ramirez?"

And Cyril not knowing why he was so ready to tell this woman of Ramirez clutching a Korean teapot, his fingers swollen with frostbite. If the boy had lived, he would have lived without hands. In any case, as of that day still a Captain, he had delivered his last report from Washington transcribed from the telecon. It was top secret. Could she keep a secret? It was about their use, the unreconstructed enemy's use of night soil in farming. Did she—?

"Human excrement. It's no secret, common practice in Germany. Beautiful cabbages and turnips. So—we're going to clean up their act?" She laughed, delighted with that phrase. "And you? You've had enough shit?"

When they ran from the cab into the Biltmore the snow had turned to a soft caressing rain, no wind whipped them through the revolving door into the smoky lounge, where they spoke to each other for an illicit hour. The speaking she would remember as well as blue eyes, large ears, his crop of thick hair growing toward nonregulation and the length of his legs shifting, until he leaned toward her eager for every word, the flow of her every perfect word spoken with faintest accent (she would never completely lose the the broad vowels, the glottal stop), speaking to this stranger from another war as though it was the most natural thing to tell of Inge's extravagant coat fashioned by a furrier in Vienna, her mother's initials sewn in the satin lining, where a secret pocket might hold a lady's handkerchief and gloves. The fox coat had been their only blanket the first Winter in New York, the feel still of that slippery pocket where Inge stashed their visas in case she must flee to yet another city, make herself known in yet another language. Speaking to the Captain, her story seemed light as an operetta, yet heady as her mother's perfume, which lingered on the grey fur. Her release of words to a stranger was time out from her life, in no way a translation. She would never see him again. "My mother speaks Texan. She is very rich now. She has married a fool." It occurred to Sylvia Waite, the wife of the hero in the war before the Captain's war, that she spoke without protection, for no gain. On the train to Connecticut, she was certain that there was nothing indiscreet in this encounter. The children would wait up for her return. She'd said that as they ran through the station to the platform, the Captain carrying her case with dull papers to be translated and routinely returned.

Same time? Same place?
I suppose.

Nothing really to lead him on in that answer. She would mail the documents back to Section 901A, North Atlantic Fisheries Commission. As the train pulled out, she waved to the tall American in uniform—heavy brow, sunken cheeks—funny, the big scoop of those ears. He had stooped to kiss her on the forehead, much as she kissed the children who were not hers. Bowing to kiss the little woman, he was Lincolnesque—that was in her mind because he spoke of reading history, the Civil War he would go back to, to studying that war, now that he had resigned his commission.

Leaning into the storm, Cyril walks toward the headlight of the train that will deliver his grandson, the Pony Express toting his current bundle of mostly useless papers. The old man in a formal black chesterfield with shabby velvet collar proving he is hardy, attempting to prove it against the odds, white hair and whiter skin insubstantial. Artie Freeman, hopping down from the commuter train, could be the handsome stranger who returned Sylvie's wave from the platform of Grand Central, who met her same time, same place half a century ago. Cyril and the boy hallooing at each other happily—look-alikes, dead ringers—a strange effect in the Winter daylight, the old man, a translucent negative of his grandson, reaching for the canvas bag full of his unending obligations. She thought of the packets of words, numbers, graphs, tables, leaflets, documents carted about by the three of them which told nothing of their story, communications of no import masking the desire to be loved, or to be free to perform that simple duty.

February 14—

In dead of Winter roses arrive at the loft. Louise does not find a card in the box which enfolds them. They are the deep red, long-stemmed roses of convention, the odorless hothouse variety signifying love. What sort of love is so uninspired? Nevertheless,

Louise plops the roses in a bucket beside the Jacuzzi, steams herself in Cornsilk Dew. Massaging her thighs with grapefruit toner: *Artie? Artie, dear, is that you?* She is rosy, softened for pleasure, for the lover who does not appear.

She will beg his forgiveness.

No way. Stock lines in her head: *How dare you? How dare you, Freeman?*

Words as formulaic as the roses which begin to open in the heat of the loft, fleshy red petals, their color bred for pasteboard candy boxes and greeting cards of this day.

She pulls the diamond ring from her finger, arranges it on a white plate next to a rose, sets a knife and fork, fans a white napkin. . . . The picture will be called *Natura Morta: Eat Me.* The first time in weeks suited up for work, one of Artie's old shirts and paint-stained overalls, she wheels a trolley of brushes and rags, turp, oils, acrylics into the proper light, rigs a stepladder up as an easel on which a small canvasboard . . . But suppose, suppose it was not Artie who sent red roses, suppose they are a calculated investment from Dealer. Suppose they are funereal, the cruel comfort of Bud Boyce or a fellow artist marking the end of her affair with Freeman, for she has neglected all her friends, imprisoned herself with the legend of her sorrow, her abandonment . . . and shame, for shame her descent into a lust for safety, the M word. Conflicting emotions given equal time as she runs to the trash can in the hall. The long white box from the florist is gone. In the basement she discovers ONLY ROSES, the box thrown with items beyond rescue — flabby sneakers, an expired houseplant, three-legged chair.

Louise returns to the loft triumphant. He loves me, loves me not. The florist is testy, out of red roses, offers blush-pink, fifty dollars a dozen. She *has* roses. Who sent her these roses? Louise put on hold. Frank Sinatra sings, *I'll be seeing you in all the old familiar places.* . . . Six weeks into the year 2000, Lou cries, for her heart is age-old broken by the shopworn tune . . . *in that small café, the park across the way* . . . cries for herself caught in this hackneyed love story, withering in an overheated loft. On hold, she imagines the order for dozens of blush-pink second-choice roses and hangs up on Old Blue Eyes as he slips into *New York, New York. Helluva town.* The gangly goof who sent the roses, was he loose-jointed, six three, four? Head in the stratosphere, thicket of black hair grows to a vee on his forehead, as satyrs are depicted? Talk about blue eyes—nerdy Caucasian, wrists dangling from short sleeves, mismatched socks, multiple soup stains, spottily shaven? Goes by the name of Fuck-up, Flub-out, IQ 160 over 90. Identify the bastard, for I am sick of love.

Heavy snowflakes slurp down the windows of the loft. Early dark. Natural light is beside the point of Louise Moffett's work. The rose on the plate is wizened, hard. Louise clips an interchangeable red rose. She lights her subject as though she is to photograph not paint the still life, perhaps a slick advertisement to be beamed out by Skylark, bounced off the moon to outposts in desert camps, to muddy mountain villages, a promo for romantic love as it is still practiced in the dying city of refrigerated flowers. The track light casts depthless artificial shadows. Louise flexes a brush, blackens her vermillion, thinking super real, hard-edged, but the rose, the red rose has opened. The petals curl back swollen with transient life. At its center the golden ring of seed is bright as any fresh garden rose.

CONVERSIONS

Cyril has not held to his journal. After the first flourish, he records only facts, the weather, for instance—rain, cold, sun as he sees it. He cannot distinguish his breath on the windowpane from delicate crystals of rime. When he remembers the journal at all, he lists his pleasures and pain, the list spilling off the blank page.

Tues.   Muffins. Light rain. To mall.
Thurs.   Left foot. Swelling severe. Bubonic Plague in Bronx.
         [Sylvie reads him the *Times*.]
Sat.   Neighbor woman cleans. Right foot swollen, less severe.

And so forth. A brisk walk up Painter Hill recorded with rise in the interest rate, Peruvian famine and his blurred vision of Sylvie throwing crumbs for the birds. *Princess buried—England. Riots squelched—New York.* Prostate, that troublesome little nut, a dribbling in the night. Muffins in the A.M. To doctors—old news, nothing he did not know about his eyes, macular degeneration, irreversible; new news, something he has only guessed from swollen extremities—his heart weak, overstrained. Warm, unseasonable day. After the unrecorded years, Cyril finds his journal a chore. Who will read into his rheumy cough the first symptoms of his decline or a touch of guilt in discovering lamb shank simmered with wine and garlic far superior to his mother's gristle in white sauce, to Mae's shriveling of costly roasts? Sylvie perhaps, who might detect a forced thought in his jottings—*That were it not,* he writes, *for my failing sight I would choose to march with poor tenants who have marched once again on City Hall demanding heat and water in the tenements of the divided city.* Seeing himself as the offspring of stage Irish, washer woman and tipsy cop, a boy from a West Side walk-up, forgetting for the sake of a few elevated sentences the man who moved to the right side of the Park, the stockbroker given to his own prosperity who engaged in no civic duty. The listing of his days would reveal nothing to his grandson of Cyril's remorse, or of this Winter romance in Connecticut making up for lost time as though instructing Freeman that he had faltered at the starting line. *Non cacoethes scribendi,* he writes on the rare morning when Sylvie rises before him and he smells her apple muffins, knowing that Artie will never get that one, a phrase resurrected from Latin IV, *I do not have the itch to write.* And then scribbles off the page *Dea ex,* the *machina* sopped into Sylvie's blotter, she, the goddess of fortunate intervention who arrived at his door—*flesh and blood,* he notes back on the page but gives his journal up for the day. Noting each happy day, accounting no event remarkable.

Until the 14th of February, when Cyril writes:

If I had a religious holiday when I was a kid it was the 12th of February, a day worthy of observation until they bollixed the calendar with Presidents' Day. I have let it pass by, the day on which Abraham Lincoln was born in that log cabin with one window, one door. As a boy I was drawn to the stories of his poverty and perseverance. As a man I was in the midst of reading Lincoln's letters when I gave over my life, did not persevere. I recall as bitter the winter when I was sent back from Korea, the snows deep and lasting. I wandered the city in a turbulence of my own which I carried with me into the cafeterias I haunted by day, into the coffee shops I frequented at night.

I had not been mustered out and wore my officer's overcoat as I went about the city. I carried with me *The Selected Letters of Abraham Lincoln,* for I could not read at home. My mother had died while I was at war, a saint, a selfless woman who served me and my boisterous father, who with her gentle prodding wanted to spirit me out of the tenement, out of the parish. She bought me Carl Sandburg's *Abraham Lincoln, The Prairie Years* long before I was able to read. My father drank his paycheck. Wherever did she get the money for that book? For the cheap jackets and flannel pants required at Catholic school? Washing, ironing, sewing for the women who lived on Central Park, mending their children's castoff clothes for her son. Freeman lives in one of the buildings where my mother served in this way. Shall I count that a story of success when neither I, nor my grandson have half the guts of Bridget O'Connor?

I am her spoiled boy. How self-pitying to come home with no victory in Korea, to climb the sagging stairs pulled atilt from the dry plaster walls, sling down my duffle and cry for myself when I found that she was dead. My father had not sent word, fearing that, "with the skirmish of the battlefield and what with riding out in the lorries at night. . . ." He had been at the drink, of course, and spoke of the war he had fled in 1916, a British bullet in his thigh earning him an appointment to the police force in New York. Keystone Kop of the silents, the comic list to his walk disappeared with a few shots of the Irish dealt to him on his beat. How often I wished myself a foundling, a babe abandoned in a tenement doorway or discovered by Bridget Malone in the bulrushes of Central Park, knowing full well that Matt O'Connor was surely my father. As though the uniform would make me other than his son, I wore it each day and came home later each night with the caffeine jitters.

"Pay for your whiskey, lad, 'tis the mark of a man." His crippled code of honor had never taken notice of her swollen knees, housemaid's knees, as she hobbled to fetch his supper, dry on the back of the stove by the time he rolled in. I imagine her puffed red fingers wound round a rosary, the permanent scald of those hands, but the picture he showed me was roses, funereal roses by the side of the coffin with the legend in gold foil—Husband. He had taken a snapshot of his floral attention. I stood by my duffle, which I never unpacked in his house. It contained at its very center an ancient green pot taken from a house in the battered frozen town of Hyesanjin, a house with the *Reader's Digest* in Korean, a few schoolbooks in English. The soldier who stole the teapot dead, the family who owned it dead, Bridget O'Connor dead. I was home, home from the army, and thought, listening to his maudlin story of her demise, his story, was it not his story, pacing the kitchen with his game leg, unable to brew himself a decent cup of tea, for she had brought water just to the boil, warmed the pot. Hippety-hop until the bars were open to welcome the retired cop and his cronies and I thought that I would not survive in these stifling small rooms that contained the overwhelming disaffection of their marriage—her selfless labor, his theatrical despair—and thought those first days home, home from my war, that I best stay a captain, for I was no one in the narrow boy's room with the old college texts set beside *The Prairie Years.*

I was a man of no rank and understood that every thump of her iron on the rich man's sheets, every adjustment of the hand-me-down jackets had been suffered to send me out into the world. She believed the world would make much of her boy. My old man nimble with whiskey, hobbling the parlor (dusty without her), and I could not follow Lincoln's exasperated letters—Executive Mansion to Major-General McClellan, October 1862—for the thoughts of myself on the ingenious swamp buggy pulling into the muddy bay at Inchon. A raw lieutenant with the ROTC commission, my men might have been toy soldiers putt-putting down the Potomac to a college game. But as the preventive war went on and on, I saw dead men hauled off like fish in nets, their bodies squirming in the air as though still alive ascending to a chopper, their salvation, for the ground was strewn with bodies frozen stiff.

The stolen teapot was clutched unbroken to the breast of a man disemboweled. Safe, his prize of war was safe. His guts lay rigid in the snow, neat as innards in a freezer. That boy had not known cold for he was Puerto Rican, one of my men who did not understand, literally could not understand my words, my orders to press on, to blow up the bridge on the Yalu River we never reached. He never reached with the teapot I wrenched from his hands, bending each frozen finger back until it looked as though the soldier offered it to me. He lay in the courtyard, what I presume was their garden, the family that fled, and I went into the ravished home to return the pot, but did not. His trophy, my trophy was the softest green stoneware incised with small white flowers. I thought my mother would value its delicate spout and lid, though never use it, not for her black tea brewed in a Woolworth pot. Now it lay in the folds of my dirty laundry and I could not read Lincoln's question, was it not a command to General McClellan—*If you desired, could you remove the army safely? It would be a delicate and very difficult matter*—without seeing the hands of Private Ramirez, Hector Ramirez, who could not read the pamphlet passed out to the troops, *Cold Facts for Keeping Warm*, his fat frozen fingers held out to me in supplication while my old man pranced, his instructions in courage oddly insistent: "Do not desert your men," he said, " 'tis a therrible croime." The brogue blooming with the drink. "To leave them in the dahrk of noight by the Asiatic river." Preaching to me so that I would stay in the service, for I still reported to my superiors who, noting my fatigue, released me to the comforts of home, later set me to running their errands. Top secrets or trivial papers delivered, I sat long in public places, nursing tepid coffee or an occasional beer, stuck in the same year of Lincoln's letters.

"A therrible business it is, leaving the lads in the noight." As though I partook of his war, his prattle of the Rising, a stirring drama of rain-drenched alleys, dark Dublin streets, of suspected betrayal and mourning women in black shawls. His war was not my war, the one I never chose to fight, stupid in its details. With the temperature -20°, we were sent in hot pursuit, a phrase in the official dispatch which urged us on to be defeated by the Chinese token troops, 400,000 as it turned out, official information differing from—

I should be writing of love. It is the 14th of February, very cold on Sylvie's hill in Connecticut, though well above zero. I can see the red dip of the giant thermometer, her present to me, but cannot see the degree of cold any more than I can read these words. As I could not read those letters of Lincoln with my father's inebriate voice in my ears. My war was not his war of the Volunteers, their leader in slouch hat and mackintosh, deputies convening in the black of night. "Who would not run from the hell of it— O'Connell Street in flames. 'Tis a therrible thing to settle your backside safely." Exhorting me to stay on at my post, and looking at the ruin of my father I understood that he had deserted his men. I had been promoted in the field for watching my men be slung in a net. Holding a celadon teapot, fragile as an ancient skull, I had been cited for bravery for taking a Commie's shot in the ass and leading what remained of my men back over denuded hills of frozen mud, no place to hide, back toward safety, toward the Demilitarized Zone, the narrow waist that divides that unfortunate country.

In the saloons of Hell's Kitchen, my old dad upgraded me to major. And when I resigned my commission, "A bither reproach, that you'll leave your men to Tommies in the Strand." His war, not my war. The shudder of his thick decaying body, "Would a fella run off with passage in his pocket?" That is how I knew my father was a coward, a deserter who had escaped his ragtag war to put on the uni-

form of New York's finest, dodging the British baton to wield a
billy club on a few blocks of the West Side, cuffing bums and small-
time punks—Hispanic and Italian. Pity the man, though when my
test came, I was no better.

I set this down on a day of hearts and flowers. If ever she reads
this scrawl, Sylvie may translate my evasive line from war to love,
shall I call it love affair, to the unsatisfying heroics of my with-
drawal. The teapot was given to Mae, who placed it in a cabinet with
the least appealing of her wedding presents—a brass trivet, a caddie
of silver plate in which to present bottles of ketchup and Worcester-
shire Sauce. And I gave up history for the market, for the news of
conflicts, skirmishes, incursions, invasions running on the old
ticker tape with General Motors, DuPont, Consolidated Edison,
IBM, until the reading of history was well-nigh impossible, my love,
as is the writing at this date.

February 16—Henry Adams born at Boston, 1838.

The secret of education still hid itself somewhere behind ignorance, and one fumbled over it as feebly as ever.
In such labyrinths, the staff is a force almost more necessary
than the legs; the pen becomes a sort of blind-man's dog, to
keep him from falling into the gutter. The pen works for itself, and acts like a hand, modeling the plastic material over
and over again to the form that suits it best.

— "The Dynamo and the Virgin"
in *The Education of Henry Adams*

February 22—The Conversion of St. Paul on the Road to Damascus.

Born Saul of Tarsus, ca. 3, martyred at Rome, ca. 66. Trained as a
tentmaker, Saul was a Jew, a Pharisee on his way to persecute the
Christians, when a great light appeared in the desert. God said,
quotably: "Saul, Saul, why doth thou persecute me?" The super-
natural light blinded Saul for three days (perhaps ophthalmia or

the aura that is said to precede an epileptic seizure), three days in which he could not see or eat, but then saw clearly, ate heartily. As a convert, Paul was holier than the Pope, who was Peter, and better than the Pope at spreading the word. They argued. Paul traveled and wrote instructive, rousing epistles in his own hand to Galatians, Corinthians, Romans but also spoke in tongues, a cult figure for a lunatic fringe. Only his conversion will concern us, the sudden flame in the sky transforming him from killer to preacher, that miraculous moment and the snakes that refused to bite him as well as other mysteries of his strenuous life, for we have been under the spell of St. Valentine's Day far too long. Even the stunning image of Henry Adams, the pen as our staff so that we will not slip as we immerse ourselves in the tepid waters of romance, cannot tear us from matters of the heart. We are obsessed with the love interest, with hearts inflamed as Dickens noted in "Valentine's Day at the Post Office," Her Majesty's daily mail in 1850 being augmented by 400,000 letters. A mad quest for love nicely toyed with in *Household Words*, which he published in part as an Almanac, poking fun, I fear, at our Franklin in his REMARKABLE PREDICTIONS, CHRONICLES OF PROGRESS, SERVICE-ABLE INFORMATION.

Love stalls us again. We would move on to conversion, to Paul's warnings against lust to the licentious in Corinth, were it not for the fact that Cyril and Sylvie have convincingly professed the loss of faith during their respective wars and that they lie with each other breast to breast, legs entwined, passion or semblance of, until they draw off like old marital familiars to the desire for a good night's sleep; that Louise who packed up, left home for her art, is faltering, uncertain in her mockery of rings and roses as she is of her body, which wastes away as though she will have done with it, buckling sack cloth of overalls on her bones for her sinful regression to copycat ordinary, to the need of astrological certainty that she will marry that guy.

Odd that only Artie Freeman, an improbable subject for

transcendence, once suffered a sea change when plying his trade in the middle kingdom of Skylark, Bertram Boyce still bucking for the Fortune Five Hundred. Alone with his machine, searching the glass screen one day, face to face with insensitive data, about to elicit a preferential option for Product to play in 7 million households—Artie quit the game. The greedy cursor beat faster than the human heart, a predatory gnat pecking away, but already he had anthropomorphized the blinking idol, given it life, access to a story it could not tell. Rising from the computer, he looked down at the Skylark carpet where B.B.'s initials were woven as the center of the galaxy, a corporate pattern repeated all the way down the hall to the executive suite, where he swept by the indignant secretary to Chairman Boyce who was in conference. He punched Bud, buddy blow to the shoulder, same as when they were kids: "It's not a belief system," Artie said, his boyish blue eyes joyful with the inner light of conversion. He looked a disheveled saint, quite understandable to the men in suits; impressive that Skylark had a zany hacker in raveled sweater and holey jeans, doing, perhaps, Big Science that would benefit them, though not within this fiscal year.

But then Artie Freeman had not known what to say . . . neuter computer? Hey, Big Guy, it's only an operational experience. What to say that did not sound either too rich and strange or insider info mouthed by the savvy clients. SO—*it's only a franchise, a piece of the action*. Then, by the grace of God or Boyce, the conference broke for lunch.

"There had been," Artie said to no one in particular, "always a hope. At the terminal, one saw an anticipation."

And that loss of faith, his conversion, came about on an ordinary day. He had not decrypted (easily, mathematically) secret tactics of the competitor's scheme, just manipulated the numbers to the client's advantage, erased lives, buried the bodies *in silico* on that extraordinary day, a time noted to be soon after Louise Moffett's twirling temporarily at the front desk of Skylark, when

Artie was first moved by the miracle of her freshness to entertain interactive though nonsequential thoughts of his body and hers. Thoughts of love.

We see what gods we can through the human haze of love
    and fear.
And imagine what we know.

                            —Virgil, *The Eclogues*

AN ANATOMY LESSON

As you turn the page of the Almanac to see when the sun came up to fix you in the universal whirl, the old ticker pumps away, that sturdy organ, no more than a muscular bag churning its four fluid ounces of blood in each ventricle, less in each auricle. While it dawns on you that Mercury, the elusive planet, was visible only at dawn (February 11–18) and that you have flubbed it again, sleeping through best intentions to see, really see what the heck goes on up there this Winter season rather than wallow in sludgy waking dreams that inevitably involve some slight or triumph of the past, or succumb to damp semiorgasmic scenes, well, all that self-indulgent time your heart's been on duty, thumping away through the night while you were afloat in the murky pool of lust and fear.

Mercury's gone to an inferior conjunction. You are heartsick, not really but there is a sour chemical suffusion in the thorax, so you say "heartsick," your regret about Mercury pretty thin, comparable to losing your heart in fifth grade or a sin of omission, forgetting to watch the final PBS episode in which the crime is solved. You will catch that damn planet come June or September, whenever the Almanac (at this date still fresh and unruffled) says it will be in a favorable position for you to observe in this hemisphere, to catch its slow luminosity as it makes its plotted way through the sky. *O, save me from being blown forever outside the loop of time.* As the heart is the center of all feeling wherein you are proved cold, chicken, fainthearted and so forth, you swear you will not fail the celestial event again. Your lapse forgotten as the day wears on and you remember to feed the birds, to stoke the fire with the ecologically preferable pellets. You help a neighbor charge his battery and are deeply troubled by the television news—a massacre in former Kurdistan, the sexual exploits of yet another senator, a warmhearted liberal. You read heartbreaking stories of banished children mugging and pilfering in the city you have fled, the cold city where kids squat in abandoned apartments cleverly pirating water and electricity (our newest Prometheans) from the city system, but many literally out in the cold. Like so much shrinkwrapped meat . . . somewhat disheartening to think of children cuddling for warmth in plastic garbage bags. Here in the burbs, you need only keep track of a warm wind off the Sound which softens the ice to a gritty porous mat at the door, heart to you an anatomically incorrect trinket, symmetrical and famously scarlet.

Love pierced with a clean Cupid's arrow.

Love as in the lithograph which Mae O'Connor hung above the marriage bed, the bleeding heart of Christ stuck with a crown of thorns.

Love sewn onto the faded cloth of a lumpy cushion which Sylvie Waite's stepdaughter gave her nearly fifty years ago, a first awkward offering from a big-boned American child to the small foreign woman who could never take the place of her mother.

Or love rent asunder as Artie imagined it doodling on the screen, a rebus ⟶👁 am ♥s 4 U, which decorated the mawkish words of many begging letters to Lou now dumped in the mass grave of his deletions. As boy-Egyptologist he'd seen the heart pictured in tomb paintings. The heart plucked from a dead body was weighed against a feather, the good heart ethereal, light—as in *Blessed are the pure of heart.* The heavy wicked heart would not balance the feather, that soul denied the happy hereafter. Artie, sensing that his heart is adulterated, gives up on love, on Louise. Click AVOIDANCE DISORDER to find your way out, your way back to the old attraction, the mysteries of his mother's past—the sketchy and compelling past where he runs to, round that track, first on automatic, then in the breathless chase—one has an anticipation—until, in the uncharted night, he can almost see the copper glint of her hair as a cloud pulls away from the moon and they will be revealed, they, for there are two figures waiting, a man and a woman holding the white tape at the finish line, his own small heart beating out of his hollowed unmuscular chest. He is only a boy, maybe eight or ten, running for the prize with always the fierce stitch in his side, the cramps gripping his thighs, always the anticipation which is now an empty prospect in the grown man, yet invoked for: Click RE-ENACTMENT OF LOSS, which images love on the simu-scape, which tests pain beyond endurance. And once again as he approaches the mark they have gone, Fiona and Mr. Freeman, gone, not turned from him or run on ahead. They are gone.

> Where is the foundling's father hidden? Our souls are like those orphans whose unwedded mothers die in bearing them; the secret of their paternity lies in their grave, and we must there to learn it.
>
> —Melville, *Moby Dick*

Or loveless Louise Moffett, who lacquers a row of cookie-cutter hearts, tokens hard as tortoiseshell, with black vermillion the color of a dead red rose, elaborating on her loss, which is now twofold. Of Artie, yes, though a hard grain of ambition is growing its lustrous surface again, protection of a sort for the bleating valve, her injured heart. Twice injured, for in the *Times*, between news of kichi-nut pesto and the carcinogens in Red Zinger tea, there is her father pictured with a pregnant creature. Harold Moffett, global milkman, breeder of lactatious good will.

> Let the milker be mild as a moonbeam in the manner of milking, but if the work is performed with a hand as hard as a handsaw . . .
>
> —*Peter Parley's Almanac*, 1836

Dr. Moffett, biotechnocrat with soft hands and heart, is about to travel with Dossie, her offspring and her clones, to the ungrazable cliffs and waste deltas of the earth. Dossie's hooves have been designed in the manner of the Rocky Mountain goat. Her third stomach is now akin to that of the Arabian camel, a good milker. Engineered for the new century, grazing arid land, she will produce 20,000 pounds of Product within the year. *Bovidae moffetta*, Dossie, is docile, an easy homey creature much like the professor. (Here Louise chucks the *Times* away.) Too bad, for Dossie's maker professes he is pleased to be interviewed in "Living," not the "Science Times," a down home dairyman in barn boots and British tweeds with an enduring love of family and his herd. (Curiosity will have its way. Louise retrieves the page of Harold and his prodigy stained with high-gloss heart's blood.) In the casual "Living" layout, an inset: photo of Quartermaster Moffett in fatigues, yet always the dairyman, who supplied 50,000 tons of powdered milk to friendly villages in Vietnam. Well, news of the Quartermaster never reached the Moffett-come-lately back on the farm. Oh, enduring love of herd, recipient of grants galore, of patents on griffin, heffalump breeding . . . but what milk of kindness to villagers with no running water, crouched by stagnant pools, did young Harold ship abroad?

Louise reckoning that, if the journal of record is accurate, she was in the womb when her father posed beside the swollen belly of a supply plane in camouflaged jungle gear; though not reckoning the lunar Asian holiday, a period of peace not respected by the Vietcong that year. '68, the year of the Tet Offensive, of mounting U.S. casualties, and in February, when Shirley Moffett was certain she would bear a late child, the Tet Counteroffensive; the year in which the Beatles rescued Pepperland from the Blue Meanies, when the computer center at NYU was captured and held for ransom, the season in which Ralph Lauren launched his Polo brand counterfeiting Ivy League, the look of old money. Now, sayeth the "Living" section, Harold Moffett, courageous herdsman, is rich as well as honored. An architect is remodeling the original family barn. He will live in the barn with his family, family runs through the story sweet and thick as first cut manure. He is a sentimental man who has recently (St. Valentine's Day) sent roses to each of his beautiful girls, a softy this rearranger of inefficient genes, this New Age Noah who is about to board a corporate ark with his Barnumesque creature. Dossie has birthed this cowamel goatheifer, begot by icy altered sperm.

One Moffett girl, Louise, can no longer be counted beautiful. Her hair stands in brittle clumps about her ears, forms a lopsided crest from her stern brow to the bony nape of her neck—a molting bird, common tufted titmouse, her flesh nibbled away. Sure, by her lost love, Artie, but she's devoured by the re-enactment, the old need to stick it to Harold. And with new targets, his self-promoting roses, his cash cow. Feverishly modeling her hearts, she forgets to eat, to bathe. There are hundreds of glossy red tokens amassed in the loft. She has lost count. That is perhaps her point, to lose count—how many pennies in the jar, how many gum balls. How many grains of salt in the vale of tears. How few the pounds of her angry flesh to weigh against the girth of Dossie.

Cyril O'Connor has written but one entry of any substance in each month of this remarkable year, making of his failed life a story he cannot read. Though he still forms his letters as instructed at St. Gregory's in careful Palmer Method, his words trail off the margins, rear-end each other, slope down and up the page. In this record there is some little confession but, as he has noted, almost nothing of love. This recurrence, late love, is inexpressible, totally amazing, not to be demoted to an essay awarded a prize book or school ribbon for effort. The only effort is making love, the nursing of each erection, a guidance of trembling hands, frayed wires intercepting the passionate message, the old sexual message sent astray, though often enough . . . It is not in Cyril's vocabulary to go on with the joyous scene.

Nor is it natural to remark upon matters of the heart, the

organ which has atrophied these many years of his retirement—
not from his family duties, not from the lows and highs of the
market—from his chosen works and days. He had thought, in
actual retirement, to catch up, persevere through Franklin to
Adams, Jefferson, arrive at Lincoln, where he had left off many
years ago, left off in mid-letter: To Robert S. Chew War Department, Washington, April 6, 1861. *But if on your arrival at
Charleston, you shall ascertain that Fort Sumpter shall have been
already evacuated, or surrendered, by the United States force; or,
shall have been attacked by an opposing force, you will seek no
interview. . . .*

But the waste, the wasting away of mind, of heart allowed him
only the pastime of history, the thread lost in timeless hours of de-
ciphering. The words of great men too rich a diet. Short of breath
before he climbs the stairs at bedtime, he clamps his trembling
hand to the banister in this strange house. The pecking cough,
the queer arrhythmias of his bloated heart wake Cyril in the night.
A crazy click-clock of his pulse is unleashed when he touches her
taut body, reaches for Sylvie, to whom he does not confess these
failures of the heart. Symptoms, Cyril figures, of his awakening.
Even the sharp jab in his ribs is caused by this Winter feast of
love, too rich a diet.

She leads him into the early dusk before supper. They walk
up Sylvie's hill.

"Breathe deep," she yells through her deafness.

"I hear you, old girl," breathing through a tick of pain.

"Sirius, the Dog Star!" Sylvie is sky wise, instructed by the
pilot, the war hero—her husband, Bob Waite. "The Great Bear!"

Cyril swivels, searching the darkness. He does not have the
heart to remind her he cannot see even the brightest planet, only
a great haze in which she is radiant in her white parka with
shadowy crown of white hair. Tugging at her elbow, his evening
star . . . he is brought back to the smaller of two small bedrooms
in the tenement, the streetlight shining on the quilt just where he
raises a hillock with his busy toes. His mother walks softly to the

window, pulls the torn shade. Now it is dark, only a glow through the paper shade and a streak of light from the bathroom across the hall where sheets, towels, underwear of strangers soak in the tub. Cyril waits for her to come, wills her to come with a prayer that is not often answered, to come sit on the edge of his bed bringing with her smells of carbolic Octagon soap and Clorox, sweet as rosewater to the boy. It was not often she could spare the time to button the top button of his pajamas, run her rough hand down his cheek, less often when she began to sing their favorite tune passed down to her as a child, the theme song of Lilian Russell. Later, seeing pictures of buxom Diamond Lil, the music hall star, the vulgarity of her jewels, flash of her hats, heavy flesh of her bare arms, Cyril could never imagine that gaudy woman singing his mother's song. His hand on her apron string, holding her by him from verse to verse, prolonging the wavering sweetness—

> *When comes the day's last light,*
> *And my star fades from my sight,*
> *My love is unabated.*
> *My evening star, I wonder who you are*
> *Set up so high like a diamond in the sky.*
> *No matter what I do-oo,*
> *I can't come up to you-oo,*
> *So come down from there my evening star.*
> *Come down, come down from there my evening star.*

The hopelessly sentimental song of a century ago plays in Cyril's head as he fumbles in the cold night air for his love, seeing Sylvie as the immigrant girl, a merciful gauze drawn over the fine network of wrinkles scoring her face, over the pink scalp showing through her thin white hair.

"Venus," she cries at a speck lurking low in the atmosphere. Our nearest neighbor, the Great White One, Sukra, Hesperos, Ishtar and, yes, the Evening Star of Webber & Field's Music Hall and tenement fame. Venus is consumed by the dying sun.

SKY WATCH

I remember one morning when almost the whole project was out of doors staring at a bright object in the sky through glasses, binoculars and whatever else they could find; and nearby Kirtland field reported to us that they had no interceptors which had enabled them to come within range of the object. Our director of personnel was an astronomer and a man of some human wisdom; and he finally came to my office and asked whether we would stop trying to shoot down Venus.

—J. Robert Oppenheimer to Eleanor Roosevelt, 1950.

Shoot the Moon. A video game Artie played with Bud Boyce—beam off pulsars, implode planets. Smart punks in Times Square, strictly off limits. The whole thing had degenerated at the apartment, cozy baked spuds with his grandfather, Cyril's musings on the market, the news of the day on TV before settling into his dozemobile, ye olde bookerama. Fiona dead. Mae dead. Shoot the Moon. Bud and Artie, recognizable Dead Heads in the Scuzz Parlor, where the first virtual v-games were played for bucks, no inverted baseball cap or humongous untied Adidas removed the sweet stench of their private school. Bud in awe of poison packs, little capsules of expensive dope with clever names, and of the bad girl guides in crotch-cracking uniform. Artie played. Bud played. They shot the moon. And Boyce made money: Place your bets on two pink-ass cyberslummers, the preppie playoffs in Pissoir Palace. Authorities called Cyril at the office. The silence was painful in the apartment before Artie was shipped back to school in the authentic colonial town with authentic rich kids and terminals that arrived on the *Mayflower*. He never knew who the old man paid off—the cops or the robbers in Slime Square. The next holiday all was forgiven the dear boy and Freeman, as he was called at school, was subdued, a should-have-said-to-Cyril running in his head: Exactly, how you must have been with my mother, on mute remote, all is forgiven time and again. Fiona suffering Pop's indulgence. Dad with a poker up his ass, rather liking the sway of his baby girl. Didn't you admire the brazen bitch? Say it. And say I am her disappointment, your shame, say one sharp word, raise your hand to smite me—some Biblical word from the fucking dead language you speak.

But if Cyril, a master of benign evasion, spoke to his grandson of personal matters at all, it was with respect for the dead, Mae and Fiona sent ahead to a dull heaven of his gentle anecdotes. Shoot the moon, Cyril O'Connor paid the damages.

Artie Freeman idles in this time tunnel to the past, which inevitably leads to the search for Fiona and its corollary, the pursuit of his absent dad. Rising from his lethargy (he has sent his last message to Louise Moffett, cast sweet words into the void), he trips over the junk pile of electronic equipment to dash from room to room rifling Mae's linen closet and silver drawer, the narrow compartment hung with dust mops and brooms, running on automatic, as though some certainty of Doctor, Lawyer, Indian Chief will finally provide the answer to all his misfortune. *Wonderlust*'s sprawl of info is easier to search than this accumulation of middle-class detritus. When at last the clues are found, they are where no man in Mae's household would think to look, in a recipe file, tucked between her staples—poultry and pudding. Multiple clues: a rough metal cross, street jewelry that might be strung on a thong: a tiny vial of yellow liquid which Freeman takes to be a psychedelic dose, sees Fiona undulating in a light show to a primitive Moog synthesizer. And the photo, shoot the fucking galaxy, in which his mother stands between two men, a bearded dude in early black leather and a macrobiotic saint in saffron drag. On the back of the photo in Mae's careful script: "The man on the left is Freeman's father."

On the left as they face the camera? On the left from the photographer's point of view? Nothing tells Freeman if A or B deserted his mother, or whether his mother (hipsters, patent-leather boots, titty, braless) dumped both sinister A and blessed B. Fiona's fiery hair, caught by the wind, blots out one eye of the emaciated B, whose wan, wincing smile may link him to his son. Distracted A turns to someone off camera, his profile—solemn or sorrowful?— could be Artie's scowl now that he's stopped dead in his tracks, alone with the strange wonder that this alternate life was lived by his mother. So Fiona, betrayed or betraying, was not a whore. Unfair, was not a statistic in a sexual trend, a comfortable rebel in a theatrical revolution given its few pages in *Wonderlust* connecting drugs, rock 'n' roll, *2001: A Space Odyssey*, Monday Night Football, tonnage of bombs dropped in Vietnam, be-in, Doves, Hawks, microwave, heart transplant, ILLIAC—39 million computations a minute—history run off with a backup of the Carpenters' festival of song. A laundry list of data, soiled and sudsy with its promise of further access, reveals no more than the brick wall behind Fiona and her men. No disheveled Victorian porch of a commune, energetic pad of coercive freedom, just this blank wall without arch or fenestration. Wind blowing Fiona's hair might be the foul breath of a subway, the exhaust of a bus, though why set a noplace brick wall in the city? The bearded guy in the genteel S/M leather is alert, on the lookout. Artie succumbs to the dated drama: political protest, surveillance, pug-ugly J. Edgar Hoover updating files on A and on B, their seditious pamphlets, coded names.

His mother is trapped by the photographer. Her dutiful off-center grin in that Summer of Love recalls Artie's ricochet from her fleeting caress to the wry smile of their Connecticut confinement. Though always bold laughter at her men, not these men, and a soft inward look that sheltered her memories, perhaps of A or of B, the dreamy look that never let him in. Her grimace in this snapshot is no easier for her boy to solve than the golden liquid in the vial, oily and rancid, or the rough edges of a heavy metal cross.

Moment: an instant in time; time measured by movement as in the movement of the heavens, the pendulum's swing. Momentum in the balancing act of anger against expectation. The emblems of his momentous discovery are packed in with his grandfather's mail. Artie fingering the photo, constantly drawing it out of a spiffy Skylark envelope to regard his father—one of two men. On the train to Connecticut, it seems the only thing he has ever wanted to know, whether A or B, and why the dark secret, horror, the horror—bones rattling in the back closet. Unseasonably mild, a touch of Spring as he pays the cab (semblance of independence), walks up Sylvie's drive. The last quarter moon has taken its place in the afternoon sky. They answer the door together, twittering lovebirds, his grandfather blinking into the sun with milky old eyes; and moments before he displays his inconclusive proof, yearning for a Donnybrook (Cyril word), Artie's fury seeps away.

Cyril's coo of delight when handed the crumpled photo, "Ah, my bold girl." Artie sees that he cannot see, though the old guy stumbles through the Windsor chairs in Sylvie's dark dining room to the late Winter light at the window. "Beautiful, wasn't she?" He holds the photo out to the impartial judge, but Sylvie is out of range, slicing cake in her low beamed colonial kitchen. Cyril addresses a corner cupboard displaying porringers and tankards of the family Waite. "It never set well with Mae, that her daughter had many men."

"Old news," Freeman says.

"I have no other."

They settle to rich chocolate cake, shouting their praise to Sylvie. Fiona and her men safely back in Artie's pocket, safe from Sylvie's shrewd eyes. She will surely ask, "Who's Evel Knievel? Buddha Bangles?"

Her insistence, "And your woman friend? Where did you leave that?"

Artie shifts in the graceful spindles of his chair.

"The cowgirl?"

Had he really told her about the cows, the blue silos, the heartwood of Lou's apple tree in the heartland? "I have," he murmurs, "other interests."

"Other girls?" Cyril prying, the barefaced curiosity of this woman contagious.

"No other girls. A loose life is not inherited." Scolding through the stoppage of sweet stuff in his throat, producing the photo again as evidence, "Promiscuity a talent on my mother's side."

"Smug kid," Sylvie directs this to her lover, who cannot see her, now reading the words "To the left, etc. . . . ," written by Mae O'Connor, words which might make all the difference to the kid forever opening his wound, the child of a somewhat pretty girl flaunting her nubile body for the moment in time when it mattered. Sylvie takes the fork from Cyril's uncertain hand, feeds him a morsel, says to the kid, "He never knew."

"You've been over it, then?"

"We've been over a good deal."

Cyril rises. "If I had known . . ." The flesh he's put on in these weeks is slack, his chin razor-nicked. He searches the room for his grandson, the vagrant, the free-floating failure. "If I knew which man . . ."

"Yes?"

"I would long ago . . . ," floundering for a scrap of honor, ". . . would long ago."

Sylvie scuttling the photo down the table. "She knew." Freeman noting—why now, why such distraction—noting gloss of cherrywood, glint of silver on the Federal sideboard. His grandfather collapses into his cough and, nurse to a sick old man, Sylvie settles him down.

"My mother knew. I believe that."

"I believe Mae knew. We have been over it, as you said."

"We do talk," Sylvie says. "From the first day. Oh yah, *wir reden und reden*. How we do talk."

Artie does not remark upon the fifty-year break in the conversation, figuring he should weep for them and for Mae's unspoken years, for Fiona's silence carried to the grave. Such fissure and absence are pure catastrophe, and suddenly he wails for his botched messages to Lou, a yelp of grief, alarming the old folks—*there, there*—fearing he will never hear again the flat vowels of her farmspeak, nourishing to the city boy.

"We must talk," he whispers, *"go over it, Lou."*

As though Sylvie has heard, "Talk isn't cheap. I never got hold of that expression. It's expensive, *teuer*. It's dear."

He is overcome with need to say, to talk to Louise, dabs at his eyes but, schooled against tears by Cyril, finishes his slice of delicious cake watching the lovers speak their dumb show of nudges and nods, hearing persistent phlegm choked up with Cyril's cough, seeing her managerial pat-pats of comfort. Chasing the last crumb of Sacher torte, Artie can no longer put down this little woman, rouged and a wee bit flirtatious even as she tends to Cyril's ailments, to the predictable turn in their story, the end of their story. The photo, as well as the cross and the vial which he never displays, are props in a less pressing drama of bastards and fools, of messages intercepted, false pride—a worn comedy of errors.

Lou-Lou, Lou—the name beats a tattoo in his muddled head as he lays the fire, knotting newspaper with care, building a tepee of kindling. Sylvie's fireplace is deep and wide, copper pot hanging to the side on a ratchet, brass knob of the poker worn through to the iron shaft. He does not light the fire, for there will be the trip to the station before they resume, this oddly suited pair, their talk which comes easy. The hearthstone is an enormous slab of granite, cold to his knees as he sets the last log, cold as the stone before he struck the wooden match to set ablaze the fire in that lost house of his Camelot—Connecticut. Then his mother began her brave warble, singing off-key against the coming of the night, against her loneliness—he liked to think that—alone despite her men. Singing not to speak the secret to her son, though the red-gold hair was more brazen in firelight, not to say under which star he was begat, by which lover under the sign of the vial or the cross.

Through the early dusk, Artie directs his grandfather to the Jeep, buckles the old fellow in. His shopping, cooking, tending to Cyril are duties of the past, no role for him in Sylvie's house save that of prodigal, the needy child. He has been welcomed with chocolate cake and money. Yes, always that reckoning as he set

Cyril's checkbook before him, Sylvie guiding the palsied pen. And for good measure, Arthur Freeman's bonus, a healthy check which he pockets much like the allowance he was to deposit when he went back to school, more than enough for candy, movies or any emergency in a pampered life. Leaning into the front seat of the Jeep, he kisses Cyril's pale cheek, brushes his lips against a sprig of Sylvie's white hair.

"*Auf Wiedersehen,*" she murmurs, then, in her raucous compensating voice, "*Auf Wieder Hören!* I hear better on the phone."

That same night we find Artie ascending in the freight elevator, the large metal box which once hauled industrial sewing machines, cutting tables, bolts of cheap cotton and wool smelling of aniline dyes up to the sweatshop where now air-conditioning, Jacuzzi, intercom, satellite swooper, cordless kettle and teched-out phones proclaim it living quarters. The immigrant workgirls climbed the many flights of stairs for the ten-hour day of cutting and stitching. Artie rises effortlessly as the foreman did, the owner and the owner's sons, though these important men did not face a wall of burnished steel set with glass bricks or metal door with long hasps, Lou's reference to barn doors on milking parlors back in Wisconsin, back home. Workgirl and boss stepped directly into the factory, cold in this season, the girls' shawls and thin coats hung on pegs about where Artie Freeman stands, key in hand. The new lock, installed against him, has been jimmied out, leaving a jagged eyehole. He peers into speckled darkness.

Upon his return to the city, he's come directly to say: If that daffy old couple have talked since they first laid clear eyes on each other, if they shout over the gulf, the impediment of years . . . then we, we may speak, Louise. Say it, whatever we must, find the words. Note: I come with no device, no feeble wit on the intercom, hat, if I had one, in hand.

The door swings open of its own accord. Ambient city light falls through the high windows in dim hopscotch patches, a giant's game on the maple floor that still bears the quaint gouges where once the shop machines were bolted down. His hope, that she is asleep in her/their bed. Stealing across squares of light, Artie allows that hope as he trips through—clattering pebbles or shells?

The turning point in his fortune; their plain talk canceled. The bed is empty, cold. When he switches on the light—the familiar placement of slippery scatter rug and serious chair. Well, they will surely speak, each to each, when Lou returns. What's a lost hour, the chill of these past weeks to the abyss of fifty years? Lightheaded, yet sober, Artie turns and the hearts, the many hearts assault him. Hundreds, maybe thousands. The inquiring statistician in his soul has died. Inestimable, the glossy red hearts in piles like candy favors. The sheer numbers of these bright, slick . . . He touches one for the landslide. Where moments ago the lights dwarfed him, now he clatters among the litter of red hearts with the rubbery oversized feet of a clown.

Little hearts, big photos. No, the walls are hung with super-real paintings of rings and roses. Mae's diamond engagement ring blown up, untwinkling facets dead as chipped glass. Prongs clasp the stone, shown to be worthless—and lifeless as the perfect rose. Scattering hearts, Artie approaches the wall. In each identical painting, the rose and the ring sit on formal dinner plates displayed on a white tablecloth—linen with folds pressed in, accurate as a detail of bourgeois housekeeping in a Dutch still life. Each canvas bears the inscription *EAT ME,* calligraphy as anonymous as *Times* italic selected from a computer menu, the font of a wedding invitation with pretense to personal. So alike, he wanders from painting to painting so alike they mock the brush stroke, choice, indecision. *EAT ME,* Louise making her mark in good-girl girl penmanship . . . so like *The man on the left is Freeman's father.* No angry flourish to Mae's capitals, her obedient apostrophe. The rage of both women disguised by pretty script; he believes he was born to be the object of their fury, their pain.

Tacked to the wall, the clipping of Harold Moffett with his engineered cow. This filler item is overshadowed on the "Living" page by odd recipes and a precise drawing of an artichoke, that thistly herb with pinnately incised leaves, its heart nutritionally undervalued, and so we must reconsider this amusing vegetable while curious Dossie remains unproven, her ability to feed the undernourished masses, or to fly with her offspring in the temperature-controlled belly of a plane. Dr. Moffett and the artichoke are information to wrap the fish in, ephemera of last year's Almanac — the first pig's skin to be successfully sewn into a football; on cold Winter days a chickadee fluffs its nearly 2,000 feathers to catch warm air from its body temperature of 107°; the moon illusion. Why does the moon seem smaller when it is directly overhead?

When Louise returns, she finds the photo of Fiona O'Connor and her men. Freeman — she can't think his name without a catch in her throat, that happy he's been here, though he has torn the photo, tossed it deliberately atop her many little hearts. Easy to piece together, even Mae's message is clear, though Lou hasn't a notion who wrote it. Artie seldom spoke of the old man he cared for or of parents, dead and unknown, all dismissed as one simple misfortune, boxing his family into a compartment smaller than her picture postcards of the farm. Louise carefully reattaches the red head of the young woman with the crooked smile to her slim white body. A petulant, willful girl in love with one of these men? Loved desperately by the other? Already she is making up, though she knows the girl's name, Fiona, the girl who displays her nipples and navel, sucks her blanched belly in, her arms rigid, favoring neither the sweet nor the sour in her counterculture, neither the zoned-out Buddhist whipped by a strand of her hair nor the disdain of the rocker who wants out, out of this up-against-nowhere. He wants to leave this pretty cock teaser, braless in a tight T, stone-washed bell bottoms glued to her thighs. All of them so *on* with their rags.

Freeman, you doofus, you darling, tearing your mother to bits — Louise somewhat elated at the destruction of Fiona until turning the rheostat so that, in the harsh lights she paints under, she sees a note on the refrigerator and damns him. Artie has written borrowed words: *Talk is Dear, Dear.* He has come and gone leaving yet another game like the puzzles in his letters, the love letters read and reread, cherished, thrown away. Been and gone tonight, the one night she ventured forth at last to an opening, stood exposed in a gallery, the viewer on view. A one woman show.

Where on earth had she been?

"To Mars?" Dealer's limp joke, "Or the heartland?" She felt, in fact, that she had just arrived in bright red shoes, pinafore and pigtails, to face the trial in this ominous city, her jury the same tired crowd of artists and critics and freeloaders with plastic glasses of Chardonnay. A one person show, the person Felicia, the post-femme toughy desecrating documents. This time out she has clotted the decrees of Western history with glue. Papier-mâché mock-ups of terminal and keyboard, TV, phone, dresser, lamp, fridge, wastebasket are assembled in small rooms. You walk the rooms discovering the Emancipation Proclamation, Chinese Exclusion, Homestead, National Recovery, whatever Act in these funky-fun objects. A bankrupt or minor breakthrough? Lou, so long in the loft, can't track the buzz.

Boyce with the Mrs. (hefty Heather in uptown Chanel), Patron of the Arts. Bud, contemplating the Charter of the League of Nations as a microwave, possible Art for Over the Couch, "Freeman? Seen him around?"

Nothing, give nothing to Artie's false friend. "Absolutely!" What's more it's true. Lou sees Artie when she runs to Pearl Paint for supplies, imagines the distraught thatch of black hair descending to the Eighth Avenue Express. His flailing limbs duck around the nachos when the pyramid of salsa jars collapse in Foodtown, and Artie, his scrawny torso white as a scallop, replaces the major pecs of boy-beautiful in the porn-shop window.

Staring down Boyce, "Freeman," she began, then blubbered, right there in the fake kitchenette with the Volstead Act gummed up as refrigerator.

Bud sidestepping Heather, "Whoa! You doin' all right? Say, if ever . . ."

Lost in the crush, if ever he meant to complete his proposition. Another go in the limo? Temp at Skylark? Well, she was a miserable sight, Mae's engagement ring worn to face the world, wound with duct tape. Whatever hair shirt, thrown on for this attempt at re-entry, dangled off her bones. Louise had spoken her love's name on the one night she left the loft and he had come as though summoned. *Talk of the devil*, but gone, gone, a convergence of the damned planets or their ruling gods were against her. Louise turns off the light, sits in the dark not to look upon the hearts, roses and rings of her making, a bitter view as she now sees it, then slouches through moonlight past the screen to where the scatter rug is scattered. Who has been sitting in her chair, who sleeping in her bed? Still sleeps—Artie. The reversal of fortune fills her. Thank whatever gods or stars, he's home.

She lies beside him. "You bastard." No point in pursuing that line, not at this moment as she reaches for the shaggy nape of his neck. In his dream, he groans with pleasure to the popping of buttons, ripping of seams, tugging at any interference to their lying naked in each other's arms. Then the awakening, a sad discovery of coccyx, sternum, corrugated ribs, both of them wasted in these weeks they have wasted. Their kisses wild, then a slow exploration of devastated valleys, brambles of hair, a neglected landscape of desire to be cultivated in the seasons to come.

When next seen, they are gobbling the remains of Sylvie's chocolate cake she packed in Artie's mail bag. Released from their isles of desolation, how they do talk: Freeman of his latest shipwreck with the insoluble riddle—which joker is Dad; Lou of surviving the loss of him with the ingenuity of Crusoe, her attempt at reinvesting the cold ring, the dead rose. Midway through the reconciliation scene which follows sex in their era, Lou licks her fingers not to smudge patched-up Fiona and friends, the photo which Artie has fingered incessantly since he retrieved it from Mae's recipe file between fricassee and floating island. The anonymous brick building is scarred at its edges. Reassembled, the three young faces have prematurely aged.

"Your mother, not those guys . . ."

"Say it."

"It's Fiona you're after. Legitimacy is some kind of discredited plot. The claim to lineage meaningless in the meritocracy. One hair of the biker's beard, one toenail clipping of the Zen zombie will determine . . ."

"Say it."

"Whether Dads is the sinner or the saint. What the hell will it mean, the genetic correspondence?"

"So why should I care if the man I nail is brilliant or a bum or a brilliant bum? I mean really care when it was Fiona who raised me not to care, to make light, wander? I mean, from the cradle, an actual cradle rocked by the fireplace in Connecticut."

"Rock 'n' roll baby?"

"Never. Folksy lyrics. Sad—I couldn't know that in the cradle, but I woke to those wilted songs. As I grew up I heard the words trail off, the words slip, dissolve. Her voice trailed off. To some-place, someone."

As they talk Louise picks up her pad to draw, drawing through the night, illustrating their stories—dairy farm, rump steak and bone, Cyril fog-eyed, Mae prim. A comic strip of their common narrative in which a lusty Winter wind sweeps across Aunt Bea's fallow acres, a night shutter rattles spookily in Connecticut. Sylvie, of course, ferretlike Sylvie of the kind gesture, rich cake, blunt tongue, the sweet talk cut out of her talk by what trials they do not know.

"Her accent?"

"Of espionage, as in the movies."

"Children?"

"I guess. The rooms of childhood upstairs. The kids have disappeared."

"So have we all." Louise swiftly sketching the cute repoussé nose of a freckled Fiona, "They would be how old? Her children."

February 29—The year 2000 includes this day on which Ann Lee, founder of the celibate Shakers, was born.

Colorless city dawn. For an instant, when Lou turns off the lights, her bleeding world of hearts and flowers goes grey. She posts two of her night cartoons: one, the swollen professorial head and tweedy shoulders of Harold Moffett; the other, peevish, pretty Fiona O'Connor, hair brushed out of her eyes. She writes on the wall: WANTED FOR FRAUD, WILLFUL ENTRAPMENT . . .

"Dot the 'i' in willful."

"It's uppercase."

"To hell with them."

"If only—"

Lou turns to the calendar where she notches her days, sees that she must flip to the new month tomorrow. As of today the starred date of her show is unseen. Today is that odd day, extra day of reversed roles that sets the world right, and she laughs, snaring her lover in a gentle half-nelson. "Say it! Say it, pretty please."

Artie will not stoop to pretty please, but hums a high prolonged mmmmmmmm, supersonic wail of the M word; so, time dictating the plot, it is plighted at last in the outmoded tradition of leap year, yet a useful myth, vaguely heard of. And they go to bed in peace, sleep through the day, their extra day, entwined.

A queer month which adjusts the imprecise calendar, February, named after the Roman festival of expiation, added to the Romalian calendar along with January at the end of the year. There Feb. sat until 425 B.C., when it skipped over Jan. making Dec. the 12th month, Nov. the 11th and so forth. Such confusion. And the heavens did not cooperate: the solar year being 365 days, 5 hours, 48 minutes, 46 seconds mean solar time, while the lunar year is 354 days or 12 lunations.

In the course of a few lunar years, New Year's Day bops to the next month and the next. Given time, snow blankets the cornfield in August, in January lilacs blooms. We in the West choose the

Sun, which rises and sets—like clockwork, we say inaccurately—
the moon trailing behind 11¼ days each year. We in the West
rightly choose the Sun, our civil year imposed on the accommodating solar system, that we may conduct the business of life in
the West. That's where we're at, folks. The stock market in Tokyo
opens to our tune, our time.

The calendar we live by set in 1582 by Pope Gregory XIII,
whose mathematical reforms tidied the year, such a relief from his
religious wars and spendthrift ways which bankrupted the eternal
city. The Gregorian year is too long by a mere 26 seconds, the
length of a sneeze if you quickly wipe your nose, less time than it
takes to sit yourself down, turn on the machine, get to the blank
page. Who cares . . . since it would take approx. 1,661 years before you feel cheated by half a day, if by then you feel it at all, the
phantom hours you had not lived? Artie Freeman, that's who
cared, figuring he could kill time after his mother's death by cor-
recting the calendar in the manner of his Egyptians, who devised
a darn good year, but was denied access to their astronomical skill.
For his mother's sake he haunted the drafty Egyptian halls with
their promise of an energetic afterlife. Grown-ups suggested the
boring terrain of heaven, bumpy cumulus clouds peopled with
idling saints, as Fiona's final resting place. In defiance, he figured,
as Pharaoh's scribes figured in their Almanacs, that from the moment of her death the insertion of 31 days in the calendar over a
period of 128 years would leave in excess less than the hours of 1
day in 100,000 years. The boy thus rescuing the event of his
mother's death, setting it in the vastness of time.

Such hopeful calculations don't soothe the here and now
with Louise as he looks on her fragile remains. Their troubles, no
more than an extended lover's quarrel, have whittled her to bare
bone. Propped above her, Artie counts the first five silver hairs,
the flesh under her eyes the murky tint she might mix for a dead
leaf or the Winter rim round the Big Pond, a site he knows only
through her correction or distortion, for he has never laid eyes on
the farm in Wisconsin. The sorority girl who lurked, fresh and cu-

rious, under the slick New York hide is gone. Penance for his/their games, for his inattention, for the times he has played with the idea of Cyril's death, betting the old guy's grit against the odds. In the cold light of day he steals to the bathroom, where he sees the burnt out dear boy, Arthur Freeman, his mother's loony idea that her son was born free of the system, would wheel free of the dominant culture, which in an off moment trapped Fiona between two mild outlaws, A and B. He runs hot water into *their* big double tub—he felt free to say it—installed in the wake of success, Lou's first *Botanicals* and a bonus from Boyce—talk about systems—upon his having infected, child's play, the Competitor's Code with an incurable virus. Lou slips into the Jacuzzi beside him. They lie side by side, no fooling around. The water whirls, engulfs them in scalding purgation.

Friendly Reader,

You prefer another go at insatiable ecstasy, the passionate reunion, bodies inflamed, feverish after long separation, swift contraction of vulva, seeping fluids of desire, but these lovers proceed with solemnity, tidying their bed at dusk, like it says in the old song, turning night into day, sweeping the litter of hearts—such rubble, Lou says—into a corner. Perhaps, *Ingenious* Reader, you will settle for Artie's old fun and games, his irrepressible song (moderate rock tempo):

> *I love, I love, I love my Calendar Girl,*
> *March, gonna march YOU down the aisle,*
> *Yeah, yeah, my heart's in a whirl—*

singing through twelve verses of the year as they tidy, earnest housekeepers in the big white space they will make their home. When the red hearts form a mighty pyramid of trinkets, Louise cries, tears blurring the photo-realism of her paintings, her cruel rendering of the ring, wedding china and silver that she wanted all along. She will set a proper table, sing off-key to children, which seems to Louise a dangerous business, beholden to the life she walked out on. The trite red rose, gift of her father, the man she will never please, trembles at the edges. To hell with him.

Every leaf, tree, barn, field, cow she has painted addressed to the Mighty Milkman, purveyor of hard cheese to those about to die in that war he believed in.

"Fiona would shout obscenities at my father."

"Or the man on the left, *my* father, toss Harold a homemade bomb."

"For God's sake," she sniffles, "let's forget it."

GROW UP!

Tolerant Reader, I take the liberty of defending these aging children, an Orphan and an Artist, who believe themselves free of conventional family tales. They cling to each other on Broadway (snowing again), off to buy breakfast at nightfall. They will not make it out of the happenstance of birth, and are headed for yet another shopworn romance, for she has asked the man to marry her, a fellow with no prospects. And he has given his heart to a woman who has turned against her work, her ambition, swept it into the corner, turned against the glitz much as the swells in Depression comedies discovered the errors of their ways. Exiled from playland, they huddle against the storm. Who can fault them? Born into Generation $X^{1}/_{2}$ or Y, into the willed innocence at the end of a century, they have lived without a war to elicit allegiance or protest, without poverty to give them just cause, though they have seen prize photos of children with bloated bellies and twiggy limbs and looked on through the one-way glass at conflicts of amazing cruelty, the bad guys and the good guys switching roles, a resident chorus of victims. Is it fair to assume Artie has inherited Matt O'Connor's besotted wisdom concerning the bravery o' the IRA lads, or Cyril's disillusionment, freezing his dick off in the limited war, or the girlish hopes of Maesie Boyle, who could not imagine our first use of flamethrowers in Korea and posted by airmail to the Pacific bright news of her charity work? Why level the charge, malevolent unconcern, at Louise? The only uniform that thrilled was the all-star's clean Wisconsin jersey when he ran sure and swift onto Camp Randall field.

Then leave them, our lovers not quite grown, leave them the

dwindling hours on their island in Bohemia, not this bedrock island, a pastoral place all their own. Before they flip the rumpled
page of the calendar, let them tuck into a second toasty bagel,
granted this day of grace that smooths out time.

> If you dried apples,
> If potted the corn,
> If corned the beef,
> Now lie by the fire,
> Keep thy love warm.

THE ENDLESS PAGE

So, they mistake the open trenches of the city for the real thing,
killers and thieves in plain view, diseased and hungry placed out
of sight though now and then one slips through the barricades so
that Louise and Artie are disarmed, no more effective than the rest
of us. Once in a blue moon, a life touches on theirs—beggar or
loon. We may wipe the screen with the flick of an eye and the
street will be ours again with myriad shops under gay awnings
emerald and gold sheltering us from the vagaries of the sky, heat
and rain; scroll down—the electric lights shining even in daytime,
a waste of wattage, never in the neotechnic age which lingers on
in the atomic, Progress Our Most Important Product (read that
backwards), sunny atmospheric lights carrying us forth into the
market, the stalls with ripe fruit—not one pear or peach bruised;
or to the boutiques—scroll down—where every shimmering gar-
ment fits to perfection, where each household adornment is authentic in its antiquity or perfectly in fashion, what was once
called state-of-the-art. Thus the attractions of our city will never
diminish, for they are continuously satisfying, as though we have
dreamt them in one of our pleasurable dreams, and the vision,
perhaps richer in texture if we see for an instant the picturesque
urchin—Sissy settling on a stoop with her grungy gear. Sissy (minus Little Man and Tony), her wandering nights and days, endurance without calendar. She seeps through the cosmetic skin of

the city, enters the host body, the city which has been inaccurately diagnosed, patched, sent on its way whoring after commerce and culture, old strumpet displaying scars slickly healed, prosthetic womb, bottomless drawer of her sex. Scroll down—Sissy (with Little Man, Tony), illustrated vignettes in Victorian novels: Little Man in a tough's tattered coat, baggy pants, smudged nose, body abnormally small; Tony—scuzz, dimwit, large head, blank button eyes; while Sissy—the pathos of her scrappy ways, her expert pilfering of all necessities, a girl, not a boy, puny, undeveloped, with fancies we best not know, fancying that Little Man will hit on her unless . . . or if she goes back to her dad . . . but no longer fancies the soldier, that was cold shit, a mind game she played like this was another city and he would *see* her, Sissy, know her name, her name signifying she was chicken, scaredy-cat or in some document—scroll down—so named as a sister, sibling. Related, a relation? *In the evening we shall be examined on love.* So Sissy has this hat, barely remembers the time, so much is incidental, when she stooped to picked it from the mud. What's souvenir without memory and the name stamped inside grown so faint she cannot speak it, not even to herself waiting in the Park for the day to be over, the day to begin—twilight or dawn. Waiting which has no boundaries, no precinct, unlike hunger or cold. On a nostalgic stroll through the Park, pointing out sights of his boyhood to Louise, Artie Freeman will not spot her in the funny hat, feel a tweak of recognition. Sissy will not wait like a fan under the silver awning to see him come out on Fifth Avenue, watch the warm vapor puff from his mouth as he claps his floppy ears against the brutal cold in which she has lingered praying for eye contact, one lousy look. No Dickensian scene in which she is rescued. Or at least treated to lunch in some swell coffee shop on Madison Ave. by the soldier, mopey no more, with his girl. Sissy will not sell whatever Little Man peddles and be found, an unidentified runaway, dead in the Park in episode nine, a random victim offered up for the ratings, Little Man having moved on, back to Fort Tryon with Tony stealing cars for the chop shops in Jersey. Only this is known for sure: the emperor will not dress in rags and go among his people; the nut job in the toga, having miscalculated the apocryphal year, will figure our doom again and come up with our number; night falls in the city where her life touches down, would touch them if she, known as Sissy, were to be seen in a vintage overseas cap by Artie or Louise disarmed (what others suffer we behold), no more effective, yes, disarming unless, or if her life, that life touches. Scroll down.

Sylvie lies awake beside Cyril. Often she does not sleep the night through, and this night that sorry kid, Artie Freeman, haunts her. He had come with his big revelation, that his father had a face but no name. It was like an old tale for children, a story to scare them at first and in the end comfort, though in the time of reading to her stepchildren she saw that many tales were simply cruel. There was no last page of happy reunion, yet some more shocking discovery as when . . . as when that big kid, the image of Cyril, understood his grandfather was sick, perhaps dying. She has ushered Cyril to bed without pity, though she knows that the day will soon come when, despite doctors, her *Liebchen, komme liebchen* will ring with pure sorrow. He takes each day and night as a gift in this afterlife, not from God, nor was it chance that brought Sylvie to his doorstep. An angel of purpose, he calls her.

Kein Engel.

At best old woman of the hill spinning her tale of the future, how all will be well and in the Spring they will fly to Austria, show the blind man the river and mountains of her youth, drawing the present to the past. *Kein Engel,* sly as Inge Boots, clever as Inge Marks, she had known where to find him, that he was alone these many years, not waiting for the merry widow, now tattle of the town, scandal of the library where she gave her time, a gobbling Mother Goose, reading to village children.

Keeping their promise—was it not her promise?—Sylvie had counted the days while Cyril lost track even of the cherished memory—his meetings with the foreign girl, a season in which he was not quite himself, some other Cyril O'Connor moody and hesitant, romantic he supposed, but the incident gone until she appeared, particulars lost as the pretty faces of his wife and daughter were lost, the particulars—pale lashes, the kewpie bow of their mouths, shared dusting of freckles, so unlikely that they were similar. Freeman had come with that picture he could not see. Fiona with strangers, strangers to him, apparently not to Mae. So they had both had their secrets by the end of their marriage, which ended with his wife's death. Heartening to know of their mutual betrayal. He is not unhappy that she had it in her, poor Mae, to conceal Fiona's sin as she would have it, which allowed her to love the love child christened John-Francis, patron of illegitimate children. Mae had taken the baby, stolen him in a manner of speaking, from his cradle and rushed to one of her priests to have him splashed with water.

"Wonderful!" Fiona's hilarity. "Freeman's soul is saved." And called her boy Arthur after a pagan king. But the women did not live to see him lost, angry as he was today, flaunting their legacy of silence, the mess they made of the past—Fiona and Mae. Dear boy, he was that in the end, laying the fire as though a father had taught him.

Sylvie listens for the rasp of Cyril's breathing. She fancies that it is loud enough for her to hear, or a miracle if she believed in crutches and canes thrown aside at a shrine, the restoration of sight, fantastic adjustment in time of need. He has been troubled by news of the past, by the Pony Express, that big baby wanting to pop the lid on secrets. Well, they had spoken the truth. Cyril did not know the man on the left, Freeman's father. He had suspected any number of men, decent enough though in ruffian clothes. Sylvie loving the word, ruffians in Mae's parlor. Though it was seldom that Fiona brought her friends, seldom she came to that embarrassing apartment on Fifth Avenue where the floors might have been carpeted with filthy greenbacks, so Cyril said, and the walls papered with stock certificates—Dow Chemical, Nestlé, General Dynamics—works of the devil he traded. BUT THE DEVIL WAS NOT

THAT SIMPLE! he had shouted tonight after the kid left, only partly so Sylvie could hear.

She had wanted to say to that Artie, *ein verlorener Sohn*, that lost boy, who was the image of the war-weary Captain hustling her into the Biltmore, but a child with a child's cause, she had wanted to say to Arthur Freeman there is a fine art to forgetting and to getting on with it, the day. She had learned that from her mother the hard way, from the widow, Mrs. Billy Ray Boots, who went under when cheap Arabian oil flooded the market in the early Eighties, and ended up with one lapdog and sufficient American dollars in Puerto Vallarta happily winning at bridge in English and German and Spanish. She had wanted to make it easy for both Cyril and that poor boy, but had only come up with *vergesst, am besten vergessen*, which startled them, forget, please forget, somehow better in German . . . not as I forget being old if the keys to the Jeep are in my pocket, if it is Wednesday, was it Wednesday cook took me to the Alter Markt and let me eat pepper sausage? If the Madonna in Stadtpfarrkirche was by . . . but I have lost the name of the painter though I see the Virgin's flimsy veil, *Mariahilf* she was called, and the child looked like a little old man, her long fingers cupping the flesh of his spare behind, and Cyril, with a scar in his *glutinous maximus* remembering that small humiliation of the Korean War though not if he has taken the pills for his heart, doubles the dose.

The rattle of his catarrh has passed, and when she sees his breath come even, Sylvie steals out of bed to wander the house, her American house which belongs to the children of the family Waite. *Meine amerikanischen Kinder*, reversions to the language of her childhood constant now, the words that float through her head those learned in the nursery and garden and at the elaborate dinner table of the Villa, but this is her home, inherited from her husband. She will return it to his children having enjoyed the use of the hall, an expression she has never understood. She slips past the bedrooms of those children, those frightened little souls who hid in the cellar when Bob Waite brought her to his house as a bride. They were discovered in the abandoned coal bin, streaked with soot, cobwebs in their hair, her stepchildren—the dark boy, Gerald, Martha, the fair girl—sleepy and soiled, already costuming themselves as victims of her cruelty and neglect.

"She's small," Gerald said as though she was an unappealing toy meant for younger kids. They had grown too old through their mother's long illness and death, their mother a strapping athletic woman, her golf clubs and tennis rackets stashed in the garage for years.

"She's weird," Martha desolate, having ruined her party dress, crying in her father's arms, that good man attempting to do right by all three of them.

Sylvie padding downstairs in the white Winter moonlight which falls through the many small panes of mullioned windows, speckling the wide floorboards and overhead beams. Yes, she was small. The low colonial ceilings suited her better than the man she married, better than Cyril and his boy. *Grosse Kinder*, why she thinks of her stepchildren tonight. There had been a large child in the house again, never easy, for she was a childless woman who in some part of her body did not understand, could not make the tactile connection to Gerald, now a banker in Beijing, to Martha in La Jolla, who measures the plains, ridges, fissures in the sunless depths of the sea. She had tried to love Bob Waite's children, but all she could do was take care, chauffeur, join in their play and puzzles, help with the homework—take on the duties of an American Mom.

The fire still burns. Artie had laid big logs to see them through the night, not knowing that as they are old they are early to bed. Only recently has Sylvie roamed her house in darkness, touching the smooth turning of banister, the worn wood of tables and chairs. The house and its furnishings are pure, strict in an American way. She has never put her mark on this austere beauty, which she knows intimately in faint moonlight, every small table Cyril clatters into. She has wondered if she should not take him home to familiar surroundings, yet knows they will never part and cannot see herself in Mae's stiff pastel comfort, has no way to imagine the proper order of those rooms now cluttered with Freeman's jumble of discarded equipment and worldly goods, or the drawers and closets turned out—old linens, heating pads, salt dishes, patent medicines evaporated in their jars, slack pink underclothes, kid gloves, silk scarves for a mild urban Winter; or the scattered recipes for Mae's chicken pot pie and apple brown betty.

A brisk white snow is falling in Connecticut on Sylvie's hill, which is higher than the canyons formed by the dead factories in the city, colder than the loft on Broadway where fat wet flakes splat against high windows. Night in the empty room of his grandparents' overheated apartment: Artie had screwed open a casement one fine day, left it open, and now snow blows in from the Park on Cyril's chair, a thick icing on the leather and books, the books that have been pulled off the shelf, the books Artie attempted to read sitting in that chair. Franklin, Lincoln's letters, *The Prairie Years* are waterlogged, pages glued together. Left open on the windowsill, Jefferson's *Notes on Virginia* is sodden, the present state of manufacture, commerce, interior and exterior trade reduced to pulp.

Sylvia Waite pokes at the embers. The warmth of the hearthstone seeps through her slippers. She is fully awake and collapses on the couch—formal, Federal, unyielding—yet this is the seat where she read to those children who were not hers. The small weird woman with the accent they mocked. *Yah, setzt euch, mit mulk und kookies.* Still, having reached the safety of her husband's home, she did care for them.

"So—we read?" She settled the giant boy and girl beside her on this couch. It was a good time reading those stories of Hedge Hog and Three Bears, old beggar women and elves. Then they were content, the stepmother and the disrespectful children, for in those tales, once you were over the worst, it often worked out. But before the just and happy end, simple words were a comfort. When, at last, they came to Alice falling queerly down the rabbit hole, obeying gravity, betraying time, they begged for more, more adventure.

But that story was long and she'd flip to a poem . . . *"You are old," said the youth, "one would hardly suppose/That your eye was as steady as ever. . . ."*

But the sun was shining on the sea and *'twas brillig and the slithy toves* . . . That was great fun together—nonsense. And in those minutes they warmed to her, so she felt. Silly untranslatable words, free of Inge's glib determination and her own compromising survival, at the fireside the children leaning into her before the stalling arguments of bedtime. *Then fill up the glasses as quick as you can / And sprinkle the table with buttons and bran. / Put cats in the coffee and mice in the tea.* It was so hard to come by until this end with Cyril. It being love, she supposed, the easy flow of words, release from the Babel in which her mother raised her, that confusion of tongues Inge spoke to advantage. The comfort of nonsensical words with children in Connecticut, where she was happy enough and where she hears faintly the tall clock striking, a fine Philadelphia clock with inlay of native flowers that might be taken for alpine rose and pansy, for edelweiss, *bitte vergesst*, but she has not forgotten the long dining table in the Villa, does not take her own advice. Sylvie traces the pretty flowers with her finger as she had when a child listening to her father, certain that he described the whole world. The Waite house is cold as the clock chimes the quarter-hour, keeping its own time, for though she jogs the pendulum and pulls the weights, the moon above the face now rises and sets to the latitude of Dr. Franklin's adopted city two centuries ago. Bob Waite had known how to regulate the old escapement, to keep time in the present.

In her head Sylvie calculates the adjustment. In real time it is midnight as she mounts the Waite stairs, which are on loan. She lies beside Cyril, who sleeps dead to the world, blind to the snow falling in slow motion on her hill in Connecticut, where they live in a dome, a sealed toy of harmless Winter, their bubble of bliss ever thinning as it grows.

MARCH

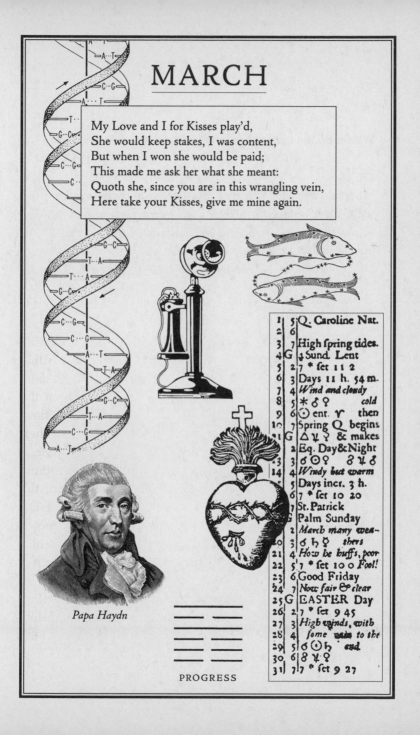

My Love and I for Kisses play'd,
She would keep stakes, I was content,
But when I won she would be paid;
This made me ask her what she meant:
Quoth she, since you are in this wrangling vein,
Here take your Kisses, give me mine again.

Papa Haydn

PROGRESS

1	5	Q. Caroline Nat.
2	6	
3	7	High spring tides.
4	G	4 Sund. Lent
5	2	☀ set 11 2
6	3	Days 11 h. 54 m.
7	4	*Wind and cloudy*
8	5	✶ ☌ ♀ cold
9	6	☉ ent. ♈ then
10	7	Spring Q begins
11	G	△ ♃ ☿ & makes
12	2	Eq. Day & Night
13	3	☌ ☉ ♀ ☗ ☼ ☌
14	4	*Windy but warm*
15	5	Days incr. 3 h.
16	6	☀ set 10 20
17	7	St. Patrick
18	G	Palm Sunday
19	2	*March many wea-*
20	3	☌ ♄ ☿ *thers*
21	4	*How he huffs, poor*
22	5	☀ set 10 0 *Fool!*
23	6	Good Friday
24	7	*Now fair & clear*
25	G	EASTER Day
26	2	☀ set 9 45
27	3	*High winds, with*
28	4	*some rain to the*
29	5	☌ ☉ ♄ *end*
30	6	☗ ♃ ♀
31	7	☀ set 9 27

We are all dying of miscellany.

— Emerson

. . . the sort of film I have always wanted to make and have never been able to, a mechanism not of facts but of moments that recount the hidden tensions of those facts, as blossoms reveal the tension of a tree.

— Antonioni, *That Bowling Alley on the Tiber*

Wind

Emily Dickinson's favorite month. She did not long for March to pass. Looking to the West from her bedroom window at the steeple of the Unitarian church, or East to the friendly undulations of the Pelham hills, she wrote five poems to the virtues of this month which we fail to see.

We like March.
His Shoes are Purple —
He is new and high —
Makes he Mud for Dog and Peddler,
Makes he Forests dry.
Knows the Adder Tongue his coming
And presents her Spot —
Stands the Sun so close and mighty
That our Minds are hot.

News is he of all the others—
Bold it were to die
With the Blue Birds exercising
On his British Sky.

version of 1872

We like March—his shoes are Purple.
He is new and high—
Makes he Mud for Dog and Peddler—
Makes he Forests Dry—
Knows the Adder's Tongue his coming
And begets her spot—
Stands the Sun so close and mighty—
That our Minds are hot.
News is he of all the others—
With the Blue Birds buccaneering
On his British sky—

version of 1878

No choice of A over B as in an Almanacky contest, turn the page upside down for the answer. Miss Dickinson plays against herself and wins with every alteration—the gorgeous opening line brought into line, the strangely generative *begets* and oh, that bold death, mercenary *buccaneering*; mock war poem for the month named for the god of war, news is he. Lenten, crocus, royal purple?

. . .

What is certain: high water 5.0 at the Battery 1:17 P.M.; the tilt of the earth, the vernal equinox set for the 20th of the month. Neither of these events will disappoint, though who are we living in the city, seldom looking up or out, to be let down by natural events? Unless we are fortunate enough to watch the high Winter sea cut away at our perch on the shore, to mark each year's measurable erosion, to celebrate scrub pine and beach plum holding ground in bitter salt air. Unless we escape to some Marina Del Rey, we live on memories of high tides for our Summer pleasure, once a day rising to the very stretch of sand we roasted on under a glaze of sunblock, waves washing in a litter of sharp shells, bottle tops, shards of glass not worn to silky perfection, Styrofoam scraps caught in rubbery seaweed; or the tide receding on schedule to expose—if you live, as Sylvia Waite does, above a small Connecticut city on Long Island Sound—the sulfurous stretch of oily sandbars speckled with the sucking black holes of inedible mussels and clams.

How easily a day was saved by high tide when Sylvie arrived with the striped umbrella, picnic basket, goggles, snorkels and the children she cared for, who were so accomplished in the water that she did not have to watch for fear . . . though often she raised her eyes from her book to enjoy the sight of Gerald whose hair was sleek as sealskin, bobbing in the waves, or the strong competitive reach of Martha's Australian crawl. If the high tide was with her, Sylvie Waite seemed like any mother or nursemaid in attendance though reading her plain white paper book, not the fat potboiler of the season. Sylvie reached for a knife intended to halve a sandwich, peel a peach and cut the pages of her French or German book. Now and then a college student or an *au pair* tending American children asked about the book, which might pass for a text assigned, perhaps an edition of Camus or Hesse or Silone in the original. Diverting any literary talk, Mrs. Waite replied in plain English that she read poorly in the sun, not wanting to be thought different, though different she was. In truth, she read in the glare of the sun as a point of pride, to keep up her languages, not for the story.

Sylvie's knife was poised over a pear when Martha snatched it from the plate, a good china plate which skimmed like a Frisbee over the sand. The girl slurped the pear, skin and all, her stepmother minding this rudeness no more than others. Gerald, bolting his excellent sandwich, wished it tuna or baloney and American cheese. Many years later he would say to Sylvie: "That was some chow, too good for us"; recalling the Westphalian ham, the garlicky chèvre, and the tide rising to where his stepmother sat calmly peeling in one long strip the skin of an apple, her book with those unreadable words tossed aside in the sand. "Some fine chow," Gerald said, visiting with his wife and kids soon after Bob Waite died in a sand trap. A bright Winter day, the golf pro and a retired doctor had propped her husband's tanned body upright on the cart with its gay awning to speed Bob to the terrace of the clubhouse in Boca Raton where Sylvie lay turning the pages of a British mystery, unable to follow the story in the sun.

Predicting tides is kiddie calculation to Martha Waite, who studies the tectonic plates which float on a sea of molten rock in the Pacific's deep ocean basins. Martha often praises her stepmother's civilizing additions to her childhood; how elegant those picnics on the beach, cloth napkins and fruit knives with dainty silver blades, and how unlike the fearful mothers; Sylvie, anchored firm in her beach chair against the rising tide, cutting her pages. Sylvie shipped the knives with mother-of-pearl handles to California at once, feeling that, when their father died, those children were well grown, in possession of their distant lives.

These weeks she has not driven to the beach where she walked daily with Bob Waite on pleasant Winter days. Enough to steer Cyril, wheezing and breathless, to the doctor, schedule the tests he must undergo, so the Winter tide can wait. He is failing before her eyes. And what would she show him? The gulls she can no longer hear without the dread electronic bug stuck in her ear? An old fisherman? There is always one old fisherman, even along this sold-out shore where clubs and clam houses abut private estates, and seaside factories have been transformed to discount palaces — one old fisherman at the outset of March readying his gear. What would Cyril see? The dark shapes of tarp and tackle box, the bright illusion of sky and sun reflected off the sea.

BLEND DAYS

If we hold to the Sky Almanac for 2000, the moon nears Mars on the evening of the 8th, the first quarter on the 13th, visible at 7:00 UT, while Spring begins on the 20th this year. Inaccurate, therefore, telling this Winter's Tale, which began on the first day of the year, ten days after the Winter Solstice. Give a little, take a little — the calendar is a practical device and it's in the nature of March (an excellent month for pruning) to be lopped off. The first three days of *Hyld-monath* (the loud and stormy month) are unlucky. No farmer in Wales will sow seeds on these *Blend* days, folklore which matters not at all to Harold Moffett, his vast acreage still under snow in Wisconsin. The arctic wind swooping down from Canada, which once threatened electrical outages, is harmless as a Spring breeze. Harold has his generators. In his barns, Bossy and Dossie and Holstein 2,209 are warm and productive.

THE BIG SNOOZE

Did you ever wonder how the dormouse comes to awaken from wintersleep? No, not even when reading the Almanac's leading question do you wonder as long as the comic mammal awakens, like Shirley Moffett, a timid creature with sleepy ways.

"You go, Shirl. Have yourself a ball." Harold speaks of his new time-share on Sanibel Island. Now he has the money: now he has no time. "There'll be folks like us, plenty of them."

"Alone, go alone? Whatever shall I do?" Nevertheless, Shirley

Moffett shops for summer clothes, packs her bag and finds herself in O'Hare hustling down a garishly lit arcade with a copy of *Vogue* and a box of peppermint patties tucked in her tote bag. She has traveled often with her husband, never alone. There is not a moment to consider what she will do in the sunny furnished rooms of the time-share lest she lose her connection, but when she is buckled into her seat next to a young man madly computing, there is a delay, the de-icing of wings, and Shirley Moffett contemplates the slick tarmac, the heaps of cleared snow blackened with exhaust, the grey industrial flatlands of Chicago strangled in highways, and she is anxious to take off, already sensing that the adventure is being alone, not whatever shall I do.

In his book, Harold Moffett makes the grand gesture, shipping his wife out of Wisconsin in the dead of Winter. And surely Bertram Boyce, at home in his flannel bathrobe, cannot be the villain of our piece? His plaid robe matches those of Heather and the two kids, the Royal Stuart tartan—a field of red crossed with green and yellow. Up early, into the cereal boxes, they look a catalogue family. Heather, who has put on weight, leaves her bran half eaten. The bowl is removed to the kitchen by Estella, a Mexican maid who hovers obediently, waiting for the children to finish a niggling argument and get dressed. She will drive them to their school. The terrace which lies just outside the breakfast room is coated with black ice. Provençal urns have swollen, split, dumped frozen soil on the terrazzo steps. The formal garden beyond is a bleak geometry in this season, chill triangles and squares. Warm and moist in the breakfast room, the thermostat set to a day in June or mid-September, but it is March and not one Boyce looks out through the French doors.

Estella watches the limousine enter the front gate, drive round the fish pond and park under the portico, where it idles, waiting for Bertram Boyce. She hopes the boss will be gone by the time she loads the kids in the Volvo, so the driver of the limo will not mumble obscenities to her in Spanish. Though she no longer prays, Estella, a graduate student in anthropology, lets an automatic *ave* run through her head—that Mr. B. will move ass so she will not be subjected to the lewd suggestions of the chauffeur, a creep in brass buttons. These days her prayer is seldom answered for the boss throws aside the *Times* and heads for his study, a room Heather has fitted out with hunting horns, a spittoon and books by the yard in tooled bindings.

Behind closed doors Boyce watches high-resolution displays of snow churning above the Great Plains, digitalized turbulence impacted over India, the Mistral blowing from North Africa across the south of France, calm waters of the South Pacific. Bud is newly addicted, a weather junkie. Skylark lacks an atmospheric hookup and Heather, who is increasingly chilly about her husband's success, maintains that "Bertie" would like to acquire a piece of the universe, more than the whole damn world. A corporate racketeer, yet not so crafty that he can commandeer the U.S. Weather Bureau; in the unexplored region of his heart, Bud yearns to be more than a glorified adman and is not as greedy as his wife and Louise Moffett make him out to be. He doesn't aim to wage a climate war (conception of John von Neumann), in which the weather of an enemy country would be altered disastrously, or to seed the clouds as the Russians did to insure rain before their sunny commemoration of V E Day, fifty years after that war. Bud Boyce is merely obsessed with predictable weather; and even Louise might soften if she could see him enchanted as a child by the distant blue and white globe, mesmerized by the current temperature in Phoenix, Maui, Bangkok, Athens, the rainfall as measured to this date in Atlanta and Houston—the still point in his day, close as he comes to meditation. Heather is wise not to break in with a small complaint about Estella or the permissive attitude of the children's private school.

Bud leans forward on the leather couch to see forecasts, national and local. He mutes "our meteorologist" to absorb the visual clips—graphics of mackerel sky at midday, hexagonal snowflakes of tomorrow. Bud's lonely pursuit lasts at the most three minutes before the gauzy atmosphere of Weathernet reappears swirling around the still, blue globe, then he's off, knowing what coat to wear, what hat if any. The long black car waiting under the portico will drive him to the Skylark garage under the Skylark building. The elements impact only if he is to fly to D.C. or L.A., to Tokyo or Delhi. He has no climatic experience after the morning fix, the rush of knowing tonight, tomorrow, the weekend, as though, for heaven's sake, he knows the future, so different in kind from the future under his command, the future technology that has arrived at Skylark. After stolen moments behind the library door—jerk-off joy in predictions, knowing the day will shine or shower upon him—Bud's up to his dressing room, where haberdashery is concealed behind chestnut paneling—sliding drawers of mono-grammed shirts, carousels of British braces and luscious ties. He throws off his Royal Stuart robe and matching jammies, pleased with his smooth well-exercised body, his rosy cheeks. Though blond curls thinning.

Bertram Boyce selecting which slubbed-silk tie for the Yale Club, or choosing black T-shirt, jeans, cashmere jacket (media movers lunching at Skylark this power day), is no worse than the world he plays in. Nothing in his strained alliance with overripe Heather, his inevitable lust for Estella's full mouth, dark as a love bruise in her contemptuous face, sets him off from men of his kind. The deals that made and maintain his considerable hold-ings are, loosely speaking, O.K., monkey see monkey do, as Louise Moffett claimed in her pathetic defense of Artie Freeman.

A trace element of loss which takes the form of missing Artie blips in Bud's tidy head as he is driven into the city, seeing for a millisecond the stock weather images he has left behind, that fic-tional hold on the future. Artie could make the fuckin' rain *rain*, infuse the screen with the deep blue of a dry sky, could figure the probability of topcoat over Burberry, but he has no patience with his pal's inclination to failure as he pulls up the first quotes of the day. Communications are down. Skylark is holding. No time to contemplate what he loved about his buddy—supersmart, an original; and what he long envied—a kid with no mother, no father, and now without Ms. Moffett, that clever piece of ass. Artie is never beholden. In Bud's view, Freeman, true to his given name, will always be free.

Bud not knowing that Artie is locked in the arms of Louise, happy lay-a-beds. Though after breakfast, as Lou lays out her brushes and paints, he is bewildered. What to do? Plug in his electronic equipment to no more purpose than scanning the *Times*? Fix the dripping faucet. On the third day of their future, he acquires a navy blue suit, fetches outmoded ties and down-at-heel brogans from Cyril's closet. He speaks to Louise earnestly, matters of life and death: the unconditional probability of medical benefits, actuarial tables, in-laws. What is she to say? Lighten up. He discovers that their extravagant loft lies in an abysmal school district . . . and will not give up on his fear of structural unemployment. Arthur Freeman, an inauthentic world beater in a Wall Street costume, takes no chances, girds up with belt and suspenders. Louise unbuckles the belt.

"Hey!"

No design on his body. She slips his résumé, a marvel of typography, into his grandfather's heavy humpbacked briefcase. "Painfully slim," she says, "the curriculum of your vita."

"It's just in my adult life, you wanna call it that, I never worked for anyone but Boyce."

Lou smooths his wild black hair, thinking first day of school, but she is not, after all, his mother. Still, it is an anxious moment as her Freeman heads out the door in search of honest employment.

Louise holds a brush above Carmine No. 2, unsure. Oh, sure about Artie, though can't see him trapped without the indulgences of Skylark. No foolin' around, no bright-boy exemptions, doing as he is bid in a stagnant cyberpool of stats and graphics. How at odds his talents, figuring hard facts and making pretty pictures on the depthless screen. Unsure—her many hearts swept into a corner pulse in the light of day—unsure of her investment in this art begun like all previous work in a nurturing fury. She fondles a little white heart fashioned by hand, sanded smooth. Should she call Dealer and cancel?

It is six o'clock in the morning, Pacific Time. Beatrice Moffett has been up since five—farmers' hours, doctors' hours. She has had three hours' sleep, sleeping in her clothes as though she is still an intern, though her hair is white as her lab coat. Up late working from the gene sequences worked out by smart lab assistants. Many of them have never worked *in vitro*, but Dr. Moffett in her white coat is a throwback to glass beakers and vials. With no disrespect she is called the Microbe Huntress, though her pursuit is not to find, not to kill a tiny living organism, but to alter and by transformation—destroy it. What's more, she works *in vivo*, with the kids she is trying to keep alive, my kids, she calls them, and they are hers, their blood, bones and cells, her brood for the time she has them, some of them responding to genetic therapy before they move on, away from Aunt Bea. She is Aunt Bea this morning, for in yesterday's mail the invitation to an opening, Lou's show, a mere eighteen days and cross-continental flight away. The glossy photo (has her niece given up on painting?) is of a ring, a rose, what Bea takes to be fine china, an advertisement for wedding tributes given the vulgar title *EAT ME*. And Aunt Bea, who pursues diseases of the blood with such passion that she has not thought of the Polish Intellectual in years, wonders if Lou feels left on the vine being single, or is deeply wounded and defiant. Remembering her own heartbreak, crying out to the moon on a Summer night, throwing her discarded body on the untilled meadow, her land. Dr. Moffett is meticulous in her professional instruction, knows and truly believes in what she teaches, but what in her wildness did she say to Louise, how instruct the girl out of her ignorance?

Living close as she can to the hospital, Aunt Bea walks the few blocks with *EAT ME* in hand. The picture is pretty enough to pin up for the children, who will not understand its implications, no more than she does. For a second she thinks she will fly to New York, to the opening, but there are set protocols of irradiation, serum factors to be administered and the shifty matter of her microbes' coats. She cannot leave her children or her lab. Yet she is fond of her remnant of family, Louise, proud of the woman who has made her way despite Harold. Her brother full of himself, and though she should be generous, Bea hates the idea that Hal feels they are in the same racket, don't you believe it. In her office, she calls Louise.

"I'm in love!" Lou cries. "But not working, not really."

"It takes its toll," Bea says and they are laughing—remembering the P.I., who, like Freeman, was unemployed. "Listen, you've got to work for payday."

She pins *EAT ME* above her desk, a delicious celebration as she now sees it, not femme formulaic, mockery of marriage, and Dr. Moffett, getting her first whiff of the ward, floral antiseptic and moist sweat of sick children, hopes that Lou's payday is more than dollars and cents. She must take greater care with what she teaches.

Should Louise call Dealer? *I have nothing to show.* She imagines him popping Zoloft, sputtering to his assistant, then his fatuous smile of relief. He never believed in her hearts and flowers, only in her meteoric career. Let him root about in the archives, the back room of dusty canvases, for a sobering retrospective of the corrupt Eighties when he was selling them wet, or further back to the vacuum of the Seventies' feeble concept of conceptual. Her happiness can't make art, not in the hedging ironies of this *commence de siècle* market. She dabs the chalky white heart in her hand with blackened Carmine No. 2. This heart will match all the others, as her mother's cultured pearls match perfectly, product simulation.

Yet Louise works on, now digging into the stiff small heart

with bloodied nails. She lines up a row of her prefab hearts to endow each with the mark of her hand, its scratch or disfigurement, knowing perfectly well that art can not exult in the dark dawn of an uncertain century. Her project is as unacceptable as a happy ending. She yearns for the undisguised Artie, just a touch of the slacker and her own exasperation. Mottling a heart with imperfections hardly visible to the naked eye, Lou figures how hard, really hard, the task at hand. It seems you must reinvent yourself to meet love's impossible demands. As she works on, she has little feeling for her work, but must make art for payday, sending Artie off in that navy blue suit and that noose of a tie will not do, though he must look the image of the Wall Street grandfather she still has not seen, Cyril O'Connor, who is old and strangely in love or in love strangely, go figure.

"Well, I figure the possibility," Artie has said, "reunion of two lovers, given the small geographic distribution, given maybe several thousand couples, after fifty years . . ."

"Several?"

"An inexact sampling, deviation from the mean. No way to take a poll . . ."

"Is he happy?"

"Without doubt, my grandfather is happy."

Happy as he steals out of bed, happily opening his neglected journal, Cyril peers through the new magnifying glass making sure that the unruled page is pristine. He will set down the day on which his clogged veins will be reamed and the day when he will fly with Sylvie to Milan on their way to Innsbruck. Plans. They have made plans for Spring. He distinguishes light: March, the *Lencthen Monath*, the month of lengthening days. His first mood of the morning is euphoric, for his days *are* to be lengthened. Let Sylvie's doctors make him a workable old man. He had waited so long for his death, impatient with the delay, waited with his books half read. Nights in the apartment he cursed the cancellation, knowing, as he turned down Mae's crocheted spread, that the sun would rise for him next day. Like a child who knows what's good for him, he is prodded by Sylvie, who crosses off the days until he will be wheeled on a gurney into the operating room, the repair swiftly accomplished. Then to see something of the world. He has been no place really—Bermuda with his wife, car trips to Maine and Quebec when Fiona was little. Korea was not a holiday. Sylvie will show him her world while he can still perceive the outline of cathedrals and ruins, the flutter of umbrellas at an outdoor café. The Alps—he would have to be more than legally blind not to feel their towering majesty.

"*Herrlich*, that is often said—magnificent. When I looked out from my window at the mountains, I thought I was no bigger than one of my dolls, no bigger than the miniature figures going up the Hungeberg in the little cars of the funicular. *Majestätisch*."

She has not wanted to see that majestic view, to feel that small again, but now she would like Cyril to see the site where her stories are set. After the war, Inge Marks reclaimed that house, sold it off for a pittance. The Villa was then said to be a school for rich foreign girls, more lately a hotel. In this season Sylvie imagines skiers lounging in the reception rooms after a day on the Seefeld, or at a snug bar in her father's study, perhaps his books placed back on the shelves. As the soldiers marched him through the hall, she had seen books thrown on the Persian carpet, but not understood, never quite understood, for Dr. Goebbels had not yet ordered torches put to the pyre of books in Berlin, works that might contaminate pure Germanic thought, until May of that year. She came to believe it was idle vandalism, the National Socialists' disrespect for too many grand words. All the free flights to Europe with Bob Waite and she had never gone near the house which lived on in her terrifying and incomplete dream. When Inge was living high in Houston, Sylvie would not travel to that city to see the replica of von Neisswonger Haus, but let her mother and Mr. Boots come to Connecticut with extravagant presents for her stepchildren, and how the kids loved his Stetson and bolo tie, the cowgirl fringes on Inge's white leather jacket, as though these amazing figures had stepped from the television screen right into the colonial parlor.

Inge, reading the hallmark on a silver teapot: "You've done all right for yourself."

"Not so bad," playing at her mother's game. No point in saying she is happy to have survived, meaning not the atrocities visited upon the lightheaded mathematician and his clever son who imitated the father's dignity as they were whisked out the front door to the Mercedes with the swastika fluttering on the aerial, not leading her mother through the garden wall while the thick soldier slept in her bed, one of Herr Professor's cigars dead in his bestial paw, a miraculous story like so many of survival. Sylvie, taking the Waites' Georgian silver from her mother's hands, meant she had survived Inge's theatrical methods of survival, that she was content with Bob Waite, cared for his children and could not bear to see them enchanted by Billy Ray Boots.

She looks forward to Milan, Paris, London when Cyril is patched up, a matter of weeks. They will arrive in Innsbruck when Spring is in the air, walk in the lovely Alpenzoo, where the otters, eagles, vultures, it is said even the bison of the region have been preserved. She will lead him up one of the gentler slopes to see the alpine primrose and gentian, to feel the grey moss fed by melting snow. She will ask the innkeeper to let her roam the Villa—to see again her father's wine cellar, the servants' nest of bedrooms in the attic, her childhood room—to discover where the bear and the elephant drank their tea, where her red wool cap was left behind, hung on a peg next to a small window which tamed the overwhelming view to a picture postcard. There the parquet was laid in a pattern of stars which the soldier trod upon as he came toward her little white bed, flipped back the eiderdown. She looks forward to remembering it all exactly, then at last forgetting. Safe in the Waite four-poster, she moans in her sleep as heavy boots tread on the stars.

While Cyril writes at her desk:

Dear Boy,

As you know, I did not see the picture of your mother and two young men, not when Mae first took it, not when you brought it to me as evidence. I believe your grandmother snapped that photo in defiance of me, attempting at that time to understand her daughter. She never knew Fiona, not from the day our child was born with a cap of red hair blessed to the touch, so soon to be an unmanageable mop, a child so unlike her mother she might have been a changeling. We had the kicker, the screamer, while somewhere a docile girl lived in a family of brawlers. Make no mistake, Mae's sandy hair and faint freckles were a pale version of Fiona's, her eyes a faded copy of her daughter's deep-brown eyes watching our mismatched lives. Our silence was a truce. Your mother knew that. Yes, I was crazy for that child, absolutely, as though she would redeem me—being bold.

Two young men, imagine. Mae pretended delight, having gone against my wishes, gone to find her daughter at a hostel, an abandoned public or parish building on the Lower East Side, where she lived in rebellious squalor. "Let her be!" *Two* young men, as though our pretty girl had *beaux*, her dance card filled for the cotillion. There is no longer any point to my *suppressio veri*. The truth is that I imagined the use my daughter was making of her body with two young men. I imagined her free of us. "Let her be!" was all I said unkindly to Mae, yet I imagined Fiona's contempt for my compromises, for my life on Wall Street and for my killing kindness. Imagine her trial, Arthur, posing with two young men in a slum her mother had never imagined, Mae drawn halfway to hell, prompting smiles, clicking her camera. No good could come from the simple enthusiasm of a woman who lived ninety blocks uptown, a world away from the mock poverty, the inflammatory pamphlets and moral highs, the sexual adventures of her only child and from, I must believe it, from Fiona's passionate beliefs.

When he hears Sylvie stirring, the flap of her slippers, Cyril gets up from her delicate desk and moves toward light at the window. The fields are carpeted in ethereal white, the crest of the hill humped against a colorless sky. Not to disturb, Sylvie passes silently and swiftly behind him. The stiff pages flip in his journal. She has never seen him so devoted to his private morning work. What words can he be writing apart from her? When they came to live together all confidences were of their shared past, a place closed off as the small landscape of a terrarium that recycles its own moist breath through the Winter. They could not sustain life in that hothouse atmosphere. A few weeks into their idyll and Sylvie Waite speaks often of the lost Villa, of Inge Boots, of her dutiful stepchildren and the Sisters Kapp—where are they now, the Three Furies, in their Saturday-night finery? Are they widowed as she is, or still squabbling in a well-appointed netherworld? Who gets the mended stocking? Who the beaded purse?

No, the present must be spoken of—foul weather and ill health. Of the grandson: "He lost his girl, so he fills the void searching for the mother, the father." And Sylvie asks: "The man on the left, how would he change the kid's life?"

Not hearing Cyril's soft answer, she answers that there is a childish thread of hope we are not who we are, neither prince nor beggar. In the bubble of spun sugar before the war, she recalls reading such improbable fairy stories with no desire to be other than the mathematician's daughter, even the beautiful Inge's daughter.

"His father," she murmurs, "he's all speculation, ghost story, a ghost."

When had she learned to speak her mind directly? Not in official translations, not raising those oversized children on nonsense words. When over the years? After Bob Waite's death, when she was no longer the pleasing suburban wife. Sylvie is known to be blunt on Painter Hill, yet she does not disturb Cyril seeing his pleasure scribbling half on, half off the blank pages bought to record weather, appointments. She grinds coffee, the kettle's shriek muffled by her deafness, and presumes that crouched over her little desk, he embellishes, *er verschönert die Tage*, making too much of each day.

A day unforeseen.

While Cyril contemplates the blanketing whiteness of Sylvie's hill, the pages have flipped. He has lost his place, but not in the story of his daughter's calling. Feeling for the edge of the page:

Mae embraced the political cause—American flags which decorated her angel cake on the Fourth of July were conspicuously dumped in the trash. The refrigerator blossomed with the U.S. dead in Vietnam—39,893, 45,929, 58,000—the escalating count that would pass by some hundred thousand the dead in Korea. She was a fervent convert. I came home to "Honky Tonk Woman," and "Give Peace a Chance," singles replacing the albums of her cheerful Broadway musicals. The mother had joined with the daughter against the domestic enemy. I had fostered the rebellion in our child, never presuming she might confuse the horrors of war with our undeclared domestic conflict, that she would "live free or die," a foolish phrase of that era. I hoped your mother would have the courage of Bridget O'Connor, that guts had skipped a generation, but it was . . .

Not to be. The pages have flipped back to the beginning of a signature, a natural divide in the gift-shop journal, back to the salutation of his written confession, back to Dear Boy. He has been inking over the thoughts already committed to the page, unable to distinguish a floating mist of words from whiteness, and does not write with his eyes upon the pen. Looking out at the dense morning sky, he feels his way to the paper's edge as he feels for fork and spoon, hoping Sylvie will not catch him. He turns in the direction of her voice. He has heard her slippers flap on the stairs, coffee grinding, kettle's whistle, and now writes on, word over word. What has the journal become? A letter that must go at once to the reader, the reader who will have practical use of this history. So Cyril inks line over line and when he is finished tears the pages from the book.

Sylvie calling from the kitchen, smell of his decaf, thump of his heart as he feels in a drawer for an envelope, quickly addressing it to Arthur Freeman, care of himself at the old apartment on Fifth Avenue, which suffered a temporary sea change during Mae's short season of protest—Indian brass votives crowding the Blessed Virgin out—but that is another installment.

"Coming," he booms, "coming, coming," supposing she hears. He fingers a roll of stamps, pastes several askew but in the correct corner of the envelope and is down the stairs clutching the rail to the newel post, turning toward the front door, directed by the chill draft blowing in where the eighteenth-century sill has rotted. "Coming," he cries to the empty dining room and the warmth of the kitchen beyond.

"I have made your muffins." *Haff, muvvins*, the lilting accent, the lure of "*your* muvvins." He smells the tart apple, the cinnamon mixed with little butter, a recipe for his heart, but does not bump through the brittle pearwood chairs past the Waites' handsome sideboard to find his way to Sylvie. He throws open the front door to the morning, which is oddly white, oddly warm and soupy. He steps into the drive.

Tapping muffins out of the pan, Sylvie sniffs Spring above the coffee and cinnamon. Not too early to order manure. This year a garden. The field at the top of the hill is given to Joe Clifford, the last farmer on Painter Hill, who will in exchange for his corn turn her soil for a small garden—early lettuce, chard. Years since Bob Waite tended his pole beans. When the ground is thawed, turn up a plot, peas go in on St. Patrick's Day about the time when Cyril would have the angioplasty, and soon after they will fly off to Milan. From Milan through the Brenner Pass . . . As a child she had not understood Inge's choice of the dangerous route through

Vienna, how charm produced their visas, through what connections her mother may have known the timetable of her husband's, her son's detention and death.

The sensible route through the Brenner Pass has been chosen with a travel agent. Sylvie will confront the Villa with Cyril at her side, check out memory, memory that has outlasted pain. The dates that will take them into Spring are set on the calendar over the dry sink. From the kitchen table, where she sets a jar of jam, she sees clear through to the front door flung open, the rug flapped back in the wind. A nuisance, he has gone to the mailbox while the muffins are warm, paying those bills the boy brought special delivery from the city. What's the big deal if the electric and telephone are not paid for an empty apartment? Paying, when already the coffee is tepid.

Sylvie does not hear the distant thump, a soft determining impact, but in a distortion of time, prolonged impossible moments, sees clearly . . . clearly strangers in the front hall, a woman with small children clinging to her sides. She cannot take in the woman's words, only the blanched outline of fear that rims her babbling mouth, her eyes propped open in the moment of disbelief, the kids' rigid bodies zipped in puffy ski jackets, and sees the thick screen of whiteness beyond the door, the morning fog lifting, not in time. *The old fool, paying his bills,* crying old fool as she runs past the strange woman, wailing to set the crows cawing, cawing unseen in the blinding whiteness. A clarity at ground level but not in time, her arms parting the white air over and over again as she runs toward the road, throwing back the drapery of sodden air as though to undo the very atmosphere, crying *Leibste, mein Herz,* old fool.

He lies on the black road, one shoe off, one shoe on, dressed as he always dressed for breakfast in jacket and tie. Her body thrown over his, she attempts the kiss of life, her breath a lover's breath not a savior's, for there is no rescue as the cars accumulate in a pack, as a burly young neighbor buttoned into a three piece suit on his way to the 7:58 pummels Cyril on the chest. She knows he is gone, soon to be gone from her in an ambulance. The siren's scream offers no hope of a medical miracle. A flashing light scours the dregs of morning fog. The mother of those stricken children on their way to school throws herself on the hood of her car, sobbing, consoling the station wagon—red, so bright a blind man could see it. A blind man did not. The cops take the children into the squad car. As Sylvia Waite is driven off to the white room of last resort where Cyril O'Connor will be declared dead, she sees a young officer go back to the red station wagon, retrieve two plastic lunch boxes from the scene of the senseless, predictable crime.

Liebste, mein Schatz, Liebste, not until Sylvie, aimlessly suspended in grief is asked to sign papers relating to her friend's death . . . *my good friend,* she says in the grip of a restricting societal moment. She feels the gritty envelope with weeping address in her hand, a message for the next of kin.

"I believe there is a grandson. . . ." The young doctor and a policeman take it that she is in doubt. She cannot hear what they ask.

The doctor getting on to her problem: "You BELIEVE there is?"

His loud word seems an accusation. She is muddled, dry-eyed, clasping Cyril's cold hand. She lets it flop on the gurney. The doctor draws up the sheet. And what is most painful? The young doctor's schooled sympathy smile, devoid of understanding. Two old people parting, he will see it often enough in this line of work.

"There is a grandson," she says. "I must call."

Sylvia Waite is led through the suburban Emergency Room, where a jogger complains of a sprained ankle and an infant with a fever whimpers in its mother's arms. In a room with comforting armchairs, pleasant end tables and lamps, she is handed a telephone on which she presses the numbers that will connect her to the apartment on Fifth Avenue, a telephone number she has known for fifty years and never called.

TELEPHONE GAMES

March 3—Alexander Graham Bell born in Edinburgh, Scotland, 1847, to a family who specialized in the mouthing of words as well as the art of elocution. Bell's "Speech is a mere motion of air" contradicted his father's system of Visible Speech, in which the mouth, tongue, nose, cheeks were configured to reproduce ten written symbols and transform them into sounds that produced a voice less supple yet more human than computerized speech. Pa Bell's method was more than a parlor trick, less than science, as was his course in elocution, a rendering of the emotions in codified gestures (mostly hot air). When his son invented the telephone—Boston, 1876—Alexander took his magical instrument modeled on the human ear from town to town with his faithful sidekick, in each show repeating the miracle of the first transmission: "Mr. Watson, come here, I need you."

Both Elisha Gray and Alexander Bell patented their telephones on the same day, a coincidence that Arthur Freeman might figure. Fame was awarded to Bell's invention, a noisy, ugly toy. The primitive black dial phone in Cyril O'Connor's apartment rings and rings. Two months ago, he would not have looked up from his book to answer. There is no answer, though Sylvie must find that big oaf who, dressed in his grandfather's grown-up clothes, kisses Lou at the door of the loft, off to the proving ground, Wall Street. In Cyril's cracked leather briefcase, Artie totes a beeper and a cellular phone the size of a bagel, a gizmo that presumes the urgent call—"Mr. Freeman, come here, I need you."

Artie has prepared a handshake, an alert nod, gestures from another of the senior Bell's programs for success, though in Alexander's science show the ebullient believer, Mr. Watson, seemed always unrehearsed, singing over the apparatus—"Auld Lang Syne" and a naughty ditty: two successful telephone pals set firmly in the encyclopedias with their endlessly improvable invention heading toward the end of an expansive century. Watson, clown to straight man, like Artie to Bud Boyce, who ingeniously buys up systems whereas Artie compu-slummed far short of invention, his illusionary demographics supporting Product with unfocused samplings of desire. His last piecework for Bud surveying the adolescent lust for sneakers, comics, comic sneakers, end-of-an-era nostalgia for old-time rock 'n' roll and for the antique art of reading hardbacks. In the final days of predicting market, Artie pixelated for consumer at point of impact, perfection of sneaker with leather-scented upper and the rich cream paper of Reelbook, on which he transmitted to Skylark a page of Dickens' *Hard Times*.

Over the wire, Mr. Bell spoke to Mr. Watson. One more telepathy show, Madame Blavatsky passing through town? No, the thick black wire of the magical instrument was visible to all. In Springfield, Hartford, Middletown, you might touch the machine, observe both ends of the call. Was it called that—the call, communication between tele-phoning devices? Sylvie Waite gives up on the phone. Weeping, at home on the unyielding couch, given at last to weeping, she looks through her loved one's private papers which the grandson carried to Connecticut. Impersonal bank statements, tax forms, telephone bill unpaid, a pity what she sees, the liveliest correspondence being from a history book club closing up shop and a *National Geographic* still addressed to Arthur Freeman, as though the boy lived at home—the *National Geographic* founded by Bell, one further entry in his energetic history—but that boy with his lifetime subscription is nowhere to be found.

While a neighbor woman, Mrs. Clifford, cleans up the mess of the ill-fated muffins, Sylvie, holding the papers addressed to next of kin, cries on the Waites' unyielding couch. She was nothing to Cyril O'Connor by blood or legal relation. She places his death in a strange history—marriage by misunderstanding to the silly wife, tragic death of the adored child, burden of the fatherless boy, her knock on his door forcing the issue of love, testing time, sad baby faces of those kids in the trooper's car, thinking of their lost lunch boxes as they tore her body off her lover's. *Ein Freier*, yes, he was once her suitor. Her cries reach the kitchen and the neighbor whose husband plants her fields, Mrs. Clifford, the last farm-woman on the Hill, comes to hold Sylvie's tough little body, embraces this childless foreign woman who came bravely to live among the few land-poor locals and the acquisitive commuters. *Sylvie, Sylvie*. Until this day Mrs. Clifford has said *Mrs. Waite* to the Mrs. Waite who tutored their gifted boy in English and math for payment in pickles and rhubarb jam—their son who is now a certified public accountant.

The dead man had been staying with Mrs. Waite these Winter weeks, a friend from the past with no accent. There is no one to claim the old man's body. Old—what does she mean? They are all old people, Mrs. Waite and her boyfriend, Joe who can barely hoist himself up on the tractor but will somehow plow the field next month, who will come home to her exhausted. "Prissy," he will say to her proudly, calling her by her sister's name, Priscilla—long dead.

The two old women bob up and down, retrieving the dead man's scattered bills and notices. The farmer's wife gathers them into the business envelope in which the boy transported Cyril's meager obligations. On the envelope the world is suspended like a Christmas ornament, silver continents glistening on blue oceans; the globe dangles from the beak of a soaring celestial bird. "Skylark," Mrs. Clifford calls above Sylvie's sniffling. "Now, that's a sweet name. Say, isn't it the make of Joe's car?"

That he had been less than original in giving his enterprise the same moniker as a modest family car, never occurred to the CEO of Skylark, who lives in a loftier orbit. His corporate name is how the phone comes to ring in Cyril O'Connor's old briefcase.

"Sit tight, man," Bud says. "Stay where you are." Cold where Artie overlooks the East River. Wind ruffles the water, whips the awnings of the shops and cafés behind him as he finishes off a wiener, having dropped his résumé at hushed personnel offices, soothing chapels of rejection. He has left unnecessary messages, dumb love speak, on the tape at the loft where Skylark got his number, message breeding message. Typical, Bud's urgency, but he's easy feeding the gulls the remains of his bun, waiting for Boyce, who always arrives when Artie is in need of salvation. Artie's love for Louise takes him out of the game. No more larks—nine to five at a workstation: dental plan, sick days, benefits he considered superfluous at Skylark.

The East River slaps at the hull of a four-masted barque, *The Peking*, a tourist attraction. An islander, Artie doesn't know he looks across at Dutch Kill, at Red Hook, that twice a day the tidal waters ebb and flow here and a hundred miles up the Hudson. Artie counting the cables of the Brooklyn Bridge when the limo arrives, makes Bud walk the cobblestones toward him. He has not seen his chum since the mock violence of New Year's Eve. Bud slouching, stopping as though to examine ice on the gilt lettering of *The Peking*, shivering in his cashmere topcoat, the reversion to Winter not accurately foretold. Artie can't wait for Bud's offer, to turn down the big shot—no more admissible fakery, borderline fraud.

But Cyril O'Connor is dead.

Artie is silent, then, recalling his calculations, his monitored fear as he leaned on the bell of his grandfather's door, he says, "I thought the old guy was immortal."

They walk solemnly to the limo. Bud speaks of the chess matches. How easily they both defeated Cyril, how often, in that hushed apartment, they played each other to a draw.

Alexander Bell imagined many improvements for his telephone, but never the technology that spews out Skylark memos in the luxurious womb of the Boycemobile, or the modest cell phone on which Artie now calls Lou, who whispers worn words of sympathy as though they are new, have never been said.

Louise Moffett, who has bought a lavender dress sprigged with white flowers so that she may be presented this coming Sunday to Cyril O'Connor in Connecticut.

Up in Nova Scotia during brisk summers with his happy family, Bell built kites, huge red silk kites shaped as circles and tunnels, hoping to reproduce the aerodynamics of birdspan for the coming air machine; and boats that almost sailed above the water, propelled on currents of air. The sometime kite flier and publisher of *Poor Richard's Almanack* would have greatly admired Bell's tetrahedron truss, which reproduced the structure of the atom fundamental to nature, as well as the hydrofoil he could not sell to the War Department. Bell developed an artificial respirator, leapt ahead to solar heat, air conditioning, atomic energy as relating to his tetrahedron cell. To Franklin and Bell, the point was to go on with curious, at times unuseful, experiments. Go on and failing, go on.

Arthur Freeman phones Sylvia Waite. Her account of the accident lapses into German, a breathless, almost lively tale. He remembers his first sight of her in sparkling ear bobs and silver eye shadow, bringing life to the dead apartment where he now holds the receiver of what he believes is the last black rotary phone on Fifth Avenue, if not in the world. Louise, at his side, knows little of Sylvie, but thinks—*She will go on. She is the sort who goes on.*

"He wrote to you, *mein liebe Kind.* His last act."

Artie moved that his final words were for *me* before walking into the fog, perhaps answers intended for me, proof of A over B, my father, family history. Cyril was devoted to history, but will no longer go on with his studies. Artie's thoughts run counter to Sylvie's love story. In a confusion of time and tenses, he thinks: *I did not go on with mathematics.*

"The body," loudly calling him to attention, "the release of the body to family," Sylvie says. "I am not."

He stands between the twin beds of his grandparents' mar-

riage, in a room he has ransacked searching for his mother and father. He listens to her sob cut off by a catch in the throat. Softly,
half spoken, he says, "You were more than family."

"*Danke schön.*"

Sylvie hangs up the phone with the amplifier on which she
has heard the boy's generous words. A complicated machine sits
next to the kitchen counter which has delivered messages this
day, updates from her dutiful stepchildren—a detailed letter from
Martha, who is mapping the earth's skewed gravitational field in
the depths of the Pacific, a note from Gerald, who is studying
Mandarin to extend mortgages to the great middle class of Chinese. She thinks it is tragic that they write of their professional
lives, so seldom of their feelings, write on their machines, seldom
call. Once in a telephone game they loved to garble words. She
was not good at let's pretend, much better at reading their story
books, yet for fifty years she pretended to herself that she would
knock at Cyril O'Connor's door and say that their marvelous tale
must resume. So it had, and for a short season she thought it no
more than a turn of the page.

Something missing, though the evening is clear, all distinction. Sylvie stands at the kitchen window. Joe Clifford hobbles the
crest of her hill, staking out the field he can't wait to plow. He
leans heavily on the rail fence—his wife is right, crazy geezer
hunched in pain, Sylvie thinks pain that is worth it, to look beyond dry stalks and frozen clots of mud to the next crop of tasseled
corn. He rests where she stood with Cyril the night the moon
went away. Time with its tricks—not that long ago fulfilling a
pledge only she had taken to heart. Something is missing as in the
party game the children played, telephone, in which a sentence
was added to and altered with each transmission until the words
were hilarious, nonsense with no ending. The meaningless messages whispered from mouth to ear could go on and on and on.

Now the farmer climbs the fence, trudging in his muddy
boots to her door. Now she must go to the bedroom, where Cyril
has neatly tucked his pajamas under his pillow. Now she must

dress in black to welcome the mourners—her library committee, garden club, bridge partners of Sylvia and Bob Waite, old friends. The tragic accident has been on the local news. Now she must go down to them and tell a story that begins with a sour belch interrupting obscenities spoken in her ear. She is twelve years old. She is twenty—*we would never have met*—in the last pew of a Catholic church, a mouse-grey coat. The hideous words break into her body never to be translated, sausage fingers devour her mouth, her head clasped to the coarse wool chest in an embrace that is almost fatherly. She is twelve—her father, unwilling to keep his mouth shut during the weeks that follow the Anschluss, has walked proudly toward the front door of the Villa, one delicate hand reaches for his son's shoulder, the other clasps a rescued book to his breast, Wittgenstein's *Tractatus*, as though going out the back door to read in the garden, though that was impossible, but Inge had told that tale to her intellectual pals in New York, not possible for she had not known the titles of her husband's most treasured books, while the boy played in the pebbled paths with the soccer ball he carries in a net, though that was not possible, it being March in Innsbruck, sharp cold unlike the day of soft flurries when the Captain with no place to go offered her a ride and having fallen in love—*I awakened you. I opened to my love*—call it love at first sight, she returned to this house, an anxious husband waiting. She is seventy-five, dressed in black, drab sweater and skirt fit for an abandoned girl who does not pray. She will speak to those who comfort her of the dry alpine *Föhn* which lifts fog, the inauspicious fog on the River Inn, which reveals nothing of the tragedy set in the Villa, why they had taken the brilliant son as well as the father, what harm to the state a boy's devotion to skiing and soccer; and nothing of the love story which opens in the imperial plaza of the United Nations softened by a powdery snow. Nothing of sorrow (there's the demon lover), chronic ailment of a girl huddled in grey fox fur, mouthing words with the raspy phonograph. *Was wollen Sie?* What do you want? *Solch ein Kummer.* What more do you want of that sorrow which

returns now but cannot diminish and she knows, even as she discovers Arthur Freeman blubbering at the foot of the stairs, that
she has lied telling him to forget, *bitte vergesst*, for she remembers
it all, yet taking that boy in her arms says, "Go on. We go on."

SALVAGE

The gold-rimmed plates and embossed wineglasses go and the
damask napkins embroidered O, O, O as though surprised when
they are brought to life from the depths of the linen closet; and the
moth-eaten afghans, the aluminum pots and pans of another time
must go; the pristine dining chairs attending the ghostly feast go.

The eerie Sacred Heart of Jesus detached from the divine *cor-
pus delicti*—"To go?"

Lou studies the bleeding heart pierced with a crown of thorns.
"To keep, a definite save."

But the tiny crystal salt shakers and the frayed bath mats go.
The shrine to Fiona in a back closet not completely dismantled in
Artie's unsuccessful search for the father—Jimmy Dean posters
and 78s, head-shop curios, the chaste uniforms of various private
schools—all those consecrated items go, along with white patent
go-go boots, rotted rubber flip-flops; clues to the mother he never
knew, up-against-the-wall Fiona, flanked by A and B. Her limited
library goes—Che, Castaneda, Marcuse, McLuhan, the *I Ching*.

"Look here!" Lou buries her nose in a silk scarf—Fiona's
musky sweat overlaid with sandalwood, a primal smell like her
mother's at the end of a day, the indelible odor of unpasteurized
barn masked by floral cologne so that Shirley would smell sweet
when the Mighty Milkman came in by the mudroom door. She
passes the cheap silk scarf, knotted to restrain his mother's brazen
hair, to Artie, who puts it in the pile to go, and then studies the
well-worn *Book of Changes*, the inscrutable pattern of I Ching
lines, hoping to capture an aura: "Gosh, there's not a chance of a
chance. *All is connected, every flip of a coin, deal of a card determined in the vast universal stream. . . .*"

"All probable." Artie getting on with the job. He must get out of this tomb with airless artifacts, the unsolved mysteries of Cyril or Mae's possessive love, their loveless marriage. "It's all probable. By chance Cyril died, the odds for fog on that hill, an old man with filmed eyes steps into the road. By chance his wild daughter dead by accident. All probable. Who the hell cares if it's A over B?" Though he stops short when a museum-shop Sphinx appears with its plaster nose lopped off.

He tells Louise of the kid who wrote in hieroglyphics, who set the Sphinx to guard Fiona's old clothes and the sacred books of her youth. "I was Thoth, a hawk or maybe an owl. My messages were destroyed by chance, not by grave robbers. I never saw her in these plaid skirts and tacky costumes." At last he understands that his mother left this tomb, lived her afterlife in the house with green shutters bought for her and her bastard boy. It was his Eden in Connecticut, his alone. Dead to the world, she sang her lovelorn ballads and crimped wet clay into unsalable pots and dressed herself as a timeless peasant in sandals and flowing sacks to disguise the beautiful body which remained uncannily rosy, ripe for the picking. Half dead to her son. Alive to the habit of sex. "She had men when she wanted them. But she was stuck with me."

The rooms that sustained the lives of Cyril and Mae O'Connor are packed up to go. The apartment on Fifth Avenue will be sold. At the door, a salvage pile: Mae's silver for twelve in a Tiffany pattern (Louise no longer fooling herself about the bourgie rewards of marriage); an ancient celadon teapot (provenance unknown); works of Franklin, Jefferson, Madison, Lincoln's letters, the discredited *Prairie Years*; blurred lithograph of a heart creepily bleeding; black tin box with titles, deeds, old tax forms, canceled checks and family papers—the certification of our lives we dare not throw away.

From New Calgary, his final resting place, a vast Catholic cemetery in Queens where he lies between his wife and daughter, Cyril pays up, rescues the dear boy. The dead man was canny: he never imagined his grandson suited up for the Market. The dead man was a throwback: he never imagined the girl, the woman, assembling whatever bits and pieces she calls art, for payday, any more than he believed his talentless daughter would sell her pots or sing her songs upon a stage. The working days of his life are unknown to those who mourn him, though they will profit from his legacy.

Money, money, money all the time!

His mother, housemaid and washer woman by profession, was not given to complaints—that short refrain, all Bridget O'Connor ever said of her meager circumstances. *Money, money, money all the time*, the apartment on Fifth Avenue will now be sold.

March 8, 1817—The Founding of the New York Stock Exchange.

Wall Street ran along a wall at the North of the city, a fortification built of stone and mud with ramparts protected by double stockades. In postcolonial days, the brokers of cotton and corn, molasses and scrip met here under a buttonwood tree. Cyril O'Connor, in what had become his avocation, the reading of history, enjoyed the origins of the Street; the buttonwood agreement of 1792, the inevitable move to Tontine's Coffee House so that business might be transacted in inclement weather; the slow but steady rise to prominence of the New York Exchange. The biography of John Jacob Astor, who parlayed seven hand-crafted flutes, his capital when he came to America, into twenty-five million, read like a fairy tale.

All such stories of the Street entertained Cyril when he first married Mae, when Frank Boyle took him into the business. In the early days of his marriage, Cyril felt he had not defaulted (in a bit of reading we will keep up our French, our philosophy) and that he might please old man Boyle with accounts of Alexander Hamilton consolidating the Revolutionary War debt by issuing bonds worth eighty million, or tales of Southern mill owners stiffing the Northern banks at the outset of the Civil War. But even the legends of Jay Gould and J. P. Morgan's successful trades failed to appeal to Mae's father, who called his son-in-law the professor. A novice on Wall Street, he had wanted to be just that, a professor of nineteenth-century history, and continued to instruct Mr. Boyle when they visited on Park Avenue or at the big shingle cottage on the North Shore: brokers still sold at the curbstone until 1850; Edison made his first real money upgrading the Battery ticker tape for Kidder, Peabody.

Frank Boyle plunked an olive into his martini: "Another day, another dollar."

Cyril had no small talk for the country-club Irish—no golf, no tennis. A scholarship boy, son of a dissolute father, he drank soda pop and continued to speak with excitement of the Panic of 1857, when a steamer went down off Cape Hatteras with eleven million dollars of California gold in its hold. The nation about to go under, General Grant came into the city. . . . Cyril lectured an inattentive audience. The men of his Wall Street of the Fifties were still licking their wounds from a more recent Black Friday. What informed them historically were the terms of last week's deal, the opening quotes of the day.

Boyle clipped the end of his cigar. Of the Market he said: "You will find it fluctuates."

Silenced, Cyril read annual reports, weekly business magazines, and survived the crisis of '57. He held his position in Lorillard, sold Xerox in the third quarter, which saved him in the Kennedy slide of '62, at which time Frank Boyle died, torn between his loyalties to hot tips on the Street and the pride of the Irish, having lost heavily in Brunswick (bowling alleys), not trusting Bobby Kennedy's deals with Bethlehem Steel. The fiscal years passed safely for his son-in-law, a man not given to speculation. It was said of O'Connor he was too much the gentleman, not one of the boys. He did not buy on margin, lived each day by the carefully considered gamble, never indulged in futures, though at the end he had a future, a life of reparation.

Close the books on his working life. It's history, over—the crash of '72, the humiliation of an undeclared war, loss of confidence in the country echoed in loss of confidence in the Market. An era which he survived as he survived the contempt of his daughter for bringing home the tainted bacon, for sheltering and feeding her love child, setting her up in a pretty shuttered house in Connecticut. When he wrote his last check for Freeman's tuition, he gave up the financial newsletters with their economic predictions as to the consumer's affluence in the telemarket of 2000 and turned at once to his bookshelves, settling into the leather chair to recoup his losses.

His life as a middleman was over. The crazed overselling of the Eighties seemed as distant to him as the trades of filler tobacco and raw cotton under the buttonwood tree. Cyril was fit to be more caricature than character in a novel, that blowsy bourgeois form in which money is ever present, lending light to happy endings, shadow to despair. He lived alone in the grand apartment, the empty rooms he called his own, but died poor, well poor for Fifth Avenue, selling off his boring high-yield assets over the years, presuming the last of his AT&T would see him to the grave, poorer than if he had followed his heart and ended a pensioned professor shuffling Civil War documents in an archival heaven.

The sun and the moon bless Shirley Moffett. Warm Winter days on Sanibel are heavenly for a woman from Wisconsin and the soft nights, reaching beyond the white shore, dipping stars into the dark ocean, are bliss. For long hours she swings in a hammock on the balcony of the time-share, baking her bones. The time-share is contractually, delightfully, not a place she can call her own. Shirl knows not one soul, though she nods to the couple who occupy the other half of the condo, folks like us who she does not see until the end of each day, when they wheel in their golf carts. In their distant, protective smiles she sees that they suspect her—a woman alone, divorced or widowed—as a possible prey. She is alone, plopped down on the tidy lawn—barefoot, in jeans—waiting for the spectacular sunset. For the first time in her life alone. A thought which startled Shirley Moffett on her first night in the time-share, when the sporty folks like us (Vermont license plate on the BMW) had not yet arrived. She was alone in a bisected building waiting for Harold's call, figuring there was no time difference — Sanibel to Cincinnati, where the world's largest cheese manufacturer consulted with her husband on the next wave of additives. Harold's old expertise with nitrates and phosphates paid for the pastel walls and rattan furniture which for two weeks are hers alone.

Alone seemed fine, she said to her husband, promising that she would change into her lemon slacks, a bit flashy in the mall at Madison, and take herself out to dinner where folks like us . . . but that first night she did not go beyond the impersonal walls. In her navy blue traveling suit, Shirley shelled peanuts left by the previous time-shares, drank down their Orvieto, the whole bottle with Sun Chips. Alone was surprisingly O.K. *Okey-dokey* came to mind as she stood on the narrow balcony and looked over the cluster of condominiums set at deceptively cozy angles to each other, all uniform grey with tasteful white trim. *Okey-dokey* was her father's expression. As the sun set, the color drained from the flower boxes and bright umbrellas and the grey condos became so like the factory half-houses in Milwaukee. Yes, much like the workers' houses which John McClure condemned to his children. When she was a kid, the McClures drove into the city once a year — Shirl stuffed in the back seat of the two-door sedan, squirming with her brothers and sister. Off the farm, farm children dazzled by the downtown traffic along Wisconsin Avenue, by the lovely hats and dresses in Shusters' big plate-glass windows. Always summer, always unbearable heat in the Chevy. They went to visit an old lady who lived alone in stifling dark rooms with sticky end-tables and tilting lamps. The McClure kids were lined up on a prickly horsehair sofa and served sour lemonade from cheese glasses, rancid cookies that crumbled into the cushions.

The old lady was so alone, yet Shirley could tell not eager to see them in her parlor, polite to her father but not in need of his company. She wore a faded wash dress and black teacher shoes, had been a teacher until. . . . The rest of the story was not told to them as children. It was the end of the Depression and the company half-house in which the woman lived was unpainted, stoop and railings rotted. Black men and white loitered in the streets. Skinny kids in rags played kick the can. "Never live on the dole," John McClure said as soon as they were stuffed back in the car. "Never live with no place to call your own, niggers in the same house — other side of the wall."

As Shirl grew older, maybe eight or ten, there was the war work and no loafers, as John McClure called them, in the scruffy neighborhood. The yearly ride to the city was more to observe the decaying half-houses, more to take heed of her father's instruction, than to visit that lady who did not particularly want them in her parlor with unraveled doilies, the sofa spilling its guts and everywhere yellowed newspapers and stacked magazines. Not the magazines her mother cherished with recipes and dress patterns and colored photos of tables with fancy food they did not eat on the farm.

"What's her name?" Shirley was the oldest and now sat up front where her father's rough hand scraped against her knee as he shifted.

"Her name is a mouthful," he said of his very own aunt born a McClure, a woman he had respected as a child, a teacher. "A fine teacher, now no school will have her."

When she learned the name it was easy, not even Milwaukee German or Polish. Italian, the teacher had married a union agitator, a man who died in a prison riot, Del'Aquilla was his name. The Italian had organized an occasion of terror called the Hunger Strike in which workers and policemen were killed.

"You never went to bed hungry on the farm," John McClure said, though that was not true.

The stern lady who lived alone had lived out of wedlock with Del'Aquilla, had only married him when he went to trial. What he was charged with Shirley never knew, but being wed his wife could not be made to testify against him. Her father had taught his children the meaning of disgrace and she had learned her lesson well, never to speak against John McClure, to shut up as they drove out of the city, back to their poverty, which was okey-dokey, almost a blessing from God their scrubbed-clean, thread-bare isolation on the farm.

Shirley Moffett finds herself alone for the first time in her life, having gone from farm family to farm family. Her two years in college came with sorority sisters, then Harold, then the kids. Her husband's fame beyond the university now leaves her in the house on her own, but there is the farm manager, his assistants, graduate students, a bookkeeper, a parking lot beside the new office, a daily maid. The rooms in the house, the original farmhouse, are peopled with beds, chairs, appliances, window treatments and seasonal coverlets that hold her hostage. Harold plans to convert the old barn, to move them into that empty space with new chestnut beams not needed for support, with the hayloft marked on a blueprint as Library, with entertainment areas and wet bars, plans to move her into this Early American artifact, as the architect terms it, to hang useless old pitchforks and scythes on the wall. Well, it was built in nineteen-ought-nine and she is no one's prize cow.

Each morning at Sanibel, Shirley Moffett hears her neighbors in the back-to-back bathrooms of the condo—his needlepoint shower, the buzz of her electric toothbrush, assigning each their own noise—his early Market report on CNN precedes her *Good Morning America*. Shirl does not wash or dress or plug in the coffeemaker until they are gone so that her noise will not counter their noise. It has been over fifty years since she has given a thought to the old lady about whom she was once so curious, Mrs. Del'Aquilla and her agitator who lived with colored people other side of the wall, a shadow on a blameless family history of Midwestern goodness and good will. But now, now as a nameless time-share woman unknown to her well-preserved neighbors, loving her own silence, Shirl wonders. She wonders what if she had trilled it like a song in the sweltering Chevy—Del'Aquilla, Del'Aquilla, Del'Aquilla, taunting her father with the lovely liquid name. . . .

Well, Shirl is only three days into wondering (a week and a half to go) and will not fulfill a reader's expectation of romance—handsome woman, once handsome, frank streak of silver in her tinted hair; transient lover appears to the faded beauty sleeping late. Shirley Moffett will experience no such poignant encounter, for she is deeply into wondering if, for instance, Del'Aquilla, as her father maintained, was a Communist. If her great-aunt read the accumulation of flaking papers and radical magazines, or if they were the man's, like Harold's farm journals.

No, Shirl believes that Mrs. Del'Aquilla read them with the agitator, an exciting thought; and that, being a fine teacher, a graduate of a state normal school, she wrote inflammatory articles in those desperate days when the factory gates were closed, when the McClures went to bed hungry on the farm, their stomachs rumbling. So much conjecture as she walks the shore searching out shells, or is suspended idly in the hammock: why her daughter, for instance, Louise, the late child who wounds her, the one she loves most, must live in a factory and continue to make her living off the manufacture of pictures that distort the farm, its barns, ponds, pastures, the very trees she once painted with care; and wonders why Beatrice Moffett no longer comes to walk her back acres and wail at the moon, now that she heads a department of oncology in Los Angeles. Does she ride the Freeway in helmet and jack boots—Harold's little sister being well over sixty? Shirley, with few details of Louise's life or Aunt Bea's, thinks of them as women alone—artist, scientist. As she is alone and happy as the day is long on this island where she avoids folks like us, where the nightly calls from Heidi with the boys' hockey scores, from Harold back at the ranch upgrading the next generation of cow/goat production, might be messages from Mars.

At the end of the first week, she hears the sporty couple arguing through the wall, the woman's gasping cries and the hushed command of the husband, "Quiet. *Quiet down,*" and wonders if the woman is sad to leave this perfect resort in the sun to return to the snows of Vermont, if it is only that which sets her off, for minutes earlier she watched them packing up their golf bags and Vuitton luggage. As though they have been the warmest of vacation friends, they wave to Shirley on her balcony, a woman they do not know—silent, self-contained in her half-house. Shirley Moffett sees them off, hail and farewell, delighted that she has a week coming to her, a week of the next time-sharers with new moans and sighs on the other side of the wall.

March 8, 1865—

Polite applause as Gregor Mendel finished reading his lecture on plant hybridization to the Natural Science Society of Brünn. He slipped the second *Pisum Paper* into a leather portfolio, a gift from his Abbott, who encouraged his scientific pursuits. Why do we prefer to see Mendel, if we see him at all, in a coarse brown robe with a cowl, puttering among his peas in the monastery garden? And savor the story of a provincial priest not recognized as a genius until many years after his death? Adulation of the little guy. If we stick to our books we may triumph like the humble monk, snipping and pruning between his spiritual duties to discover the basic stuff of our parentage in the field not yet called genetics.

The announcement of Mendel's great discovery and the Founding of the New York Stock Exchange share the day, an occurrence which you will recognize, *Devoted* Readers of Almanacs, who savor last year's advice and predictions rereading the tattered pages while the bowels ease. You will have no problem with shared occupancy under the quarter moon of Uranus, of both saints and sinners, treaties and declarations of war, heroes and demons. Almanac is about occurrence. Occurrence is all. Occurrence as information (read that backwards) allowing no hint of chaos. Between its reliable yellow covers, Almanac is system and antisystem, regulated as to the movement of the heavens, yet allowing for editorial fancy, indeed courting oddities of nature—the eighty-pound squash, birch secreting maple sap, cat with ten lives, milky spore of milkweed poisoning as it heals, swallows returning by magnetic fields to a highway underpass where their cliff of shale is no more. The stuff of legends, not so the Almanac tells us with pulpy authority: a bible for our days.

Almanac's informative correction of the pea-pod legend: Mendel—son of an indentured farmer who knew little Gregor was more than garden-variety bright. His vocation was for Natural Science. Entered the Augustinian order to complete his education. In Vienna studied physics and mathematics, including statistics with Doppler. Too frail a spirit to sustain the tribulations of parish life, he was released to his common peas. Of 28,000 plants, 12,835 were examined. Round seeds bred with angular resulted in round seeds (dominant). Second generation yielded round to angular (recessive) in a ratio of 3:1 and so forth. In a text funning up a drab subject, the *Pisum Papers* were reduced to a cartoon of Mendel in friar's garb counting fat green peas. A. Freeman disliked that dumb book which sat under a musty bong on his desk in New Haven, for he admired Gregor Mendel's innovative use of stats in his theory of heredity. As a young man, Cyril O'Connor's dominant black hair in a widow's peak was exactly like Artie's own. His grandson's unathletic body the very image of his loose-jointed limbs strung onto a long torso; big ears, the pinched bone at the bridge of the nose and eyes dark as wet peat—black Irish, bog boy, expressions of Cyril's not quite lost in Artie's heritage. Pale Mae, freckled Fiona, his unknown dad were recessive genotypes. When he walked with his grandfather in the Park, strangers smiled at the strong resemblance, peas in a pod, and Artie took pride that according to Mendel he was no freak.

The cloistered miracle man and the Stock Exchange are fit bedfellows, for the good monk of Brno had his mind on a yield from *pisum* quite apart from his genius in introducing statistical methods to science. He aimed to improve the crops of Moravia and to increase the income of the monastery. When he became abbé of Brno, he was much concerned with government taxation of church property, his administrative duties taken on so that he might afford the education of his nephews and nieces, whose mother had sacrificed her dowry to educate him as a boy. Money, money, money—though never giving up on science, he read Darwin's great work on Natural Selection while Darwin remained unenlightened about the math of heredity. Mendel went on to bees and to fruit trees, developing hybrids, much as his father had with a few cuttings. The commodities markets are more secure in the futures of corn, rye and wheat when bred for the strong kernel, yet they depend on the weather. Toward the end of his days in the abbey, Mendel observed sun spots and ozone, kept meteorological records which belittled the vulgate Almanac used by the farmers of Central Europe. He proposed weather stations, the relay of information by telegraph toward the prediction of the season's cherry harvest, a money crop in Moravia.

Which brings us round to Bud Boyce, who cannot name any but the most ordinary trees or flowers on his property, who thinks an annual returns each year of its own accord, for the geraniums by the pool and those purple ones in the Provençal urns appear like clockwork. Living in a comfort zone—72°–75°, Bud is currently obsessed with weather, what will come to pass. His wife believes the control of the Sun and the seas are beyond the clicking dick of his remote. Heather's harsh. It's the predictable bucks her husband yearns for, the yield from an unconquered segment of media.

Bud at the supermarket. One for the books. Bud with the kids and Estella (occasion to fantasy-fuck the maid while squeezing the melons). The boss wheeling the pet-food aisle, heaving sacks of kibbles, is blind to Estella's sullen smile. She is light-years from the cruel fluorescence of Price Chopper, from this slick gringo in his rustic weekend outfit. She laughs when he reaches for the *Farmer's Almanac* at the checkout, where it is displayed with miracle diets and the tabloids—primitive back-country stories, Solstice voodoo. On a recent day off, Estella has attended a lecture on the influence of the Mayan calendar on postcolonial agribusiness. Shocking, even tragic: major corporations in Mexico and Brazil as well as international banks now employ astrologers, believing their predictions to be as sound as economic indicators.

"*Ficciones!*" Estella laughs as Señor Boyce puts out for the *Almanac*.

The boss fumbles for his smart card, drops his Swiss knife out of his fisherman's pocket. In the past week Estella has been ordered to bring Mr. Boyce a second cup of coffee in his dark study. Loosening the belt of his plaid robe, he looks from the Winter storms sliding across the continent to the ravine of her crotch, to her breasts as though they are the snow-capped Rockies. She need not fear, will be glad of his romance with the little golden book published every year since 1792 with its sketches of the seasons on the cover. Mr. B. will become devoted to checking the upbeat page of the Almanac against the screen's tropical depression. He will not look up at the woman who serves him. Despite the heraldic crest on his pocket, she will think he is like a village priest in a dusty soutane, mumbling his breviary, the daily sop to the deaf god of poverty and ignorance.

"*Gracias.*" The boss paying no mind to Estella or his coffee.

"*De nada.*"

On a clear blue day, Estella lets the kids take off their Winter jackets before she races them to the Volvo. She would like to tell that poor excuse for a father and husband to look out the window of his bogus *biblioteca*, see his wife, pleased for a moment, bending to a green shoot. But the chief executive of Skylark orbits without direct observation, dresses for sleet and freezing rain, trusting the *Almanac* above the U.S. Weather Bureau. Unlike Franklin, Mendel, Edison, Bell, who were well acquainted with failure, Bud is certain he will profit by his morning affair, the little thing he has going with the weather.

LET NOT YOUR HEARTS TOO SOON REJOICE

Arthur Freeman has inherited. He has not totally forgotten the great novels assigned in prep school and college in which money is not salvation—the hero duped by expectations or the heroine reduced to folly by her legacy—and so believes that in seeking work he is saved from his mother's thankless dependence.

"Why Wall Street?" Lou says, "There's Skylark."

"You're kidding."

Surely kidding, but Artie was such a darling in his short-sleeve shirts with the pocket protectors, the saggy socks and run-down sneakers. He may never fill his grandfather's brogans and why should he? Since his return, he is only mildly entertaining and Lou likes to think that he's mourning the old man, not the loss of his lightness. The prodigal returned, but there is no father to welcome him and she proposes, only to herself, a place far from Wall Street with ponds and trees, shutters, barns, the honk of a yellow school bus at the end of the driveway, sets Artie in an upstairs bedroom interfacing with the world, a player once again in the digital culture, but can't imagine herself without the wonderful confinements of this city. They find little to say to each other as they go about their separate adventures. It is less than two weeks to her show conceived in sorrow, born out of loneliness. The slick surface of her red roses, the sparkle of immaterial crystal and silver look Kodachrome shallow—out of this time and place, referencing references, endless appropriations, quoting what others have said with no substance of her own, yet she's in and out of the loft to the glazier, the welder, the photography studio, bent on the project she must believe in. Lettering a sign LO when Artie leaves in the morning, LOVE complete when he returns at the end of the day's rejection. Love in bloom? Love is blind? She will not say.

The Street: awash in techies, kids who speak a computerese of constant obsolescence. Artie has not kept up with the chipster trades. POW! The joy stick misses the scaly old demon as in an arcade game played with Bud years ago. He is unfit for combat. The great firms of Wall Street possess software with answers to questions as yet unposed. Thousands of children generate cows, brindled or black Angus; run the numbers, diddle the demographics to form suitable pillars of profit and loss. As he seeks his fortune on Wall Street, Artie's loss of faith is a match for Lou's. Heavy cloud cover in the loft as they go off about their business. Let not your heart too soon rejoice, when they speak they say little. Their silence is civil.

THE IDES

A gentle warning, the single word of an actor in a minor role. *Beware.* Sylvia Neisswonger cancels her trip to Austria. She will not go alone, has never felt so alone, not when abandoned by Inge, not as translator in a sterile studio apartment, not alone on the hill after Bob Waite's death. Beware—the worst has happened again, though this time loss of her lover is merely personal, yet she feels it as keenly as the extinction of her father and brother at Mauthausen, the camp on the Danube of Viennese song. *"Ich bin geworden,"* she murmurs. "Soft, I have softened." These years in America, lost track of that war and her husband's heroic flights over the burning city of Dresden and Captain O'Connor's retreat in a bloody unresolved conflict. This last death is divorced from worldly event and it seems to Sylvie that her story may have begun this New Year's Day in a wild storm, a youthful dream about to transpire, long, too long delayed, and that she has turned from her own history as one curtains a dark scene, turns to the soft lamplight like Inge veiled, hat atilt in the cosmeticized present. No, she must remember it all—she is twenty, not hearing the words of the Latin Mass, she is thirty, her stepchildren inflating a beach ball while the waves lap at her feet, splash the canvas of her chair, the tide rising to engulf her; reading her British murder mystery in Boca Raton, she is about to become a widow of sixty. *"Geworden und alt."* Yes, she is the old woman in nightgown and slippers, throwing herself on her lover's body, kissing the last warmth of his spittle, old fool, and the state trooper kindly places his jacket over her bare shoulders, over her shame. But she is soft now, perhaps too old to remember it all, and what is there to fear but the empty day?

·   ·   ·

Doomsday for Shirley Moffett, packing to go home while, in New York, Louise steals out of bed, where Artie dreams a twitchy wake-up dream of his résumé written in invisible ink. In chalky morning light, the days lengthening at last, Louise answers the phone. The second week of the time-share has been heavenly, Shirley proclaiming it pure bliss, which is not exactly what she means. She does not have the heart to tell her daughter of her discovery, that it is pleasurable alone. And though she loved farm and family once, it seems once upon a time, so her call, her one call out from the impersonal pastel haven, is to Louise, who detects not bliss, but hysteria in her mother's nattering on.

"The second week *not* folks like us, not at all. Dilly and Moe know *exactly* the block you live on in the city with the Tong and the Mafia clam house. Folks who write letters to *stop* the nitrates and phosphates contaminating our food and could not abide your father, poor man, he's not here. Not here, thank God, no time to waste with the sand and the sea, Hal has no time for the time-share and believe me not a moment to waste on folks like Dilly and Moe."

"Mom?"

"Dilly was *detained* in '69. Moe split for Canada."

"Daddy's war?"

"Exactly."

Louise peevish: "Mom, I had to read about the quartermaster in *The New York Times*.

"Exactly. We never spoke of Nam. Nam. Nam, I was alone with two cows, a new baby and a barn full of cats. Forget that picture in the *Times*. Hal sat at a desk in Washington, believe me."

"I do."

Shirley up at farmers' hours on her island, her time sadly at an end. Lou believes her mother's complaints, though the postcard words, *heavenly* and *bliss*, do not reflect Shirley's agitation. She believes that Dilly and Moe know shit-all of disorganized crime on lower Broadway. She believes about the people on the other

side of the wall, folks like and unlike us, the latter story incorporating a poor woman in Milwaukee who married into a Commie
slum, a courageous woman alone who served stale cookies and
warm lemonade in the Great Depression, her couch sprouting
"coarse pubic hair."

"Mom?"

She believes that her mother in Sanibel has missed choir
practice for the Easter service at First Methodist, but sang the
"Hallelujah Chorus" on the balcony, her soprano to Dilly's alto,
the woman through the wall detained briefly in the war, "bravely
imprisoned while Harold Moffett shipped what order of untested
crap. . . ."

"Mom?"

"Crap with what lethal preservatives, that did not preserve
diddly-squat in the jungle." This radical alto and Shirley going it
a capella during the gold-to-purple sunset, though Moe and Dilly
were atheists from Brooklyn, which did not diminish their appreciation of Handel. Moe says screw the hallelujahs—art is art.

"Mom. Mom?" Louise looks down the length of the loft.
Yesterday, the hearts, roses, wedding signifiers of her manufacture
were shipped off to the back rooms of the gallery to await installation. Now her cleared space, call it home with Artie, seems cluttered with her mother's anger and elation. The words assaulting
her have no place in her mother's mouth, a woman who does not
belong with a godless couple from Brooklyn.

"Your father was one good looker, the body of a god." Louise
does not believe that, but believes that he was taken from his desk
in the Pentagon, costumed in combat gear and photographed for a
patriotic promo pushing chemical foodstuffs, and that home on
leave he begat . . . To her daughter, Shirley Moffett sounds like
one of those shrill women on a talk show, unburdening themselves
of a lifetime of injustice. And Harold begat Louise out of Shirley
while on leave, abandoning the farm and the university for the patriotic service he was exempt from, having the cats, cows, etc., two

kids and a breeding wife. What is there not to believe in? Shirl's history of blood relatives who lived in prehistoric condominiums? Commies, perfectly happy to have "niggers through the wall."

"Mom! You want me to come down there?"

"Certainly not. My time is up." The hard edge to Shirley Moffett's voice softens. "It's been heaven," she says dreamily to her daughter, "pure *bliss.*"

By a cast-iron radiator in the loft, the salvage from the Fifth Avenue apartment: pale green teapot, works of the Founding Fathers, fetishistic Heart of Jesus and the black tin strongbox with family papers look to Louise like props for improvisational theater. They beg reinvention. After her mother's mad call, she is drawn to these objects—the weight of family stuff. Poor Shirley, even, she thinks, poor Harold, their marriage blown by the time-share. She has always considered their alliance a perfect conspiracy. Hardly the moment to say—Guess what? I am going to marry. And what has she to celebrate of the heart's expectations that her mother has not trashed? How can she have it both ways when her time is almost up? In less than a week she will be judged by her show, the show which mocks the commodities of marriage, though she has stashed the O'Connor silver in her kitchen drawer, though she wears Mae's diamond and is so hopelessly in love with Freeman that he seems to her a handsome man.

Lou opens the black tin box with a faint gold line by way of decoration. Artie finds her leafing through his family documents seen often enough in the search for Mom and Dad: the immigration papers of Bridget Malone, the dishonorable discharge—no surprise—of Matthew O'Connor from the New York City Police Force for conduct unbecoming, a survey of the Boyles' estate on Long Island lost in the market of '62, canceled checks which spill from a dry rubber band. His own birth certificate with a tiny footprint no bigger than his thumb: Boy O'Connor—before Fiona saddled him with the name of her Camelot king, pagan and cuckold.

Lou says with a vengeance, "My mother called."

"Old Shirl?"

"She's losing her mind." A swift kick at the black box: "What's all this old stuff? A burden." Though she carries the ancient Korean teapot out of harm's way. "Old Shirl no longer loves the Big Cheese." Her last word.

Her fury recalls Artie's eviction, which preceded the long silence marking their season of disagreement. When she marches off to wherever she goes these days, he takes possession of a shelf for his inherited words-in-a-row — Franklin, Jefferson, and so forth, their faded bindings shamed by Lou's glossy art books. He closes the black box. All that is current has been handed to Cyril's lawyer. A definite burden the heart tug of his tiny foot, his great-grandfather's disgrace. Gains and losses. He sweeps up the scattered checks. His hand hovers above the wastebasket. Now, that is strange, all signed by Mae O'Connor in '68, '69. Artie, shuffling his grandmother's canceled checks, notes that they are made out in her obedient hand to the same two names again and again — one a Rev. Russo; the other Murphy, S.J.

He thinks A. He thinks B.

Quick with possibilities: His mother in her hipsters was flanked by men of the cloth. A priest begat a bastard. The checks end six months before his birth. The end of Mae's charity or patience?

Trail's end: the detective remaps the plot so that the dim reader who has not picked up on the clues . . . The daughter, given her coming of age in the late revolutionary era, given the mother's piety, the father's disbelief, given the stale air which a girl of spirit could not breathe watching a man and woman cheerlessly assume their burden, knowing that she was their last hope, that she must pay off. Given the collusion of Wall Street and Washington, greed and arrogance of a country, not hers if she could help it, fighting a bloody imperialist war, you see the simple marriage of personal and public outrage in Fiona O'Connor's aberrant behavior. She was showing, the child a thickening at her waist. Mae O'Connor had gone down to the abandoned school where her daughter lived with the chosen people dedicated to living better than she had lived, as though they could start from scratch, take a man, a woman, a bean, love and a daisy. The daughter in full bloom, adept at inflammatory sloganeering though she had read almost nothing of Trotsky, of Marx before removing herself from college to the red brick school, giving up academic blab for action, term papers for broadsides "Mao Now," "Christ was a Communist."

Her son is left with canceled checks, figuring one priest or another. Fiona, bent on breaking the rules, fucked the good father. He has nothing on Russo or Murphy, searches the loft for the photo, but it has disappeared in the exodus of hearts and flowers packed off to Lou's show. It will not be needed to prove that the girl with the superior smile created a scandal, that he was an injury from the day he was conceived.

As a kid he had lied: *My father? Commander of the Goodyear blimp. My dad brought dust back from the moon.* Before settling on dead. He is dead. And now damns mother and daughter resting in New Calgary with their shocking little secret. Cyril, too, though he had no use for Mae's priests and prayers. Fiona's silence transforms her into a dutiful daughter, hiding her shame. She took the conventional U-turn—rebellion to conformity. Artie knots his grandfather's narrow tie, dresses for the hunt, but he does not, this day or in the days which follow, sit at the computer to begin the endgame, the search for A (celibate), or B (his priestly dad). The dread day has come and he stalls.

"Found Art." Lou props the heart of Jesus against the gallery wall. Dealer mutters unconvincingly of his confidence in her work, his belief in the installation of Moffett's hearts and flowers, nuptial produce, the carnival chance of it all, her amusing blue Tiffany boxes—the jest of a Warhol rip-off.

"I think no," he says of the glutinous heart stuck with thorns.

"I think yes."

"May I think of my reputation?"

"It's a concept. You're getting," Lou says, "one-tenth of the concept."

He wears a French farmer's smock of coarse hopsack. As they spar before the morning cappuccino, a witch's ring of welts crawls round Dealer's throat. This woman is strangling him. He would like to throw her trinkets out of his gallery, ship the bitch back to her lover, an unattractive man she's fallen for again, *fallen* the operative word, but he's put his money down.

Louise deflates the foam on her coffee. Her mother bad-mouthing her father. Shirl carrying on because she must part from virtual strangers in some retirement ghetto. Her own sharp and insufficient words to Artie, the world has shifted on its axis and it's less than a week to her show. And by God, she will show them. She got on the bus to show them, but for now she must duke it out with Dealer. Clutching Mae O'Connor's livid heart of Jesus to her breast as though that kitsch under glass will restore her, she speaks of the earthy and mystical heart, the sacred and profane, thorns and arrows, the iconography of saints, and hears her Aunt Bea's voice, the woman of science: DON'T YOU BELIEVE IT.

AVOIDANCE DISORDER

The ides (from *idus*, to divide) occurred on the 15th of May, July, October as well as March. In all other months they occurred on the 13th until Julius Caesar set the year by the sun. Artie knew that stuff when he was a kid, even the dopey way the Romans named the dates—three days before the ides, two days after, ten before the calends, which were the first days of each month. After he had been denied his Egyptians, he began to reckon each day as pre- and post-Fiona. Days after her holiday in the Caribbean mounted to months and years, until the accounting became as unmanageable as days once counted by the French and the Russians from the beginning of time, the date of their revolutions.

Now that the date will come up on his screen in his search for a Murphy, a Russo—he lets the days flip by. He wanders the financial district, not turning up for an interview, his one humiliating nibble to word-process for a client of Skylark. *Beware!* He says nothing to Louise of his unfound fathers. She says nothing to Artie of her enterprise when she returns past midnight, drained by her mysterious tasks. On the morning of the 18th she is at the door before he's hitched into his suspenders.

"Where to?"

"The library," she says.

He turns to the boxed-in datasphere, a third party in her/their loft, and offers himself for whatever it's worth—his talent in the information line.

"It's my show."

Beware! Their clipped exchanges are more ominous than their season of crossed wires, their squabbles serial, the conventions of sit-com; in each script Miss Moffett declaring her artistic independence to the sweet zhlub, Freeman, who aims to become a slave of the system. How many days since they have shared the Jacuzzi? How many nights have they slept side by side as though alone? What is it Louise must know, so arcane it must come from the tomb? What is it Freeman does not want to know, wandering the streets of lower Manhattan? Whether the answer proves to be A or B, he will no longer be the self-romanticizing bastard, the foundling from Planet X.

He ducks into Trinity Church out of a sputtering rain. Businessmen and -women come for the noon service to pray, he imagines, for bonds to hold, a rise in housing starts or the GNP; his grandfather's lingo, though Cyril never spoke of the Street itself, the stately old buildings or junk stores with bins of discontinued items—mouthwash, calculators, spongy sweaters of uncertain dye, or of the imperial underground mall—weatherless, seasonless—the World Trade Center, which shelters Artie from the cold. This, too, was his grandfather's world. He should have said you selfish old man not telling me where you went each day,

Artie figuring his should-have-said-to-Cyril was more than useless, death deleting all possibility. The high-pitched cry of the gulls mixing with the whoops of children playing in Battery Park on an almost Spring day seems to Freeman pressing news of his grandfather, not an avoidance of A or B. He tours the Old Customs House, trailing a pack of schoolchildren who believe that 140 tons of glass and metal in the skylight of the Beaux Arts building is data downloaded from an alien world, who giggle at naked statuary in which Christianity triumphs over man and beast, who listen to the guide's memorized spiel—*the shipping of Manhattan north and west, and the heights of Brooklyn to the south and east, that a hundred years hence, or ever so many hundred years hence,* others will see them as Artie Freeman now believes his grandfather saw and enjoyed the Winter dusk turn gold at the end of his working day, *of the sunset, the pouring-in of the flood-tide, the falling back to sea of the ebb-tide.* Whitman's exuberant lines losing the rowdy kids completely, while Artie mourns the departure of Cyril, who never told of this phantasmagoric landscape that was his unacknowledged city, his home.

March 19—Edgar Rice Burroughs, born Chicago, 1875.

Wrote for the pulps, *Tarzan of the Apes,* and *John Carter of Mars.* J.C. was an earthling, a fighting man by profession, always at war with science:

> I believed that Mars was habitable and uninhabited; then a newer and more reputable school of scientists convinced me that it was neither. Without losing hope, I was yet forced to believe them until I came to Mars to live. . . .
>
> I hate to do this to my long-suffering scientific friends; but if they would only consult me first rather than dogmatically postulating theories which do not meet with popular acclaim, they would save themselves much embarrassment.

John Carter triumphs over evil. The world in a haunted house— slithery arms, bulbous head, taped groans and maniacal laughter.

When I recognized that the effects of the genre, the wing flap of a thousand giant bats, the trickle of sticky blood in the cave, the hot white sting of the ray gun, held neither fear nor magic, I gave up the serial adventures of John Carter, knowing how it all comes out. They were books long outgrown by my brother, boy stuff discarded by the boy who was allowed with supervision to drive the car. Reading Burroughs was sort of sneaky like looking through his dresser drawers for cigs, fingering the hard rim of a condom in its tight packet. So I'd had it with sci-fi, with the incomparable princess wandering the war zone of lesser Helium in spikes and C-cup bra, with J.C. sucked under in the Lost Sea of Korus, which lies in the Valley of Dor, not to mention the flat-and-fancy way the stories were told, for I had discovered sentences, whole paragraphs in my English Reader *(Twain, Hawthorne and Cather, not one of them English) which I knew to be grand,* la vrai chose, *even when I did not understand the jokes, the parables, the writers' passion for words or their passions. So I chucked Burroughs until one day in the library, a warm day at the end of Winter and I'd been home for a week with the flu watching reruns and reading excerpts in* The English Reader. *The day being fine, I was allowed the branch library, a short walk from home. I grazed the shelves looking for Cather and there was Burroughs in a black binding:* She puts on a record, metallic cocaine beebop. She greases the dingus . . . shoves the boy's legs over his head. . . .

It didn't take me long to figure the wrong Burroughs, but choice stuff, WOW. This is a yen of the brain alone, a need without feeling and without body, earthbound ghost need, rancid ectoplasm swept out by an old junky coughing and spitting into the sick morning. . . .

Miss Stangle looked at me over her glasses, actually said, "Tut-tut!" with the puckered smile. I tut-tut years later telling how I approached her desk boldly to check out Burroughs, screw Willa Cather and the Slovak settlers of the Great Plains, and was denied, for my library card was that of a child, a pale infantile blue.

Though I have found the original Burroughs. A tag sale. I

am with my brother and his kids, adolescent girl and boy. The boy, a quiet shuffling athlete, the girl a bit of a princess who has turned the corner to gorgeous and knows it. A true believer, I had wanted to stop at this house spilling forth junk; always hopeful that under the broken plastic toys strewn on wobbly tables, behind the fake Wedgwood vase, perhaps concealed by the driftwood lamp or the humidor inlaid with a ship's barometer—I will find treasure.

My brother is actively bored, his kids disgusted by the costume jewelry of a lost age, huge chunks of green and blue glass affixed to Chanel chains, fake Barbara Bush pearls, crystals dangling on leather thongs, but they are patient with me since the divorce, accommodating to my whims when I visit—now that the worst is over—the tears, the accusations. The woman who is dumping this trash stands with a cash box cradled in her arms. Once pretty in a bookish way, her salt-and-pepper hair drawn back, severe. Tortoiserim glasses enlarge her inquisitive eyes, looking, with what I take to be a wry smile, at each purchase of her belongings. Why do you want these things, things I want out of my life? The card table with the useless wedding presents of silver plate, the carefully ironed cocktail napkins with embroidered cock crowing, glasses for Irish coffee still in the tourist-shop box—like mine exactly, though I have not had the heart to give them up. She is dealing, making change for golf shoes that belonged to her husband. Resolute, ringless. I check that out. Divorced, widowed, moving on.

My niece has found a white cardigan sweater, pearl buttons, Peter Pan collar—fashionable when I was her age, and of course, she may have it. Then there are the woman's books—Twain, Hawthorne, Cather early and late, all of V. Woolf, Whitman's Leaves of Grass in facsimile edition. They are my books exactly, books I have not looked at in ages, but will carry on my back if I must when I move on. I turn to pay up for nostalgia time, that white sweater. The woman has been watching me fondle her books. Somewhat affronted, I stumble over years of the National Geographic, the familiar yellow covers tumbling, exposing, in the slick pasteboard cover that I remember, John Carter of Mars, *which I buy for ten cents. Eyes meet through our tortoiseshell glasses and she seems the wiser woman, the seller of pulp fiction, not the buyer, as well as the seller of all those good books.*

Despite the heat, my niece puts on the white wool sweater, which recaptures an air of innocence she lost early in childhood. In the car, my nephew tunes in a Yankee game as my brother drives me home, returns me to the empty house that my husband has left not so long ago, left me to the forlorn rooms of my children, whom he has taken off for the weekend on some unbeatable adventure. I switch on the lights in the dining room and kitchen as though with wattage I can people the tables and chairs as though the house will never empty of my addiction to the happy ending. Though I once laughed at the games of sci-fi and laugh still at the dime novel in my hand in which character is drained by action breeding plotful, plotless action, in which there is no darkness unless you credit the shadow at the end of John Carter. *I set the book by my bed unread. Then in the sleepless waiting I read every miserable word. As I listen to hear the soft grumble of tires on driveway gravel, shadows cast by the moons of Mars roll and tumble in an ever changing fantasy . . . as I wait, listen, and wait, two pasteboard lovers appear on the royal balcony. Oh, it is the earthling and the Princess of Dor who turn to each other in shadow and slowly predictably merge, merge into one as I listen, wait and listen for the rusty cry of screen door.*

And on this day—Louise Moffett wears the violet rayon dress fabricated in India, prim as though designed for a tea party in the last days of the Raj, or for church—listening for her mother's faint soprano lost in the hearty choir of First Methodist. She has worn the dress with its subdued pattern of white flowers just once, when a man she hoped to meet was buried in New Calvary, a wet day and the heels of her pretty shoes sank into the ground where the bright green Astroturf failed to cover the hump of dirt from his ex-cavated grave. Only now does she wipe off her shoes, the dried mud pale and sandy—poor soil, she thinks, the farmer's daughter.

Poor clay, thinks the artist, Moffett. She is alone in the loft. Artie went off in the blue suit, bravely swinging the briefcase, and in a sympathetic mood she slipped into the sensible dress, which is entirely inappropriate for mucking about with her crew at the gallery. The dress was meant to display her as presentable, so it is yet another costume, though in no way extravagant like the blue cocktail dress which she threw in the gutter on Broadway. Lou feels that they are both strange in their clothes, though not estranged, not yet. Their silence has settled in and they are almost comfortable with their secrets, like an old married couple pursuing separate lives. Thinking she has failed at love, Lou shucks this plain dress-up for that of a haggard woman in overalls who wants no one and everyone to know who she is, not even as Artie first knew her—the Prairie Princess with *Postcards*. Her show is day after tomorrow and suppose she takes a pratfall, fails for Artie and the world to see.

March 20, 1727—Sir Isaac Newton died after suffering the excruciating complaint of stone.

He was, by his own account, an idle boy who came to realize his powers when he was teased by a fellow student, then fought and won the day. How fisticuffs led to his early joy in mathematics remains a great mystery, though we suppose the confidence of the fatherless boy was transferred from the physical to the mental plane, or more properly that they were brought into an excellent union to the great profit of mankind.

Dark room, pinhole of light at the window, Newton's prism captures the colors of the spectrum. A Lord of Limit, training dark and light, he devises the calculus to measure the fundamentals of limits and change, but it's the apple we wait for, for the second-most-famous apple to fall. After the fall there was gravity explicit, the planets swinging in their clockwork ellipses, the movements of the stars and the tides in this universe made certain.

On A. Freeman's bulletin board in New Haven next to Madonna in her prime and a VR pizza, Newton in breeches and periwig thought deeply under the apple tree (a tree invented by Voltaire), its slivers preserved and sold like pieces of the True Cross. Sir Isaac, having secured us in the world—are we not in it?—cared deeply about the Cross, about proof of the Deity, and wrote many theological tracts—suppressing as impolitic the paper in which he disproved the Trinity, for he was a fellow of Trinity. Let Beatrice Moffett proclaim it in the Milky Way, DON'T YOU BE-LIEVE IT, to the simpleminded theologian who seduced her lover, but it is true about Sir Isaac's other worldliness, and though Dr. Moffett knows her physics, working with blood in the world of fluid boundaries, a science of questionable calculus and uncertainties where life blossoms or dies, she cares nothing for Isaac Newton's bio, that 40% of his work was devoted to astrology, to tales and predictions drifting at God knows what speed down from the stars. And like the rest of us, Aunt Bea believes in our Newtonian universe: if we slip, we fall.

March 20—The Vernal Equinox.

Equal allotment of night and day. Never touching, they lie next to each other, a quilt which old Shirl stitched drawn up to their chins. Louise twists her ring, a small movement under the covers. This is the day of her merciless exposure, her show. They are both awake at the first light and she wants to say that she is sorry for her silence, though not sorry for her work. She wants to say that she's glad of her mother's complaints from the happy island, that she was a fool not to know—what child wants to know the knots in the cord of marriage?—but speaks instead of the time when she packed up one knapsack and left the farm, a story never told to Artie, how she dumped the handsome hunk she was to wed, telling this to the high ceiling, to the shaft of light that now travels the white walls, telling Artie for the first time, if he cares to listen, how she had walked down the long drive leading to the State Road to board the bus. She had turned once and saw her mother in night clothes, arms whirring in the morning mist. June, the mornings still cold in Wisconsin. Now, with Shirl's troubling confession, she thinks her mother was waving her off, wishing her well. On the bus she had watched carefully as the house, the barns, the silos and pastures grew distant, and when they were seen no more she was sick, retching up bile from an empty stomach. The bus driver stopped. He looked at his watch. They were no more than a few miles from her father's farm. "You want me to take you back?"

"No. I said no. My eyes watery and the trembles, the way it is after you vomit. A woman my mother knew, First Methodist or one of her clubs, cleaned me up, a woman I remembered who had a bunch of small snotty kids."

"So?"

"So I stayed on the bus. Now I have nowhere to go."

Which does not warm Artie's heart. Equal time: it seems a retaliation when he drops his silence to tell her he has turned up the bogeymen, A and B, has known for some days of his Fathers—far out, farther than moondust, dirigible, any imagined occupation—Fathers Russo and Murphy.

"Priests!" The girl raised vaguely Protestant, the New Yorker who's seen it all, sits up in bed.

"Priests, and easy enough to access their sacred files—diocesan and Jesuitical. I feel like a spook, like I've maybe sinned, that the simple facts are not ... not secular." Priests. They hold each other, babes in the woods, and he tells the little he knows, all that he has avoided.

Russo, whom he designates A, left the priesthood in the early Seventies, when Boy O'Connor was a baby. His current residence, eerie, is in Connecticut not far from the magic white house with green shutters where Fiona strummed mournful ballads, where Artie watched at her bedroom door as she dressed to go out with her men; and not far from the country road where, in a second white house with faded green shutters, his grandfather found contentment, before he fumbled like Mr. Magoo into a fog, though Magoo in cartoon fashion tripped laughing and grousing into the next adventure. He thinks of this Russo, a writer of best-selling bandaids, therapeutic trash, who lives within spitting distance of the day school Artie attended, that Russo may have stopped to watch a soccer game, caught sight of an abstracted little boy who missed an easy punt, before driving on to the comforts of home and a wife not Fiona.

Murphy is B, still in orders, sent to a foreign land on some missionary mission, for some years now back in the city. He lives in a community on the way to the Boyce brownstone where Artie and Bud played with a big old pre-DOS computer, their first hookup, on which they spun baby algorithms or wrote a serial involving Gatorade with the properties of uranium and a punk princess to be saved from intergalactic danger. He had run to Bud's house by the rectory where the priests lived, by their school where B teaches, wondering why Mae did not send him to the priests to be educated, scooting by the stern statue of Ignatius Loyola, to issue the further heroics of Slive (acronym for *Elvis*), who must defend the glowing isotonic drink from Nazi thieves. Twelve, thirteen would be his age, a route he took daily on vacations. The Catholic kids in uniform did not share his holidays and he pushed his way through them, a priest at the door unable to monitor the end-of-day elation. Murphy may have seen him. Loyola, his grandfather's school, then why had they not sent him . . . because some blessed son of a bitch would be reminded every day that he had broken his vows. Of course by that time, the time of Slive, he had declared his father dead.

On the morning of the 20th, Artie pours out these miserable bones of a story, then quickly reverts to his silly old self, attempting to set an egg on end, but the egg rolls down the table gently, nudging the celadon teapot. The laws of gravity have not altered for the Equinox, for the trick of a balanced egg, but he's made Lou laugh, not forgetting that this is her day.

She does not forget Russo or Murphy: "You should attend to your business. When—?"

"That's the question, isn't it?"

"Answer the question with a question. Oh, Artie."

"Be serious?"

Lou buckles herself into paint-stained overalls: "Perhaps he will be just ordinary, this father."

Dodging the subject: "The show's hung. Why the work clothes?"

Silence and a cool kiss goodbye, like she's about to hop that bus that will take her from him.

"No preview?"

"Come when it opens, come when the crowd comes."

She's out the door.

"I'm one of the crowd?" he calls.

"Mind your business."

It's the fast talk that once engaged them, the system that broke down. What should he have said to Louise? Let's crawl back under the covers and tell each other stories till we are scared to death.

Now they mind their business. The day is timed as in a scavenger hunt, Artie and Lou in pursuit of separate prizes. Diving into the uptown subway he thinks of her nerve, the girl on the Badger bus who would not turn back to the farm; Lou is haunted by the hurt of the boy who thought his father better dead. She enters the gallery, where Dealer is knee-deep in hearts and flowers, mounting her show which may prove the whole sick bus ride out of Wisconsin a disaster.

THE NUMBERS GAME

Father stands at the door of his classroom. If you looked over Mae O'Connor's shoulder, he would be the man on the left; or, from the perspective of the brick wall, the gaunt fellow in Buddhist saffron who looked straight at the nervous woman fussing with her lens, smiling gently as he smiles now. He wears topsiders, corduroys, a sweater buttoned precisely over a black dickey, the turned-around collar of a cleric.

Father.

High school kids offer their papers to him with groans and sighs, a quiz in precalculus. By a bulletin board in the hall, a man, neither faculty nor student, examines a picture of the French Club in Montreal, the Debate Society with trophy, yearbook deadlines. Father has a comforting word for those students who have given the test their all and go on their way. He is a man of sixty—no, when turned to the young man in the corridor, older than sixty—pure white hair cropped close as it was the day he entered the novitiate, shorn for the military obedience to the Society of Jesus. Once a conventionally handsome man, his even, unremarkable features are blurred by a haze of fine wrinkles, the ruin of flesh that has been long in the sun. His soft grey eyes weary, he takes a step toward the visitor, perhaps an alumnus of Loyola, who loiters at the bulletin board reading timeless notices of basketball practice, the senior prom.

May I be of any help?

The man is stunned, hefts his briefcase as though to produce his credentials, then looks to the classroom beyond. They are not alone. One last girl hunches over the test.

If you'll pardon me. Father abandons the visitor to stand patiently by his desk. He is not as tall as the man who waits in the corridor. In a lineup with Fiona O'Connor and Gene Russo, he was the tallest of three figures. He wore an orange-yellow tunic that hung loose over gauzy material of orange-yellow pants. And sandals, he wore sturdy sandals when at Anima Mundi, the Project for Peace in our day. Wearing the color of another priesthood sympathetically, never denying his faith, yet he was something of an undercover man, or, as his provincial put it smoothly, on loan from the order, tending to a commune of Catholics who might stray. With them he read the sutras from one of the abridged versions of the Noble Truths which circulated in the bookshops of the East Village and which he considered harmless as beans, common as salt. *Just as the great ocean has one taste, the taste of salt, so has this doctrine and discipline one flavor, the flavor of emancipation.* Freedom from the Wrong Path, which could be cleverly construed as kin to Christian. He had been sent on this mission because he was known to be clever, though not a Doctor of Theology, that would come later. He would be sent to the Gregorian University in Rome. As though in preparation, he was to go among these militants for peace who presumed to start society from scratch, or from the simple formula: take a man, a woman, a bean, a grain of rice, love and a daisy. *The Society shall adapt itself to the times and not the times to the Society.*

The student's pencil rolls to the floor. She's stalling. Father picks it up, lays it beside her idle hand. She is sallow, stringy, not pretty, not smart. Determined and deluded, she will repeat the class next year and not get it. She wipes tears into the sleeve of her grey flannel blazer.

Vera, the test is over. It's time, well over time.

Father? Please.

He erases an equation left from his class. He is a teacher of math in holy orders. With a grain of salt he wore an Asian tunic and fell in love with a girl. He took money from her mother, a wealthy woman thrilled by Anima Mundi, the spirit with which they all ate and prayed and sang, her daughter among them. He took the woman's money and her girl. In Salvador, where he was sent out of harm's way—the discipline swift and discreet—he wore a black soutane to teach children English and math. Later, he asked to wear the loose clothes and sandals of the peasants to teach in the villages which lay in the region of Aguilares. Then he grew his hair long like the rural priests and drove from village to village in a rusted-out Ford with books and pencils. Pencils and penicillin marked him as a subversive, as a Communist for teaching two plus two. He sat in a dusty yard counting out coffee beans with children who could not add or subtract for want of food. He had thought to be a Doctor of Theology, to study the great

writings of the East, not as they had been scanned with the absence of ultimate seriousness by the inmates of Anima Mundi, but
to read closely of the soul as discussed in the conversations of the
Greek King Menander with Nagasena, the Buddhist teacher. He
had thought lecture halls, seminar rooms would be the scene of
his scholastic calling as a student, then as a teacher.

Now then, Vera, the geometry folks will be coming in soon.
Folks, always a soppy word slips from his mouth to soften.

Father. Father.

He is no one's father, has little authority parental or parochial.
He knows they call him Murph, Joe the Murph, Padre—for he
speaks to the Hispanic students in fluent Spanish. He was in the
territory of Aguilares in '77, during the siege. Strip-searched,
blindfolded, he heard the shouts of the peasants who had foolishly
made demands, who were called pigs in official communiqués,
men and women being tortured. He heard the planes, but could
not see the helicopters of a full-fledged military operation. For a
short time after the terror, he drank the cheap corn liquor which
the Indians distilled with human bones. Between ragtag classes he
would find the bottle tucked in with the pencils, penicillin and
his breviary and sip at the scalding stuff, just enough he believed
to take the edge off, to believe he was blessing miserable lives, to
believe he was not a Doctor of Theology. By his own will, not by
the grace of God, he has not had a drink in twenty years.

Does it count if I get the idea but can't figure?

Vera, fair is fair. Perhaps St. Hubert, the patron saint of mathe-
maticians, was with you today.

No saint, certainly not Hubert, about whom nothing reliable
is known, can save this child. Fair is not fair. She thanks Father,
an old-timer who is mocked for his wimpy niceness. Too nice, he
had once considered the telephone an occasion of sin: on home
leave he called the woman who wrote him generous checks for
Anima Mundi, the frightened pious woman wanting to buy into
the rice-and-bean culture, even into the bold pamphlets promoting peace in our day, wanting to buy back her daughter. That

war in East Asia long over, he called, but she was dead. He dare
not ask after the girl, then the man who answered said softly,
as though beyond comprehension that both mother and daughter were dead. It was cruel calling the father those many years
later, a strange party asking as though she was still living, asking
for the mother when he wanted beyond all temptation to speak to
the girl.

He had taken her with him one night when a woman was
dying. A frightened child was sent to fetch a priest, though how
they knew he was one in his saffron motley, and he'd put on his
priestly stole, let Fiona bring the blessed candles, the black kit for
Extreme Unction, and they walked past the curious in the street,
past the club where Hell's Angels, past the bodegas and bright
blue storefront *iglesia*. The woman, wasted by drugs, lay in a filthy
bed, the child weeping at her side as he performed the last rites.
She died while he was anointing the lesions on her feet with holy
oil and, looking up to the girl who was his acolyte, he thought, *My
God, this girl playing at revolution is beautiful in candlelight,
though perhaps she is not playing and perhaps she knows I am a
fraud, but am not this night, this night washing the dead with her.*
He had told her as they walked home, home being the communal
rooms of Anima Mundi, that the powers that be said the rite was
no longer limited to death but was to heal the living and he had
given her the vial of holy oil as a keepsake, a love token. Which
was sacrilege. They had all been in love with that redhead, every
man, woman and child who reinvented life in the red brick
school of a discontinued parish.

He is a failed priest who inscribes a right triangle on the black-
board, the Pythagorean theorem and the most gamelike of its uses
are under review. If Pat is ten miles north of the devil's disco and
Mike is thirteen miles east, then calculate . . . They will snicker at
the devil and his dated disco. Chalk dust settles on his black
dickey. Vigilant, he stands at the door of his classroom waiting for
geometry folks. The young man, loitering, speaks to Vera. She
bobs her head as though she is getting it, the simple matter of a

rate of change, how fast or slow she is going to Bloomingdale's on the IRT, enters her empty head. Son of a gun, how did he get by the uniformed guard who protects the front hall of Loyola? And how does he make what has been an impossible trip from here to there at five miles an hour easy for the unfortunate girl? A better teacher of the calculus than the Padre, perhaps an alumnus, they come back to wonder at the boys they were.

Or a harmless stray, not about to molest the fleshless girl eaten with ambition who runs off, the short grey skirt of her uniform slapping at knobby knees.

You sure I can't be of help?

No, Father.

Our Vera wants to be pre-med. When she goes to college, that is. She wants it so darn much, but we are not all equally endowed.

The luck of the draw.

Yes, that's it.

As geometry straggles in, he thinks that as a priest he should have said that we are equal in the eyes of God, but it has been years since he spoke such words in Spanish to farmers without land, to children never allowed to taste an egg but sent to sell them in the market. He is living out his days as a teacher of math with no edge on his subject, one step behind the whiz kids with the patron saint of calculus guiding them from the computer in a dead digital voice. As a priest he cannot demonstrate logical certainties and so believes his mission has come to entertaining geometry folks with Zeno's paradox, that delightful problem, and trusts that the bell will ring, the last class of the morning for Joe the Murph, who silences the noisy kids and tells them, in one of the Padre's pedagogical warmups, that Pythagoras, who discovered that we live here on earth, was a vegetarian, but therein lay a great mystery, for he ordained that his brotherhood must never eat beans.

In the year when Archbishop Romero was martyred, Joseph Aloysius Murphy, S.J., the Yanqui Father, had been relieved of his provincial duties, reassigned, once more in the black soutane teaching English in San Salvador to wealthy children who came to school with bodyguards. At each Mass the bishop prayed for the poor and the powerless. At each Mass Romero insisted on reading the list of the week's missing and dead. It was 1980, March, a sweet month in that part of the world, *be not afraid*, the bishop was celebrating Holy Mass in the chapel of the San Salvador Hospital, Fathers Murphy and Sánchez in attendance. Romero was shot in his robes on the altar, having preached against the military that day, the killing of brother by brother, ending his short homily as usual—*be not afraid*.

Murph would like to take this class—they are very bright— beyond plane geometry, *be not afraid*, for this is his calling, perhaps as the fellow said, the luck of the draw. When he travels to Rhode Island to visit his mother, who is ninety years old, and his sister, a practical nurse, he wears the black suit, the Roman collar. They fuss over his soda water and rare sirloin, the Irish sweet bread baked for the occasion. Such pleasure they take in serving him, he might be a Doctor of Theology, yet he has never tasted philosophical emancipation, only the one flavor, salt.

Freeman runs down the steps of the school where Cyril was once the prize pupil, hails a cab to Grand Central. No chance that he is the son of that spent priest with stone-grey eyes, not his blue eyes or Cyril's. Like begets like, unlike governed by insufficient determinants; mathematics presenting a problem, but you don't inherit learned skills and the Father is slow as an antediluvian UNIVAC, throwback to pencil on paper, precalculator calculus, whereas Freeman as a boy once computed pi, which can never be computed, to the billionth on Boyce's PC, or said he did to better his buddy. What he has seen and heard this morning is the disproof of B. Unable to concentrate on the *Times*, he is traveling how many short miles at breakneck speed per hour, toward A, his father most certainly.

There is nothing that gives the feel of Connecticut like coming home to it. It is a question of coming home to the American self in the sort of place it was formed.

                                        —Wallace Stevens, *Opus Posthumus*

Looming blood-red, no shutters—the reference is barn. Russo's house sits above a considerable piece of land for suburban Connecticut. Shifting Sylvie's Jeep, Artie makes it through the open gate to the top of a sharply peaked hill, no other like it, the hill recently moved here along with full-grown trees and shrubs, pond with geese in the distance, sheepdog bounding, no sheep. It is the Spring Equinox—too early for lawn and meadow, yet the smell is sweet decay, faint barnyard, as though the coming season sprayed from a giant aerosol can.

What will I call the man? An intruder, he drives the Jeep in fits and starts like a bump'em car, swings into a copse.

Is this a copse, Dad?

This grove of trees which conceals a four-car garage in a pristine henhouse, no hens.

I took a wrong turn, Pop.

Four vehicles—Jaguar to RV—a fair chance that Russo is at home, though the day has been unprofitable so far, Murphy in the uncool cardigan yoked with the holy collar having it both ways, as Artie suspected he'd had it with his mother until that proposition was disproved by every aspect of the bloodless Father.

At least Russo's done himself proud. The Jeep (Sylvie's bewilderment at his borrowing her relic) has set off an ultrasound that scatters the birds in the thicket into the crisp Spring breeze and flushes out Russo, the man himself.

You the photographer?

I came up from the depot.

Fumbling with a Cyril word, the depot where Sylvie picked him up, he now faces the bearded man in the photo who, process of elimination, must be the lost father at last. Russo, the booted thug, the toucher, one slick black leather sleeve circling Fiona's waist, zips into a jacket of supple tan suede. The reference is money. Corduroys, topsiders. *Is there a costume trunk labeled A. Freeman's Dad?* Work shirt open at the neck, exposing sandy hair, beard trim, distinguished snowy lights. Russo is beautifully bald, that is to say bald enough to look fatherly, sage, concerned, at this moment concerned with the seedy trespasser, concern one of his major attitudes. He is often pictured on his book jackets with concerned eyes upon each reader, no distraction in his programmed care from you, Dear Buyer of Inspirational Books. Alternate looks are compassion, the notch up from concern, and, before the spiritual meat of a lecture, the wobbling head of joshing self-deprecation, because if we cannot see ourselves then we . . . We inevitably leading to I, to Russo's little throwaway confession.

You are not the photographer?

Cyril's scuffed briefcase not a photographer's bag. Russo has trouble with interlopers, hostile readers who do not achieve in life what he promises on the page.

This is a private road.

I took a wrong turn.

Uninvited, Freeman gets out of the Jeep. He stands a head taller than this stocky man, looking down at the polished scalp. Failed implants have left a pox on top of the smooth pate, for Russo is, in fact, bald as an egg, his ears small with tiny lobes, still it is possible. Artie strokes the slim ridge of his bog-boy nose. Russo's is stumpy, still, still . . .

I'm looking for Long Ridge.

Artie fully aware that he is not on Long Ridge Road, where Fiona sent him to the private day school, where he told the boys who did not want him on their soccer team that his father was a Mafia hit man now dead.

This is High Ridge. Said with exasperation by Russo, who, for all the good counsel widely professed in his books, is decidedly unhelpful.

I'm looking for . . . for a Mrs. Waite.

Russo softens, not that he knows the Waites. As a celebrity he keeps his distance from neighbors, but it comes over him that he is testy simply because the photographer who is to take head shots promoting the lecture tour has forgotten the day or is late. No, here's the rub—this guy now loping toward the house, sniffing the country air, about to use his phone, has not spotted him as Gene Russo, his face now famous as a minor movie star's. The old sin of pride, if sin were not written out of his philosophy. We must pass on, after injury, failure, sorrow, pass on—that is Russo's absolving message in *Three Roads, Five Paths, Seven Ways*, which have lingered for years on the best-seller list and are accessed by millions on ROMs in which he speaks in a book-lined study with intimacy of his own failures and sorrows. We must pass on, as he passed from the priesthood after his worship of Fiona O'Connor. He was her confessor at Anima Mundi and her secrets will die with him, though she has been useful through the years, that is her life has been of use, first appearing in *Three Roads* as the story of a young she-wolf at play—prowling, seductive—in a prolongation of adolescence, searching spiritual food for her beautiful animal body. The anthropomorphic fables of this slight volume wildly successful, but Russo knows to pass on in style, not theme, as he knew to cross the river into Manhattan to join the Project. Where would he be now, if he had not searched out the red brick school with that crew who lived on the edge of disbelief in all things declared holy? A parish priest in an Italian neighborhood already going, gone in the dead center of Newark or Jersey City. Preaching what? That it is not over, the lingering Christian guilt of the late-capitalist era? That God is Love in the projects? *Take not away my soul, O Lord, with the wicked, nor my life with men of blood.* Pronouncing dead words to a few old women not afraid to walk the streets to early Mass? Pass on.

Artie Freeman enters a wired environment, near Skylarky. Beyond glass doors a centerfold blonde in black tights, the bib of her dainty apron held aloft by fantasy boobs. More immediate, a garrulous fat man in a wheelchair who, mistaking him for the photographer, explains that he is answering Russo's e-mail, a full-time job dealing with fans. A pale secretarial girl does not turn from her scrolling computer racing toward some text which arrives on a big monitor, Russo then reading aloud, his pastoral voice caressing each plain English word:

> If I had to live my life again I would have made a rule to read some poetry and listen to some music at least once every week; for perhaps the part of my brain now atrophied could have been kept active through use. The loss of these tastes is a loss of happiness.
>
> —Charles Darwin, *Autobiography*

Super!

Russo has forgotten the interloper with the briefcase. He will forget Darwin's meditation, which doesn't cut it, a rueful selection unfit for *Ten Byways*. He is deeply committed to the writing of *Ten*, for in these byways he will pass on to stories of the afterlife which he now picks like common daisies from many fields—the Egyptian Book of the Dead, the Incas' upper world in which peace of mind and body overcome ambition and lust, Christian vaults with stars and the heavenly hosts. One more river to cross for a man worn by seven children, three wives, four cars, many agents and aides, by numbered days on the calendar assigned to cities where he will lecture for a healthy sum every weekday of the Spring, forgetting which little jokes go over in St. Louis, which tender memory delights the Denver Junior League. Alone in hotel rooms on the weekend, he loses track of who will next meet him at what airport and longs for an afterlife seen as retirement. Paradise is a golf course, cap on the bald head to keep off the Carolina sun, the garden reclaimed with neither alimony nor tuitions. But celebrity, much like a priestly calling, goes on to the end.

The Muslims disappoint, not coming through with significant tens, though the Quran had proved a gold mine for *Three*, *Five*, *Seven*—what use he has made of its mystic numbers. We cannot lose ourselves on Russo's ways. The trees, en route to our corrective fulfillment, are marked in his forest. Three—the unifying principle of the Trinity; water, air, earth; thought, word, deed; the

Platonic good, true, beautiful—for there are always in Russo's system references to the past and to cultures other than that of his myopic constituency. It gives *us*, he is never patronizing, "vista, a sense of the continuum, the inner strength to pass on," words of the master Artie reads on a dust jacket.

He has been abandoned. What luck, the luck of three wishes. He does not wish for the blonde with amazing knockers licking white frosting off her fingers, for he thinks of the spare body of his Lou, her ribs skeletal, these last weeks giving each day to her work body and soul, solo—and of the terrible test she has set for herself this day, a day of judgment on Moffett's hearts and flowers. His wish is to be invisible, which almost comes true, for he steals about Russo's control room speed-reading the bonkers numerology, the uplift at the end of every journey. And taking in the photos: wives and children—three wives, one plain woman and two pretty—the blonde is the third, about his own age, Freeman guesses. Seven children. Of all those kids with Russo's retroussé nose and lobeless ears, he would be the oldest, the rightful heir, if . . . Five senses, five fingers, five toes. The first number which is made up of odds and evens. The mystical pentagram, Pentateuch, Star of David.

> Live, primrose, then, and thrive
> With thy true number five,
> And women, whom this flower doth represent
> With this mysterious number be content.
>
> —John Donne, "The Primrose"

Super. Always the reach for coherence as in Almanac's grid of days, the numbers game imposed on flux, the scatter shot of connections pleading for the larger view as we take the marker from the page at bedtime to cure love lost or unattainable, to read on in the troubled night. A page of Russo might be any page, one parable flowing to the next before the repeat of his abracadabra self-revelation—loss of faith, passion, infidelity, divorce. Fess up where you've been, flip ahead to commitment, unity, renewal, procreation. Pass on.

The correspondent shifts heavily in his wheelchair, suspects the black-haired intruder. There have been incidents, troublemakers stuck in their lives who want to punish Gene Russo. He swings round from personalizing a letter to a devoted fan, thrusts a phone rudely at the perpetrator with the briefcase poking through passages of the master as if he could travel the many paths to the mesa of understanding in an irreverent flip of a page. Some sneak from the IRS, surely not the photographer. Artie, phone in hand, does not go through the charade of calling Sylvia Waite, pretending he has lost his way when he is lost utterly in this sad caper. Russo is the living end. His hairpiece sits limply atop the Finnish edition of *Seven*. Seven pillars of wisdom, seven lively arts, seven days of the week, ages of man, terraces of the Buddhist paradise which the parish priest approached in his carnal knowledge of Fiona, a wild, hurtful woman he can no longer name, for she has circulated under many names in his ever-profitable work.

Or would not want to name, the one who got away. When Father Russo went to the apartment on Fifth Avenue in a grey flannel suit bought for the occasion, ready to offer that girl the world, the mother said she was no longer in the city, the mother who had given him money, hush money, wanting to control her daughter's life at Anima Mundi, now offered him money to stay away. He sat, uninvited, on her tight button-back couch and took out the cross, a satanic Eighth Street cross the misguided woman had given to her daughter, the daughter passing it on to Father Russo. *Be what you receive and receive what you are*, the girl had said to him, the girl who knew that he had come on board for his advantage, on board for her revolution full of white-hot hatred and love; and that every one of them would fail her dedication and fall away. Or be forever canceled, as he was canceled as a man when she hung the cross on his neck not in mockery. In truth there was no play in the girl, the rest of them given to political theatrics. Listening to her sins, he felt her very soul tremble like a flame between purity and corruption, then burn steady with a loss of faith, and knew there was a priestly act he must perform for this beautiful girl, an act of self-abnegation which as a man he could not do. He passed on, marrying out of spite a plain woman, a helpful woman, the story of her maternal affection may be read in *Three*, the tale of the good golden hen.

   . *Super!* The secretary, ethereal as a ghostwriter, preens. She
  · ·   has searched out the ascent to heaven, the ideal ten of
· · ·   the Song of Songs, the ten commandments, Mo-
· · · ·   hammed's "ten who are promised paradise," and in
the Pythagorean geometry, a containment, perfection.

Arthur Freeman offers "Ten Little Indians" as he sprints out the door, where a blond boy (unlobed and pug-nosed *à la* Russo) jumps off the school bus to embrace the rollicking sheepdog to the delight of his amazing blonde mom, a perfect ten. He does wish that the Jeep would not grind its gears as he zooms past the photographer's vintage Ferrari, away from the impossible father, the hawker of happiness. Talk about irrational numbers! Artie has used up two of three wishes, but doesn't need the third, figuring that baldness is inherited from the mother's side, that O'Connors and Boyles die with full heads of hair. Seven marshmallow noses, fourteen unfleshed ears provide an adequate sampling: he is in no way kin to these fraudulent brothers and sisters, or to A, who writes fairy tales for frightened children. Given the day's choices he calls it quits. Different from passing on.

Artie turns off High Ridge Road onto Painter Hill and parks at the entrance to the Waite homestead, where his grandfather was killed. He goes to the listing mailbox, where the old man was headed with the final letter that he can't read. All his life he has wanted to face the father who begot him, give a name to absence. He chinks a rock into the earth to set the mailbox straight. All his life he has wanted to know what others know without resort to decoding glyphs, to entertaining puzzles or predicting probability in the flip of a fair coin. One follicle of Murphy's hair, one millimeter of Russo's blood holds the marker with no margin for error. He quits the believing . . . if ever it was belief in the phantom father, more like an incurable yen. He wants no such test, no proof, yet his sorrow is immense, real as the knowledge that he can't subtract loss from what he never gained.

Sylvie is stationed by the door, dressed for their evening trip into town. Her earrings brilliant, her wrap a faded scarlet coat missing half its gilt buttons—a coat which Bob Waite admired. She wonders what this big kid has been up to as he jerks from gear to gear bucking clear up to her door, but senses as she takes the driver's seat that his silence stills some unspeakable pain—the finality with which he flings the battered briefcase into the back of the Jeep. The Wall Street item which contains evidence—Mae's bountiful checks, Boy O'Connor's birth certificate, the death notice of his mother, family photos, though not the incriminating photo of proposition not A, not B. When Sylvie draws into an incredible parking place directly in front of Lou's gallery, all that reliable evidence will be stolen on this day in which the hours of light equal the hours of darkness. Pass on.

THE PROGRESS OF LOVE

A crowd has gathered at the window of the gallery which looks out on West Broadway. They watch a woman in overalls mold little red hearts and throw them in a galvanized pail. She's fast. The hearts nick easily, one out of three or four losing their humps, no matter—tossed in the pail. Artie Freeman stands above the crowd seeing what he has seen often enough, though not recently in the loft: woman at work. Lou in her bubble of concentration, do not disturb. He looks for Sylvie, thinking he will lift her above the crowd like a child to see the action which these people on the street find compelling, but she has ducked into the gallery. Her scarlet satin coat, her froth of white hair can be seen bobbing among the privileged invited to the opening, the inner circle with white wine in plastic glasses who turn now and again to watch the performance of the artist in her aura.

Wait now, she'll do it.

Wondering what will *she* do, Freeman dares not think of the woman exhibiting herself as his Lou, her skit or dumb show in a world removed, more distant than the animated figures in arcade games of his youth in which it was possible to beat the machine.

Now! Wait now. She'll do it.

Louise Moffett rises from the table on which she molds her hearts, a kitchen table of the Thirties with a hygienic enamel top the color of rich cream. She lifts her pail and marches off the platform, finds her way through the crowd, which is and isn't her audience, then climbs a wooden ladder and dumps the hearts in a bin.

So?

So, she restocks, goods in a store.

Goods?

Artie enters. On a small placard the exhibition announces itself: *The Progress of Love* lettered in her own eccentric script listing to the left, bold in its capitals, impatient with the end of words. He thinks to go to her at once, to where she sits back at the table dipping into a bucket of red muck. She does not look up from the task at hand. He thinks not to go to her—a blooper, walking on camera in the middle of a scene. Dealer, speaking effusive French, approaches her with a sleek grey man—a client, a critic? They stop short of Lou's platform, of her intensity, her devotion. Befuddled Dealer is ecstatic, his eyes popped as though he has swallowed a pit of pure gold. Moffett's work is his to promote, to further his reputation, though Moffett is Collection of the Artist: don't touch the woman. You may only look on.

Freeman looks away from his love, closed to him as if she is a replica of the farm girl turned artist. This is what he sees: A ladder, Plexiglas bins—two large translucent beakers which tower above him. A clawed scoop hovers over one bin, then dips into the red hearts where there are rings, keys, stars, moons—charms and favors you cannot win. Moffett has rigged her primitive vending device with pulleys. Prying open the claw, plunging it into the mass of hearts, angling for your gold star is a skill you might acquire, get better at, like Pick-up Sticks or even Scrabble. The spectators are amused, art folks carelessly cuing up to have a go at the game. Hands on the controls, or lack of control, for how often the brass key, the silver spoon slips through the claws. Then, too, the player cannot get his prize any more than he can snatch the ripe russet pear or the peach with high blush from a mouth-watering still life. There is no exit from the beaker, no tunnel or slide for the claw to dispense your take as in the gum-ball machine. Satisfaction, if any, is holding aloft the unattainable—a gilded moon, brindled cow, wee silver knife or spoon. The prize must be the trial itself, while in the second beaker . . .

This is what he sees: The second vessel is not chock-a-block full. Louise, climbing the wooden ladder, continues to pour in newly manufactured hearts. A hand lettered sign: *Guess how many red hots in the jar?* But the numbers change with every addition, so that even if he were to toy with rate of innovation, with distribution of a random variable, she wouldn't give him a fair chance. A cheap shot, which is not how those milling about the test tubes see this work in progress.

Brilliant! Process. Moffett plying her trade.

He supposes brilliant, as they say, these friends of Moffett's, of his, he's not seen since the start of the year when he was evicted from their company. Lou and Artie kept to themselves when love returned, then withdrew to themselves in silence. Now these trendies are eager to air-kiss, congratulations in order. Felicia, the unforgivable woman with the death-camp tattoo, presses her emaciated body against him. She simulates awe: "The walls! The walls are to weep."

Sylvie is dry-eyed at the wall where he finds her studying *the* photo, rather a blowup of that photo in which she discerns Freeman's crude rip and Lou's Scotch Tape, which reattaches his mother to her impossible men. The blowup is a grainy monster exposing the crumpled love triangle, all three equally flawed. Russo, in black leather, digs his fingers possessively into Fiona's waist, where it can be seen that the top button of her hipster is undone to accommodate the slight swell of her belly. Murphy in mellow yellow tolerates the wisp of red hair that cuts across his handsome face, resigned to his punishment.

"Come along," Sylvie says.

He cannot walk away from the story, which has been bigger than his life. His mother's crooked smile belies the welling sorrow, now it can be seen, in her eyes and the one tear that has fallen and hangs from the tip of her freckled nose.

"*Kommen Sie.*" A teacher who knows the answer, Sylvie asks, "So what is our *Macher* in the overalls saying?"

"Mocker?"

This is what they see:

Loot: Acrylic on canvas: Crystal, china, silver, diamond, hothouse rose, folded napkin—one slick airbrushed painting like another, the hefty price of each posted in Moffett's hand. *Loot*, subtitled *EAT ME 1, 2, 3* and so forth, through twelve consecutive numbers. All bear the circular red sticker. They are sold.

Studio: Black and white photo on matte stock: Bridal portraits of Mae Boyle and Shirley Moffett (née McClure) in which the veils, bouquets, sweeps of white satin (from the salon in Bendel's, the seamstress in Wisconsin), slim waists and the dark lipstick of '52 and '62 appear almost identical in a halo of photographer's light, as does their assurance.

Milch Cow: Ink on newsprint: Harold Moffett in *The New York Times* with his loved one, Dossie. The shy nuzzle of his professorial head against her goatlike skull, his tweedy arm caressing the beast's curried shoulder.

Happy Days: Kodachrome snapshot: Beatrice Moffett Strobinski, M.D., mounted on a Monster Cycle with Polish Intellectual.

This is what Arthur Freeman sees:

Sylvie stumbling into a stack of blue Tiffany boxes set next to the black box which lies open so that anyone may rifle through what remains of his family's records. Sylvie backs away, indignant at the interference of Moffett's art, a trap in her attempt to view this progress.

Ach, Schwindler!

Artie relieved that she does not hear the patronizing titter of the seasoned patrons, who know to look from one black box to the many others, from the information in the battered tin strongbox to the information on the wall of mute black monitors.

This is what they see:

Colorful sidebars repeating down the screens: *Borrowed, Blue, Old, New.* While, center screen, in serious black on white, the birth, marriage and death dates of those pictured in Moffett's gallery. Each date an event fixed by events. Mary Therese Boyle: b. New York City, 1930: Grant Wood—*American Gothic,* Chrysler Building, Marx Brothers—*Animal Crackers,* Mussolini, bread lines, "Mood Indigo," von Sternberg, Capra, Babe Ruth—forty-nine homers, Sigmund Freud—*Civilization and Its Discontents.*

Blue, Old, Borrowed, New. The video spins, speedy, uncontrollable. Fiona O'Connor, d. 1982: *Star Wars,* 4,150 married by Rev. Moon, "Just Say No," *E.T.,* Sinai returned to Egypt, gypsy moth devastation, antinuke march—Central Park, "You Were Always on My Mind."

Borrowed, Blue, etc. Beatrice and Ignatz Strobinski divorce 1986: *Challenger* shuttle misfires, oil falls $11 per barrel, aerobics, microwave pizza, weapons sales to Iran, "Cheers," Desi Arnaz & Georgia O'Keeffe die, 40,000 homeless NYC.

What is she up to, placing the players in her Progress of Love in real time? Freeman thinking, borrowed time, samplings cribbed off the net. No—out of the LIBRARY, shouting to Sylvie: "So—what's NEW?"

"The dirty overalls."

And on she goes in the red satin coat, just the ticket for a reception to celebrate the admission of Austria to the U.N. in

1955 ... while Freeman lingers, letting the pop tunes, heavy-weight champs of the world, movies and Broadway plays, illustri-ous names reel by. Particular attention paid to war—the Second World War, Korea, Vietnam, Gulf—the familiar short list, un-nourishing information. There is not one platinum record or baseball score or forgotten Pulitzer Prize novel or Salk's vaccine, *Ich bin ein Berliner.* Warhol *100 Cans,* Yalta, Arafat on the White House lawn in this garage sale of history that cannot be accessed with ease, yet all public events rub up, uncomfortably personal. He cannot figure whether their lives—his life and Lou's—are made smaller or bigger by this show.

"Moffett," he yells.

Old, Blue, Borrowed. Cyril O'Connor, b. 1925, New York City: Bessie Smith, *Mein Kampf,* Scopes Trial, transmitted televi-sion image, Charles Chaplin—*The Gold Rush* ... Artie lifts the black metal box. "Moffett!"

She is atop the ladder, spilling an infusion of plasticene hearts, her reverie closing him out. Artie aims the black box at the electronic box.

Bud Boyce at his side: "Happy Millennium! A repeat performance?"

"This ... this *exhibition* ... ," but Artie gets no further, for Boy O'Connor, b. 1970, comes up on the screen: Floppy disc, Kent State, Cambodia, *Love Story,* Afro ... and he is only human, interested as we all are in any old news, if news of ourselves.

The crowd is thinning. Time to move on to the bars, the bistros, or to contemplate for a minute *The Progress of Love.* What does she mean, if we may use that overdirectional word? We are born into this world and forget it? That we are trivial and grand? Hardly grand, her muted TVs, schlock videoblast. Surely she's not pushing synchronicity, meaning loaded in any-which-way se-quence of events, a discredited notion ... move on before decid-ing whether dinner will be Indonesian or pricy Italian as we walk further downtown, for we are downtown in long black coats and this year's black patent boots, somewhat melancholy, though who cares what the artist intended. The beginning or the end of perspective? The old lady, a hoot in the red satin coat, a feminist reading of Mother Time? That costume jewelry making a comeback, though not in our set. Brisk for March, the beginning of the end, the end of the season. There will be other openings this Spring, nothing we care for. Moffett is either genius or fraud. It was old, don't you know, a worn idea—trash-heap bricolage, acquisition.

However—the Plexiglas bins. You nabbed one of the rings, held it in those pincers. That was fun and the father, *hers*, making cow eyes at his animal—a musk ox or griffin, unnatural, yet she did not seem angry, the artist that is, going about her business.

Walking through the night past vendors of earmuffs, sunglasses, off-brand shampoos, irregular towels . . . Why was Moffett unruffled when we find ourselves disturbed having attended *The Progress of Love*, the place to be tonight? Nothing profound in the drawing of a Zodiac Man with the face of her lover. He was there, you know, the gawk in the business suit. Touching, how strong she rendered his homely features: India ink on paper.

Sweet. Yes, that was sweet.

Louise Moffett has no control over those who choose to sentimentalize her work, or those who leave her show early seeing only love run out in the spill of time. She has set up a single black monitor with a steady reassuring heartbeat jogging along on the screen. From its dials hangs *Misericordia*: Lithograph, thorned heart overpainted with blood.

"Sacred and profane. You see," Dealer chatting Freeman up, "the living and the dead." For Jesus only knows why Moffett must have this man. . . . Quite beyond him, the perversions that make his artists produce their best work. If the show travels Louise must travel with her ephemeral environment. "She is the living fixture, the performative . . . ," he informs this rude man who turns away, trots off to the end of the exhibit.

And this is what Artie sees:

Love Letter: Ballpoint on blank book. Cyril's letter, the final page of that letter not posted the day of his death, the words scrambled, illegible except . . . except Lou has lifted word from word, as though carefully brushing the dust off a treasured codex in an ancient grave to produce a clear transcription:

I see that my task is not over. I have always thought of you as my son, but failed you by living out of my time, turning to my books which did not save me from wanting my life to be over. I had long been the difficult child and you the responsible father. Did I ever thank you for the clean clothes and the fine victuals? I thank you now though I am happy and well fed. I must not compare the present with the past though I think often of my wife and daughter. *Non amittuntur sed*—as it was once said—they are not lost but sent before. And we must move on, Arthur. Take a page from my book.

Let us go back to the beginning, for you are in need of the father you will not find. I know that your mother loved him as only my girl could. Whichever man it may be in that picture, she would not distract him from his calling. She would not ruin his life. In love we are all deluded. For Fiona, the romance could never end.

Let us go back, dear boy. Though it may be a great treat, I have second thoughts as to seeing the world which I will never see clearly. While Sylvie sees the old world, I will return to the apartment. We will cook up our dinners of old, the nightly steak and baked potato that sustained us in our years together when you were my boy.

Now to the early mail. I believe there is a gentle mist, the day verging on Spring.

C.

The wall is to weep. Lou stands by his side. The show is over. She will mold little hearts in the window here on West Broadway for the duration, put their lives on display in old borrowed gestures. But their day of reckoning is not past.

"Did you tend to your business?"

"Yes."

"And you found?"

"No one." He's not on the planet with Murphy or Russo. No one. Later he will tell her of his sampling of fathers, his closing the book before the end of that story. Later he will say that his mother could not have been ruined by either one of those men, that she was never ruined, merely unlucky. But this is Lou's show, so later he will say that he found no one who will do, no one worthy. Who could be? The problem was beautiful without its solution. Now she moves him on to the last item on the gallery wall, where they see:

The Founding Father: 10-point linotron Galliard set on acid-free Ecusta Nyalite, paper meeting the minimum requirements of the American National Standard for Information Sciences—permanence of paper for printed Library Materials: Illustration of Benjamin Franklin as sculpted by Houdon; a tired old man with peeled back eyes of white marble. She has destroyed a book. One of Cyril's books. The photo of Franklin's bust is placed beside a torn page, the passage marked by his grandfather's hand:

And be not thou disturbed, O grave and sober Reader, if among the many serious Sentences in my Book, thou findest me trifling now and then, and talking idly. In all the Dishes I have hitherto cook'd for thee, there is solid Meat Enough for thy Money.

—*Poor Richard's Almanack*, 1739

Freeman loops his arm around Moffett. He may never understand her scraps and pieces, but she has given him back the day, a day teetering on the edge of extinction. They move on, though she persists, "No one? You found no one."

"A remote possibility."

"Oh, Artie! Not again." For if again, she has failed and her *Progress of Love* is no more than a commission fulfilled for the gallery, a business deal, her slick paintings of hearts and flowers sold by the dozen to Boyce, who will install them in the reception area of Skylark.

"Not again, Lou. I'm a happy bastard. A scramble, unsequential DNA."

"Seriously?"

"Seriously, Lou."

With many thanks, they decline the invitation to dine with Dealer, Critic, Curator, et al. Sylvie is their charge. She has nested on the chair at the kitchen table, a bright bird with drooping head saddened by her lover's letter. Second thoughts! *Ein Blinder*, he was well enough fed, coddled, but he was about to leave her, to resume his parental duties. *Ein Blinder Norr*, so like the blind, forever in love with that daughter. Sylvie does not believe that the artist in dirty overalls meant to be cruel mounting her accumulations. What progress? And naturally, she was written out of the little family drama. What might her wall reveal, hung with the beautiful Inge, b. 1899—*The Merry Widow*, Herzl, Zionism, androgynous boys, Pan-Germany; the nipples, navels and pubic hair of Gustav Klimt's women sucking men in, yes, School of Inge, triumphant in her hand-beaded wedding dress of the Twenties under the arched doorway of the Villa, positioned a step above von Neisswonger, gentleman mathematician; or Inge by the pool with Marks, Garbo and Thomas Mann in their Hollywood berets; or with Billy Ray Boots, Stetsons on their empty heads. In Sylvie's show, Babs Waite would hang next to that wife, Mae Boyle, her athletic shoulders straining the lace of a family gown and somewhere in an album with sticky pages there is a photo, her own, of a determined young woman in a blue taffeta afternoon dress, wasp waist, appropriate for her marriage to Bob Waite, who stood beside her smiling his embarrassed smile, the kindest of men. And she did love him, that is what the walls must say, or the televisions they have turned off for the night. Do not forget that she came to care for that sturdy corporate man she had efficiently married. As Cyril, the dutiful man who has betrayed her twice, in his way honored his wife's innocence and simple faith, their days lived together under one roof, do not forget . . . *das Haus*, but she cannot retrieve the line in her native tongue.

The lights dim. They are coming to her, the artist and that lost boy, hand in hand coming around the candy jars she does not fancy, two pillars of fire damped down for the night, the entrance to *das Haus*. . . . Do not forget *das Haus des Friedens in Stille*. The house of peace in stillness.

At home we find no messages, checking before we take off our heavy coat. A favor in the pocket, not the cheap key or star we could not extract from the giant bin of hearts. A postcard, Moffett being known for her *Postcards*, a stack of them offered as we came to the end of the show, a little something to take home from the party. *The Progress of Love* (1795), Fragonard, a series of wall panels in which lovers are restored to the garden where they play erotic games un- der a china-blue sky. We have chosen blindly, *Love Letters*. The woman is perched on a plinth reading one of those letters, her silk skirt in studied disarray. The man embraces her, his elaborately dressed curls resting on her bare shoulder. Are they his letters to her? Hers to him? Must they read aloud what has been committed to the page? The garden (their stage) is in full bloom. Lapdog, lyre, Oriental parasol in attendance. A goddess in classical drapery looks down from a higher plinth on the human scene of sentimental communication, an inedible apple of white marble in her hand. Moffett affects overalls. We see how diminished our time, how black-and-white earnest the libidinal nature of consumerism. She has borrowed the title, painted nothing herself of filtered sunshine and sweet deception. The dream world of our 3×5 postcard is long gone from view. The lovers must be rereading dear words that they know. Moffett, once so painterly, a pity she has given up on Nature, here painted only the hard-edged rewards of Romance—the bridal registry of china and crystal with the crude words *EAT ME* and the suggestive vulva of the florist's too-perfect red rose.

If we choose, we can make up stories about those people we do not know—Harold and Mae and Fiona—whether they loved lightly or for the duration; how they got from there to here, to Moffett's wall. What world would they wish to live in? They seem to us both generic and particular. *Washington* was the Father of Our Country. The postcard of the Fragonard is signed on the back *L. Moffett*, some nerve. Unsettling as the vending machine that withheld our prize, or her impossible guessing game—how many hearts.

Perhaps that is why I can't settle to the morning paper, new news, its small pleasure on a late night, getting a jump on tomorrow. And can't sleep, figuring the date of my birth—the pop tunes, the B movies, the kidnapping of the Lindbergh baby, the unhonored treaty. None of this random account is my accomplishment or my fault. Or yours—not cloying roses or the sting of red hots. Then why, digesting the rich Italian cheese cake, am I blue. And wasn't her show meant to send us out into the night, to more than an expensive meal, with a sweet and sour aftertaste? The hazy backlight of my bridal photo, the clarity of my gaze. Short dark curls, the Italian cut of that year, spring from my illusion veil. Our stainless-steel sink, our Bendix tumbling the wash. The date of our daughter's birth—Snoopy, Cuban Missile Crisis, Eleanor Roosevelt dies in the year when it was presumed we could colonize Mars, bring our problems to that planet as in science fiction. That in our progress we would defect or die or seem to, lost on our islands. For Christ's sake, bring me, bring me one rose.

THE ENDLESS PAGE

The Royal Books. Rival Libraries. Egypt curtails exports to stop plagiarism, forgery. Books burned to keep public baths warm, Alexandria. Books burned as wasteland of individualism, Berlin, May 10, 1933. Sissy apprehended in St. Agnes Library, Amsterdam Avenue, Upper West Side, N.Y.C. How you get to be a radical: by preferential option for the poor, though Sissy, if not entirely forgotten, remains more statistic than documented case in which residence unknown, names of Dad or whoever, recidivist—times of departure from domicile and intermittent return. She is a standard deviation, dot on a curve. In her gear a soldier's hat will be found to no purpose or revelation when she is cuffed in the St. Agnes Library, a warm resting place, Sissy sitting over *Men* to *Och* of the *Britannica* with Shotgun and vials of "El Dorado," a courier for Little Man, operating from Beepersville. Tony, dumb fuck, turning her in, copping his plea. The book in no way an extension of her eye, Sissy opening to whatever page, never reading the entry which tells her that in 1930 the city of New York installed its first traffic lights due to the congestion, such fun to know but that charming fact unknown to Sissy, dot on an ascending curve sent out the revolving door of the city, now living upstate whether in comfort or distress we do not know in an establishment found for her correction. In the blank upcountry days which may be some kind of hell for a girl who worked the precinct like it was Gay Paree; or some kind of heaven, pure bliss, where a single technician can milk 80 cows in an hour and what is a weed? A plant whose virtues have not yet been discovered. *Sich verreist*, out of reach, her city. Or out of mind like Innsbruck, the quaint city not traveled to by Sylvie, with a house called Little Golden Roof adorned by 3,450 gilt shingles. Dumpling soup and gambols in the snow, so much to correct, *The Sound of Music* moviescape of Alps her stepchildren believed in and how could she say, *Nein, nein*—the Tyrol *mit* more Kappelmeisters than churches, a great chorus of jolly songs to correct, the nightwarmth of eiderdown turning the metal buckle of the thick soldier's uniform cruelly cold on her body before it was harshly unclasped. *Doe, a deer, a female deer*, such lessons she dare not correct. And in answer to Almanac's question: the dormouse is eaten in Europe before Winter dormancy, when it is fat. Remember not to forget, keep up your Latin, forget that you may remember platitudes: wisdom demoted to knowledge to information, write it down not to forget the need, Homo Narrator, to correct—October 31, 1992, John Paul II proclaimed to an assembly in Rome that the church was in error concerning Galileo's heresy (March 5, 1616) that *the earth is not the centre of the world nor immovable* and wished to reconcile the differences between Holy Scripture and science. Nam. Nam. Nam.

We were terribly wrong—Robert McNamara, April 3, 1995. *The next time the novelist rings the bell I will not stir though the meeting house burn down.*—Thoreau, *Journals*, November 1851. Only correct—the climate cycle is affected through variations in the accretion of interplanetary dust and a leap second to be added to the year due to the slowing of the earth's spin (June 30, 1997). "There will be Weather this Week tho' I say nothing about it."—*The Almanack of Dr. Ames*, March 1731. *Sir—Interceptive actions, such as hitting a moving target or catching a ball, need to be adequately timed in order to be successful. Because there is a significant time delay in the transmission of information along the visual pathways there could be a critical difference between the perceptual and the actual position of the moving object.*—*Nature*, December 1995. Only correct to recall Sissy upstate, to set her under the Sap Moon of March perhaps tasting her first maple syrup poured on the snow or Sissy set to music—malling with a matron, a motherly figure—in a vast arcade where *the climate must be perfect all the year,* filching nothing in the biosphere under which ficus trees native to North Africa, stopping perhaps in a bright beckoning bookstore where the ingeniously competitive dust jackets recall nothing of the headachy steam heat in the poor branch library of St. Agnes, recall not for a moment the spurious link to the lost libraries of Byzantium and Thebes, Shadwell and Sarajevo, disasters never to be called up like salt in the oversalted stew corrected by a potato which absorbs salt like a sponge thus supper saved, the damage ended, the song ended—*with the sad funny ending, a rich man in a poor man's shirt,* Bruce Springsteen, 1991, correct The Boss, the bosses, guard against unwarranted optimism, the sport ended—as when wearing a silly cocktail dress or serious violet dress, serious old soldier's cap, silly overseas cap—you must choose, not hedge your bets. Speak your mind. Say serious dress or silly hat, no ironic attitude toward your own conviction as in (not) believing in astrological advisements—Castrate, Breed, Pollinate, Seek Pleasures, Wean, Slaughter—and thus correct the endless page, forfeit the game. Choose.

The Earth   The Heaven

Illustrations: Comenius; *Orbis Sensualium Pictus*

Time:

I turn my glasse, and give my Scene such growing
As you had slept between—

—*The Winter's Tale*, Act IV, Scene I

Artie hesitates at the door, dressed as a gent today on his way to
Skylark. One last time he steals across the creaking floorboards to
the darkened corner where the baby sleeps in a cradle he has almost outgrown. He dare not touch the sparse downy tufts he
claims to be his son's full head of red hair. He dare not breathe
above the astonishing fingers and toes with their minuscule pink
nails. Lou is sleeping. The baby sleeps by the cast-iron radiator,
where it is warm. Artie is in a doped-up state of contentment and
exhaustion—sleep-deprived, baggy-eyed, sallow. He and Lou have
produced this remarkable person who blows bubbles from his
puckered mouth and knows precisely how to suck his mother's tit.
Most days Artie stays home manipulating his power machine for
Bud Boyce, imaging weather, but today . . . Weather is super-
animated these days, streams of ice particles fall from cirrus
clouds, forked lightning zooms in and out of the screen to make
the pitch as though to sell the unstable skies. Bud has achieved
his dream, a weather station of his own—storms, heat waves,

twisters of his prediction, or the fairly accurate predictions of Skylark's resident meteorologist hired out of the U.S. Geological Headquarters in Atlanta. As Artie sees it, his pix art is inessential to Bud's forecasting and now-casting, in which Doppler isobarics and thermal maps are simultaneously shown. He is the mere virtual man, simple simulacra, outdated as turtle graphics—pen up, pen down. By the time his pictures hit the screen they are old news.

Slipping out of the steel fire door, descending in the industrial elevator, walking to the subway through a soft rain—March again, the end of the month, one of the borrowed days, the three days that the Basque and French and Scots said were stolen from April, farmers yearning for Spring. When it clears, Lou will take Cyril out in his sling, warm against her breast, while Artie makes it plain to Bud that he's opting out of the weather team. There is a standing army of digital artists on the aural/tactile frontline. What Bertram Boyce refuses to understand: even if you know what's coming your way, you are at the mercy of weather. So—he will discontinue the pretty pictures, the animation of tropical depressions and gentle zephyrs.

Artie will not confess to Bud that he has gone back to school. He is old for math, though Newton was forty-two when he published his First Law of Motion, von Neumann, the *Wunderkind*, didn't get around to his algebras until he was Artie's age exactly. He must begin again with differential equations and the Golden Rectangle. Back to square one, where some friction stopped him in moving forward. Or fictions of the past. Artie can't figure what lies in store if he attends to his business, applied mathematics. To playing WHAT IF seriously: what if transient events on the Sun, solar winds (or Mendel's sunspots) molding the earth's magnetic field, induce currents which saturate transformers? The total collapse of electricity—that's what if! In the subway, he checks his grandfather's pocket watch against the battery clock. The watch with slim Roman numerals on its face is accurate, a gift from Maesie Boyle to her fiancé, Cpt. O'Connor. Artie wants to catch

Boyce in his early morning mood just in from the burb, to say to the big guy himself that it's quits, *finito*. To say that he's a surd, nuts as an irrational number, but intends to go on to maybe quantum mechanics, unprovable verities, dark matter. Then, swinging uncertainly from a post on the B train, Artie Freeman considers pure math and the holy grail of conjectures which may lie beyond his grasp, the sexiest Theory. Of Everything, everything—well, some made up reality that's faulty, correctible. What if he does not have an original mind? He may be sent back to GO, end up imaging fractals, very pretty pictures of seashores and mountains, or teaching, just teaching. Still, he has chosen the world he cares for and there's a hell of a lot not known about the mysteries of pi and about our old friend gravity which Artie may never know if he's an amateur like the history buff, his grandfather, whose books, word after word, frail page upon page, stand unread on a shelf.

March 28—Johann Amos Comenius, b. 1592 at Comna or Niwnitz in Moravia.

The philosopher who first introduced the ordinary things of life into the teaching of children. His *"Orbis Sensualium Pictus*, being a Picture and Nomenclature of all the chief things in the World, and of Mens Actions in their way of living!,"* was the model for *The New England Primer*.

> With such Book, and in such a dress may I hope to serve, To entice witty Children to it, that they may not conceit a torment to be in the School, but dainty-fare. For it is apparent, that Children (even from their Infancy almost) are delighted with Pictures, and willingly please their eyes with these sights, And it will be very well worth the pains to have once brought it to pass, that scarecrows may be taken away out of wisdomes Gardens.

He traveled to teach in Holland, fled to Poland upon the Spanish Persecution of the Protestants. In his *Light in Shadows*, Comenius predicted the millennium in 1672, at which time the papacy and Austria would come to ruin.

Sylvie Waite strolls under the palms in La Jolla, where she picks up her stepdaughter from the lab. Security lets her pass without ID, queer old lady in pedal pushers hiking up from the parking lot to the Oceanographic Institute. Sylvie believes she will make this trip to visit Martha every winter until she dies, for she loves the gentle hills looking out to the Channel Islands. On her machines Martha shows her the steady slippage of a fault along the coast, so slow it may not issue seismic waves. Slippage, even gaps may or may not predict a quake, the system chaotic, the crust of the earth constantly shifting. Sylvie turns up her flesh-colored ear bug to hear Martha tell that, though her machines measure thousands of small earthquakes, as yet they do not record environmental degradation. Given her say, Sylvie tells that she had not yet graduated college when she took the subway, her first job at the U.N., way the hell out in Queens, an old factory at Lake Success, to type her translations on machines without the accent marks of any nation. Such is their talk. Sylvie is most attentive to the ridges snaking the dark seabed of the Pacific, though thinks it a pity this brilliant woman can't speak a personal word, that all her friends are colleagues at the lab, professional chums met at conferences or on expeditions. This large woman is the child she raised—shy, studious, a smart girl without a lick of charm. And though she curled Martha's obstinate hair, bought her pumps and maxis and minis, Sylvie remembers clearly that these gestures seemed wrong. Then she let the kid be. Now their visits are easy, the good stepmother listening to Martha: we are in the Ice Age, that is, if the ice on our earth melted we would be unable to swim to safety, for the land mass would disappear. Sylvie is undisturbed by such enormities and by Martha's study of the ocean floor, a history of violent eruptions. She is more than a respectful child to Sylvie, who brings family treasures of silver, pewter, brittle china to the bungalow which looks out on the lower bay.

The clock, the Philadelphia clock, has been shipped ahead of Sylvie's Winter visit. It sits squarely on Mexican tiles. The hours, adjusted to Pacific Time, chime in thin stucco walls. The children, as Sylvie calls Gerald and Martha Waite, do not want the family place. The house and her hill will be sold when she dies. Gerald will take the sideboard, the corner cupboard, the unyielding Federal couch when he returns from Beijing. Sylvie will remain to the end pacing the empty rooms she has cared for. In this past year she has thought of moving into the difficult city for the museums, coffeehouses, the opera—with the infrared headset she would hear German, Italian, French, no need for the simultaneous translation. Stick the damn hearing aid in her ear for lectures at Goethe House. Perhaps she took a wrong turn and was never meant for country life. More likely, she is heir to a small dividend of her mother's tactics of survival, so she dreams of a studio apartment in range of the room on Columbus Avenue where she first landed on this side of the Atlantic with Inge, a short walk to the park bench at 86th Street. *Natürlich*, she would never have been bold enough to speak to Cyril O'Connor. *Ganz bestimmt*, she will not move. She will stay in her house on her hill.

And drive the Jeep into town through the energetic city to visit those children she cares for more than her own, to check out that long-limbed baby who will tower above them all. The day before Cyril was born, Sylvie drove through a flutter of snow and sat with Louise in the loft, drinking tea and waiting, Lou enormous with child waddling from bed to the window, looking down on the fresh Winter scene, Christmas approaching. Then Sylvie told of her brother, Otto von Neisswonger, who was killed at sixteen, the brightest boy in the *Gymnasium* but given completely to soccer. It was all he cared for, so what did they want with him? With her father, yes, an intellectual who did not take his inquisitors seriously—perhaps that was his crime. But they never knew.

"*We* never knew. You see, there was Inge, my mother, and she never knew why they were taken to the camp when so many were leaving, allowed to leave in those months. It's not in the books, though I read, at one time, every word I could find—*ein Anschlusstudentin*—how it could be, *ich weiss es nicht*, how it could be outside of history that they were taken. A political mistake? *Wer weiss? Wer weiss?* A winter illness? It is possible."

Sipping noisily at her tea, "*Vergewaltigung* is the word. The rape," Sylvie wailed in clear English, telling of the little white bed in the Villa, the soft glow of the comforting night light in the hall, for the first time telling—the stench of the man, the weight of his body, the foul whisper—*Hure Nutte, kleine Mose, kleine Mure!*—that she may have dreamed these common words *Du kleine Fotze*—breathed at a little girl—cunt, whore—translation vanishes in the act. How to make clear that she lay in silence until it was safe to wipe her body, which for many years was never washed clean. The velvet princess dress chosen by her foolish mother for their journey. What journey did Frau von Neisswonger imagine and to what parties in exile might her daughter wear the dress with lace collar stolen by *das grosse Ungeheuer?* Then she, the child, repacked the little suitcase with useful warm clothes, led Inge in that damn fox fur through the garden wall.

"I have lost the word for scapegoat, but I ask you," she cried, "isn't it too easy, always to place the blame on Mrs. Billy Ray Boots?"

A question Louise was unable to answer.

"And why did my mother listen to a child?"

Inge, the beautiful mother, who never when they came to America, never spoke of her boy, as though unable to say *Otto*, and in the end did not remember the son with bruised knees and elbows as she, Sylvie, did not remember the filthy words whispered in her ear. But her will, the will of a child, led the mother on when they should have stayed, if not for the lost cause of the father, then for the son, for Otto.

"Otto!" Why call his name on the eve of a happy occasion? *Ein Südenbock!* Scapegoat, Mother what injury we have done to each other, "Nonsense. Don't listen to me! Don't listen!"

Louise in her slow rolling gait came to Sylvie, to thank her for the afternoon of drinking tea and waiting, knowing that she must bend, if bend she can, to kiss her for the bits of story that she must piece together, a sorry story, a horror that had never been told.

But today Sylvie has baked in Martha's bungalow. The freezer is stuffed with tortes and hazelnut cookies and she must fetch her stepdaughter from the Institute. Born in a cold country, she is overcome by the oleander in bloom on the Freeway and walking under the palms, by the geraniums spilling down a slope to the sea. She must remember, at times it is hard to remember—ask Martha, when she finds her in the cool observatory, if the machines which predict all of this crumbling—flowers, hills, bay, bungalow—measure in centuries or in our days to the hours and minutes.

Up the coast, close to a gap in the San Andreas Fault, Beatrice Moffett continues to direct work on her gene sequences and to analyze the blood of children who will die before Sylvie. Aunt Bea, much honored, does not rest on her laurels. Still somewhat flamboyant as she takes the young docs on grand rounds, but what they will remember is not her flash or her early papers on cyto-genetics, but the deft move of her tiny hand taking the pulse of a child, holding the thin wrist like the stem of a delicate flower. Impossible to believe the stories—that she was ever married, that she was married to a flim-flam spiritual adviser, or was it a thug in studded leather when she famously rode a Harley Davidson hog. Beatrice has given her back acres to the child, Cyril Moffett, a living will she calls it, for she has no intention of returning to the farm. The here and now is L.A., Latitude 34 degrees, 3 minutes North; Longitude 118 degrees, 14 seconds West; Venus not visible at an inferior conjunction. She is in it, and from time to time looks up in perfect silence at the stars: the constellations in the

Milky Way are in place as seen from the playroom window of the children's ward where she beds down for the night when a death is imminent.

March 31—Franz Joseph Haydn, b. 1732 at Rohrau, Austria.

He married, unhappily, the sister of the woman he loved. As far as we know, Papa Haydn was without issue, so called because he was protective of his unappreciated and underpaid musicians who worked for him during the many years he served as Kappelmeister at the great palace at Esterhaza. Haydn seems to have been in all ways a generous man, praising the young Mozart as his master, admiring Beethoven as Europe's great composer of the future. When he no longer worked for the Esterhazys and was living peacefully in Vienna, he traveled to England upon invitation, where he was much celebrated and where, at the age of sixty, he fell in love with a charming widow. Their love letters are full of passionate concern and intimate domestic details, but we may find Haydn's *London Notebooks* even more endearing. To know that the man who brought the sonata form to a state of perfection took note of the price of a roasting chicken and a plucked duck, that a dry measure of coal cost £7, that the city of London consumed 8 times one hundred thousand cartloads of coal each year, that Lord Barrymore gave a ball at which 2,000 baskets of gooseberries were served, 5 shillings a basket, is to be enchanted by a practical man who loved both customs and statistics in a strange, hospitable country.

> In order to preserve cream or milk for a long time, one takes a bottle full of milk and puts it in an earthenware pot or copper vessel containing water enough to cover more than half of the bottle, and then places it over a fire and lets it simmer half-an-hour. Then one takes the bottle out and seals it securely, so that no air can escape, and in this way

the milk will keep for many months. N.B. The bottle must be securely corked before it is placed in the water.

—*London Notebook*, 1792

This quaint excerpt, Kind Patron, may demote the great man, make a final entry of Haydn, a light postscript to the Winter months, prelude to better days. How can you trust our editorial judgment if we promote the words of Papa Haydn: *Since God has given me a cheerful heart, He will forgive me for serving Him cheerfully.* No, in honesty we cannot, in these hellish, postindustrialist days, sell you the elixir, the tonic of Haydn, the pop composer of the *Surprise* Symphony with its simple spoof—a double ending. For God's sake, a happy ending. When we leave off laughing we must cut Franz Joseph down to fit the page of our Almanac, as we have trimmed Franklin, Edison, Bell, von Neumann, noting their failures and amusing foibles, their contracts with the Almighty, Brother Mendel's true vocation being sweet peas. Though, when we have set ourselves up, we are poorer in the manner of Almanac makers, mere compilers, avoiding the heavy weather of troubling days, deleting for instance *The Seasons* set to Haydn's glorious music:

> Let not your hearts too soon rejoice,
> And oft, and often, veiled in vapours grey,
> Ole Winter swift steals back;
> On tender bud and blade he sheds his venom's chill.

Shirley Moffett has come to the end of this year's time-share in Sanibel, hers alone, for Harold has gone aconferencing again. His calendar full, now that Dossie is dead. All dead, Dossie and her nameless numbered progeny he led down the genetic cow path. The King of Curd almost got it right. Almost is not good enough. Still, his daring husbandry is timely, and hopeful news on the agribusiness circuit, where the global milk carton and fat-free rump are in inexhaustible demand. His creature is more valuable dead than alive, for Harold Moffett's stock has risen, his failure meeting with adulation, for Dossie dissected, his daring translocation of her cells, is a biological advance.

The island has been divine for Shirl, who plotted her time-share to be with folks like herself, Dilly and Moe. She has unburdened herself of the year's events in Wisconsin—Heidi's trial separation from her philandering husband; a threat of milk fever in the big barn; Hal on antidepressants after Bea signed over the back acres to the baby, a beautiful boy with strong lungs. Those kids really got down to business. Shirl has been to New York, to the expansive white space where Louise lives with her family. She has slept on a futon, walked the factory floor with the child so that the parents might sleep. "They are not married." This a proud declaration. "And they will not marry."

Moe and Dilly, as it turns out, have never wed, got to the Registry Office in Toronto and turned away on principle. Packing her bag with the lemon linen slacks, the flowered shirts which she will never wear poolside back on the farm, Shirley Moffett recalls with good humor the preening woman so pleased that her older children chose appropriate mates. Artie is a darling man but so odd, so oddly brought up. On the eve of departure for home, a moment between worlds, she fears for Louise in the old way. Then, standing on the balcony of the insubstantial half-house, she lets the phone ring and ring itself out (the nightly call from Heidi or Hal), and thinks with joy of her New York daughter, a woman alone. A guilty thought: not without problems, Shirl's double life. She will go back to the converted barn, which is almost completed, a strangely luminous place with high windows, an alien space haunted by stalls and haylofts, by the sharp odor of bloody cauls and the fetid droppings of mice, by the broken chains of children's bicycles and the slick oil spill from the first of their secondhand tractors, yet—yet a kitchen any woman would die for. The alto part of Mozart's "Oh, Christ is risen" floats into the languid air of the tropical night. Dilly singing what they sang together earlier in the evening, the orato-

rio Shirl will sing with the choir in a field at a chill sunrise service on Easter in Wisconsin. She turns to answer the insistent
ring. She will say with some truth to Harold that she is packed
and longs for home.

Louise wipes milky bubbles from the baby's mouth.

"Piggy." He grabs for her breast. Time is of his making. She is
hoping to get to Pearl Paint on Canal, buy a sheet of good rag paper to draw a card for Artie's birthday.

"Daddy's birthday," she coos in the simpering voice which
comes with motherhood. She does get out into the day where, at
the wide crossing on Canal, the exhaust seems whisked away by
fresh Spring air. Cyril sleeps in his cuddly as she makes it past the
noisy shops, metal bits and parts of mysterious fixtures spilling
onto the sidewalk. Pearl Paint is her old haunt, discovered when
she first came to the city, but she's wary, a stranger recently to the
acrylics, oils, fixatives as she makes her way to the one sheet of
fine paper on which she will draw something zany for Freeman's
party, a party for two plus their suckling child. All the magic mak-
ings are before her. She picks not one, but five sheets of rich rag
paper. Cow, she's a perfect cow, months since she thought to do
art—paint, assemble. Her hand caresses tubes of cadmium yellow
and French ultramarine, then the edge of a white sable brush, soft
as the baby's fine hair, then a whiff of linseed oil gets her and she's
lost to greed, pure possession.

Cyril Moffett wakes on Broadway, looks sideways at the face of
his mother, already familiar and it is only familiarity, her being
there that matters, and the bright sting of blue sky before sleep
again, before hunger. But Louise, balancing a rough watercolor
roll and two heavy bags of assorted supplies, is far away—alone in
her room drawing a Zodiac Man, turning at the end of the drive
for a last look at the silos and barns. She's alone, watching her
blue silk dress be rescued from the trash, flutter off to its afterlife.
Then—climbing the ladder in her staged *Progress of Love* in

progress—alone with her useless, useful art. Work, such work and what will it come to? Not little *Postcards*, not overwhelming *Botanicals*, perhaps never the really big thing.

Setting down her bags on the sidewalk, she peeks, as new mothers will, into the warm bundle to check the baby's breathing. And home she goes to work. Give us this day. To set Cyril in Sylvie Waite's cradle. To draw a cartoon strip: *April Fool*: charcoal on paper. Artie (flapping ears, sharp bony nose) juggles pretty numbers under the arc of a horseshoe which brings luck even to those who don't believe in it. In the second panel, her darling is suspended in the stratosphere, a lanky Lincolnesque cherub sprouting wings. From his cloud he contemplates a luscious apple about to fall into a pie, then takes aim with an arrow, his arrow in midflight, aloft in the air, still, poised . . . which is where we leave the artist, Louise Moffett, in mid-stroke, a soiled ashen hand now cupping a breast to feed her crying child mother's milk, give us this day. Strong flood current in the Narrows, N.Y. Harbor. High tide at Dutchman's Kill, 5:45 P.M. Give us the last quarter moon, inauspicious for planting cauliflower, sweeping cirrus clouds, Uranus in the house of Pisces, warm front, stands the sun so high and mighty. Mars approaching Jupiter. Give us, give us this day.

June 28, 1997

"In Dead of Winter" by Maureen Howard first appeared in *The New York Times*.

Grateful acknowledgment is made for permission to reprint excerpts from the following copyrighted works:

"Camelot" by Alan Jay Lerner and Frederick Loewe. © 1960, 1961 (copyright renewed) by Alan Jay Lerner and Frederick Loewe. Chappell & Co. owner of publication and allied rights throughout the world. All rights reserved. Used by permission of Warner Bros. Publications U.S. Inc., Miami, Florida.

"About to Move" from *And the Stars Were Shining* by John Ashbery. Copyright © 1994 by John Ashbery. Reprinted by permission of Farrar, Straus & Giroux, Inc.

"I'll Be Seeing You" by Irving Kahal and Sammy Fain. Copyright © 1938 (renewed 1966) Fred Ahlert Music Corporation on behalf of The New Irving Kahal Music Company. Fain Music Company on behalf of Sammy Fain.

"Calendar Girl," words and music by Howard Greenfield and Neil Sedaka. © 1961 (renewed 1989) Screen Gems-EMI Music Inc. and Careers-BMG Music Publishing, Inc. (BMI). All rights reserved. International copyright secured. Used by permission.

Poem no. 1213 from *The Poems of Emily Dickinson*, Thomas H. Johnson, ed., Cambridge, Mass.: The Belknap Press of Harvard University Press. Copyright © 1951, 1955, 1979, 1983 by the President and Fellows of Harvard College. Reprinted by permission of the publishers and the Trustees of Amherst College.

"Do-Re-Mi" by Richard Rodgers and Oscar Hammerstein II. Copyright © 1959 by Richard Rodgers and Oscar Hammerstein II. Copyright renewed. Williamson Music owner of publication and allied rights throughout the world. International copyright secured. Used by permission. All rights reserved.

Illustration credits

Pages 5, 71, 175, and 258: *Orbis Sensualium Pictus* of Jan Amos Comenius, 1659; pages 1, 67, and 173: Signs of the Zodiac by C. J. Hyginus from *Poeticon Astronomicon*, 1485; page 67: Almanac illustrated, *Poor Richard's*, 1733; Man of Signs (Zodiac Man) courtesy of *The Old Farmer's Almanac*; light bulb courtesy The Edison National Historic Site.

A PENGUIN READERS GUIDE TO

A LOVER'S ALMANAC

Maureen Howard

AN INTRODUCTION TO
A LOVER'S ALMANAC

January 1, 2000 (leap year), 224th year of American Independence, in the city and environs of New York.

Louise Moffett teeters in stiletto heels through her confetti-littered loft, lamenting the details of her disastrous millennium bash and the heartbreaking fallout that accompanies her entry into the new century. Across town, her lover, Artie, awakens with a hangover and the cloudy memory of a botched marriage proposal the night before. So begins *A Lover's Almanac,* a romantic, thinking-person's love story about fate—how and why we live the lives we do and fall in love with the people we do.

The lapsed lovers are two thirty-somethings in New York City. Louise, a Midwestern farm girl, is a hot artist. Artie, an orphan raised by his grandfather after the death of his hippie mother, is a hapless computer wizard. As we follow their romance, we draw back to learn about their parents' and grandparents' lives, about the events, public and private, that have affected their fates. At intervals, we turn from the characters' stories to consider the lives of the geniuses who have so profoundly affected our society: Edison, Einstein, Franklin, and other creative thinkers of the past. In this "broad meditation on Western thought" (*Los Angeles Times*), Howard asks: How do we make our own histories—and how do we connect to history writ large? To what extent do we control our destinies? As we plumb the depths of Maureen Howard's lush prose to discern the curious, looping narrative strands at the novel's heart, we find a witty, moving, and brilliantly simple love story. In the grander sense, as we ponder the fate of the characters in light of the novel's intricate historical backdrop, "a modern version of the great panoramas of the past" (*The New York Times Book Review*) is revealed, one that braids love, memory, and fate into a rich tapestry encompassing all our histories.

An Interview with Maureen Howard

Part of the unique beauty of A Lover's Almanac *is the fascinating detail that you use — like entries in an almanac — throughout the novel. What is your own conception of the significance of the almanac as cultural and historical repository, and what did you hope to achieve by shaping your novel in the almanac's image?*

The almanac is a lively elastic form which combines both fact and fiction. I believe I call it, not irreverently, a bible for our days. On the one hand, its astronomy gives us the movements of the planets with great accuracy; on the other hand, it charts our fabulous stories in astrology. Though the novel makes mention of many ancient almanacs — Egyptian, Indian — it is the entertaining book of the American people, Ben Franklin's and *The Old Farmer's Almanac*, that appealed to me as a perfect system to display the little stories by which we mark our days along with the almost operatic accomplishments of technology and the never ending tragedies of our society as we come to the end of this era. My gathering of facts with fiction in this playful form, the almanac, is a gesture against chaos. Call it a survival manual.

An important aspect of Cyril's character is his love of history — an idea that reverberates throughout the novel through your use of historical detail. Was this primarily a plot device, or a reflection of your own personal passion for history?

Cyril O'Connor's love of history strikes a thematic chord that I hope resonates throughout the novel. Cyril, the old lover in the story, had wanted to be a historian when he was young, but lost track of that dream in the getting and spending of life. He had wanted to understand the Founding Fathers and the vast story of events that formed the time and place he was born into. When he attempts to go back to American history, he's beyond making sense of it. My young lovers, Lou and Artie, have no sense of history at the start of their troubles. They treat the fifties, in which they enact their millennial party, as though it is a movie set, getting "the look" of it right and the spirit of that time all wrong. But yes, I am fairly passionate about the use of history in my work, about all the discoveries that might tell us who we are.

*Your novel is, at heart, a love story. But it's also been called "a tribute to progress" (*Miami Herald*), and "an exuberant look at where we have been and where we may be going when the present millennium is over" (*San Francisco Chronicle*). Can you comment on your intentions when you first sat down to write? Was this the love story you've always wanted to tell, or, rather, your way of conveying larger ideas about history and fate?*

The love story was absolutely essential from the start. I went back to that harsh late comedy of Shakespeare's, *A Winter's Tale*, which has both old and young lovers, and ends with a bittersweet reconciliation. That glorious work was only a touchstone, for I've bent the Bard's lovers quite out of shape, though Cyril and Sylvie — my golden oldies — have lived middling fair lives without each other for fifty years. And my young lovers — urban, savvy, cynical — are children still who have not tested the depths of love as the novel opens. Larger ideas? The idea seems to me so simple: that these characters' lives are to a great part shaped by the culture they live in, live through. Still, they must find their way.

The timing of the novel has a narrative significance, and also serves to emphasize certain themes and motifs. What inspired you to place the story at the turn of the millennium?

We started some years ago to plan the celebration, congratulating ourselves on making it to that spectacular date. Science and its servant, technology, can predict the placement of the stars, the full moon, even the tides, but we will be imprecise, even bewildered, about where we are headed. As Artie and Lou predict, the media will be all over the millennium. They fear that the virtual world, the glut of images, will distort the experience of the millennium, yet they distort it with their party. Finally, in *A Lover's Almanac*, both the old and the young must take stock of who they are.

A Lover's Almanac *has much to say about individual choice. Historically, the almanac itself was used to predict future events, yet many of your characters seem to be at their best when taking it upon themselves to decide their fates. What are you thoughts on this fundamental question?*

The question is too weighty. I write fiction, not the blustery self-help books of the successful writer in my almanac. Like Louise, who, as a kid, uses astrology to take swipes at her family, I disbelieve in predictions which limit us, rob us of choice. We may be creatures of our time and place, but we make choices, not always for the best, when we love and work. Sylvie, Cyril's old love, boldly rings his doorbell so that their romance may begin again; and Louise, in her *Progress of Love*, shows literally that in the end she understands the impact of the past on present lives, of the public world on the personal. She makes her art in the midst of her audience. As we make our lives? I suppose. And as I made my almanac "to summon aptly," as Robert Frost says of his work, "from the vast chaos of all I have lived through."

A Lover's Almanac *is the first in a series of novels that you plan to write, each taking place during a separate season of the year. What themes do you see as unique to the Winter installment, and can you comment on your vision of what will unite the cycle?*

Yes, I'm writing the seasons, writing Spring to be exact, the season of rebirth, picking up from birth at the end of *A Lover's Almanac*. Spring will be three tales that continue the themes of inheritance, of what we must recall to live with some honesty in the present. I'm interested in what stories we choose to tell, when we choose to tell them, and what dreams and memories we keep to ourselves. The natural world of the seasons is a grid, like the almanac, in which we live our days. Richer, grander in imagery than any novel, the seasons present us with their comforting and perilous stories. I hope to tap a few in my small way. Like Louise, I live on the dangerous edge between belief and disbelief in my project.

QUESTIONS FOR DISCUSSION

1) In the past, the almanac was an indispensable tool for interacting with the practical world. Today it has become more a compendium of minutiae, a source of entertainment. How does Maureen Howard play with these different definitions of the almanac? What does each of these competing conceptions lend to the novel?

2) A surface look at *A Lover's Almanac* reveals a variety of characters and story lines, some seemingly unrelated to each other, or touching for only brief, glancing moments. Through this, what is Maureen Howard saying about life in the context of our interactions with others? What is Sissy symbolic of? Does her presence confirm the idea of lives interrelated, or question it?

3) How does Louise's vocation as an artist relate to the larger themes of creativity and inspiration that permeate the novel?

4) What does Maureen Howard achieve through her use of historical references in *A Lover's Almanac*? Considering the point in time

at which the story takes place, what is the author saying about the importance of looking back if we hope to move forward? How is this idea, on a personal scale, carried out in the lives of the characters?

5) Is Louise's art show *The Progress of Love* meant by Maureen Howard to be ironic? In what ways have Louise and Artie progressed through the course of the novel?

6) How does Maureen Howard play with the idea of fate throughout the novel? Do her characters make their own histories, or are they playing into destinies laid out for them?

7) What is the significance of Howard's many evocations of inventors and men of ideas?

8) In what ways do Louise and Artie embody their generation? Are those nearing adulthood late in this century lacking a sense of their place in history? In the culture of 2000, does this matter?

Also available from Penguin:

Bridgeport Bus   The luminous, funny story of a woman's midlife rebellion and self-discovery. ISBN 0-14-005566-5

The Facts of Life   Howard's brilliant, award-winning memoir. (July 1999) ISBN 0-14-005500-2

For more information about other Penguin Readers Guides, please call the Penguin Marketing Department at (800) 778-6425

Visit our Web site: http://www. penguinputnam.com and click on Club PPI for a complete list of Penguin Readers Guides that are available online.

FOR THE BEST IN PAPERBACKS, LOOK FOR THE

In every corner of the world, on every subject under the sun, Penguin represents quality and variety—the very best in publishing today.

For complete information about books available from Penguin—including Puffins, Penguin Classics, and Arkana—and how to order them, write to us at the appropriate address below. Please note that for copyright reasons the selection of books varies from country to country.

In the United Kingdom: Please write to *Dept. JC, Penguin Books Ltd, FREEPOST, West Drayton, Middlesex UB7 0BR.*

If you have any difficulty in obtaining a title, please send your order with the correct money, plus ten percent for postage and packaging, to *P.O. Box No. 11, West Drayton, Middlesex UB7 0BR*

In the United States: Please write to *Consumer Sales, Penguin USA, P.O. Box 999, Dept. 17109, Bergenfield, New Jersey 07621-0120.* VISA and MasterCard holders call 1-800-253-6476 to order all Penguin titles

In Canada: Please write to *Penguin Books Canada Ltd, 10 Alcorn Avenue, Suite 300, Toronto, Ontario M4V 3B2*

In Australia: Please write to *Penguin Books Australia Ltd, P.O. Box 257, Ringwood, Victoria 3134*

In New Zealand: Please write to *Penguin Books (NZ) Ltd, Private Bag 102902, North Shore Mail Centre, Auckland 10*

In India: Please write to *Penguin Books India Pvt Ltd, 706 Eros Apartments, 56 Nehru Place, New Delhi 110 019*

In the Netherlands: Please write to *Penguin Books Netherlands bv, Postbus 3507, NL-1001 AH Amsterdam*

In Germany: Please write to *Penguin Books Deutschland GmbH, Metzlerstrasse 26, 60594 Frankfurt am Main*

In Spain: Please write to *Penguin Books S.A., Bravo Murillo 19, 1° B, 28015 Madrid*

In Italy: Please write to *Penguin Italia s.r.l., Via Felice Casati 20, I-20124 Milano*

In France: Please write to *Penguin France S.A., 17 rue Lejeune, F-31000 Toulouse*

In Japan: Please write to *Penguin Books Japan, Ishikiribashi Building, 2-5-4, Suido, Bunkyo-ku, Tokyo 112*

In Greece: Please write to *Penguin Hellas Ltd, Dimocritou 3, GR-106 71 Athens*

In South Africa: Please write to *Longman Penguin Southern Africa (Pty) Ltd, Private Bag X08, Bertsham 2013*